Finding Brooklyn

THE CLUB KINGS
BOOK TWO

CHARLOTTE ST. PIERRE

Contents

To A - For always protecting the space I need to be me, supporting each idea I come up with, and holding my hand along the way.

Author's Note

Reader friends - this is a "why choose" romance, where the main female character will end up with multiple romantic partners. In this book there are descriptions of child abuse, domestic violence, rape, attempted murder, torture and detailed sex scenes. If these subject are difficult for you, this may not be the book for you.

If you are still reading...I hope you love Brooklyn and The Club Kings as much as I have enjoyed bringing them to the page!

CHAPTER

One

Brooklyn

SWEAT SHIMMERED ALONG MY SKIN. I stared at the mirror in front of me as my feet pounded against the treadmill. "I See Red" by Everybody Loves an Outlaw blared through the gym speakers. It was just one benefit of dating some of the most wealthy men in the city, a private gym.

The Brooklyn Reeves from a few months before would have chosen an outdoor run any other day. That was before I was hiding from a murderous ex-boyfriend. Memories slipped into my concentration and I shivered, pushing them back into the box so I didn't trip and fall spectacularly in my boyfriends' basement. It had been two months since Lyle's bathroom attack. My Knights weren't keen on me going back to my apartment, so I had been living under their roof ever since.

Aiden, Gideon, Oliver and Jaxon Knight, the Club Kings of the city. A name they earned by owning the most successful night-clubs across the country under their umbrella corporation 4K. I didn't know that when I initially met two of them at one of their clubs. All I knew was they were the most gorgeous men I'd seen in my life.

The Club Kings had earned their reputation by their hard work and dedication to their businesses. However, I wasn't the only one that didn't know much about them before meeting them. They were notoriously private, and their histories were kept out of the public eye. Now that I had gotten to know them, I knew there were skeletons they didn't want flashing around the city. That privacy only made them more interesting to the public, and they were envied by men and wanted by most of the women that saw them.

When I thought about that first night, it made me smile and almost laugh out loud, recalling how I had run from the club and from them, afraid they would see all the things I was hiding from the world. Now that I looked at myself in the mirror, all of my scars, old and healing, were on display. I wore a sports bra, to support my not too large breasts, and short Lycra running shorts that hugged my upper thighs and ass. I had worked hard to have the figure I did, even with the things I wanted to hide.

The burn scar on my thigh from childhood was always the least of my worries. What happened to me as a child wasn't my fault. Therapy made me understand that I was the one that should have been taken care of, not the one caring for my addict mother. That scar reminded me that when it came down to things, I figured out how to feed myself and kept myself alive, even when I was too little to drain hot water in the sink.

Nightmares were attached to the scar that made its way from behind my right ear, down across my collarbone, ending just above my cleavage. Lyle's first murder attempt. And now I had the scars of his second on my abdomen. Those were still pink and working to heal, a perfect reflection of what was happening on the inside of me as well.

Despite all of what had happened, Lyle getting out of prison, stalking and attacking me, I felt a happiness I wasn't always sure how to deal with. I had found four men who wanted me, despite all the trouble I had brought to their doorstep. While Lyle was busy stalking me, he was also seeing me with each of them and that made them targets.

I continued running, letting my thoughts roll around each of my guys. Jaxon Knight, my serious man, with his full color tatted sleeve and perfect 5 o'clock shadow. During my recovery, he kept the meds on schedule and made sure they followed each instruction from the doctors. He knew how to bring calm when I was spiraling, and I had appreciated him as I struggled with the after effects of the attack.

Oliver Knight, the one always good for a joke and the perfect afternoon nap cuddle. His feelings were more on the surface than he would like people to believe, but I was understanding him more each day. I had to admit I found him sexiest when he didn't put in his contacts and wore his glasses. They made him look businesslike until he opened his mouth and then, typically, he had me laughing or moaning.

My big man, Gideon Knight, was all protection and strength. We were still working through his emotions around the attack. He blamed himself for not standing up to me and demanding that I didn't go to lunch with my assistant that day. A lot of the attack was fuzzy, coming in spurts through nightmares. However, the one thing I held onto was the moment I saw Gideon racing into the room. I had known without doubt he would save me.

The unelected leader of the chosen brothers, Aiden Knight, was the toughest to crack. It was him that brought the guys together as children, creating the family none of them had growing up. We had a brand new thing going on and I thoroughly enjoyed his attention to detail when it came to hot sex. But something tugged at me about the distance he often kept between them. I tried not to put too much thought into it, as what we had was the newest out of the brothers.

Not having to choose between them had been confusing for me in the beginning. And sometimes it felt too complicated. As I had gotten to know each of them and been intimate with them, the idea of having to choose was impossible. My heart was full and each of them had a piece of it. I couldn't choose one, just as I couldn't make the choice for part of my heart to stop beating.

I knew I was flying close to the big four letter word, a place I hadn't been in since Lyle. When I thought of that time now, I knew what I had felt for Lyle wasn't real love. He didn't cherish or value me. He didn't protect me when I needed him. My feelings for Lyle weren't something I could put a name to, because it was too dark and unworthy.

What I felt for the Knights was something completely foreign to me, which was why I refused to put a name to it yet. The guys didn't get jealous about each other or act ridiculous in their relationships. That didn't mean they weren't real men when it came down to it. And the idea of them running from me if I put my heart on the table, scared me more the anything.

Living with my guys threw my sex drive into a frenzy. I had never particularly enjoyed sex, never really knew what I could be missing. My best friend Ash had tried to explain and make me understand what was out there. My hang ups kept me from any sort of physical relationship until I met the Knights. Now I couldn't get enough of them. Luckily, none of them complained.

As the music shifted and "Wave" by Meghan Trainor pumped through the speakers, I slowed my pace to a cool down. I picked up the water bottle that was in the holder in front of me, drinking deeply before looking in the mirror again. Movement caught my eye and breath caught in my throat. I felt a flash of panic until my eyes locked onto who had entered the gym.

Oliver leaned against the door frame, naked except for a pair of gray lounge pants. His short, dirty blond curls were mussed on his head and I couldn't help but remember fisting it as his head was between my thighs the night before. His glasses were pushed up on the bridge of his nose, a sign that he rolled directly out of bed to come and find me.

I stopped the treadmill and bent to pick up a towel. I could see Oliver's reflection as he tilted his head to stare at my ass. His gaze turned hot and I couldn't help the smile that spread across my face. Wiping the sweat from my neck, I spun to look at him.

"Morning," I said.

"You left me alone in bed," he growled.

"I did not," I replied.

"Gideon doesn't count," he said, as he began to walk slowly toward me.

I thought about running, making Oliver work for it. However, I was feeling hot, just by the way he was looking at me now. It was the same with all of them. Each of them were chiseled from a mold to look like gods, I knew it had to be sinful. And if it was, I would burn happily in hell after I had my fill of each one of them.

Oliver bent his face toward me and ran his nose along my sweaty neck and nipped at my ear, before pulling back.

"You smell tasty," he said.

"I smell sweaty," I argued.

"Perfect," he replied.

Before I could think of a different response, Oliver bent and threw me over his shoulder. I squealed and wrapped my arms around his trim hips, trusting him to not drop me on my head. It was this playfulness that I had gotten so used to with Oliver. He made me laugh, and it made me feel lighter in all situations.

As he climbed the gym stairs, I had to watch the ground upside down. When we entered the main level, I heard a gruff laugh and lifted just enough to see Jaxon with a cup of coffee, walking out of the kitchen.

"You gonna help me?" I screeched.

"Sorry, love. Looks like my brother has other plans," Jaxon called after her.

"Traitor!" I yelled back with a laugh.

Oliver took that moment to slap a hand down on my ass. Instead of squealing, I couldn't help the moan that slipped from my lips. Oliver's chest rumbled with a chuckle.

"My baby liked that," he said, before kissing my hip.

"Oliver, you need to put me down," I said in mock annoyance.

"Once I get to the bed," he replied.

As we climbed to the second floor, Oliver shifted to one side to allow Aiden to pass. He bent so he could see my face. His handsome smile was easy, and it made my heart flutter a bit in my chest.

"Have fun, sweetheart," he said, before kissing my cheek.

"Why does no one help me in this house?" I cried out, causing Aiden and Jaxon to both laugh on the first floor.

I allowed my hands to span the planes of Oliver's muscled abdomen, my fingers running along the delicious V that was visible above his lounge pants. At the landing of the second floor, Oliver seemed to hesitate before heading for his own room. I knew that meant he wanted me to himself, since Gideon was likely still asleep in my bed.

Kicking the door closed behind us, Oliver walked straight to the bed and tossed me onto it. I squeaked as I ungracefully bounced and then laughed out loud.

"Ya know, you could have just asked me to come to bed," I said.

"Where's the fun in that?" Oliver asked.

His eyes told me the only fun on his mind was the naked kind. I lifted up onto my elbows and looked over at him. I could see the tension in him as he held himself back from jumping onto me. The thought made a smile cross my face, and Oliver turned to set his glasses down. I kicked off my running shoes and Oliver peeled the socks from my feet.

Oliver lifted one of my feet and pressed his thumbs into the arch, and I flopped back with a groan. He continued the massage on the other foot and I couldn't help but go limp in the middle of the bed. His fingers crawled up my calves, pressing and massaging my muscles. I was tight after my run and his hands were doing wonderful things to my body.

When he reached my thighs, his thumbs glided close to my center, but he didn't touch where I wanted. I lifted my hips to him, but he just darkly chuckled and pulled back. Opening my eyes, I hadn't even realized had closed, I looked down at him. He was watching my face and his eyes were hot on mine.

I reached down to grab his curly hair and urged him up my body. When he was over me, I pulled his mouth to mine in an almost violent kiss. It was always this. I couldn't hold back with how badly I wanted him. Oliver liked to tease and play before giving into what I desired. The proof was pressed against my hip that he wasn't going to hold back too much longer.

Oliver

WHEN I WAS GOING to look for Brooklyn, I hadn't expected the rush of desire the moment I found her running the gym. It wasn't strange to wake up alone with one of my brothers on the other side of the bed. Brooklyn tended to run early or slip into bed with Gideon when she had a nightmare. However, when I woke up, all I could smell was her all around me and I instantly needed to find her.

Seeing her in the skimpy running gear, I immediately needed

her in my bed. Having her spread out below me was exactly what I wanted to see each moment of the day. I pulled away from our kiss and looked down at her. Her blonde hair was piled on top of her head in a messy bun, pieces that had escaped stuck to her neck. Her icy blue eyes were heavy with desire as she focused on me.

I couldn't help but thrust my cock against her hip and watch as her eyes flared slightly. It was never enough with Brooklyn. With my gaze never leaving hers, I ran a hand down her chest until I could tug the front of her sports bra down, allowing her breasts to spill forward. I grinned at her before ducking my head and sucking a taunt nipple into my mouth.

Brooklyn's back bowed off the bed, pushing her breast into me, while her hand fisted in my hair. She always loved pulling on my curls and it only made me hotter to know how badly she wanted whatever I was doing to her. I slid my mouth across her skin until I could tease her other nipple. A throaty moan escaped my girl's mouth. I pulled the bra off and tossed it to the ground. I wanted her bare for me.

I continued my exploration with my hands as I slid my palms down her sides to the top of her running shorts. Slowly, I peeled them from her skin, down her toned legs, until I could drop them to the ground. Brooklyn watched the movement the entire time. Keeping my gaze on hers, I slid a finger through her wetness and I reveled in how her eyes rolled back into her head and her thighs fell open for me.

She was soaked before I even touched her. I circled her clit with my fingertip and I watched as her breasts rose and fell in harsh breaths. When I slid two fingers into her, she lifted her hips with a groan. I looked down to watch as my fingers penetrated her beautiful pussy. I crooked my fingers inside her, knowing the moment I found her g-spot by the way she trembled.

"I want you to cum on my fingers, baby," I growled.

"I'm so close, Oliver, please don't stop," she said, her head thrown back and her eyes closed again.

I continued the motion against her g-spot. Twisting my wrist, I ran my thumb along her clit and it was the final push Brooklyn needed to fall over the cliff. Her pussy walls clamped down on my fingers, and I continued to fuck her slowly as she came down from her orgasm.

Quickly, I shed my lounge pants and crawled up her body until my hips were between her perfect thighs. She lifted her legs, wrapping them around my back, and tried to pull me into her. I allowed my cock to slide along her sweet pussy and she moaned when I hit her clit, but I slid away, not burying myself into her yet.

"Oliver," she moaned when I didn't give her exactly what she wanted.

"Yes, baby?"

"Please," she begged.

Leaning up on my knees, I grabbed her hips and flipped her to her stomach. She let out a groan as I grabbed her and pulled her to her knees, so that her ass was pressed against my cock. Remembering her reaction on the stairs, I smacked my hand down on her ass. Brooklyn buried her face in the bed, muffling her moans.

"Damn, that's fucking hot," I said.

"Stop teasing and fuck me," she said, turning her head to look back at me.

My girl had gotten dirty since she started letting down her guard with us, and I loved every minute. Gripping my cock, I notched the tip at her entrance. She was so wet, I was able to slam into her to the hilt in one thrust. She cried out, my name on her lips. The sound only encouraged me to pull out and slam into her again. Brooklyn was ready for it, and she pushed her hips back into me. Her tightness squeezed me and I had to breathe to keep control of myself.

I leaned over her, propping myself up on one arm. She turned her face and I captured her mouth in a hot kiss, allowing my tongue to slide along hers while I slowly fucked her with hard, deep strokes. I could feel her walls trembling around me. Sliding my free hand around her hip, I pressed my fingers against her clit and she immediately exploded around my hardness.

Going back to my knees, I dug my fingers into her hips and slammed into her harder, chasing my own orgasm. When I exploded into her, we both collapsed onto my bed. I rolled onto my back and Brooklyn immediately draped herself across my chest. I wrapped an arm around her and she leaned up to kiss me softly.

"I do have to get ready for work," she said with a smile.

"And now you're nice and relaxed for the day," I replied.

"Maybe too relaxed. I could fall asleep again," she said, letting her head rest on my chest.

I let her cuddle into me for a few moments. I looked over at the clock and sighed, knowing she wouldn't be happy to be late. Sliding out from under her, she watched me with hooded eyes. I slid my arms under her and pulled her up into me. She immediately threw her arms around my neck and rested her head on my shoulder.

Despite our naked state, I walked down the hall to her bedroom. I kicked open the door with a foot, not caring that the door bounced off the wall, which woke Gideon. He peered at us from under an arm. He sat up when he caught sight of a naked Brooklyn, his long hair wild around his face. Brooklyn waggled a finger at him as we passed the bed to the bathroom.

Inside, I sat her on her feet and turned on the shower. She began to pull her hair from the bun, and I watched as it fell and flowed over her shoulders. Once there was steam coming from behind the glass, I lead her under the spray. She let the water flow over her head, and when she opened her eyes, I saw her focus on something behind me.

As anticipated, Gideon was awake. I moved to give him access to Brooklyn as he joined us in the shower. My brother was a beast of a man, but luckily the shower in this bathroom was huge. He ran his hands over Brooklyn's shoulders and leaned down to kiss her sweetly. She smiled up at him before wrapping her arms around his middle and hugging her naked body to his.

I grabbed the shampoo and began to massage it into her hair and she leaned back slightly to give me access, though she didn't let go of Gideon. We all knew that their relationship was a bit more difficult now. Gideon was weighed down with guilt for the attack on Brooklyn. None of us blamed him, our girl included. But there were times we could see him putting distance between them. Brooklyn would yank him right back. She was perfect for him.

Brooklyn leaned back to allow the shampoo to rinse from her hair. Gideon took the opportunity to lean down and run his tongue around her nipple. I watched as her mouth opened on a surprised gasp. Turning her face toward me, I pressed my mouth to hers. She immediately opened her mouth, allowing our tongues to duel.

Breaking away from our kiss, Brooklyn turned to Gideon, who was sliding a hand down her abdomen. I could see the way her eyes brightened as his fingers found her folds. I stood behind her, cupping her beautiful breasts in my hands, and kissing along her neck. It didn't take long for Brooklyn to begin panting under our touches.

Gideon hissed out a sound when Brooklyn's hand closed around his cock. She grinned up at him and his eyes were fire on her. Without warning, Gideon slid his hands under her ass and lifted her off her feet. He turned her, so that her back was against the shower wall, her legs spread around his hips. Brooklyn's voice echoed as Gideon thrust his cock into her.

I watched as our girl cried out, Gideon fucking her roughly. My own hand circled my hardened cock, stroking, knowing how good it felt to be buried in her. Gideon's face was buried in her neck and Brooklyn's eyes found me. She bit her lip, watching intently as my hand stroked up and down my cock. As I erupted, I caught my cum in my hand to prevent it from going all over the shower. Brooklyn moaned loudly, watching the scene unfold as Gideon was deep inside her.

She threw her head back, leaning against the wall, and Gideon cursed. I knew she had come and was likely squeezing the life from his cock. His growl followed as he thrust a few more times before stilling inside her. When she opened her eyes and looked down at Gideon, adoration shown in her gaze. She grazed her lips over his and he carefully slid her back to the floor.

When we tried to help her shower, she shooed us out of the bathroom.

"I know what will happen if I keep letting you two touch me. Get out. Find your own shower. I'll be down soon," she giggled.

With towels around our waists, we headed down the hallway. We broke away without words into our own rooms. Mine still smelled of Brooklyn's lavender body products and sex. I could get used to my room smelling like that at all times. I climbed into my own shower, just to finish the job before getting ready for the day.

As I picked out my clothes, I thought about how much time my brothers and I were spending together now. Family dinners were almost an every night occurrence, with all of us getting off work in time to be at the house and eat with Brooklyn. We had been close as children and those bonds had grown as we became adults, but often work was what controlled most of our time. Brooklyn brought a glue to us that we hadn't had before.

I opted for a v-neck cashmere sweater with slacks. I had a light day. And even if I didn't, I would be home in time for family dinner and maybe a movie night with our girl. My brothers were my family, but somehow things just felt more complete with Brooklyn in our lives.

Brooklyn

ONCE MY MEN left the bathroom, I was able to finish my shower. As I cleaned between my legs, I felt sore in all the right ways and I couldn't wipe the smile from my face. Morning sex was something I was getting used to, but it often made me run behind schedule.

I quickly dried what I could of my hair before twisting it up into a messy but professional French twist. Light make-up was next, and I was thankful that my morning routine wasn't long and drawn out. I was never one to wear heavy layers of makeup, normally going for a more natural look for work days.

In my closet, I found a pencil skirt and tucked a loose tank top into it. I added a cardigan to the outfit and pulled shoes from one of the numerous boxes the guys had gotten me. They had told me I wasn't going to be allowed to pay them back, but I recognized a lot of the labels of the shoes and clothes, and I knew it wasn't a cheap wardrobe.

Of course, replacing a wardrobe wasn't something I thought I would need to do. Lyle had other ideas when he broke into my apartment and ripped everything I owned to shreds. I shivered slightly, thinking about the night I found my room vandalized. Pushing away the negative memories, I focused on what was right in front of me.

Entering the kitchen, all four of my men were going through their morning rituals. Aiden, as always, sat at the island with his mug of coffee and newspaper. I had wondered why he read a physical newspaper, but once the reasoning was explained, I never mentioned it again. It was hard for me to picture a young Aiden, searching the classified ads, hoping his father was looking for him.

Gideon was at the stove, cooking what smelled like sausage and likely eggs to go with. I wasn't used to eating a real breakfast before work. When I lived with Ash, our morning routine was usually a muffin and a cup of coffee. Now, Gideon insisted I eat something before my day started. I refused to admit that it was true. I did feel better throughout the morning with a full stomach.

Oliver's hair was unruly and still a little wet, but he sat at the island scrolling through his phone. I walked up behind him and kissed him on the back of the neck. He leaned back just slightly, and I hugged him. He didn't take his eyes off the phone, checking through his work emails from the evening and morning.

I made my way to the coffeemaker, where Jaxon was already holding a mug of black coffee for me. His eyes warmed as he gazed down at me. Still walking around barefoot, I was at least a head shorter than any of my guys, Gideon being the exception who more than towered over me. I lifted up on my toes so I could quickly kiss Jaxon. He didn't let the chance go by without wrapping an arm around my waist and deepening the kiss for a moment.

When he let me go, I was slightly breathless and could feel the blush on my cheeks. He grinned down at me and handed me my coffee. I sat on a stool next to Aiden, who flipped down the paper for a second to smile at me. As I carefully sipped my coffee, his hand found my thigh. He squeezed softly, his easy affection often getting to me.

This was how our mornings often were. Quiet, but with purpose to get the day started off right. I enjoyed the time when I could just watch each of them, without their full attention being on me. In the few months I had been living with them, it was a routine I was becoming very fond of. My internal instincts tried to warn me of enjoying it too much. I was living under their roof for protection and eventually I was sure they would insist I go home to my apartment with Ash.

Gideon slid my breakfast in front of me, a kiss on my temple as he stepped away. He also added toast to the plate. They all knew that I had no problems with eating, I enjoyed food immensely. Also, a reason I needed to run every morning. The food I enjoyed would also enjoy sticking to parts of my body I didn't want it to. As it was, I felt like I had gained weight during my recovery from Lyle's attack. None of my guys complained though, each of them loving my naked body whenever they had the chance.

"Frank will be with you today," Gideon said.

This was also routine. The typical conversation we had first thing in the morning. We went over my schedule, and Gideon had hired security to escort me everywhere I was going. Frank was my normal guard, and we had struck up an easy friendship. Like all the Knights' employees, he didn't question what went on behind closed doors or why a different brother was kissing me at the door each morning.

The conversation also started up butterflies in my stomach. I pulled up my calendar on my phone to ensure there weren't any outside meetings I had. I already knew I didn't, but I had a hard time looking at Gideon, knowing I was keeping a secret from him. I confirmed I had no outside meetings and agreed to stay with Frank if I left the office.

Gideon looked satisfied, a small smile sliding along his face. I reached over and pulled his beard lightly, as I always loved to do. It was perfectly trimmed and combed. He was my wild man, even when he had his long hair pulled back in a bun like he did in the morning. I smiled a little too brightly, but luckily Gideon didn't notice.

There had been adjustments made to learn to live with the Knights. They were incredibly protective of me. I couldn't say they didn't have a reason to be. Lyle was still on the run, hiding from even Gideon's deep dives into searching. However, I wasn't used to being a kept woman anymore. In my head, I knew the difference between Lyle and his controlling relationship and the relationships I was in now. However, sometimes a panic would settle in, feeling like I was in over my head.

So, I had a secret. One that I was pretty sure the guys would be furious to hear about. They really only had themselves to blame. When I had healed from the attack, I wanted to learn to defend myself. The answer was a resounding no from them all. Gideon offered to teach me some things, but after two lessons, it was clear he was holding back and I wouldn't learn anything that way. When I brought up outside lessons again, the answer was the same.

The only one that knew what I was up to was Frank. Because I'm not stupid. I knew that I couldn't go out alone. Lyle was likely still stalking me and was keeping an eye on all my movements. Frank only kept the secret, because I was clear if he didn't take me where I wanted to go, without telling the Knights, I would be going on my own. Which would also get him fired.

I didn't feel good about the deception. It made me nervous each day. But the power I felt from what I was learning was worth it. Frank tried to talk me out of it almost daily, but he knew it was a lost cause.

"Stellina?" Gideon's voice broke into my inner thoughts.

His nickname for me, "little star" in Italian, was the one he used when he was especially trying to be sweet. I looked over at him and saw that all four of the guys were watching me.

"Sorry, what?" I asked.

"Lunch?" Gideon asked.

I looked down at my phone and scrolled, knowing damn well I had nothing for lunch. But I needed a way out of having lunch with Gideon, so I didn't miss my class.

"I have a lunch meeting with my team today. Sorry big man," I said, without making eye contact.

Lying had never been something I was good at. I was afraid to look at any of the guys, sure that I would blurt out the truth. The idea of hurting them made me feel slightly ill. Then a small voice in my head bolstered me and sent the reminder that this wouldn't be happening if they hadn't tried to control me.

I pasted a smile on my face and lifted my eyes. Gideon sent me a small smile and nodded, never one to argue about work, as long as I wasn't leaving the office. Aiden was still in his paper, and both Jaxon and Oliver were looking at their own devices. Relief washed over me, realizing no one had picked up on my deception.

The doorbell rang, the signal that Frank had arrived. I downed the last bit of my coffee and popped a piece of sausage into my mouth.

"Thank you for breakfast, big man," I said, kissing Gideon on the cheek as I walked by.

His big arm snaked out and looped around my waist, pulling

me back to him. He kissed the back of my neck and squeezed me tight for a moment.

"Have a good day, stellina," he said.

I patted his arm and nodded, still feeling the weight of what I knew I would be doing later in the day. I went to Aiden and pulled down the newspaper. His eyes were light and his smile was easy, something that wasn't normal for him. I pressed a quick kiss to his lips. I repeated the sentiment with Oliver, who also smacked my ass as I walked away. I threw a hot gaze over my shoulder and that had him laughing.

Jaxon stood and took my hand, walking me toward the front door. He opened it and Frank stood in his normal black suit and black sunglasses. If I didn't know he was personal security, I'd wonder if he was in the FBI, with his serious face and eyes that took in everything around. Frank was light on the details with me about what his past was about, but it was good enough that Gideon trusted him with my welfare.

Frank nodded to me in greeting and went down the steps to the dark sedan we drove everywhere. Jaxon turned me so I was in his arms. He smelled clean with the hint of woodsy scent that came from his products. I had to remind myself I needed to go to work, or I'd want to climb all over him. Lifting a hand, I rubbed at his stubble, always perfectly trimmed. He smiled down at me.

The way his dark eyes seemed to search mine, gave my anxiety a twirl. I tried to wipe away any signs of deception with a small smile in return.

"Be good today," he said.

"Aren't I good every day?" I asked.

"Up for debate," he joked.

Then he took my face in his hands and kissed me deeply. I gripped the back of his sweater, pulling his body flush against mine. He moaned as he slanted his mouth over mine and I opened for him. His tongue slid sensually against mine before he pulled back, nipping my bottom lip and ending the kiss.

"See you at dinner," he said, his voice taking on a gruff tone.

I nodded and stepped around him to pick up my bag. Slipping the shoes on my feet, I stood and adjusted my skirt and glanced at myself in the mirror that hung on the entry way wall. I could see Jaxon behind me, and when I met his gaze, he adjusted his pants in an obvious sign that he wanted me now.

"No, no, no. I gotta get to work," I said with a laugh.

Jaxon pretended to lunge for me, but I got out the door with his laughter following me. I turned and blew him a kiss, which made him grin. Frank had the back door open for me and I threw my bags in before sliding into the seat. I waved my fingers at Jaxon, who stood on the front steps watching as we drove away.

As soon as we were through the front gate, my guilt flooded me and the smile fell from my face. Why did doing what I needed to do, need to feel so shitty?

Brooklyn

I WAS LOST in thought until Frank cleared his throat from the front seat. I had insisted a few times that I didn't need to sit in the back when he drove me. However, he said it was easier for to him to see through the front windows without a person sitting in the passenger seat. His interruption to my self condemnation had my eyes meeting his in the rearview mirror.

"Lunch lessons today?" He asked.

"Yes," I replied.

"You don't look happy about it. I'm sure Gideon would be more than willing to pick up the education," Frank said.

It was the same song and dance we went through at least once a week. Frank knew my answer would be no. I knew Frank felt obligated to ask. Gideon had hired him. However, I was his charge. And I had made it fairly clear I would go AWOL if he didn't accompany me. The idea of being caught without me worried Frank more than my lessons being discovered.

I looked out the window as we approached the outskirts of the city. When I brought up self-defense to Gideon, he acted hurt. It took time for me to explain that it wasn't that I didn't trust him to protect her. The attack wasn't his fault. I had been unprepared for the danger that Lyle posed. And I didn't want to be in that position again.

I had expected the guys to understand where I was coming from. When I was met with a no that was nonnegotiable, I felt myself bristle. I could make decisions for myself and I knew what I needed the most. Living in the house with my guys did go a long way to my safety, but I couldn't hide behind their walls all the time. Even with four of them, they couldn't be with me at all times.

They had been clear they didn't want me wandering from the house or my office unless previously scheduled. If I wanted to see Ash, I had to tell them before, and Frank had to take me. If I wanted to have lunch outside of the office with co-workers, Frank was right with me. The whole thing felt ridiculous until I remembered it was Gideon who found me with a knife in my stomach. Knowing where they were coming from helped tamp down some of my need to rebel against their hold.

However, the self-defense classes were not an option. Gideon couldn't teach me. It had become obvious that he couldn't handle me throwing a punch or taking one. Even if he held back, he still wouldn't attack me the way Lyle had. And if he wouldn't threaten me enough, how would I learn to defend myself from that type of attack? Our lessons only caused more friction between us, so I quit them.

We pulled up to my office and Frank showed his ID to get into the parking garage. Security had been increased since everything had come out about Lyle. He hadn't specifically come to my office, but he had somehow delivered a dead rat at one point. When I came clean about everything with the President of the company, he was horrified that I had been keeping everything secret.

Part of me was worried they would see me as too much of a risk. But it was the exact opposite. The employees closed ranks around me, being even more careful of calls that came to me or deliveries that came to the front desk. My assistant, Pam, opened all of my mail and packages now. And the President had informed the building owners that increased security was needed on the garage and the front lobby.

My job didn't allow me to fade into the background, but now I felt even more on display when I walked into the office. Frank walked with me until I was through reception and into my office. He normally stationed himself in the reception area and had created quite a friendship with the receptionist and Pam. It made having him shadowing my every step a bit easier.

Now that everything was out in the open, I no longer felt the need to hide the scar across my throat. I didn't call attention to it, but I didn't worry about wearing uncomfortable high collared shirts and large ornate jewelry to hide it. The sense of being comfortable in my own skin had given me more confidence than I could remember having.

I knew a lot of the confidence was also coming from the Knights. The way they wanted me, every piece of me, all the time, made me feel powerful and sexy. It was something I had only read about in books or seen in romance movies. And I had it times four. The relationships could be a bit overwhelming at times, as I tried to learn to navigate things, but each of them made me feel at ease with whatever decisions I made.

Sitting at my desk, I threw myself into my schedule. I

reviewed my to-do list for the day and messages I had received in the evening. We often worked with business people that didn't find the time to call or return messages until after hours. I sorted through the ones that I needed to return immediately and got to work.

Mid morning rolled around and Pam stuck her head into my office. I was on a call, but I beckoned her in. When she entered, her arms were full of a vase of flowers. I eyed it warily, though I knew Pam would have read the card and ensured it wasn't anything nefarious. She sat them on the small coffee table and smiled brightly over at me before leaving and closing the office door.

Pam was more adamant on protecting me, after the attack at the small café she had insisted we eat lunch at. The woman had inadvertently helped Lyle's plan by taking a call from a fake friend. The person wanted to surprise Brooklyn. Well, he had surprised me with a knife to the stomach. Pam felt as much, if not more, guilt than Gideon.

I ended my call and went to the flowers. Written on the card in black pen was a quick message. "You're amazing, babe. - O" My heart fluttered in my chest. I leaned down to smell the roses. They reminded me of fire, with the center of the bud a bright orange, bleeding into the outer petals that were a deep red. They were beautiful, and the gesture was thoughtful coming from Oliver. He liked to play, but his feelings were clearer than any of the others.

Leaving the flowers on the coffee table so I could see them in front of me, I sat back down at my desk. Thinking about Oliver made me think about the morning sex. I closed my eyes and remembered what it was like to be against the wall with Gideon, him fucking me hard, while I looked over his shoulder at Oliver, bringing himself to orgasm under the water spray.

Unconsciously, I squeezed my thighs together, turned on by the memory. Why hadn't someone told me that watching a man touch himself, while staring at you, was such a turn on? Oliver was always very vocal and physical about his attraction to me.

For some reason, watching him finish himself while I was having sex with his brother was climbing my list of turn ons. It was like I found something new to enjoy each day with my guys and I wasn't complaining.

My phone rang, and I had to pull myself together and get my mind off sex, at least for the rest of the work day. While I spoke with our events manager, my eyes continued to stray to the roses and I couldn't keep the smile out of my voice. By the time the short call ended, my events manager was just as bubbly and I was sure she thought I was that happy about her ideas.

The rest of the morning went by without incident and when lunch came, I grabbed my gym bag and left my office. Frank was already on his feet, with his normal surly look. I was used to his attitude, which would last until we were back in my office after lunch. I waved at the receptionist, who smiled at us as we went to the elevators.

The drive to the gym was quiet, Frank already knowing his arguments weren't going to stop the lesson of the day. He walked me to the 'door of the locker room inside the gym. He always waited right outside while I changed, to ensure nothing happened to me for the moments he couldn't be right next to me. Once I came out and joined the class, he would settle into the seating area and watch the lesson.

After researching self-defense, I had settled on Muay Thai classes. There were so many options for women in my situation. However, when I pictured how Lyle held me by my throat, I knew I needed techniques for close combat. Muay Thai also had long range combat skills, which made me think about preventing Lyle from ever getting close enough to force a kiss on me again.

I stepped onto the padded mat with the other students of the afternoon class. I was one of three women. When we had to partner up, one of us was always with a man. Today was my day. The man was twice my size but had kind eyes. He smiled at me as the instructor gave us directions on which skills we were to be practicing.

For our warm up, we were working on sparring with only our lead hand. I fell into my stance and began to circle with my partner. We weren't meant to connect, and each of us threw jabs while the other dodged and ducked to miss the slight impact that might come from the punch. We then rolled into regular boxing and were able to add our second hand to the mix. I had started to feel more confident in my punching, with all the bag work we did during our classes.

We switched into a third drill, where one of us could only throw punches and one could only use kicks. This was one of my favorite warm-ups, because it made you think about how to get close to avoid being kicked if you were the one throwing punches. If you were the one only allowed to kick, you had to dodge back to avoid punches, but also stay close enough to land your own blows.

My partner's reach was well beyond mine and at first, he was taking it easy on me. I had punches first, so after the first time, I dodged into his space and threw a series of punches, he started to take me a bit more seriously. When we switched and I could only kick, things got a bit more complicated. His reach was way longer, and I had to get creative with ducking in to land any kicks.

We took time on the bags, which was always something that got my blood pumping. With the same partner, one of us held the bag while the other kicked and hit the bag with more force than we could use on our partners. Our instructor moved from bag to bag, giving tips and motivation.

"Brooklyn, you're not throwing your hips enough with your kicks. The punches are getting better," he said as he walked by me.

I nodded and focused on my hips and kicks to ensure I was getting the full power behind each blow. I pictured defending myself against Lyle in the bathroom. There was enough space for me to kick him and take him down before he even got to me. But I didn't have the skills on how to do it. I landed one strong kick, causing my partner to step back a bit.

"Whoa, getting some aggression out?" He said.

"A bit, I guess," I replied, as I paused to catch my breath.

The last bit of the lesson was practicing clinching and grappling. We were learning how to counter different holds and I paid attention closely as I followed the steps to escape the holds my partner put on me. He was larger than Lyle would ever be, but knowing I could have the steps to escape an attack made me feel even more confident in my training.

After class, I said goodbye to the people I recognized and our instructor before ducking back into the locker room. This was where I washed away all evidence of the lesson, redid my hair and make-up and walked out as if nothing had happened. The look on Frank's face always reminded me he knew what I did.

Five

Aiden

THE FIGURES on the screen started blurring and I rubbed my eyes. It had already been a full day of work and I still had a few hours to go. I leaned back in my office chair and looked around my office that was in Club 4. It was my only office away from home, though there were offices in the back of every location we opened.

Club 4 was our first big venture. It had started slowly, without a reputation or anything to attract customers. Now it's always at the top of our revenue streams, building a name for the best place to be on a weekend night. I was proud of what we had built together, my brothers and I.

The office door opened, and Jaxon walked in. He plopped down in a chair on the opposite side of my desk. He held a folder in one hand, so I knew his visit was business. Each of us had specific responsibilities within our company, 4K. While I was the face of the business and technical CEO, each of us held the same amount of sway over the business. I wanted it that way, to ensure we did everything as partners.

Jaxon was in charge of HR and employee relations across all of our businesses. Gideon naturally fell into security, physical and virtual. Oliver was great with people, so he was good at being the face with our vendors and contracts we held. Together we worked as a well-oiled machine and kept all 4K properties running and prosperous.

"I've got the list of final employees for the new location. I'm probably going to have to go and do the orientation in person," Jaxon said, his voice grim.

I didn't say anything for a moment, just nodded and looked back at the figures on my screen. We were expanding to a new location outside of our state. It opened a new revenue source for us, however the learning curve of a new state with its taxes and laws, made all of us feel the stress. I knew I needed to go too, see the location, ensure the renovations were being done correctly.

There was only one reason neither Jaxon or I were ready to travel. Brooklyn. We were all slightly damaged after going through the attack on her and the feeling of the chance of losing her. Until that moment, I hadn't been willing to admit to myself that I wanted her as badly as my brothers. And it still took until she was healed for me to make any moves on her to solidify those feelings.

"Aiden?" Jaxon's voice broke into my inner thoughts.

"I know you need to go. I need to go too. I guess we just shouldn't travel at the same time?" I suggested.

"You don't want to go any more than I do," Jaxon replied.

I nodded again. The idea of leaving her while she was still in danger made my heart feel like it was being ripped from my chest. I wasn't prepared for the emotions Brooklyn created inside me. The habit of pushing them down was one I was very familiar with. Over years of abuse and neglect, I had learned how to manage the way I allowed my emotions to rule my life.

"We'll need to plan it. Let me know what you think is best and I'll go with that," I said.

Jaxon just nodded and stood to leave the office. After the door shut, I leaned back in my chair again, staring at the ceiling. The four of us had overcome all the odds against us to get to where we were. I wanted to believe we were far away from who we were, but those men would always be inside us.

If I was being honest about Club 4, we all knew it wasn't opened in the most legitimate way possible. The previous owner of the club was in debt to Jaxon's father. At that time, Jaxon's father was a mid-level drug operation and was intent on climbing the ladder.

That plan included Jaxon, Oliver, Gideon and myself. Each of us filled a roll in his enterprise and we were only helping it grow by leaps and bounds. It was working for him that I learned I had a head for business.

I barely graduated high school, probably wouldn't have if Gideon hadn't worked hard to keep me on track. Lord knew my mother wasn't one to support me. I was lucky if she didn't beat me so badly that I couldn't go to school. By the time I was a teenager and towered over her, I was busy just keeping off her radar, mostly so she didn't steal any of the money I was making slinging drugs and running the books.

Gideon was used as muscle and when Jaxon's father decided to call in a debt, he'd send Gideon to do the dirty work. This time, when Gideon went to the collect on the owner of the club, the owner groveled and offered the business as payment. In a split-second decision, Gideon changed our trajectory and created a new future for the four of us.

Together, we pooled our funds and paid the debt the club owner should have paid to Jaxon's father. We never told him about the club or how it had been transferred to Gideon's name. To initially fund the running of the club, the way the owner had run it, the four of us continued to work in the business with Jaxon's father.

After a few years of trying to balance, I called a meeting for the four of us and we were all in agreement that it was too much. Gideon had just barely escaped a murder charge the year before, after Jaxon's father sent him to dole out justice. Jaxon was sampling product, more than any of us were comfortable with. The life was leaving Oliver's eyes. And my mother had finally killed herself with the same product we were supporting. We all knew we couldn't do it anymore.

That was where things got complicated. I had every piece of information to put Jaxon's father away for good. I had quietly been collecting names, dates, amounts, locations and more on the entire drug enterprise. When I started collecting the data, I didn't specifically know what I would do with it. But if I could use it to protect my brothers, I knew there was a purpose.

The blackmail only went so far, and I was reminded of that as I looked at my current figures again. We still had secret payments leaving 4K that we hid through shell companies. I hated it. But while I had dirt on Jaxon's father, he hadn't been just trusting us all those years either. He had enough to put us all away for good. He stayed away as long as we kept up our payments.

I rubbed my eyes again, feeling the familiar sick feeling I got when I thought about our past. It wasn't just the drug dealing, beatings, killings or the number of things we had to do for Jaxon's father. We did what we had to for survival, what all four of us had done since birth. Maybe those things should bother me more. It was knowing that no matter how good we were now, deep down we all had that darkness inside us.

That darkness is what rose to the surface as I picked up the files Gideon had compiled on Lyle. I flipped through some of the earlier history, memories about Brooklyn that I didn't need to be reminded of at the moment. When I got to the end of the trail, I felt the same frustration I did when Gideon first told us he lost track of the fucker.

It was clear now that Lyle had a partner, a female for sure. I looked at the images of Lyle fleeing down the street after stabbing Brooklyn in the cafe bathroom. His face was burned into my brain and I would recognize him anywhere. But who was hiding him? Who was helping him stay off our radar? I couldn't help but wonder if this somehow was connected to us, as well as Brooklyn. Could it be someone from our past helping Lyle get at Brooklyn, in the hopes of hurting my brothers and I as well?

I wasn't opposed to getting my hands dirty, we'd all done it before. Blood and death weren't strangers; however, we had put that behind us as we built the lives we wanted to live. Now, we had people to pay to handle things when necessary. Lyle was one I wouldn't mind handling myself.

Shaking those feelings off, I tried to focus on the last bits of work I needed to do. Nothing would make sense, and I was at the point of knowing I needed to walk away. An idea popped into my head and I immediately jumped up and gathered my things. If I couldn't work here, I'd find a better way of spending my time.

CHAPTER
Six

Brooklyn

A KNOCK on my door was the only warning I had before it swung open. I had papers spread across my desk, working out donor gifts that were most affordable as well as attractive. I glanced up, expecting Pam in the doorway, but my gaze froze when I found Aiden.

"Aiden? Is something wrong?" I asked, immediately worried about why he was in my office at the end of the day.

As I stood to round my desk, he stepped in and closed the

door behind him. He looked dark and like he'd had a long day. His dark hair was messy, as if he had been running his hands through it. I noticed stress tight around his gray eyes, though his gaze on me was softer. He was wearing a black on black suit and shirt, his shirt open at the throat.

He walked to the roses on my table and quickly read the card. When he turned to me, he had a small smile on his face.

"My brothers always know the things to do," he said.

For just a moment, I could see through the walls Aiden always built around himself. Exhaustion, concern, and anger shined through for a moment. I stepped closer to him, placing my palm against his cheek, looking into his swirling eyes.

"Are you ok?" I asked quietly.

His hand came to my waist, holding my gaze. I could see questions and I waited for him to say whatever he had come to say. One of his hands slid up my side, slowly coming up my chest, over my collarbone, until his fingers caressed my throat. My pulse increased with each moment he carefully touched me. I waited for him to say something, anything, to explain the way he was looking at me.

His fingers closed around my neck and he pulled me into him. His lips descended to mine. The touch was soft at first, exploring, greeting my lips with his own. I let my arms go around his waist, my hands going under his suit jacket to feel his back through his dress shirt.

Aiden growled low in his throat as my hands slid over him and he slanted his mouth over mine, deepening the kiss. His tongue slid along my lips, asking for entry. I opened for him and I couldn't stop the moan as he began to explore my mouth. He nipped at my bottom lip, then slid his tongue along the spot to ease the sting, before sliding his tongue back against mine.

I pushed up on my toes, even my heels not making me as tall as Aiden, rubbing my body along his in the process. I could feel his wanting me pressed against my stomach. His fingers around my neck pressed softly into my skin, controlling me in the kiss, not allowing me the chance to put any space between us. When Aiden was like this, I could feel my heart burst with the emotions he brought out of me.

Finally, he pulled away, ending the kiss. We were both gasping for air and his gray eyes looked lighter than when he first came into my office. I was thankful I could wipe away some of the worry he seemed to be having. His smile was slow and sexy as he looked down at me. I knew my lips were likely swollen and my cheeks were pink from the blush that had crept up my neck.

"Are you ready to go home?" He asked.

My brain misfired a few times before I looked over my shoulder at the work I really needed to finish. It only took a moment for me to decide I could easily finish the work from home. I looked back at Aiden and nodded.

"Good. I told Frank to take an early night. My car is downstairs," he said.

He leaned down and kissed my neck, his lips caressing over my pulse and I sighed in contentment. He straightened and motioned toward my desk. It took all of my concentration to not trip over my own feet as I went to my desk to pack the documents I needed and my laptop into my briefcase.

When I was ready, Aiden led me to the door, but kept his hands to himself so not to cause a stir in the office. My co-workers knew I was close to the Knights and was staying with them currently due to safety concerns. But we were careful not to show affection that would cause rumors to fly throughout the office.

I said goodbye to Pam and waved to the receptionist. Once in the elevator, Aiden turned to me and pressed me against the elevator wall. I gasped at the sudden onslaught, and he took the moment to dive for my mouth again. His lips slid down my jaw to my ear, where he sucked the lobe between his teeth.

"Why do I want you, as badly as I do, all the time?" He growled into my ear.

"I, honestly, don't know," I replied, my words ragged and breathy.

He pulled back and looked down at me seriously.

"You really don't, do you?"

I shook my head, not knowing what to even say. I didn't see myself as anything special, but for some reason Aiden's eyes were saying something completely different.

"You're a damn goddess, sweetheart," he said gruffly.

I could feel the blush on my cheeks and I tried to look away. But Aiden grabbed my face and forced me to look him in the eye. He didn't say another word, just stared down at me with an intensity that had my knees wobbling. The only thing that saved me from becoming a puddle on the elevator floor was the ding of the door, announcing the arrival at the parking garage level.

Aiden slipped his hand down my arm, causing goosebumps to rise, before taking my hand and leading me into the garage. Normally, Aiden left the driving up to an employee. Either a town car or a limo was his day to day ride. Today, he lead me to his dark blue Porsche Cayman, a slick sports car that he liked to drive faster than the law really allowed.

He put my bags in the small trunk space of the car before helping me into the passenger seat. The purr of the engine was the initial excitement of knowing we were going to be shooting out of the parking garage and flying around the city. As he put the car into drive, Aiden seemed to hesitate. I looked over, waiting for him to either break the silence or pull from the parking spot.

"I'd like to take you somewhere," he finally said quietly.

"Ok," I replied.

There was a small crack in the heavy facade that Aiden always had around him. The newness of our relationship made me walk a thin line, not pushing him further than he wanted to go. My heart was already at risk, reaching out to him every time he was around.

As he pulled out of the parking garage, his hand found my bare knee. The warmth crept into my body and I had a hard time keeping my breathing under control. As if he knew my struggles, he began to push up my skirt, revealing my bare thighs under-neath. His fingers glided between my legs, clearly on a mission.

I looked over at Aiden's profile and I could see the sexy smirk he was wearing, but he didn't turn to look at me. When his fingers found my panties, he softly pet me through the silky material, causing me to hum in appreciation. I couldn't help my reaction, as I let my thighs slip further apart.

His fingers moved to find the edge of my panties and when he slid through my wetness, I threw my head back with a gasp.

"So wet, sweetheart," Aiden murmured.

I could see he was still staring at the road, his other hand tight on the steering wheel, knuckles white and straining.

"Aiden," his name came out more like a moan as his finger found my entrance and dipped in shallowly.

I gripped his forearm with one hand and the car seat with the other. My hips involuntarily lifted, trying to get more from his fingers. His laugh was gruff, and I knew this was getting to him. I felt the car speed increase as we began to leave the city and head into the outskirts of town. But my trust in Aiden didn't leave room for me to be worried about crashing in the sports car.

He began pumping two fingers into me and I was quickly climbing toward a climax I couldn't control. When he removed his fingers and slid up to my clit, I was teetering on the edge of a cliff I so badly wanted to fall over. His fingers circled the bud and suddenly pinched, causing me to cry out as my body began to shudder from the deliciousness of release.

Aiden pulled back, waiting for me to release the death grip I had on his forearm. When I finally did, I saw a full-blown smile come across his handsome face. He finally glanced over at me, as he put his fingers in his mouth, cleaning my wetness with his tongue. I could only stare as he licked my taste from his fingers and then growled one word.

"Delicious."

The car began to slow, and I pulled my gaze from Aiden to look around. He had taken us up a mountain on the outside of town. The sun was just beginning to set, and he pulled the sports car into a small dirt parking area. The view over the city was incredible, cast in pink and dark purple hues from the setting sun's rays.

Aiden wasn't looking at the view. His hand came to my chin, turning me to look at him. He leaned forward and captured my mouth in a demanding kiss. I pushed closer to him, willing to give him everything he needed from me. Thrusting one of my hands into his dark hair, I slanted my mouth against his, deepening our kiss.

Aiden's fingers found the buttons on my cardigan, and he pushed it off my shoulders. His mouth followed his hands down my chest, until he could pull down my tank top and bra, to expose my pebbled nipple. Running a tongue around it, he brought it to an even tighter peak, before sucking it into his mouth. Moving to the other, he lavished it with the same attention.

Suddenly, he pulled away and opened his car door. He shrugged out of his suit jacket and dropped it in his seat. I then sat and stared at him as he rounded the front of the Porsche and came to my door.

"Get out, sweetheart," he said.

I turned and took the hand he offered. He led me to the hood of the car, turning me to look at the city in the waning light. His big arms wrapped around me from behind, one around my chest and the other around my hips. The embrace felt incredibly intimate as he kissed the sensitive area behind my ear.

We stood quietly, watching as it got dark around us, before he began to kiss down my neck, to my shoulder. I tilted my head to give him better access to the delicate areas that he was giving attention.

"I'm going to fuck you on the hood of my car, sweetheart," he said.

The heat that pooled in my stomach told me how badly I wanted that. He spun me, his hand on my throat again, something he seemed to love to do for a sense of control, before he slammed his mouth down on mine again. We battled, tongues, lips and teeth, as he led me back to the car. When the backs of my knees hit the bumper, he encouraged me to sit.

Crouching in front of me, Aiden slid his hands up my skirt until he found my panties. He slid them down my legs and over my stiletto heels before pocketing the material. I reached forward, wanting to touch him badly. Unbuckling his belt and unbuttoning his pants went faster than I thought possible. I slid my hand into his boxer briefs and palmed his heavy erection. His breathing became ragged as I stroked him a few times before he pushed me back on the car hood.

With his hardness released, he slid between my thighs, pulling my knees up to wrap my legs around his lower back. He notched the head of his cock at my entrance and slowly slid into me until he was seated deep.

"Thank fuck for IUDs. You feel so damn incredible," he moaned against my mouth.

"Aiden, please god, move," I begged.

I felt so full, and the friction of each movement sent shivers throughout my body. I moved my hips, trying to get the contact I wanted. He smiled against my lips before kissing me slowly again. Then he slowly pulled out of me and slowly pumped back in, his movements controlled and sensual. Aiden had always been an attentive lover, but this felt different somehow.

He leaned down and freed my breasts again as he continued the slow thrusts into my depths. He kissed from one nipple to the other, before kissing up my chest and neck to my mouth. I grabbed his hair and kissed him with all the passion that was building up in me with his slow thrusting. My point getting across, he pulled out again and slammed into me hard.

"Is that what you want, sweetheart?" He murmured.

"Oh my fuck, yes," I moaned as he did it again.

"My girl has a dirty mouth," he laughed, though the sound was strained. I knew he was holding himself back.

"Baby, you said you'd fuck me on this car. So do it," I said, opening my eyes and staring into his gray depths.

I could see the heat simmering in his eyes, and it sparked as soon as I spoke. He leaned up then, grabbed my hips and began to fuck me with long, hard strokes. I couldn't get leverage on the car hood, so I was completely at his mercy. He grabbed my legs and brought them up, so my ankles were on his shoulders. The position caused him to slide even deeper into me and I cried out as he swung his hips harder.

"Come for me again, sweetheart. Squeeze my cock with that perfect pussy," he growled.

One of his hands snuck between us and he found my clit. He strummed the bud with his thrusts and within moments, I was cresting the wave of orgasm, crying out his name and throwing my head back. He slammed into me and almost collapsed on top of me on the car. I wrapped my legs and arms around him, letting us both float down from the orgasm high.

"Fuck, Brooklyn," he groaned into my neck.

Aiden propped himself up so he could look down at me. For a moment, his gaze was completely open and I could see emotions swirling in his eyes. It was more than he ever usually showed me and I could feel tears prick my eyes from the deepness of it. But just as I was about to speak, I saw him shut down.

Pulling back, Aiden tucked himself back into his pants, buttoning and fixing his belt. He held a handkerchief out to me and my panties. The coldness from him was stark compared to the way he felt against me just seconds before. I was shaky as I cleaned myself up and slipped my panties back on. The evening temperature seemed to take a dive, and I started to shiver. He took my elbow to help me off the car and walked me to my side of the Porsche.

Once we were both in the car, Aiden threw it into reverse and soon we were racing toward home. I could feel myself still shivering as I slipped back into my cardigan, the feeling in the car cold and distant.

"Aiden, what happened?" I asked.

"I thought the two orgasms were pretty clear?" He said, his voice laced with arrogance.

His tone stung, and I stared at him for a moment. His face was a mask of indifference and a coldness settled in my chest. I turned to look out the passenger window, leaning toward the door, wishing the car was larger than it actually was. I was thankful when I saw the gate leading to home come into view.

When Aiden put the car into park and turned off the engine, he sat like stone behind the wheel. I looked at him, hoping he would say something, anything, to take away the sick feeling I had in my stomach. There was a moment where I almost felt like he was making love to me, instead of just having fun. I let myself get lost in the sensation of that feeling. Now, he was ripping that away, and I didn't know what was happening.

The silence was more than I could bear. I got out of the car and slammed the door before retrieving my bags. By the time I reached the garage door, Aiden still hadn't left the car, and I didn't wait to see what he would do. I snuck from the mudroom, through the kitchen, glad I didn't run into anyone else at home. When I got to my room, I quietly closed the door and locked it. Even if Aiden had regrets, I wasn't letting him in now.

I undressed and stepped into a burning hot shower. I left my hair piled on top of my head, not wanting to get it all wet, but needing to wash away what had happened with Aiden. I had never felt like my relationships with any of the guys was just sex until now. Even if what I had with Aiden was fairly new, I didn't anticipate being used.

By the time I was dressing in sweats, I found a resolution inside myself. I wouldn't allow myself to be just another piece of ass. If Aiden wanted something casual, he could find it somewhere else. I cared for the Knights, Aiden included. But that didn't mean he could treat me as if I was just some girl he picked up for the night at the club.

Bolstered by my renewed confidence, I made my way to the

kitchen. The house was quiet, except for the sound of someone cooking. When I entered, I found the chef moving around, earbuds in his ears, as he pulled out the ingredients for dinner. I caught his attention, and he froze before smiling and removing the buds and putting them in his pocket.

"Miss Reeves, good evening," he said.

The Knights' chef couldn't be much older than me, but he was always extremely polite and businesslike. I smiled at him and took a seat at the island.

"Hi, Chris. Do you mind if I hang out in here while you make dinner?" I asked.

"Of course not. Would you like a glass of wine?" He asked, motioning to a bottle he had opened for dinner.

I nodded and soon I was sipping on a deep red wine that helped warm some of the ice that was still sitting in my chest. Chris had just made a joke involving food, and I was laughing when Jaxon appeared at the entrance of the mudroom. I watched as his eyes shifted between the young chef and me. The only indication of any emotion was the slight tightening of his eyes, before he entered the kitchen and came straight to me.

"Hey, love," he whispered against my lips as he leaned to kiss me.

His kiss was deep and searing. Without even going to his room to change, Jaxon took the stool next to me and his hand landed on my thigh. I smile over at him, realizing that my even tempered man was actually jealous.

CHAPTER
Seven

Jaxon

WALKING into the kitchen and finding Brooklyn laughing with the chef made a fairly unusual feeling rise in my chest. I wasn't typically a jealous person. But the green-eyed monster started to claw up my throat, and I had to swallow it down as I walked to Brooklyn.

After I sat next to her, the twinkle in her eyes told me she knew why I was sitting next to her. I couldn't leave now. That would just look even more strange. So, I shrugged out of my suit jacket and hung it on a hook by the mudroom door, before sitting back down with her.

"How was your day, love?" I asked.

Almost immediately, her blue eyes clouded and I knew something was wrong. But Brooklyn was a strong one, and she immediately pushed away whatever was upsetting her, smiling a little too brightly at me.

"Fine. Had to bring some work home, but that's ok," she replied.

She lifted her wineglass to her mouth and took a long sip. She swirled the dark liquid and stared into the glass, not making eye contact. I gripped each of her thighs and twisted her on the stool until she was facing me. Taking the glass from her hand, I set it on the island before the red wine spilled all over her. She looked up at me in surprised as I shifted until my stool put me right between her legs.

"What is it?" I asked softly, using a hand to push her chin up until she was looking into my eyes.

"Just a rough day," she replied.

I stared down at her, watching as tears seemed to gather in her ice blue depths, but she blinked and they were gone so suddenly, I had to wonder if I had seen them in the first place. I kissed her lips softly once, then let my mouth wander to her ear.

"Let it go, love," I whispered.

I could feel her tremble slightly, then her arms went around my shoulders and she was pulling me to her. Instead, I lifted her from her stool and let her climb onto my lap, until she was curled happily with her face in my neck. She took a deep breath and I could feel as her body relaxed.

"You always smell so good, Jaxon," she said.

I had to laugh a little at that. I didn't really wear cologne, but I did like the specific scent of my body wash and hair products. If my girl liked it, I'd never change the brand. Hell, I'd buy it in bulk right now.

I rubbed her back, sliding my palm under the oversized sweat-shirt she was wearing. Goosebumps broke out on her skin, but she just sighed and leaned into me more fully. We sat like that, as Chris moved around the kitchen, continuing dinner. I noticed that he had put his earbuds back in, taking the hint that this was a private moment. With the jealous feeling gone, I felt slightly guilty for thinking about firing Chris for a split second, just for making Brooklyn laugh. My inner thoughts could be ridiculous.

Brooklyn's hand moved to her wine glass, and she took another sip, but didn't try to move from my lap. I was perfectly content having her as close as possible, at least with clothes on. I wasn't sure what was bothering her. But I knew she was home, and she was physically safe. Anything else we could handle.

Moments later, the rumble of Gideon's motorcycle could be heard in the garage. Brooklyn's head picked up, but she didn't make a move to go back to her stool. When the rumble stopped and Gideon appeared in the kitchen, he took in the scene, and I could see the concern cross his face. He came to us and Brooklyn angled her face toward him so he could kiss her hello.

"Hi," she said in a small voice.

"Stellina, long day?" He asked.

She just nodded, and he trailed a finger down her cheek.

"I'm going to change and be back down in just a few," he said.

Brooklyn nodded and burrowed back into my neck. Gideon and I met eyes over her head and I could only shrug slightly, to let him know I really wasn't sure what was going on with her. He disappeared and when he reappeared, Oliver was also with him, who had apparently entered the house through the front door and changed before coming to the kitchen.

Chris began to serve dinner and Brooklyn started to move from my lap. I circled an arm around her waist, content with her just staying. She leaned back again and kissed my cheek. I pulled her plate over to next to mine and picked up a piece of potato to feed her. She obediently opened her mouth and chewed before I gave her a bite of chicken.

"Where's Aiden?" Oliver asked.

I felt Brooklyn's body stiffen at the mention of Aiden and suddenly I was more worried about what was going on.

"His car is in the garage. Probably in his office," Gideon replied.

Oliver picked up his phone, presumably to text Aiden to get his ass to family dinner. I continued to feed Brooklyn and myself, as my mind whirled around the possibilities. If they had fought, I wasn't sure Brooklyn would confide in me, Oliver, or Gideon. Whatever had happened between them was enough to send Brooklyn into a spiral and I didn't like it.

Aiden appeared at the entrance of the kitchen and his eyes immediately went to Brooklyn. But where usually his gaze is light and happy when he looks at her, now it was dark and shutdown. He already had a scotch in his hand and he took his plate to a stool across from Brooklyn, instead of sitting on the one she had vacated.

Brooklyn had turned into stone on my lap and she shook her head when I tried to give her more food. She sipped her wine and turned her face away from the table and I had the suspicion she was avoiding looking at Aiden at all. Over her head, I could see Oliver and Gideon exchanging looks before they both looked at me.

Downing her wine, Brooklyn put her glass down and pulled out of my embrace.

"I have some work to do. I'm going to head upstairs," she announced.

"You haven't finished your dinner," Oliver pointed out.

"I'm not really hungry," she murmured, as she put her feet down, standing between my legs.

"Do you want me to come with you?" I whispered quietly, hugging her carefully.

"No, babe. Finish your dinner. I'm just going to work," she said.

She kissed my cheek before leaving the kitchen in a rush. I

couldn't help but follow her with my eyes as she left. Oliver and Gideon both did as well and when they turned back to their plates, we all just stared at Aiden, who was just staring into his scotch.

I pushed around my food for a moment, trying to decide how to broach the subject of what the fuck was happening right now. Things had been on a positive track with Brooklyn. She had become comfortable in our home, behaving as if it were her own, exactly how we wanted things. The way she had come out of her shell was amazing, and we were drawn to her like moths to a damn flame. Tonight, she had felt like the same doe in the head-lights as when she ran from us at the club the first night.

"What did you do?" I finally growled, not realizing how my anger was rising.

"Who?" Oliver said, his fork halfway to his mouth, looking around, confused.

"Him," I said as I jabbed my fork in the direction of the brooding Aiden.

Aiden lifted his gaze, and instead of the shutdown look he had when he had entered, his eyes were now ablaze with fury.

"What the fuck is it any of your business?" He asked.

The tone of his anger had Gideon's eyes snapping up from his plate. He looked between us, waiting to see how this conversation was going to unfold.

"It's all of our fucking business when she starts avoiding us the way she did just now," I said.

"Seems like that's not a me problem," Aiden sneered.

"Whoa, what the fuck, Aiden," Oliver cut in.

I could feel my anger seeping into my veins and I knew this was going to go too far. Standing, I took my plate and Brooklyn's to the sink. She had barely eaten anything, so I took her food and put it into a small glass container to save in the fridge in case she got hungry later. The motion helped me clear my head before turning back to my brothers.

"It's clear you have a harder time being in a relationship. But that doesn't mean you get to fuck this up for the rest of us. I will not lose her, because you're a prick," I said.

Aiden had the audacity to roll his eyes, and I wanted to punch him in the face. Gideon eyed me, and I knew for a split second he could read my mind. I knew Gideon wasn't happy with the news Aiden wasn't treating Brooklyn right, but he had always defended Aiden, since they were children. He wouldn't sit by if I decided to follow through with my thoughts.

"If you can't hold on to your girlfriend, that is definitely not my issue. Sounds like you should work a little harder and get her screaming your name, Jax," Aiden said.

I didn't even know I was moving until Gideon was in front of me, pushing me back. Oliver was on his feet as well, looking at the stairs, probably worried Brooklyn would hear us fighting. Aiden just sat with his scotch, eyeing me as if I were nothing but a fly for him to flick aside.

"That's enough, Aiden. You're being a dick. Go be a dick somewhere else," Gideon growled.

"Whatever. You all are too fucking sensitive. I got no time for it," Aiden replied.

Standing, he took his scotch and left his plate on the island. He disappeared down the hall into his office. The door slammed behind him, putting an end to the conversation. Gideon, Oliver and I stood in the kitchen, silence surrounding us except for my heavy breathing.

"What are you thinking happened?" Gideon asked quietly.

"I have no idea. But it's clear it was him who upset her today and him she's avoiding. Did they spend time together today?" I asked.

"Yeah, Aiden texted me to let me know he sent Frank home and that he was bringing Brooklyn home," Gideon said.

We went silent again, all of us in our own minds trying to figure out what could have happened during a drive home. It was enough to send Brooklyn into a spiral.

"Jaxon, why don't you go see if you can talk to Brooklyn? See if you can figure out what's going on and maybe help clear up whatever it is?" Oliver said.

I nodded, not that I needed his suggestion, I was already planning on going to her. Gideon finally stepped back, once he was sure I wasn't going to storm after Aiden and try to beat the crap out of him in his office. Even if I did think he deserved it, it wasn't going to accomplish anything. And I was sure Brooklyn wouldn't be thrilled with us physically fighting in the house.

Leaving the kitchen, I took the stairs two at a time until I was on the second floor landing. Brooklyn's room was right in the middle of the floor, which is why it was previously the guest room. It was her room now. I couldn't see it as a guest room ever again. I knocked lightly on the door and once I heard her quiet voice, I entered.

The room was dark, and I knew immediately she wasn't actually working. I could see her laying in the middle of the huge bed we had gotten custom made. Since she started staying with us, there was never a night she was alone and more often than not, two of us were with her. The larger bed made all activities much easier to accomplish.

Right now, the only activity I was thinking about was consoling her. She lifted her head to look over at me. I went to the bathroom and flicked on a small light so I could see her face. Her eyes were puffy, a sure sign that she had been crying. My anger threatened to overflow again, but as she watched me, I knew I couldn't let her see that.

"Hey, love. Can I join you?" I asked.

She just nodded and flipped back the comforter. I quickly shed my clothes. As usual, I wasn't wearing underwear, but I wasn't climbing into bed with Brooklyn for sex. I slid under the comforter and pulled Brooklyn close. She laid her head on my chest and curled an arm around my stomach.

"What's going on, Brooklyn?" I asked when she just laid silently for a long moment.

She was quiet long enough that I started to wonder if she'd confide in me.

"Is it right for me to talk to you about one of your brothers?" She finally asked.

That was a decent question. We had never been in a relationship that was healthy like it was with Brooklyn. Before, when we were all in a relationship with the woman named Missy. It was a constant unhealthy stream of events. Jealousy, competition, comparisons and more. We didn't know what was really happening until the end, when she tried to pull us all apart. She wanted us all, but she wanted us to fight over her.

That was the exact opposite of Brooklyn. What we had was working. My brothers and I didn't feel like any of us were less in the relationship. None of us felt like we had to fight for dominance or Brooklyn's attention. We all had our piece with her, and it all added up to one whole.

That meant there were things we hadn't been faced with before. When we were dating Missy, if she talked to one of us about another, it was always her talking shit, a lot of it untrue, and just to create chaos in our family. I didn't believe Brooklyn would be that way, evident by the fact that she was even asking if it was ok to talk to me.

I had to make an executive decision. Sometimes she was going to need to confide in someone. There were four of us and if she needed something, I wanted to be sure she was getting that from us, emotional or physical.

"I think it's ok if you need to talk and it has to do with one of my brothers," I finally replied.

"Ok...well, Aiden picked me up from work today. When he came to the office, it was clear something was weighing on him. But then he was sweet, and we had some fun together," she said, her voice taking on a slightly wistful tone.

"That sounds like a nice afternoon," I said, trying to encourage her.

"It was. It really was. It's just, for a moment, I thought I saw more of Aiden. I feel like he's always keeping me at arm's length. But as soon as he started to open a bit, he shut down. And he shut down hard," she explained.

I didn't really need her to explain how Aiden could be. Since we were teenagers, Aiden knew how to use words to cut to the bone. He was quick witted and way too fucking smart for most people in the room. And since the debacle with Missy, where Aiden was sure he was in love, he had avoided complications in the relationship department. I thought he was willing to try with Brooklyn and that was why he had started dating her as well.

"And I don't like the feeling it gave me," she continued.

Brooklyn propped herself up now, so she could look into my face while she spoke. I could see that tears were threatening again, and I reached my hand up and cupped her cheek. She leaned into the caress and closed her eyes for a moment.

"None of you have ever made me feel like what we have is wrong. But how Aiden treated me, I just felt dirty. And it made me hate everything I thought he and I were building together. I think I was wrong about him. But I hope I wasn't wrong about all of you," she said, her voice getting small at the end.

Anger and panic flared in me. I was back to wanting to storm into Aiden's office and punch him in the jaw. I didn't speak for all of my brothers, but I was pretty positive Oliver and Gideon felt the way I felt. Brooklyn was perfect for us, perfect for our family, perfect for our home. I wanted her to feel cherished and as priceless as she was at all times.

"Don't do that. Aiden has his own fucking issues. That has nothing to do with me, Oliver, or Gideon. I promise you," I said, my voice harsher than I meant.

I pulled her face down to mine so I could kiss her sweetly, holding back all the desire I always had in me when she was around. I just wanted to pour unspoken emotions into her without scaring her from the house completely.

When she leaned back, she smiled sweetly down at me, before laying back down on my chest.

"Could we just sleep and cuddle tonight?" She asked.

There wasn't anything she could ask for that I wasn't going to give her.

Brooklyn

PLEASURE COURSED THROUGH MY BODY. I was fuzzy, just waking up, trying to distinguish reality from dream. As I tried to shift, a steel band came across my hips. I opened my eyes and realized I was lying on my back in the middle of my bed in the Knights' house.

Another wave of pleasure coasted through me and my back bowed involuntarily, a moan escaping my mouth. A chuckle from between my thighs had my gaze snapping down my body. I was met with the sight of Jaxon's face buried at my core, his tattooed arm holding my hips down.

His tongue circled my clit before dipping into my entrance, and I moaned again. His eyes lifted to meet mine and desire shown in his chocolate brown depths. I was now fully awake and able to participate in the sexual delight that was happening.

As he moved back to my clit, I grabbed at his short brown hair, trying to guide him where I wanted him to stay. I grounded myself against his mouth, grasping at the orgasm that was causing my thighs to start to tremble. I cried out as I fell over into bliss and Jaxon slowly kissed up my body, until he was laying next to me.

"Good morning, love," he growled in my ear.

"Mmmm," I mumbled.

"I'm not done with you yet."

He turned me so I was on my side, my ass cradled against his hips. His hand slid up my shirt, to my hardened nipples, pinching them before drifting down my stomach. His palm glided along my hip, until he could pull my leg back over his, then he pushed my upper back away from him, giving him the perfect access to my wetness.

My orgasm made his entry smooth and slick, both of us groaning as he bottomed out.

"I can't get over how fucking good you feel. I could sink into your pussy every day for the rest of my life," he groaned.

Hearing his dirty words only turned me on further, causing me to rotate my hips back. His fingers dug into the flesh of my hips and I knew he was enjoying my movements. His breathing sped up as I ground against him.

Once he was ready, he stilled my hips with his hand and began to thrust deeply into me. I moved my hips in time with him, causing him to hit even deeper inside me. Each motion rubbed all the right places, and I was quickly climbing to a second orgasm. As his cock hit my g-spot, I cried out and clenched down on him.

"Fuck, I love when you come on my cock," he growled.

His thrusts became erratic as he slammed into me and then stilled as he spilled into me. I could feel his cock twitching, and it made me squeeze down again. He groaned, his face now buried in my upper back.

After he slid out of me, I turned so I could face him. He kissed me deeply before smiling brightly at me.

"I couldn't help myself. You're gorgeous when you're sleeping."

"I'm not complaining," I laughed.

My happiness came down just a bit as I remembered the day before and remembered why Jaxon was in bed with me alone in the first place. He was always the one to do the sensible things and coming to talk to me about why I was upset would be right in his wheelhouse.

He could see through me without a word. Just like the night before, though he was initially jealous of me talking to the chef, he saw quickly that I wasn't right. I tried not to let that darken the happiness I woke with. I smiled up at him and nuzzled his neck with my lips.

I had to force Jaxon to leave the bedroom so I could get ready for work on time. Alone, the events of the previous day rushed back, and I tried to compartmentalize, so it wasn't so painful. I finished off my make up and chose a floral dress for the day. It swirled around my knees and would work great with the black stilettos Oliver had bought me.

Taking a deep breath, I started down the stairs. I steeled myself for the cold shoulder I would get from Aiden. I still couldn't understand how we had gone backward so quickly. He was different from his brothers. When Gideon got into his guilt and tried to pull away, I knew I could bring him back to me. I knew we had a connection that I could lean on when times were tough. Aiden and I didn't have that.

I entered the kitchen quietly but froze when I realized Aiden was completely missing. His newspaper was on the island, where he would normally sit to read. Jaxon was sitting at the island, a laptop open in front of him. Gideon was toasting a bagel and was sipping his coffee at the counter. Oliver was looking at a tablet, swiping every so often.

Gideon saw me and he forced a smile onto his face. He wasn't great at hiding his emotions all the time, especially when he was concerned or stressed. I could see the worry around his eyes now. Jaxon looked at me and his smile was brighter, not as concerned, and I was sure our happy morning helped with that.

Oliver didn't notice me right away. I snuck up behind him and nipped at his neck, only causing him to jump slightly.

"Gideon, what did I say about keeping your teeth to yourself?" He said.

And just like that, I burst out laughing. Gideon just made some sort of gagging noise across the kitchen, and Jaxon laughed along with me. Oliver turned on his stool until he planted his feet on either side of mine.

"Oh, well, it's you. I guess that's alright," he said dramatically, with a roll of his eyes.

I was still giggling when Oliver wrapped a hand around the back of my neck to pull my mouth to his. The kiss was more than a hello. It was a statement, a reminder, a promise, and I was there for it. I gripped the front of his button-up shirt and held on as he deepened the kiss. When he pulled away, I was panting, and he had a sexy grin on his face.

Carefully, I made my way to Gideon, who had a bagel and coffee ready for me. There was something about his inherent need to feed me that made me feel close to him. It was his way of showing his affection, while also making sure I was taking care of myself.

I took the plate and mug from his hands and set them down on the island where I would sit. I then turned back to him and leaned into his chest. His big arms circled me as he hugged me tight. Looking up at him, I tugged on his beard lightly, until he leaned down and allowed me to kiss him. When the kiss ended, I just hugged him around the neck, wishing I could just crawl up his body and stay there all day.

Gideon guided me back to the island so I wouldn't forget my food. Aiden's spot stayed empty, and I forced my eyes not to wander to it. It was a glaring reminder of how badly things had gone between him and me, after an amazing time under the open sky with the sun setting behind us.

I took a bite of my bagel and ripped it with more force than needed. I was fucking angry and could admit that to myself. Aiden had taken that moment from me, a moment that felt like a damn movie scene. My heart was too wrapped up in all of it and Aiden ripped that all away from me. So, I decided instead of feeling sad, I was just going to be mad.

Under Gideon's watchful gaze, I finished my bagel, even though it fell like a stone in my stomach. I tried to enjoy my coffee while looking at the three men in the kitchen.

"Oh, don't forget. I'm going to dinner with Ash tonight," I said.

All three sets of eyes looked up at me. I saw the moment Jaxon and Oliver looked to Gideon, and the whole situation rankled me. In my already angry state, it wouldn't take much to push me to fuming. Gideon looked at me thoughtfully and finally just nodded once.

"Didn't realize I needed your approval. I was really just letting you know," I said.

With that, I stood up and went to the entryway to get my shoes and bags. I knew Frank was already outside waiting for me and I wasn't in the mood for some sweet goodbye. I could feel Gideon's presence before I turned to see him.

"It's not about approval, Brooklyn. We just want to make sure you're safe," he said in a low voice.

When I didn't respond, and just stooped to slip my feet into my shoes, Gideon took the extra two steps to be right next to me. Once I stood, his big body crowded around me and I took a step back. I knew I probably seemed like a defiant child, but I was really tired of feeling yanked around and controlled.

Gideon's eyes narrowed as I tried to put distance. One of his large hands came up to my throat, and he guided me back until my back was against the front door. I just continued to glare up at him. Nothing about Gideon frightened me. What worried me more was the moan I had to swallow down as I hit the door.

"Don't be a brat. It's not like you," he growled.

"No? Maybe I just haven't had the chance to show that side yet," I said.

His fingers flexed around my throat, but my defiance didn't simmer. I set my feet and glared up at him. His glare was hot down on my face.

"Maybe. If that's true, I guess we have something to work on," he said.

"Good luck," I shot back.

Before I could take in a breath, Gideon's mouth slammed down on mine. He used his hand around my throat to angle my chin up so he could deepen the kiss however he wanted, controlling my response. His free hand gripped my ass through the thin material of the dress I chose for work. When that wasn't enough, he pulled up the material until he could grab my bare flesh.

I fought back with my mouth, nipping at him, trying to block his entry to me, fighting for the control I thought I was losing. My hands came up, and I pulled his hair that was still down loose. The growl that came from his throat was menacing, but sent heat directly to my core. He pushed a thigh between my legs, rubbing it against my heat.

The moan that came from my mouth caused Gideon to pull back with a satisfied grin on his face.

"I'd fuck you against this door right now, if I thought you wouldn't be pissed about being late for work," he said.

I just looked up at him, the anger leaving my stance. Instead, I melted against him, using my arms around his neck to pull myself closer, until he released my throat and circled my waist with his big arms. He lifted me off my feet, so my entire body was pressed against his, with his face buried in my neck.

"You're mine, stellina. I'm not trying to control you. But I protect what is mine," he said into my skin.

I just nodded. I couldn't trust my voice. The tremor that ran through my body to hear him claim me was more than just physical. It touched my heart in a way I needed after the incident with Aiden, reminding me that not all the Knights were the same. And the three of them cared for me deeply.

When he put me down, I let my hands slide from his shoulders, down his broad chest, digging my finger tips in just slightly. Another quiet growl came from his lips and I looked up to find him watching me, his eyes hot with hunger.

"We can continue this later, big guy," I said with a smile.

I tugged on his beard softly and he kissed me once more before stepping back and letting me get straightened out for work. He stood at the open door as I got into the town car with Frank and I turned to watch him disappear from view when we got to the gate.

Flopping back in the seat, I sighed and tried to straighten my thoughts so I could get ready for the day ahead. I knew my face looked like I had been making out, because Gideon's beard always rubbed my skin a bit red. I glanced in a pocket mirror and had to smile, but also hoped the color calmed down by the time I got to the office.

Work was a whirlwind all morning. The stuff I hadn't finished the night before got piled up with additional tasks. When lunch rolled around, I was running from my office, not willing to miss my Muay Thai lesson. Frank had to drive faster than usual, because I was running late. My mind was all over the place between work and Aiden. I realized I hadn't even worried about Lyle, because I was so wrapped up in everything else.

In class, I was paired up with a man about the same height as me, but much bulkier. We were practicing kicks and blocks. My mind was all over the place, something I typically was able to control during lessons. I was kicking first and was feeling frustrated that my kicks weren't looking as polished as they usually do. Seeming to notice, the instructor wandered to our pair to watch, which only made me feel more off.

When we switched, I bounced lightly on my toes. I blocked the first two kicks, but the third slid in and was harder than I expected. I fell to the ground, the wind knocked out of me. My partner came to my side quickly, apologizing that he hadn't meant to actually land the kick. The instructor motioned him toward a bag before leaning down over me.

"You're distracted," he said simply.

I just nodded, knowing I had no excuse for missing the block.

"You need to come in here, clear minded. Or injuries happen, Brooklyn."

My ribs ached where my partner's shin had connected. He apologized profusely at the end of class as well, and I just smiled and shrugged it off. In the locker room, as I quickly showered and put myself back together, I cursed the person really at fault, Aiden Knight.

Brooklyn

THE SQUEAL ASH let loose when I entered the restaurant for dinner was louder than necessary and caught the attention of other patrons. I cringed, but made my way quickly to our table and hugged my best friend tightly. Frank followed, requesting a small table nearby.

"Hi Frank," Ash said, waggling her fingers at him.

The man actually blushed as he acknowledged her, but then looked away. I couldn't help the laugh that bubbled out. I never saw Frank off his game, except when Ash flirted with him. I tried to see him through Ash's eyes and I could see the appeal. He wasn't a bad-looking man, his build filling out his black suits in the right ways, slightly graying hair at his temples. It was his smile that really did Ash in, though, which is why she flirted, just to get him to flash her a smile.

I sat down and glanced at the menu, but since this was one of our regular spots, I already knew what I would be eating. Ash had already ordered drinks, and I sipped before smiling across the table at her.

"Hi, girl! You need to tell those boyfriends of yours that they need to let you out more often," she said.

"You know why they're being so careful," I reminded.

Ash was somber for a moment with a nod. Then she brightened again when the waiter came to take our dinner order.

"It's really good to see you. How's work?" I asked.

Ash dove into the position she had trained for in Europe. It was easy to tell how much she loved it, her happiness bubbling up in her words. It made me happy, to see her content with her chosen profession.

"I do miss coffee mornings with my best friend, though," she finished.

"I miss you too! I promise we'll do this more often," I replied.

"So, how are things with your men?" Ash asked, raising her eyebrows.

I sighed and picked up my drink.

"That's not the face of bliss," Ash commented.

"No. I mean, I am happy. Gideon, Jaxon and Oliver, they're amazing. They make me...feel things...I didn't really know possible before," I said.

"Ah, the sex is still going strong, huh?" Ash laughed.

I could feel the blush on my cheeks as I thought about how I started my morning with Jaxon's head between my thighs.

"That's definitely a strong part of it. It's more, though."

Ash looked at me over her glass, her eyes widening.

"Are you in love with them?"

"How do I even know? In my entire life, I've never had one healthy relationship, present company excluded, to teach me what it is to love. A lot of therapy taught me how to at least love myself and even that's hard at times," I explained.

"You know more than you think you do, Brooklyn. You've always been a dear friend to me, giving your heart to our friendship. There's no reason you couldn't do that with a man, well, your men."

I thought about the relationships in my life that should have taught me what it felt like to love. My mother never took care of me as a mother should, only teaching me what it was like to fend for myself to survive. The first person to take interest in me was violent and abusive. My friendship with Ash had been the most healthy thing I had in my life. Until I met the Knights.

I was saved from having to say anything else by our meal being served. We continued to chat about how things had been since we were apart. I told her about my Muay Thai lessons and she was astounded by how I was keeping them a secret. When I explained that their protective behavior went a little above and beyond, Ash frowned.

"I like that they are keeping you safe, at least until Lyle can be found and handled. But don't let them push you around. I'm glad you're taking lessons. That must make you feel like you're taking control," she said.

"Yes! That's exactly it. The guys don't understand that," I agreed.

It was so nice talking to someone that could see things from my perspective, understand how I was feeling. Our conversation steered lighter, and we were laughing loudly, with tears in our eyes. It was always like that with Ash. She could make me forget everything else and just have fun.

The check came, and we were finishing our drinks, when Ash made a noise and grabbed my hand.

"I don't want our night to be over. Let's go dancing!"

"It's a week night, Ash. We both work tomorrow!" I laughed.

"Oh, come on. We aren't old ladies yet. Let's live a little," she replied.

I thought about it for a moment and knew the biggest problem would be telling the guys I was going out. Pulling out my cellphone, I saw I had missed a few messages from the guys while eating dinner, just telling me to have a good time and other sweet things. I created a quick group text with Gideon, Jaxon and Oliver, purposely leaving off Aiden because I didn't want to sour my mood with him.

———

Me: Ash wants to go dancing. Going to hit Club 4. I'll be home after. Frank can come with us.

———

I hit send before I could doubt myself. I wanted to go dancing, wanted to hang out with my best friend, wanted a bit of freedom. Club 4 was the safest club we could go to, as Gideon's security team was well aware of Lyle and the threat he was to me. And with Frank shadowing us, it would be unlikely anyone would come near me.

My phone rang in my hand, and I groaned when I saw Gideon's name. I had texted, so that I could avoid the conversation I knew he would want to have. With nerves in my belly, I let the call go to voicemail. It immediately started to ring again, the action pushing the nerves out and replacing it with irritation. I locked my phone and pushed it back into my purse.

Ash did a little cheer across from me, encouraging my defiance. I wasn't going to have one of my boyfriends tell me I couldn't go dancing. I picked up my drink and downed the last bit, watching while Ash did the same. Suddenly, her eyes focused on something beside me and I looked over to find Frank with his phone in his hand.

"You're kidding me," I said.

"Gideon is trying to reach you," Frank said.

Though Frank was all business, it was clear he was uncomfortable being the middle man. He held out his phone, and I glared at the offending device.

"It would be better for us all if you just talked to him now," Frank said in a low voice.

I ripped the phone from his hand, glaring up at him now, feeling as if he had switched sides on me. He held up his hands in an innocent motion, but I wasn't buying it. I put the phone to my ear.

"Yes, Gideon," I said.

"Stellina, I was trying to call your phone. Is it not working?"

"I already told you what I was doing. I wasn't sure what else there was to talk about," I said.

The line got quiet for a moment and I almost pulled the phone from my ear to see if the call had dropped.

"I thought I made my position clear this morning, Brooklyn. We're just trying to keep you safe," he said, his voice low and slightly menacing.

"And I said I would take Frank. Plus, aren't your guys at Club 4 really good at what they do? Lyle can't get in there," I reasoned.

"Still feels like a risk."

"Well, sometimes life is risky. And I want to have fun with my best friend, end of story. So, we're going. Can we use the VIP area?" I asked, throwing in a fake sweet tone at the end to get what I wanted.

"Yes. We'll see you there."

Then the line did go dead. I pulled the phone from my ear and stared at it. That son of a bitch. Because he couldn't control me over the phone, he was going to crash my night out to make a point. I held the phone out to Frank, who took it gingerly, as if I was going to explode. He wasn't far off.

"Frank, we're going to Club 4."

On the drive to the club, I explained that our night was about to get busier with three Knights in tow. Ash took it all in stride, though she was giving me feminist accolades for standing up against Gideon, even though he was big and intimidating.

"Nothing wrong with having that eye candy around. And if they keep you occupied, I can find my own," she joked.

I pushed her shoulder and laughed just as Frank opened the sedan door for me. We were parked in the back of the club, in the 4K parking. I rolled my eyes, but I could admit having rich boyfriends that owned our favorite club did have its perks. We entered through the private back entrance and went up the stairs until we were on the owners VIP level.

For now, the level was empty, minus Viv, the normal waitress. She came up to us with a huge smile. I gave her a side hug. She had always been very nice to me whenever we were in the club, which was often enough. She didn't question the relationships or why I had free rein, which I appreciated.

"Do you ever take a night off?" I said loudly, to be heard over the bumping music below.

"Sunday and Mondays every week. You are never here on a weeknight! Special occasion?" She asked.

"Just a night out with my best friend," I replied, motioning to Ash.

I did quick introductions and Viv was off to grab us two of my favorite fruity drink. If I was going to be in the club on a weekday, I was going to enjoy myself. We settled ourselves into a booth with our drinks, laughing and talking more about life. When "Dirrty" by Christina Aguilera and Redman came on, Ash jumped up and grabbed my hand to go down to the dance floor.

As we made our way down the VIP stairs, I noticed the security guards watching us closely, no doubt instructions from Gideon before we arrived. Frank followed loosely, keeping us in sight the entire time. Pushing through the crowd, that was even packed for it not being a weekend, Ash and I started dancing.

Almost immediately, a man came up behind Ash, and his arm snaked around her waist. When she met my eyes, I scrunched my nose, knowing he wasn't her type. She grabbed my hand, and I swung her out of the embrace until we were grinding together. She looked over at the guy, smiled sweetly, and waved him off. He turned around dejectedly, and Ash and I couldn't help but giggle together.

The next guy that approached Ash caught her eye and she looked over at me for agreement. I gave her a smile. For a moment, I couldn't find one thing attractive about the guy. My mind just compared him to my guys, and in every area I could see, he was lacking. But as I tried to pull that lens back, I could see where Ash would be attracted to him, so I nodded my head with a brighter smile this time.

The music slowed a bit, catching the crowd off guard with "Impatient" by Jeremih. Ash was in the arms of the new guy and they were swaying and grinding to the beat. A moment later, arms circled my waist, and I froze. I looked down and immediately didn't recognize the person touching me. I spun away, and the guy followed, trying to hold on to me and grind against me with the beat.

Clearly not taking the hint, I stopped moving and tried to just push his hands off of me. Instead of getting the idea, the guy grabbed at my dress, trying to pull me closer.

"No, thanks," I called over the music.

"Come on, pretty girl. Just a dance," he said, but his fingers were dancing on my bare thigh and I knew he was thinking about a lot more than a dance.

"I said no," I yelled more forcefully.

The guy just grinned at me, clearly intoxicated beyond the point of having any reason. The next time he stepped close, I allowed him to. But I quickly put into action one of my many practiced moves. Grabbing his neck to control his body, I slammed a knee up into his stomach. I felt the breath whoosh out of his mouth near my head and he stumbled back.

On instinct, I stepped back into a fighting stance, in case that hint was also not strong enough. The jerk rubbed at his stomach, his eyes wide as he gasped for air. We were still surrounded by dancers that had no idea what was going on, it had all happened so fast.

"Stupid bitch," he said, though there was no sound, and I was only reading his lips.

He began to step forward, and I pivoted to avoid any attack he could launch. As I moved, I collided with a solid chest. Looking up, I found Gideon towering over me. He was flanked by two security members that looked like they had just fought through the crowd themselves. Gideon just looked as if he had appeared, out of thin air, to be by my side. Though, at the moment, his eyes weren't on me.

The jerk, to his credit, realized quickly that he was in trouble. He was no larger than me, so Gideon's towering form was intimidating. Jerk started to back up, his hands up. Gideon didn't give him a chance to get away. His large arm snapped forward, easily reaching the guy's collar. Gideon pulled the guy to his chest and then lifted him clear off his feet, with the jerk holding onto his arm for dear life.

"When I woman says no, that's the end of it. When that woman is MINE, that's the end of you."

Gideon's menacing voice was loud enough to be heard over the music, but he wasn't yelling. I watched as the jerk went completely white. My mind whirled with the possibilities of what Gideon was meaning, causing me to step forward and touch his free arm. His angry gaze snapped to me, but as soon as it saw it was me, his face transformed into affection.

"I don't think you need to beat every drunk guy that hits on me to a pulp, big guy. Maybe put him down?" I said.

Gideon seemed to consider my words and then turned and practically tossed the jerk to his security guards.

"86 him. Trespass if he returns to any of our clubs," Gideon yelled.

The jerk started to sputter, becoming sober enough to realize that the judgement was fairly harsh. But he didn't have a chance to speak, as one of the guards punched him in the solar plexus. I cringed, but didn't have a chance to see them take him out, as Gideon grabbed me roughly. His hand came to my chin, forcing me to look up at him.

"You're mine. I don't let other men touch what's mine," he growled.

"Well, other than your brothers," I replied.

"You know what I mean, Brooklyn," he said, his voice laced with what sounded like his last nerve.

"I know, big guy. Can you kiss me now? That was hot," I said, grabbing him by his jacket lapels.

As Gideon's mouth crashed down on mine, I allowed the last fleeting thoughts to leave my mind. No, I didn't want to be controlled, told what I could and couldn't do. And Gideon's multiple declarations that I was his should have raised my hackles. So why was I melting under his touch, ready to take him back to the stairwell and climb up his body?

I let the confusion go, so I could just enjoy the feeling of Gideon. His lips against mine. His beard rubbing against the sensitive skin of my face. His hands on my hips, holding me tightly against him. His hardness I could feel against my stomach. I could feel myself getting hot and I wasn't sure how long I would be able to last in the club without ripping off his clothes.

Gideon

I HAD no idea where the caveman, she's mine, attitude was coming from. When I saw Brooklyn fighting off the advances from the owner's level, I practically jumped down the stairs. As I ran by, the VIP guards caught that something was wrong and they followed. Frank wasn't far behind, tossing people out of the way until we were near Brooklyn.

The guy had just gotten more pissed as Brooklyn kneed him in the stomach, while even I could admit it was hot to see her doing it. The sick fear in me turned to rage as I saw the guy continue to stalk toward her. As soon as I had my hands on her, I could barely control myself. I wanted to pull her skirt up and bury myself in her, just to brand her as mine.

Brooklyn was fighting against me, every step of the way. I knew she understood it was about her safety, so she accepted most of the steps we'd taken. But even as timid as she thought she was, it was clear there was a fire inside that was ready to burn me alive if I went too far. And I loved each flame.

The music on the dance floor shifted again with "Whisper" by Able Heart playing and cheers from the crowd rising around us. Brooklyn pulled back from my kiss to smile up at me. She began to sway her hips and rubbed against me in all the right places. I wasn't the best dancer, but I could press my body against hers and move as she did. Luckily for me, my girl didn't seem to care.

She turned and threw an arm back to grab around my neck, pulling my face to her neck. I obliged and began to kiss and lick at her skin, feeling her tremble under my hands, that were splayed across her stomach. She released my neck, and I looked up to find my brothers making their way through the crowd. Oliver and Jaxon both stared at her, and she beckoned them forward with a finger.

Suddenly, Ash was next to her and I could hear only a part of the quick conversation.

"This is about to get interesting, isn't it?" Ash laughed.

I couldn't hear Brooklyn's response, but there was a smile on her face and Ash threw back her head to laugh.

"I think I'm going to head home," Ash said, her eyebrows going up and her eyes motioning to the man she had been dancing with.

Brooklyn's body went still, and she looked the man over, as if she could tell if he was a psycho serial killer just by staring at him. Before she could respond, I pulled out my phone and shot a text to Frank, telling him to meet Ash and this guy on the owner's level and take them to Ash's place, if that's what she wanted.

"Stellina, Frank will take them," I said in Brooklyn's ear.

She looked over her shoulder at me, a grateful smile on her face. She tugged on my beard in the way that turned me on each time, before turning back to Ash. After Brooklyn explained, Ash smiled and waved a little at me, to which I just inclined my head, not wanting to take my hands off my girl. With Ash moving away through the crowd, Brooklyn turned back to the three of us in the middle of the dance floor.

"Feel Me" by Selena Gomez came through the speakers and I could see a sexy glint come into Brooklyn's eyes. She slowly swayed with her ass against me, my arms wrapped around her waist. Oliver grabbed one of her hands, kissing the inside of her wrist before leaning toward her ear. I didn't hear what he said to her, but Brooklyn shivered and turned to kiss him hard. Jaxon joined, and she swung out of my hands to wrap a leg around Jaxon and dance for a moment.

She moved from each of us, touching and rubbing as she danced. We created a small exclusive circle, not noticing anything outside of us. She came back to me, and her hands were on my chest, sliding south, until she was cupping me through my dress pants. I couldn't help my mouth from dropping open as she gave me a sly smile and motioned for me to bend closer to her.

"Take me somewhere, private, now," she said.

I didn't think twice. I grabbed her wrist and started for the stairs. Our offices were on the third floor of the club, with windows overlooking the dance floor. No one would enter them without our permission. On the stairs, Oliver and Jaxon were hot on our heels. I could hear Brooklyn's laugh, as I didn't slow when we hit the third floor, dragging her by her wrist behind me.

Slamming my office door open, I dragged her in behind me, grabbed her by the back of the neck and crushed my mouth to hers. She immediately opened for me and was on her toes, trying to deepen and control the kiss. The door shut behind us, Oliver and Jaxon both entering. Jaxon went to the wall length window and shut the curtains before everyone would get a show.

Oliver came behind Brooklyn, his hands cupping her breasts while he kissed a path down her neck. One of his hands continued to trail down until he could pull up her skirt. I knew the moment he made contact with her heat, because she moaned into my mouth.

"She's fucking soaked," Oliver said.

I stepped back, breaking the kiss, and handed her to Jaxon. Brooklyn smiled at him and he began to kiss her softly while Oliver fingered her from behind. I could see her hips moving with the movement, and I knew it wouldn't take long for her to come. I went to my desk and moved the few items that were on the surface.

"Oh god, Oliver, don't stop," Brooklyn moaned.

"Never, babe. I wanna feel you come on my hand," he said into her ear.

His words seemed to push her over, and she shuttered and cried out. Oliver wrapped his free arm around her hips, keeping her on her feet. Jaxon pushed her hair from her face and kissed her again as she came down from her high.

"On the desk. Now," I demanded.

Oliver smirked and pulled his hand from Brooklyn, licking her orgasm from his fingers, causing Brooklyn to moan and spin to kiss him frantically. As he kissed her, Oliver slowly backed her to the desk. When her butt hit the surface, he lifted her with ease. He bent over her, slowly pushing her to her back, where Jaxon grabbed her hands and pulled them above her head.

"Ok, love?" He asked.

She looked up at him, passion and need shining from her gaze while she nodded her agreement.

"My turn. I need a taste," I said, moving Oliver to the side.

Brooklyn looked down her body at me and I kept her gaze while I reached up her floral dress to pull down her panties. I tossed them to the side before spreading her before me. I lifted one of her knees and draped her leg over my shoulder, and she did the same with the other. Kneeling in front of the desk, I could gaze up at her face, but also had a perfect view of her glistening pussy.

She tried to pull her wrists from Jaxon's hold, but he just bent over her face and said no before plundering her mouth again. I watched as Jaxon removed his loose tie and carefully tied it around her wrists. I hadn't even touched her, but she moaned and it was clear our girl didn't mind a little bondage.

With her more secure, Jaxon leaned over her and pulled the front of her dress and bra down, letting her breast free. He latched onto one nipple while Oliver joined and began to tease the other. I dipped my head and let my tongue run through her outer lips, causing her hips to buck toward my mouth. I grinned and obliged my sexy woman by sliding my tongue into her entrance, slowly tongue fucking her.

"Jaxon?" She moaned.

"Yes, love?"

"I want to suck your cock. But I might need my hands for that," she said with force.

Jaxon's eyes widened as he looked down at her. Oliver barked out a laugh, his answer whenever he's feeling overly tense.

"I think we can work with what we have, love," Jaxon replied, his voice rough.

I continued my ministrations, causing Brooklyn to moan and grind against my mouth. It was my favorite place to be and I could stay there all night. But I could tell she was getting close again. I circled her clit with my tongue, softly at first. Then I flattened my tongue and pressed it roughly to the tight bud, causing her to jerk on the desk.

Next to her head, Jaxon had undone his pants and pulled out his cock. She licked her lips, and he moved forward. Moving her hair away from her face, Jaxon slowly fed his cock to Brooklyn, until she couldn't fit anymore in her mouth. He didn't force her further, but Brooklyn tried. He pulled out and slid back in, holding her face still as he fucked her mouth.

Sliding two fingers into her tight channel, Brooklyn groaned on Jaxon's cock and he threw his head back. I could imagine the vibrations she was making were enough to push him to orgasm as well. I curled my fingers, finding her g-spot at the same time as I sucked her clit into my mouth. She cried out as much as she could with a cock in her mouth and Jaxon picked up his pace until he was coming down her throat, our girl swallowing every drop.

When he pulled back, Jaxon dropped down to kiss Brooklyn and Oliver moved to take my place between her legs. He ran the head of his cock along her pussy and her hips fell further open. When he didn't push into her the moment she wanted, she looked down at him.

"Oliver, stop teasing me, or I won't let you finish," she said, in her most annoyed tone.

"Yes, ma'am," Oliver replied, before thrusting into my heat.

Her body bowed across the desk and I couldn't help but stare at the beauty she was. Her dress was up around her hips, with Oliver's fingers dug into her flesh. Her breasts bounced with every thrust. Her arms were over her head, her wrists still bound and her behaving even though I knew she didn't want to.

I went to her hands, leaning over her upside down, until I could palm her breasts, pinching her nipples between my fingers. I stepped back until I could drop my mouth onto hers. She poured all of her pent up passion into the kiss, matching me for each stroke as Oliver fucked her roughly. The only sounds in the office were slapping flesh and Brooklyn keening moans as she started getting close again.

"Oliver, I'm going to come. Oh god," she cried.

Jaxon joined Oliver and slid his hand down Brooklyn's body until he found her clit. The moment he touched her, she started to thrash her head back and forth and cry out.

"Fuck, babe. You're strangling me," Oliver groaned.

He picked up his pace and collapsed over her as he poured into her. I went to the other side of the desk again, waiting for Oliver to pick himself up. Once he moved from Brooklyn, I leaned over her, grabbing her chin, making her look at me.

"We aren't done, stellina."

"Gideon," she moaned, lost in her pleasurable bliss.

I ran my hands up her arms until I got to her wrists. Pulling her hands down, I helped her stand. She was unsteady as she looked up at me, waiting to follow my lead. I walked over to my oversized office chair that I was rarely ever in. The best way I could think of using the chair was with Brooklyn.

Before sitting, I undid my pants. Sitting, I pulled out my hardness and grabbed Brooklyn's tied wrists again, leading her to my lap. I turned her, so she would sit backward, giving my brother's access to her still. Lining my cock up with her entrance, I pulled her down onto my lap.

She threw her head back and her hair fell around us as I hissed as her tightness closed around me. Jaxon moved to kneel in front of her, gripping her hair and pulling her mouth to his, while I began to thrust deeply into her pussy. I pushed her legs further apart and slid even deeper into her, causing her to buck and push back onto me.

"One more time, baby," Jaxon said.

He sucked one of her nipples into his mouth, as Oliver joined to kiss her. Jaxon's fingers found her clit again and he began to stroke her in pace with my movements. Jaxon moved until he was pressed against her front, his mouth at her ear.

"Love, do you know what it feels like when you come on our cocks?"

Brooklyn gasped and shook her head slightly, while Oliver grinned at her and kissed down her chest.

"Your pussy is tight all the time, but when you come, damn love, it's like a vice. It squeezes us tight, sucking us deeper into you, like you don't want to let go. You don't want to stop, do you?" Jaxon loudly whispered against the shell of her ear.

"Fuck no," she said.

"If we could do nothing else but fuck you, that's what we would do. Just to feel that hot pussy around our cocks. It's perfect. Just like the rest of you."

Brooklyn's eyes looked like they were shining with tears, but she smiled sexily at Jaxon as he pulled back from her ear to look into her face. He kissed her deeply and began to strum her clit again, evident by the way her pussy walls quivered around my cock. Moments later she was exploding again, throwing herself back into my lap, keeping me bottomed out in her.

I wasn't able to hold back. I stood with her in my lap and slipped from her body. I stood her on her feet and used my foot to spread her legs. I reached around and put her bound hands on the desk and lifted her dress to show her perfect ass.

I didn't take any time to slam into her again. Holding onto her ass, I slammed into her roughly until she was screaming my name as she either orgasmed again or her previous one just continued. I was too lost in the feeling of her to know what was happening.

Burying myself into her, I erupted with a bellow and I barely kept us both standing upright. Brooklyn collapsed onto the desk, her cheek pressing against the wood. Her breathing was heavy and erratic and her eyes were closed. A sweet smile was on her lips and I knew in that moment I loved her.

CHAPTER
Eleven

Brooklyn

I WAS FLOODED with chaotic emotions. As Jaxon helped me stand up and carefully untied my wrists, I felt amazed at myself. Having my hands controlled had turned me on beyond what I thought was possible. Jaxon lifted my wrists to his mouth, kissing where his tie had been. I smiled at him shyly, not really knowing what to say after his dirty talk.

Gideon knelt in front of me, using a towel from his personal bathroom to clean between my legs. He was careful and tender. I was overwhelmed as I looked down at him and saw his own feelings shining back at me. My big man was always tough, but just for the moment, he was showing his soft side to me. I tugged on his beard softly, which caused him to smile, and he turned his face into my palm, kissing me.

My dress was pulled up and straightened with quick hands. I looked over at Oliver, thankful for his thoroughness with checking that everything was put back where it should be. After Gideon went to the bathroom to put the towel away, Oliver helped me back into my panties. I threw my arms around his neck and buried my face in his shoulder.

"Hey, babe, what's up?" He asked.

"Nothing. I just feel really good. Can we go home now?" I asked.

"Of course," Oliver said.

We walked out of the office together, laughing at a joke Oliver had just dropped. Walking into the owner's VIP level, I froze, taking in what I was seeing. Gideon bumped into me, but then his arm snaked around me to keep me from stumbling.

"What the fuck?" His deep voice vibrated in his chest.

"Is that?" Oliver started to ask.

"Apparently," Jaxon answered, anticipating the question.

The person in question was a petite brunette that was currently sitting against Aiden's side in one of the booths we could see. Viv walked up with two drinks and I could see from her face that she wasn't thrilled with the woman being there either. I took note to thank her for being a good friend later. Right now, I wanted to find out who in the fuck the woman was with Aiden.

I tried to pull away, but Gideon's arm around me tightened. He could read my thoughts before I had the chance to act on them. Aiden's dark gaze had landed on us and I watched as a number of emotions flickered across his face, before he settled on indifference. The woman, noticing his attention being pulled away, looked over.

I stared in astonishment as a huge, bright smile spread across her face. She bounced up to her feet, tottering on heels that made her a few inches taller, but still shorter than me. Her walk was like that of something expected on a runway. She was small and dressed in a skimpy skirt and a backless top, her small breasts clearly free under the thin material.

When she got to Oliver, who was standing furthest forward, she threw her arms around him. To his credit, he didn't embrace her, but became a statue. She pulled back with a mock frown and looked up at him.

"Oli, aren't you happy to see me?" She pouted.

Oli? I thought to myself. No one called him that. His face was stone as he looked down at the woman.

"Don't call me that," he said through gritted teeth.

Looking over at Aiden again, I saw him down the drink Viv had just brought him. His hair was disheveled, and I immediately assumed it was from her hands. A pit of dread and sickness spread through my stomach. I knew Aiden had pushed me away, but I didn't know that meant we were completely over.

The small woman was now moving toward Jaxon, leaving Oliver looking like he'd just swallowed something rancid. Jaxon side stepped her and stalked toward Aiden. She looked after him for a moment, before focusing on Gideon, who was still holding me.

"Hi muscle man," she crooned.

"Why are you here?" Gideon asked.

"Couldn't I just come and see my boys because I missed you?"

Her boys? My brain was screaming at me. Why would this woman be calling them her boys? I remembered that briefly it was mentioned by one or more of them that they had shared a girl-friend before. But I never thought to get more details. Never thought I'd need to be worried. But here I was faced with a woman that was all over Aiden and trying to touch all of my guys.

I could see Jaxon motioning wildly by the booth, but Aiden's gaze was glued to me. Or was he staring at the woman standing in front of us? I couldn't see her from the back, but maybe it was impressive. I leaned back into Gideon's comforting embrace, happy he wasn't shying away from me or trying to embrace the woman.

"If that was even close to the truth, it still wouldn't make any sense," Gideon shot back.

He then moved to take my hand and walk around the woman. I could hear her talking to Oliver behind us, but Gideon kept moving. As we approached, I could hear some of Jaxon's rant to Aiden.

"You know what she did to us before. And now that we have money and success, suddenly she pops up. This stinks Aiden," Jaxon was saying.

Gideon tried to pull me past the booth, but I stopped and yanked back on him. He stopped and looked at me and shook his head in warning. But I was already angry and confused. Nothing was going to stop me from saying something to Aiden.

I walked to Aiden's side, just as the small woman was sitting back down next to him. To his credit, he looked uncomfortable, and he lowered his arm from the back of the booth so it didn't look like he was embracing her any longer. I bent, so my words could be for him and not for her.

"I didn't realize we had come to this, Aiden. But I've gotten the message, loud and clear," I said.

As I straightened, his hand snapped out and grabbed me by the forearm. Gideon was at my side in a split second.

"Aiden," he warned.

"Back off, Gideon. I wouldn't hurt her," Aiden said.

I realized then his words were slightly slurred. Aiden was actually drunk, something that was very rare for him. He stood swiftly and pulled me away from Gideon, to the rail of the balcony.

"You seem to have everything figured out, sweetheart. Why don't you clue me in?" He demanded.

I ripped my arm from his grasp and he didn't try to touch me again.

"You don't want me. That's fine. I thought we might have hit a bump on our new road. But instead, you've gone off on a detour that I'm not following. So fine. I know the score," I said.

Aiden studied me for a moment, indecision on his face.

"I didn't fuck her," he growled.

When he turned to look away from me, I spotted red lipstick on his cheek and I felt frozen in my spot for a moment.

"Yet," I shot back.

He didn't deny it, and it was like he reached into my heart and yanked part of it back out. I gasped for air for a moment, stepping away from him. I had been so wrong about Aiden Knight. I turned on my heel and practically ran for Gideon. He opened his arms, and I threw myself into him. He curled his body around me, holding me to him before turning me toward the private exit from the club.

In the parking area, the limo waited, and Gideon guided me into the vehicle. Jaxon and Oliver joined us quickly and soon we were driving away from the train wreck that was my heartbreak. I just stared out as the city flew by and tried to find a way to disconnect the feelings I thought I had for Aiden.

At dinner, I had just been telling Ash that I have no idea what love is. And if this was the way it felt when it fell apart, I wasn't sure I wanted it. I clearly didn't know what love was, because I wouldn't have felt it so quickly for Aiden and I wouldn't have allowed myself to be so hurt by him.

When we got home, I stood in the entryway, trying to decide where to go. On one hand, going to bed alone seemed like a good idea, but then it also made me want to sob. Jaxon came to me and kissed my temple.

"I have a bit of work to handle before bed. Gideon, why don't you take her up to your room?" He suggested.

Jaxon and Oliver exchanged a look, and I didn't have the energy to figure out what it meant. Gideon nodded and without a word, he lifted me into his arms and started to climb the stairs. My body was sore in all the right places and one not right place. I tried to adjust to keep him from pressing too hard on my ribs that I was pretty sure were bruised.

In his room, Gideon gingerly put me on my feet in the bathroom. He helped with the zipper of my dress and I let it fall to the floor. As I reached back to undo my bra, I noticed Gideon had frozen and was just staring at me. I looked at him strangely for a moment and then looked down at myself, immediately seeing what caught his attention.

My side had seemed to burst into color with purples, blues and reds. The bruise had blossomed just over my ribs and was angry looking. I stared at it for a long moment, wondering why I hadn't felt more pain until Gideon had picked me up to carry me. The bruise looked much worse than the way I actually felt.

"What the fuck happened?" Gideon demanded.

I went still, not prepared for how to face down what I was going to have to come clean about. But then, why did I have to tell him every little thing going on with me? This was my body, my life. If I had an injury, it was my business. I could feel defiance rising and my spine began to stiffen.

"Nothing. I'm fine," I replied.

My answer sounded lame to my own ears, so I knew it wasn't going to satisfy Gideon. He stepped back, no longer touching me, to stare down at me.

"Brooklyn," he said. His voice took on a demanding tone, and it only caused me to bristle further.

"Gideon. This is my body. And if I say nothing happened, nothing happened," I shot back.

I stepped toward the bedroom, prepared to just end the conversation. Gideon had different ideas, throwing an arm across the doorway. I stopped, shot him a glare, and ducked under before he could stop me. I put my dress back on, zipping up the back, so I wasn't arguing half naked. Being dressed made me feel more in control.

Gideon stalked into the bedroom after me, anger radiating off of him. I wasn't sure if the anger was directed at me or if he thought someone had hurt me. And technically, maybe someone else had done it, but it wasn't without my acknowledgement. Of course, the big man didn't know that, and I wasn't ready to show my hand quite yet.

I crossed my arms across my chest, trying to determine if the evening was at a loss. Gideon opened his mouth once, but snapped it shut. He tore the elastic from his bun and his hair flowed around his shoulders. He ran his hand through it in an aggravated manner as he paced across the room from me.

"Who did it, Brooklyn?" He finally said.

"That's none of your business," I replied.

Gideon's eyes snapped to me and narrowed. I knew right away it was the wrong answer, however, I didn't trust that Gideon wouldn't track down my sparring partner and hurt him for leaving a mark on me. Which was utterly ridiculous, but fell right within Gideon's capabilities.

"My business? You are my business, Brooklyn. Your safety is my business. You can be your independent little self, but when it comes to you being hurt, I will know how it happened," he practically yelled.

I was so torn. Having someone care about my safety was a warm feeling. But the control of how he did it sat like a rock in my stomach. He didn't say anything else. His thick arms were crossed across his chest and his legs were planted. If we weren't in the middle of a fight, I would be focusing on how fucking hot he looked.

"This conversation is done. It's going nowhere. I'm sleeping alone. Do not follow me," I finally said.

I spun, just as I saw the pain lance across his face and I felt tears burn at the back of my eyes. But I refused to allow him to see it. I went to the door and flung it open with more force than necessary. The bang of it reverberated through the room and made me jump. Steeling myself, I stepped into the hallway and practically ran to my room before Gideon could stop me. I threw the lock on the door the moment I entered, though it wasn't really going to stop them if they wanted to get in.

My room. It wasn't really though, was it? All the clothing inside had been purchased and chosen by Oliver. And though I appreciated the gesture and thankfully he had fantastic taste, I never even got the chance to have a say in it. Since Lyle had broken into my apartment and destroyed all of my things, I had only bought myself a handful of items, things that caught my eye or basics I just didn't have anymore.

I looked around at everything and I felt more angry as the moments went on. I kicked my shoes off and shoved them into the closet, closing the doors so I wouldn't be reminded of every-thing that I hadn't controlled in the last few months. I threw the dress into my hamper and ran myself a hot bath.

As I lowered myself into the water, my side sang with pain and I knew I really needed to apply ice instead. But there was no way in hell I would leave my room now. I thought I heard the door handle in the bedroom jiggle once and I ducked lower into the tub, as if that would ward off any of the arguments that were coming. But no one entered, and the sound stopped. I let out a pent up breath and laid my head back to let the tears fall.

CHAPTER
Twelve

Oliver

DOWNSTAIRS IN OUR OFFICE, we could hear doors slamming upstairs and what sounded strangely like Brooklyn running down the hallway. I looked over at Jaxon, who was behind his laptop.

"That doesn't sound good," I said.

"No, it doesn't," he said, his face wearing the worry I was also feeling.

We had heard raised voices moments before, but we dismissed

them, thinking Gideon was having more fun with Brooklyn before bed. Jaxon and I were both totally distracted by what we were trying to dig up online.

Missy. Seeing her at Club 4 was a gut punch. I hadn't thought of the woman, not in a serious manner in years. When she hugged me, she smelled exactly the same, and it went to my head for a moment, pulling back memories. Most of those memories were horrible, so I didn't feel the need to stick around and have a catch up with the snake.

As soon as we got back to the house and Gideon took Brooklyn upstairs, Jaxon and I went to work to try to figure out what Missy could be up to. Aiden had been three sheets to the wind when we had found him with Missy. I hoped that didn't mean he couldn't distinguish reality from fantasy where she was concerned.

I hadn't missed the pain in Brooklyn's face when she saw how Aiden let Missy hang on him. Aiden could be a bastard on his own at times. I loved him. He was my brother, if not by blood but by choice. I had never regretted the way we tied our lives together. However, his behavior with Brooklyn was confusing to the rest of us.

"I can't find shit," Jaxon growled as he slammed a fist on his desk.

"She couldn't have disappeared and then just reappear when she felt like it," I replied.

I scrolled through the search I had tried, but her name wasn't unique enough to be sure I was even looking at the right person. We needed more details on her, and Gideon was the one that had those. I looked toward the stairs, wondering if I should go and get his file on Missy. Gideon had files on anyone that could be a threat to our family. And there was a time Missy knew some of our deepest secrets.

"Think she saw Brooklyn in the tabloids? Wanted to come and mess with what we had going on?" I asked.

"Missy is sadistic and self serving enough to do exactly that.

The way she behaved tonight could be explained by that."

The ending of our relationship with Missy was explosive and definitely not amicable. After she had broken it off with Gideon and Jaxon, she tried to pit Aiden and me against each other. We were young and dumb, thinking with our cocks, so her drama just about worked. It was Jaxon's cool head that was able to break through the haze and make us see what she was doing.

Back then, we were just four guys in our late teens, working the drug business with Jaxon's father. Missy had initially been a customer, but Jaxon had taken an interest in her. Jaxon was busy using the same products we were slinging, so he and Missy hit it off. The four of us lived in a dingy apartment together, but we were paying for it on our own, so it felt like the best place any of us had lived.

Missy started to stay over, walking around the apartment in nothing but her panties, tempting the three of us. At first, Jaxon was too high to even care that he was sharing his girlfriend. By the time he was sober to understand, all four of us were deeply involved with her. However, the issues weren't with us. It was Missy's drama that caused the fiery end that came.

Dating Missy together, for a time, made the four of us feel closer. We were caring and providing for the same woman, something we could do as a team. And it was something that didn't have to do with the business we were buried in with Jaxon's father. It was something we were building as a family. I could admit that if Missy hadn't been as fucking nuts as she was, we would have stayed together because we felt stronger together.

The break up had been the big push that got us out of drugs and on our own. Aiden had been scrimping and saving, using his financial skills, to build us a nest egg. No doubt that if Missy had known about the money, it would have been spent. That thought lead me down another thought process.

"What if it's about the money? She's come back because she wants what we've built?" I asked.

Jaxon nodded, and I knew he'd already considered that. That

would be in Missy's bag of tricks. Now it was just up to us to make sure she didn't get her claws into any of us. Aiden included. Even if he didn't want to be with Brooklyn for some insane reason, Missy wasn't a decent alternative.

A shadow fell into the office, and I looked over to see a disheveled Gideon in our doorway. I swiveled in my chair to look him over. He looked upset and furious. I heard a crack and looked down to see his hand squeezing his phone as if it had insulted him and he decided to teach it a lesson.

"Lighten up, man. Your device wasn't built for violence," I quipped.

"Just got off with Frank. Brooklyn's been taking secret self-defense classes every day at lunch," he said quietly.

Jaxon's head snapped up now, and we both stared at him.

"Secret? How was she doing that?" Jaxon asked.

"She convinced Frank to take her. I'm moments away from firing him. At least he fessed up when I called to find out what had happened to her side."

"Wait, what happened to her side?" I asked.

"When we were undressing for bed, I found a huge bruise over her ribs. According to Frank, she wasn't focusing on class today and her sparring partner nailed her with a kick she was supposed to defend against," Gideon explained.

"What the fuck? She was sparring? That's exactly what we were trying to prevent," Jaxon said.

"I should have known something was up when I saw her fighting off the guy in the club," Gideon continued.

"Wait, what do you mean, fighting off a guy in the club? Why do I feel so fucking confused right now?" I asked.

"Sorry, didn't get a chance to explain between dancing, fucking Brooklyn in my office and Missy showing up. Shit! Missy showed up. What the fuck is up with that?" Gideon rambled.

"Back up. You said Brooklyn fought someone. What happened?" Jaxon said, preventing Gideon from completely derailing.

Gideon ran through a quick story of a man being too forward with his advances. When he talked about Brooklyn kneeing the guy in the stomach, I let out a low whistle. My brothers and I had agreed that the idea of Brooklyn getting hurt, because she was trying to do right for herself, wasn't how we wanted to protect her. We wanted to make sure it never got to that point. But here she was showing that even in the middle of our own club, with Gideon and his men watching her, she needed to handle business, and she did.

"Maybe we were wrong about the self-defense," I mused.

"Wrong about what?" A slurring Aiden said, as he entered the office as well.

Great, it's a damn party now, I thought to myself.

"Tell me you don't have that evil witch with you," Jaxon said, standing to look beyond Aiden.

"Huh? Who?" Aiden asked, his alcohol infused brain addled and lost in normal conversation.

"For shit's sake, Aiden. You smell like a fucking liquor store. Go to bed," Gideon barked angrily.

Aiden blinked up at him and even I had to stare. It was unlike Gideon to be very harsh with Aiden. He would tell Aiden the truth, even when it hurt. But it was always done in a calm, neutral manner. Gideon had never gotten beyond his need to protect Aiden, as he had done since they were in grade school together.

"I'm an adult, Gideon. I can drink as I'd like," Aiden shot back.

"Maybe if you weren't making yourself and Brooklyn so miserable, you wouldn't need to drink. Just a thought," I said.

That earned a middle finger from Aiden, but he didn't deny my accusation. I knew the reason he was so out of sorts was because he pushed Brooklyn away and he regretted it. Instead of fixing things, he drank and tried to ignore it.

"Where's Missy, Aiden?" Jaxon asked.

"How should I know?" Aiden replied.

"Because you, man who can't stand straight, were with her when we left the club," I said.

Aiden wavered a bit again and squinted at me. I would swear I hadn't seen him this trashed since we were kids.

"Oh. Yeah. I told her to get lost."

"Thank fuck," Jaxon breathed.

"Why? Did you think I'd bring her home or something? Brooklyn's here, isn't she?" Aiden asked. His voice was incredulous, as if we weren't watching him weave around in one spot.

"We just had to be sure," Jaxon said.

"What did she want, Aiden?" Gideon asked.

"She didn't really say. Kept calling us her boys, and I told her to fucking stop. She pouted. Then I told her she needed to leave our level cause I was going home. I think she said she'd see us later, not sure what that means," Aiden said.

"I should put her face at the door, so they don't let her in again," Gideon said.

Jaxon and I both nodded our agreement. Then, without a word, Aiden swayed in a circle and headed toward the stairs. I watched, wondering if we were going to see him tumble to his death. I wanted to strangle him. I knew he had his issues, emotional demons that haunted him, but it wasn't fair for him to take those out on Brooklyn.

"What are we going to do about him?" I asked.

Gideon stared out the door, as if he were picturing Aiden getting to his room and stumbling safely inside. Aiden's safety was always one of his biggest burdens, though most of the time Aiden didn't make it this difficult. To hear even Gideon get angry with our brother, I knew things were bad.

"He's the least of my worries right now. If he wants to drink himself to death, that's his choice," Gideon finally said.

"And how are we going to talk to Brooklyn?" Jaxon asked.

"Her door is locked. I checked. So, she's not talking tonight," Gideon said, his voice dejected.

"We should give her the night. She did these lessons, behind our backs, on purpose. Tomorrow, we can have the semblance of a civil conversation," Jaxon replied.

I leaned back in my chair, imagining the three of us confronting Brooklyn about secrets she's keeping from us. I had a sinking feeling the conversation wasn't going to be as civil as Jaxon was hoping. Protecting Brooklyn was our only goal and with Lyle still in hiding, the lunch lessons were just one more place the fucker could find her.

In bed that night, I was restless, wanting to be with Brooklyn, but knowing she likely hadn't unlocked her door. I didn't like having to wait for the conversation we needed to have. The longer things rolled around in my mind, the more worried I got. She had pushed us away once. I knew she was capable of doing it again. And I wasn't sure I could handle that.

Aiden

I TOOK my normal seat at the kitchen island and avoided looking at any of my brothers. My head was splitting, and I had no one to blame but myself. The guilt of how I had treated Brooklyn pushed me to trying to drink and forget. The problem was, once I was sober again, I realized I had done more dumb shit.

In the very beginning, I tried to tell Brooklyn in my own way that I wasn't good enough for her. My heart wasn't capable of loving anymore. The moment I felt it thud with feelings for Brooklyn, I felt panic clawing at my throat and I was sure I would suffocate.

The evening at the city viewpoint, fucking her on my car had been the hottest moment of my life. When I looked down into her eyes, I saw too much shining back at me. I was moments away from blurting out some sort of random romantic adage that applied to how I was feeling. But it was just heavy enough that I had to lock it down and shove it deep.

I wouldn't admit to anyone that I had fisted my cock in the shower before coming down for coffee, stroking myself, thinking about how beautiful Brooklyn looked leaning back on the hood of my car. I came against the shower wall, thinking about how tight and hot she was around my cock. Afterward, I felt guilty as fuck. I needed to figure out my shit.

Hurting Brooklyn didn't feel good. Fuck, I hadn't felt that bad in years. The shine of her eyes, unshed tears, that she felt because of me. It was almost more than I could handle. But I kept shoving at her until she abandoned me. And then I felt a crack deep in my chest that couldn't have been anything other than the heart I thought didn't feel any longer.

That pain had nothing on the headache I suffered from, while Gideon banged around pots and pans and Jaxon stared daggers at me. The only one that didn't seem like he needed to be angry with me was Oliver. When I studied him over the newspaper, he looked pale and lost in his own world.

When Brooklyn entered the kitchen, a blush to her cheeks, her lips flattened and stoic, I realized I had missed something. I slowly put down the newspaper as my brothers all froze and turned to watch her. She seemed to straighten her spine and push her shoulders back. She had a black gym bag, which she unceremoniously dropped at the entrance of the kitchen. I stared at it, confused by what was happening.

Brooklyn didn't speak to anyone, just went to the coffeemaker and poured her own mug. Normally, one of my brothers got her coffee and breakfast. But no one seemed to be speaking at the moment. She sat down with her mug and held her phone in her palm, focusing on whatever she was reviewing.

Gideon sat a plate near her and she just eyed him cautiously. He then sat down on his normal stool next to her with a sigh.

"We know about the classes, Brooklyn. Frank told me when I called him. He won't be guarding you any longer. I'll be assigning someone new," Gideon said.

Classes? I vaguely remembered interrupting a conversation when I stumbled into Jaxon and Oliver's office the night before. But they started talking about Missy and I was confused about what was happening with her. I felt completely out of the story-line of what was happening around me.

I knew the moment Gideon's words left his mouth, they were the wrong ones. The blush in Brooklyn's cheeks increased and her hands tightened around her mug until her knuckles went white. She stared at the countertop and took a number of deep breaths, clearly trying to control whatever her reaction was going to be.

"Frank will be with me daily, or I'll have no one," she finally said, her voice dangerous and low.

"I'm sorry, Stellina. Frank didn't follow the clear directions set for him. He can't be trusted."

Brooklyn's eyes snapped over to Gideon and I almost had to lean back, feeling the heat from her look. Gideon had the sense to fidget under her focus, feeling the pressure of what was happening.

"How dare you! You don't get to give instructions about my life and then fire someone because I don't follow your directive. I get to be my own person still, Gideon. And that means I'm going to continue taking the Muay Thai classes," she said harshly.

Whoa, Muay Thai? I thought to myself. I didn't know much about martial arts, but I knew that one was a serious, competitive sport.

"We've only been trying to keep you safe," Jaxon tried to interject.

Brooklyn's hand flew up, and she pointed at him.

"You've tried to control me. I want to learn to keep myself safe and you said no. That's not a decision any of you get to make for me," she said.

"The injury on your ribs..." Gideon started.

"Was the first one I've ever gotten. And if I hadn't been distracted by shit happening in this house, I wouldn't have gotten hit in the first damn place," she yelled, standing up.

She went to the sink and dumped her coffee out, standing with her back to us for a split second. I looked around at my brothers and they were all exchanging looks and I could see this going down the wrong direction.

"That's enough. You're going to quit the classes and that's the end of it. Gideon will get a new security guard who can follow instructions and keep you safe," I said.

I snapped up the newspaper again, considering the matter closed. The paper was ripped from my hands and a red faced Brooklyn stood in front of me.

"I'm not sure who you think you are. You can be with whatever woman is throwing herself at you for the moment and you think you can tell me what the fuck to do? It's ok for that same woman to be touching Oliver, and calling you all her boys, but I can't go to a self defense class? You have all lost your fucking minds," she said, before turning on her heel and storming out of the kitchen.

I stared after her, dumbstruck at the way she had raised her voice, and told us all off. The situation with Missy was a misunderstanding and eventually that would get cleared up. I hadn't intended for Brooklyn to see her. However, when I saw my brothers taking Brooklyn to the offices, jealousy had risen up in me and I felt angry to not be with her. When Missy appeared, I was already partially drunk and her presence only made me drink more.

My brothers all stood and followed in Brooklyn's wake, but before they even got out of the kitchen, the front door slammed. I heard the door open and heard raised voices, but a car door slammed and soon the front door closed once more. I sat rooted in my spot, just processing everything I had just learned in ten minutes sitting in the kitchen.

When my brothers came back in, all three of them looked torn and despondent. They all sat down and just looked at each other. The silence was more than I could handle, with only the blood pounding in my head for sound.

"I will admit, I'm pretty confused to what the fuck is going on."

Brooklyn

WHEN I FLUNG open the front door, I was grateful to find a confused Frank standing next to his usual car. Before I saw him, I didn't have a solid plan on how I was getting away from the house and getting to work. My vision was blurry with tears that were fighting through, but I pushed them back with all the rage I was feeling.

"Frank, please take me to work," I said as I stalked toward the sedan.

He watched me warily, making a decision to not say a word, just nodded and opened the backdoor of the car. Just as I was sliding in the, the front door had opened and Gideon, Jaxon and Oliver streamed out. Frank froze and looked between them and me.

"Brooklyn, we aren't done talking," Gideon called to me.

"That wasn't talking. That was dictating. And I'm done with it," I yelled back.

I reached out and grabbed the door handle, pulled it from Frank's grasp, and slammed it shut. I manually locked the door, in case any of them got the wild idea to try to pull me out of the car. I stared straight ahead, so I didn't know what exchange there was with Frank, but it was only a few seconds before he was climbing behind the wheel.

Once we were through the gates, I finally let myself collapse against the seat, laying my head back.

"Are you ok?" Frank asked.

"No. But I guess you already knew what was coming," I said.

"Sorry. I couldn't lie when Gideon called. Especially if the bruise is as bad as he said," Frank replied.

"I'm not mad at you, Frank. I never should have had to keep the secret in the first place. And I brought you into it. So, I'm sorry."

The drive to the office was quiet and entirely too short. I was still seething over Aiden making his demands on me. What game was he even playing? I still didn't know who the woman was and why she was on the owner's level. The Knights didn't just let anyone up there, so she was either business or pleasure. And Aiden had been too drunk for it to be business.

My heart constricted again at the thought of Aiden having sex with the small woman. I had tried to not feel too much for any of them too soon. But now I felt like I was drowning and everything hurt. I turned my face toward the window and leaned my forehead against the cool glass, trying to control myself before getting to my office.

Once inside the parking garage, Frank came around my side of the car and helped me out. I had my gym bag over my shoulder and he saw it, his eyes widening.

"You want to go to class today?" He asked.

"Seems I might as well. They all know about it now. And it's what I want to do. That matters," I replied.

Frank seemed to mull over my answer, but nodded and walked me to the elevator. On my office floor, he planted himself in reception and I went to my office alone. I immediately closed myself in, even though I didn't have any morning calls. The silence I was met with was exactly what I needed for my chaotic thoughts.

I knew exactly what I needed to do, and it was going to hurt like hell. I picked up my cellphone and dialed Ash.

"Brooklyn Reeves, I demand to know how hot last night was after I left," Ash's singing voice came across the phone.

I couldn't hold it back any longer and I choked on the tears that were starting to flow.

"Wait, what the fuck? Are you crying? Do I need to murder someone?" Ash demanded, her voice losing its happy quality.

I let everything pour out. Without a lot of description, I told her what had happened the night before. And then I admitted to her that I was taking the self-defense classes the guys had forbid. Ash didn't say anything until I was struggling to take a deep breath at the end.

"What do you need, girl?" She asked quietly.

"Can I come stay with you for a bit?" I asked.

"You don't even need to ask. Just come whenever you want. You could have my room. I know yours might upset you..." she said, her voice trailing off.

I knew what I would be facing if I went back to Ash's apartment. Though we had wiped all evidence of the break-in from my room, I hadn't been back since. I wasn't sure the room wouldn't still feel violated, but I didn't have much choice. And I couldn't kick Ash from her own room.

"No, that's ok. You're a good friend. I'll sleep in my old room," I said.

"What are the guys going to think about this?" She asked.

That was the big question, wasn't it? I propped my elbow on my desk and let my forehead fall into my hand.

"Probably nothing great. But I can't keep doing this with them. I appreciate the protection they've offered me, but I still need my freedom."

"I understand."

"I'm going to ask Frank to keep working with me. I have a feeling Gideon will want that and will keep him on payroll. I hate to ask to come back. I don't want you in danger," I said.

"Lyle has been pretty clear who his target is. You're my best friend. I will do whatever I can to help you," she replied.

"Thank you, Ash. I'll come tonight after I pick up some stuff from the house."

"Just avoid those guys before you get out the door, girl. I have a feeling they would lock you in if they knew you were taking a break from them," she said.

Though the comment sounded like it could be a joke, there was no humor in Ash's voice. I was sure she was more than half right about that. Gideon and Aiden would likely try to keep me in the house. Jaxon would try to reason with me, though when that failed, he'd probably agree with Gideon and Aiden and throw away the key.

Oliver was the one I focused on for a moment. When I had taken a break from them in the beginning, it was Oliver that was clear to me about how badly it hurt him. The look of hurt on his face was almost enough to make me fold, and not follow through with what I knew I needed to do. This wasn't about hurting them or about me not having strong feelings for them, it was about them hearing me.

"Brooklyn? You still there?" Ash's voice shook me from my thoughts.

"Yeah, sorry. I'll see you tonight," I said, with more strength than I felt.

We said our goodbyes and hung up. I tried to work the morning away, keeping my mind focused on my tasks and not on what was to come. Lunch came, and I was relieved to leave the confines of my office. Frank drove me to my class without a word, but his silence was enough for me to know he really didn't approve of this continuing.

I was determined to not get hurt again in this class, so as I dressed I pushed everything from my mind. When I got to the mat and was paired up with a partner, my mind was completely in the movements and I wasn't caught off guard again. I took out my aggression during our bag work, and my partner commented on me needing to lighten up a bit.

My teacher stopped me as I was going into the locker room. He waited while all the other students left and I stood and stared at him, waiting for whatever was coming.

"Brooklyn, nice job today. You seemed a bit aggressive, but that's ok. Everything good?" He asked.

"Yes, sir. I'm sorry. I'll be more careful next time," I replied.

"No, no. I want to see you bring that much strength to every class. I wouldn't be doing my job if I didn't check in with my students once in a while," he said, laying a hand on my upper arm.

The gesture was casual, but his hand lingered. I fought the urge to look down at my arm and make an obvious issue with him touching me. He smiled kindly at me. I knew he wasn't much older than I was, but I looked at him as an authority figure and the private moment started to feel uncomfortable. I was just debating on stepping back, when he dropped his hand.

"I was also wondering, hopefully, I'm not being too forward, if you would like to get a drink with me one evening. After you're off work, of course," he said.

Before the shock could paint itself across my features, I schooled my face into kind resignation.

"Oh, thank you for the offer, really. But I have a boyfriend," I replied.

Disappointment flashed across his eyes, but he smiled brightly again and nodded.

"Understood. Good job, again. See you at the next class," he said, before turning to move toward the gym office.

I let out a huge gush of air, glad the uncomfortable moment was over. In the locker room, I slowly dressed and let the moment replay in my mind. The instructor was handsome and fit. Often, he fought without a shirt and it was hard not to notice the way his muscles were sculpted. However, noticing wasn't the same as being attracted to him, which I wasn't. All I saw was all the ways my guys were more attractive to me.

Which only made going to Ash's even harder. I wanted to be with them, even if they were pigheaded and controlling. The desire to just run into their arms at every opportunity was still in me. They had ignited a sexual awakening that most people probably had when they were younger than me. But even that didn't mean they controlled me as a person. There needed to be respect and understanding between us as well.

In the car on the way back to the office, I decided to drop the bomb on Frank.

"Frank, instead of going back to the office, can you take me to the house?" I asked.

Frank glanced up at me in the rearview mirror, his brow furrowed in question.

"Are you done for the day?"

"No. But I need to get some things from the house before the guys get home," I replied.

I knew I was hedging and not coming right out with it, but I needed Frank on my side for this. Gideon would freak out about my safety, but if Frank was already agreeing to watch the apartment and still drive me, it might make it easier on the big man.

"Ok. What's going on, Brooklyn?" Frank asked bluntly.

"I'm going to stay with Ash for a few days until things calm down at the house. I'm hoping you'll keep your position with me, but at the apartment," I said.

Frank didn't say anything, but I did see he was changing our direction, taking a turn that would lead him away from the office.

"I can't cover that on my own, Brooklyn. I have to sleep. Gideon will need to hire a second man," Frank finally said.

Shit, I thought to myself. I hadn't considered that Frank didn't watch the house when I was there. It was protected by a wall and an alarm and four guys that could handle anything that came our way. I chewed the edge of my thumbnail, thinking. Frank continued driving toward the house while I pondered.

When he pulled through the gate, I held my breath, worried one of them would come out of the front door as soon as we pulled up. But when Frank opened my door, there was no movement anywhere. I felt relieved, but also sick about leaving without facing them. I just knew if I saw them, I'd cave and that wouldn't solve anything.

In my room, I quickly packed a few outfits from the closet and grabbed items that I needed from the dresser. Once I had everything packed in a suitcase, I stood and stared around the room. I tried not to let my eyes linger on the bed, where I had spent so many nights in the arms of my guys.

And they were mine. Even though I was angry with them at the moment, and needed to get some space, it didn't stop how I felt about them. I knew that would be hard for them to understand. Thinking of that, I set down the suitcase again and went to the small desk my room had. I fished out a small piece of paper and wrote a short message. I knew one of them would be looking for me eventually, especially after the blow up during breakfast.

I only spared one last look at my room before jogging down the stairs with my suitcase. Tension thrummed through my body, holding me taunt as I looked around every corner. I didn't fear seeing them, I didn't fear them hurting me. I was more afraid that they would find a way to stop me.

In the foyer, I hesitated and glanced around. Everything was still and silent, the only noise the beeping of the buttons as I set the alarm again. Closing the door behind me was the hardest thing I had done. Frank took my suitcase as I leaned against the front door, trying to comfort my heart before I had even left.

As Frank pulled through the gate, tears streamed down my face. He watched me in the rearview mirror, his eyes full of concern, but I just turned to look out the window. My heart was breaking into tiny pieces as we left the gated property behind us. My mind knew what I needed to do, but that didn't stop me from knowing how badly I was hurting them and myself by doing it.

Jaxon

MY CHEST HAD ACHED all day, and I rubbed my hand across it again. The fight with Brooklyn was all I could replay in my mind all day. The look of fury on her face as she slammed the car door on us was etched in my brain, and I could barely focus on anything else.

Things hadn't gotten any better once Brooklyn had stormed out. My brothers and I rarely fought, but we were at each other's throats, laying blame on each other. Now that I had time to reflect,

I knew this was a joint fuck up. The four of us had agreed to protecting Brooklyn and keeping her under guard.

What none of us realized was she would grow to resent the situation. Gideon was still pushing against us, believing we were doing what was best to protect her. In my mind, I agreed with him. With Lyle out in the world, we could only assume he was waiting for his perfect chance to get near Brooklyn again. But she was her own person, and she didn't take kindly to being dictated to.

I stared into the glass of dark liquor I had poured myself. It was entirely too early to be drinking, but my mind was an absolute mess. I normally knew the things to say, the things to do, to workout difficult situations. Calm and dependable Jaxon. I couldn't seem to tap into any of those strengths now.

There was a time I wasn't the dependable one. A time when I was high more often than I was sober, when my brothers could only be sure I would show to deal, so I could get my hands on product. It was a time in my life that all I wanted to do was hide from reality and drugs helped me do that.

Looking at my computer screen and the photo I had pulled up, I remembered how influences in my life didn't show me the right path to go down. I set down the glass and leaned forward to look closer at the most recent photo of Missy I could find. She was staring into the camera with a small smirk on her face.

When Missy had been the woman I thought I loved, we loved the drugs together. She would encourage me to do more and the sex we had would be messy and unfulfilling. At the time, I had no idea what could be, and I tried to hold on to Missy tightly, even as things began to unravel. When she almost fractured my brothers and me, I finally pushed the veil of drugs out of my vision so I could see what was happening to us.

Missy didn't look like the addict she had been the last time I laid eyes on her. Gideon had a slim file on her, but she never seemed to be someone we would need to worry about, so time wasn't wasted on her. Now, she had reappeared into our lives, not only at the club, but we each had received text messages from an unknown number that seemed to be her.

The message that came to my phone had read "Don't you miss us, Jaxon? Miss the high?" It was sickening to me and I had immediately deleted it. We all had come too far and built something too important together to allow Missy to weasel in and hurt us. We were on the path of building a family we could be happy with, in love with, by adding Brooklyn.

Which brought me to staring at a recent photo of her in a tabloid. Somehow, Missy had created a social media following and now was considered an influencer. When I browsed through her content, it turned out she used her recovery from addiction as a way to pull people in. Kicking addiction was admirable, but Missy used it as a ploy to gain followers.

I clicked on another tab that showed me her net worth. She wasn't in the big leagues, but she had come far from the girl they had known. Her income streams were mostly advertising through digital sources. She had picked up one or two endorsements and they were big paydays for her. Seemed after those were banked, she started to show up on the paparazzi circuit.

One site actually had Missy connected to us, though it was written as very mysterious. I would hedge my guess that it was actually Missy feeding the information to the tabloids. As far as I was aware, there were no pictures to place us together, even in our past. Taking selfies or memorializing our lives hadn't been on our list of priorities.

We had been successful in keeping our past from the spotlight, as we rose to power within the city. Now we had friends in politics, law enforcement and even a few judges. Those friends had all been made by legal means, most by supporting the same charitable foundations or being on boards supporting causes we all agreed on.

I opened one tabloid site and stared at the front page again. I would have to bring it to the attention of Gideon, to see if he could find out how it happened. But there was a photo of Missy sitting with Aiden in the VIP section of Club 4. The story didn't have details about who Missy was, but they tied Aiden back to Brooklyn and the headline was about them being on the outs. I shuddered to think of Brooklyn seeing the story.

The timing of Missy's appearance sat wrong with the four of us. We had been successful for quite a few years and she hadn't come out of the woodwork. I couldn't wrap my mind around why she wouldn't want to show up until she was also successful on her own. That wouldn't matter to Missy. The way I saw it, she was always out for what she could get from a situation. If she wanted us back, it was only because we had money now, not because of some unrequited love.

I had no doubts that Brooklyn was also a reason Missy showed up. We paid off enough photographers to keep the stories about her to a minimum in the tabloids. But some photos leaked here and there, linking her to one or multiple of us. Brooklyn just shook her head at the situation and didn't seem overly concerned about the public's opinion. However, if Missy saw just a few of the photos, it may have given her more incentive to come and disrupt our lives now.

Shutting my laptop, I finished my drink and sat back, rubbing my chest again. My heart hurt with the way we had left things with Brooklyn. I picked up my phone and felt disappointment when I saw my pleading text message to her had gone unanswered. It made me feel weak, but I couldn't have her going an entire day not knowing how important she was to us. And that's what Brooklyn did to me, exposed me for all of my emotions. Things I could usually keep in check, were right on the surface with her.

The image of her connected to wires with a beep telling us if her heart was still beating was on my mind constantly. It took mere moments for Lyle to get access to her and almost kill her. I wished Gideon had just killed him then. It would have been self defense. But when the story came out, I knew Gideon had to act quickly to help Brooklyn and I couldn't blame him for that. We were just stuck watching our backs, waiting for Lyle to resurface. None of us believed he had given up on our woman.

I decided that my one drink wasn't enough to stop me from driving home and left my office. My brothers weren't around, which was a good thing. I was too lost in my mind and a lot of it contained anger at how we all dealt with the morning conversation. Most of that anger was directed at Aiden for pulling the shit he did with Brooklyn. Making her doubt our feelings for her, even for a moment, was too much for me.

In my car, I rehearsed all the things I wanted to say to Brooklyn when I got home. I wanted to apologize, to explain why we were overreacting. I needed to tell her that the thought of her injured made me sick to my stomach. That I needed her to lean on me, on us, to protect her. I wanted to slay any demons that came for her.

Pulling my car into its spot, I noticed I was the first home. I had no idea where my brothers were, but it gave me hope that I would have time with Brooklyn before they arrived. I walked through the kitchen without acknowledging Chris, who was busy with dinner prep, only glancing around to make sure Brooklyn wasn't keeping him company again.

As I climbed the stairs, an uncomfortable feeling was settling in my stomach. Somehow, before I even opened Brooklyn's door, I knew what I would find. Inside, I immediately noticed her closet doors not shut and a number of items missing from hangers. It wasn't everything, which gave me a small sliver of hope that wherever she had gone wasn't meant to be permanent.

Turning, I found a slip of paper on her recently made bed. The bed we had specially made so she could have us with her whenever she wanted. I picked up the paper and collapsed on the bed, reading her words over and over, trying to understand what she was trying to tell us.

———

I had to go. I care for you all, but this is too much. I need my space and need to be sure of what I want. Please don't follow me. xo - Brooklyn

———

Pain lanced through me as I began to understand she had left us. The last line explained why she wasn't responding to any messages. She didn't want us to contact her. She had been pushed to a breaking point, and she had moved out before any of us could even talk to her.

"What's going on?" Gideon's voice came into the room.

I looked up at him as he glanced around the room. The noise of his motorcycle hadn't carried up the stairs. It was clear my brother came looking for the same person I was. I held up the note, and he snatched it from my hand.

"Fuck," he breathed.

"Yeah, fuck," I replied.

He immediately pulled out his cellphone and from the side of the conversation I could hear, he was speaking with Frank. He stalked out of the room and I zoned out, looking back at the bed I had just been in with Brooklyn a day before. I could clearly see her body arching as I put my mouth on her early in the morning. The memory now felt painful and far away, but I didn't want to lose it.

Gideon reappeared with Oliver on his heels. My brother was pale, his lips in a tight line. He was holding the note that Gideon had passed over, his eyes going over the words again and again as he sat down next to me.

"Frank is outside Ash's apartment building. Brooklyn asked him to take her there with her stuff. She's staying there for now. Frank is agreeing to be her daytime guard still. I called in someone to cover the night," Gideon explained.

"Did you let Brooklyn know? She might not like being watched," I said quietly.

"She won't answer my calls. I asked Frank to inform her,"

Gideon said. His words came out sharp and I could see the pain in his features.

We all sat in silence for a few minutes, each lost in our own thoughts about what was happening. I found myself fearful, wondering if we could even fix it and bring Brooklyn back to us.

"What are we going to do?" Oliver said, voicing my thoughts.

"She was pretty specific about what she wanted. For us to not follow her. She wants space from us," I said.

"What do you think she means about being sure what she wants? She doesn't want us anymore?" Oliver asked.

I looked over at him and I could tell he was struggling to hold on to his emotions. Out of the four of us, Oliver's heart was the closest to the surface. Something that had been abundantly clear with the affection he showered Brooklyn with. Though the words hadn't been spoken between any of us, I knew without a doubt that Oliver loved her. If I analyzed my own feelings, I would say I likely would too if I allowed myself.

"Too much happened at once, a perfect storm," Gideon said.

"Right. Aiden and her fight, Missy showing up, us piling on her about the Muay Thai lessons," I replied.

Gideon jerked his chin in a nod, his silent way of agreeing to the hand he had in the fight that was the final straw for Brooklyn.

"Will she be safe?" Oliver asked.

"As safe as I can make her, without being with her every minute of the day," Gideon immediately replied.

I knew Gideon had men from all walks of life working for us at the clubs, as well as the private security we employed. Frank was a good example of the type Gideon would pick for the most important assignments. I felt somewhat secure knowing he would pick someone of the same caliber to protect the building at night.

"The apartment will be harder to protect, but my men will do everything in their power. I trust them with the job," Gideon continued.

Together, the three of us went to the kitchen, but I didn't think any of us had appetites for dinner. Sitting at the island, I thought about what I had researched all day and decided to tell my brothers what I had found on Missy. We had multiple issues to address if we were going to bring Brooklyn back and that snake was just one of them.

As I was talking about the money Missy had made, Aiden entered the kitchen and the three of us fell silent. He looked around, and a frown came to his face. He sat at his seat and watched me, waiting for me to continue. Once I finished, he looked around again.

"Where's Brooklyn?"

"Gone. Like you wanted," Oliver said, his voice laced with more venom than I had ever heard him speak with.

Gideon didn't even look up, his hand gripping his fork so tightly, I was sure it was going to bend in half. Oliver glared at Aiden, looking like he could launch across the island at any moment. Aiden's face went ashen, and I had to appreciate that he at least acted like he was upset by the news.

"I didn't want her to leave. Why would I want that?" He asked.

"Why is exactly the question of the day isn't it? Why did you push her away? Why were you so horrible to her? Why did you allow her to believe you would fuck Missy? Why?" Oliver ranted.

"She made that assumption. I didn't do anything to make her believe that!"

"But you didn't do shit to make it clear that you didn't want that bitch. You know Missy showing up is only to fuck up our lives, Aiden. Why wouldn't you have made that clear to the woman we do want?" Oliver asked.

"Oliver, this isn't helping," I said quietly, hoping I could keep calm in my voice, a calm I didn't feel at all.

Aiden looked down at his plate without speaking again. Oliver shot me a look, but he clamped his mouth shut, keeping his anger in for the moment.

"We need to get rid of Missy. Make sure she's not coming around. Then we need to tell Brooklyn the truth about who she is.

She deserves to know, especially with the tabloid rumors flying around," I said.

Aiden didn't acknowledge what I had said, but Oliver and Gideon both inclined their heads to me, agreeing. The problem was, how would we tell Brooklyn anything, if she wouldn't answer our calls? If we gave our girl the space she wanted, would a chasm open that could never be closed again?

Brooklyn

BEFORE FRANK even knocked on the apartment door, I knew the guys had found my note. My phone suddenly got quiet, the constant calls and text messages that I had been avoiding all day, stopping completely. When I let Frank into the apartment, his face was sullen and I felt some small amount of guilt for making him be in the middle of me and Gideon.

"Gideon called," he said.

"I figured," I replied, just as Ash entered the room with a bottle of wine and two stemless wine glasses.

"He doesn't want to overwhelm you or overstep, his words. But he has assigned a man to be outside during the night. I'll be back, normal time, to take you to work in the morning," he explained.

I sighed, thinking about how Gideon must have sounded on the phone. It was the emotions I was sure he conveyed that prevented me from answering any phone call. I hadn't listened to any voicemails either. I knew I was too weak when it came to them, and it would kill me to hear that they were hurting.

"Ok, Frank. Thank you. I appreciate you staying on, even though this wasn't the original assignment," I said.

He looked indecisive, and we stood in silence for a moment. I could hear Ash fidgeting with things behind me, clearly reading the room. Finally, Frank moved to go back to the door, but stopped just as his hand touched the doorknob.

"We all just want you to be safe, that's all The Knights have wanted. I hope you realize that," he said.

"I know," I replied quietly.

I did know. My safety was a top priority to them. They all just went about it the wrong way, treating me as if I had no say in my own preservation. I tried really hard to understand where they were coming from. But I had spent way too much money in therapy to learn how to be my own person, without three overbearing men showing up, forcing me to go backward.

Frank nodded to me before leaving and closing the door behind him. I quickly locked it. Though I wanted to find a way to hold on to my independence, I didn't feel completely safe. I had grown complacent living behind the walls around The Knights' home. I didn't want to be controlled, but I would miss feeling as safe as I did.

Turning, I found Ash looking at me. Without saying anything, she came to stand next to me and showed me again how to use the new security system Gideon had installed for her after I had left. It was similar to what the house had, so I didn't need to learn much, just remember my code. Seeing the system only made me think of my big man, and I had to step away as my eyes filled with tears.

Ash followed me to the couch, where I collapsed and laid my head back on the cushions. I heard her twisting the top off our favorite cheap bottle of wine and pour two generous servings. Without opening my eyes, I held out my hand until the cool glass slid into my palm. I sat up so I could sip the white wine and Ash met my eye.

"So. We going to talk about it?" She asked.

"Not sure what else there is to say," I replied.

"You love them?"

I thought about that. I still wasn't sure. What did love feel like? Or the loss of it? Was it the pain in my chest that felt like I was hollow? When I was with them, was it the elation I felt whenever they were near? I didn't know the answers to those questions and jumping to love was too scary for me.

"I don't know," I finally responded.

Ash didn't say anything, just nodded and sipped her wine.

"Even if I do, all of this is too much," I added.

"All of what? Men who care, protecting you the best they know how?" She asked.

"You agree with them?" I asked, my eyebrows shooting up as I stared at my best friend.

"Not at all. The controlling your movements and always knowing where you are, that's just weird and over the top. But I guess a part of me can understand why they went that far."

"Explain," I said, needing to understand more.

"Brooklyn, you aren't used to anyone caring about you first. I realize that. Maybe they do too, but I would guess they are dense men and don't. When you were attacked, it was clear that the four of them were devastated, especially because they felt like they had let you down," she said.

"That's ridiculous. I've told Gideon so many times it's not his fault," I interjected.

"Doesn't really matter what you say to him. It's clear he's taken on the responsibility of protecting you and he doesn't want to fail," she replied with a soft smile.

"I'm not their responsibility. If anything, I just wanted to be a girlfriend," I said, feeling exasperated.

"It's not really uncommon for men to be possessive about their girlfriends, and that's not always in the bad way you've experienced," she said, her voice taking on a quieter tone.

She didn't need to say much to toss me back into my memories. Early in my relationship with Lyle, before I really learned to be scared of him, I had to report everything back to him. At the time, I thought it was because he loved me and wanted to be with me all the time. Of course, I learned that it was his way of controlling me, as if I were a possession to him.

Once, I didn't go straight home after my classes, instead stopping at the grocery store to buy a few things we were low on. I didn't think anything about the time it took to deviate from my normal pattern. When I got home, Lyle was waiting for me at the door. I smiled, under the impression he was greeting me. Instead, he knocked the groceries from my arms, causing eggs to fly everywhere and a can of tomato sauce to fall painfully on the top of my foot.

Lyle had screamed at me for being late and then added in the mess that he had just made. He didn't hit me, but sometimes I thought physical violence would have been easier to handle. I was so afraid of being alone, I apologized over and over, begging him to forgive me. I promised to never go anywhere without telling him first. Then he forced me to my hands and knees to clean up the eggs. He stood over me, drinking a beer, until I had the mess cleaned up.

When I was done, he shoved me into the kitchen and told me to get dinner going or he was going to be pissed again. There were plenty of times I thought about leaving Lyle. But the fear of being alone, having to face the unknown without someone familiar, was too daunting for me. As always, after the outburst from Lyle, he found a way to try to smooth things over. That night, during dinner, he sat and held my hand, telling me how much he loved me. I accepted it and believed every word he said.

"He said he owned me," I whispered.

"Who? Lyle?" Ash asked.

I nodded. It made my stomach roil to even think about the times he claimed he owned my body and soul. For a long time, I thought both were tainted because of what he had done to them. It wasn't until I met Oliver and Jaxon that I realized anyone could look at me differently.

"You know that's not true, right girl? That was bullshit back then, and it still is. Someone is going to find that fucker and end him. I put my money on your men," she said with a grin before taking another long sip of wine.

A chill went down my spine, thinking of The Knights finding Lyle. They had told me some of their past and I didn't doubt they could handle the situation. But did I want them doing that for me? Did I want them putting themselves in the line of fire to protect me?

"Only three of them," I said, going back to what Ash had said.

"What?"

"It's only three of them. Aiden and I, I think we broke up," I said, my voice hitching as tears threatened to spill.

Ash slid closer to me and slung an arm around my shoulders. I laid my head on her and a tear escaped my eye, making a trail down my cheek.

"Tell me what happened? Maybe I can help," she said.

I recounted the night Aiden and I had sex on his car and I felt a shiver go through Ash's body. I laughed and sat up and looked at her.

"Ok, sorry, that's hot though," she said with a smile.

"It really was. But the moment I thought we were making a connection, Aiden pulled back and slammed a door between us.

He made me feel cheap and as if he only wanted me as a piece of ass. Then there was the woman that showed up at the club the other night, after you left."

"Whoa, what woman?" Ash said, setting down her glass as she got animated.

I shrugged before setting my own glass down. "I'm not sure who she is. None of the guys gave me any information. All I know is she was with Aiden on the owner's level, and he had lipstick on his damn face. Then she called them her boys, and I almost lost it."

Ash sat back, her face screwed up in confusion, the look perfectly reflecting what I had going on inside my head.

"But Gideon, Jaxon and Oliver?" She asked.

"Each reassured me after the whole thing with Aiden. But when we got home from the club, Gideon found the bruise and that fight started, which brought me here," I said, shrugging my shoulders.

"You know you're always welcome here, girl, but I just can't imagine these guys are controlling like what you've known," Ash said, reaching for her wine again.

I snuggled into the couch, pulling a blanket over me, and sipped my wine as well. In my head, I knew my guys were nothing like Lyle or the abuse I suffered from him. Still, something about being told what I could do and having my location always watched felt too similar. It raised all of my defenses and that led me to running from them completely.

"It's not the same. It doesn't feel right, though," I finally admit.

"And there was no talking to them?"

"Not last night or this morning. I just couldn't keep fighting. It's three against one and I know they aren't going to change their tunes."

Ash didn't reply right away, and I turned my head so I could look at her. She was stretching her legs and not meeting my eye, which told me she had something to say that I likely wouldn't care to hear.

"Spit it out," I finally said.

"Well, look, like I said, you're always welcome here. I'm happy you're here. I've missed our morning routine the most. But I know those guys were making you happier than you've been in your life. I wonder if you didn't leave a bit quick, running from a good thing, because you felt that familiar feeling of things closing in around you. You've experienced trauma, Brooklyn. That doesn't just go away. There are things that will trigger you, and I think this might have been one of those times where your fight or flight kicked in," she said.

I didn't reply, just looked into my wine glass, absorbing her words. It took me a long time to admit with therapy that I had been a victim, that I had experienced a traumatic experience over a number of years, in addition to my childhood. I wanted to believe I was stronger than anything that happened to me and having the label of trauma over me made me feel weak. A lot of therapy helped me think of that in a different way, even if I did slip into old habits.

We finished our wine and Ash hugged me tightly before we split off to go to bed. I had been delaying this moment, and I felt a knot form in my gut as I moved toward my old bedroom. Pushing open the door, I stood outside for a long moment before reminding myself it was just a bedroom and all the windows were now armed with motion sensors that Ash had armed after Frank left. No one was in the room except me.

The walls were all a stark white now, no photos or artwork hung any longer, most of it ruined when Lyle broke in. The bed was new, just a box spring and mattress on a bare metal frame. Ash said the bed set had been there when the room was cleaned, so I knew one of the guys had purchased it and made the bed. Something about that made me feel a little more calm as I slid between the sheets.

I slipped my earbuds into my ears, wanting to block out the extreme silence of the room. I hit play on a random list and felt tears bubbling up as soon as the strains of "It'll Be Ok" by Shawn

Mendes came to my ears. I couldn't stop the faces of The Knights from flashing through my mind and tears from streaming down my cheeks. Maybe I didn't trust myself to know what love was, but the amount of pain I was feeling I knew somewhere in my subconscious that it couldn't be anything else.

Brooklyn

MY BREATHING WAS COMING in gasps and I felt as if I had just run five miles. I looked around myself and I felt confused by my surroundings. But in the distance, I could see the dull outline of a group of people. Instinctually, I knew it was The Knights, and I started to walk toward them, though no matter how fast I walked, I didn't get any closer to them.

Suddenly, I was whirled away, and I was crying out for them as I was slammed into a new place, a place I wanted to forget had ever existed. A hand clamped down on my shoulder and I cried out in fear as I was swung around. Everything around me moved slowly and I couldn't ignore the drab apartment I had lived in once upon a time.

The hand on my shoulder stopped me and I was face to face with Lyle, his face twisted in an angry sneer, his hair clinging limply to his forehead and a large stain on his shirt. Without a doubt, I knew what had happened, and I started to beg for forgiveness. I had been making dinner and when I turned with the plates loaded with food, Lyle walked into me and the food had splashed across his shirt.

"I'm so sorry, Lyle. It was an accident," I heard myself saying.

"You fucking stupid bitch, you can't do a damn thing right," he yelled at me.

"I'll wash your shirt and I'll clean up the mess right now," I stuttered.

His fingers dug into my shoulder and he pulled my face close to his. Lyle wasn't much taller than me, but he tried to make me feel as if he could easily control me physically. I never fought him, giving him the power he seemed so desperately to need over me. He dug his forehead into mine, glaring at me.

"There's only one thing you're good for," he said, his voice low and threatening.

I could feel my body start to shake and I knew what was coming. His other hand fell to my shoulder and both of his hands pushed me until I was kneeling in front of him. I could barely keep myself from falling over and I wanted badly to back away. However, I knew the punishment would be even worse if I ran.

Lyle's hands went to his belt, taking his time unbuckling his belt and releasing the button on his jeans. He pulled out his dick, that was already semi hard just from the idea of forcing me to do something he knew I didn't want to do. He got off on my fear, but even though I knew that, I couldn't hide how petrified I was.

He reached out and grabbed a handful of my hair, forcing my face forward until his dick was rubbing along my cheek. I wanted to turn away, but his grip tightened as he ran the tip of his short length against my lips.

"Open your mouth and do something right for once," he said.

I swallowed down the bile that was rising in my throat and slowly let my mouth fall open. Lyle grunted as he slammed his hips forward, his dick sliding between my lips before I was ready. My teeth grazed him and he pulled back and slammed into my mouth again, hitting my nose with his pubic bone each time. He ground against my face, enjoying as I started to gag and fight for air.

"Fuck, at least your mouth is good for one thing. It's perfect when I don't have to listen to you whining," he groaned.

Using my hair, Lyle controlled the pace. At one point, I felt my lip split from the battering it was taking and I could taste the metallic blood taste as Lyle's dick went through the cut. Even as tears streamed from my eyes, Lyle continued to thrust into my mouth. I tried to go somewhere else in my head, hoping this was the only thing he did to my body for the night.

As his dick swelled, he held my head firmly, my nose pressed into his pubic hair. He began to come, and I coughed and choked as it was forced down my throat.

"Swallow every drop, every fucking drop," he moaned, as he continued small thrusts through his orgasm.

Once he was done, he yanked my head back by my hair and tossed me to the side. I fell, fighting the vomit that wanted to burst from my mouth. I took deep breaths through my nose, focusing. I tried not to think of the taste left on my tongue or what was now sitting in my stomach.

However, I let my guard down for too long, thinking Lyle had moved on. Instead, I felt my leggings being tugged, and I looked over to find Lyle working to pull off my clothes as he stroked his semi hard dick.

"No, no, Lyle. Please. I just want to go to bed," I begged.

My pleading only incensed him further, and he ripped my leggings at the seam until he could get to my panties. He spit into the hand he was stroking himself with before pulling my panties to the side. I tried to crawl away, but that only made it easier for him to pull my hips up and make me take him from behind.

With no prep for me, he forced his dick into me dry, tearing at my pussy, until I was crying out in pain. But he loved it when I cried, and he thrust harder, until he was fully seated. When I collapsed, he just pushed one of my legs up so he could still thrust deeply into me. I laid crying into the dirty carpet as Lyle groaned and fucked me.

I shot up in my bed, in Ash's apartment, covering my mouth to prevent the scream I wanted to let loose. My eyes flew around the room and a moment later I was falling out of the bed and tripping into the bathroom. I flung the toilet seat up in time to vomit up the wine and dinner I had with Ash.

My nightmares hadn't been as bad with the guys in bed with me every night. It didn't surprise me to have one the moment I left their home and decided to sleep alone. Flushing away the evidence of my nightmare, I laid my head on the cool toilet cover for a moment. I was clammy and sweat coated my skin.

The shivering started next as the scenes from my dream replayed. Really, it wasn't a dream, but memories coming to the surface while I slept. I had once told Jaxon of the times Lyle had taken me by force, raped me. I hadn't been specific, because there were too many times to make a list. He was already angry enough to learn what I had suffered that wasn't listed in the police file they found.

I couldn't stop with the filthy feeling in my gut. Standing on shaky legs, I stripped out of my pajamas and turned on the shower. Once the water was scalding, I stepped under the stream and winced from the pain. But I stayed. So much time had passed, but I could still feel Lyle's hands on my skin. The damage he made still hurt, the scars he left felt new. The hot water sluiced down my skin and I scrubbed with a loofa.

The hot water was turning cold, pushing me from the shower. I would have stayed there for the rest of the night just to avoid any additional nightmares. The bathroom was full of steam that felt immediately suffocating. I found clean pajamas and wrapped my wet hair in a towel before laying back in my bed.

It was impossible not to think about how I had handled nightmares while with my guys. The thought made me pick up my phone and scroll through my contacts. I clicked on Gideon and stared at his phone number. He had sent me a goodnight text, without any other context. They were respecting my boundaries as I had set them, but now I found myself doubting the need for them. I pressed the phone against my chest, holding onto it like a lifeline.

I so badly wanted to hear Gideon's deep voice, to know he was there to protect me. Without a doubt, I knew he would come to the apartment and hold me if I asked him. But I knew that wasn't fair. Not to him and not to me. I couldn't always fall back to them to hold me. I had to figure out how to put myself back together.

Pulling together all the strength I had, I put the phone back on the charger and rolled away from it, just to make sure I didn't pick it up and fold under pressure. I could almost feel Gideon's arms gathering me to his chest as he rumbled words of reassurance. A tear trickled from my eye. I had to admit to myself at least how badly this all hurt.

Sleep didn't come again, and I laid still, staring at the bedroom door. Even though I wasn't asleep, I still jumped when my alarm blared. I sat up in bed and scrubbed at my face. I had a big day at work and I was going to have to figure out a way to rally. In the bathroom, I grimaced at my reflection. Dark circles lined my bloodshot eyes and my hair was a ratted mess.

I tamed my hair into a semblance of a bun, feeling glad that my day would be spent outside of the office. I tried to bolster the excitement of the day. The planning for the week had been going on for a long time and I was happy to be included, even if I wasn't feeling like that at the moment. I took extra time on my make up, so the evidence of my hard night wasn't clear to everyone around.

When I came out of my bedroom, I was dressed in skinny jeans and a sweater. Ash took in my appearance and immediately handed me a mug of coffee.

"I heard the water running in the middle of the night," she said.

I just nodded as I sipped my coffee.

"Nightmare?" She asked.

I nodded again. She reached over and squeezed my arm, her eyes full of sympathy.

"I had been doing better with the guys. I think all the emotional turmoil just got to me," I said with a shrug of my shoulders.

I didn't mention to her that I almost caved and called Gideon, not wanting her to hear how pathetic I really was. We finished our coffee and muffins she had bought, before both heading out the door at the same time. Frank was on our landing, waiting for me, and I smiled brightly at him. The look he gave me told me he knew I was faking the greeting.

In the car, Frank gave me a brief review of the night, and I was happy that he reported there was nothing strange around or inside the apartment building. I had been tense with the idea of Lyle or whoever he was working with, trying to get into the apartment again. I trusted the men Gideon trusted, but no one was infallible.

Frank continued to give me his review and then informed me of the plan for the day. I knew this week would be difficult for Frank and my security. If I hadn't been working on the project for as long as I had, I would have gladly had someone else attend. But I wanted to see things progress for myself.

So often the work I did was behind the scenes and I rarely saw the outcomes come to fruition. This time though, I got to be entirely hands on. A few months prior, the idea of animal therapy had been brought to my attention. I did some long hours of reading before deciding it would be a great program to try with some of the teens in our programs. Studies seemed to point to animal therapy helping with boredom, decreasing feelings of anxiety, worry and fear, all things our kids struggled with.

The goal was to take a handful of kids to a working ranch, where the owners would allow the kids to learn and work with the animals on property. I had found the perfect place to take our first group and had worked closely with one of the owners over the phone. Despite how bad I was feeling, I felt a pang of excitement to meet her in person.

"Brooklyn, does that work for you?" Frank's voice broke into my thoughts.

"Oh, hmmm, sure," I replied, not really hearing everything he said.

Frank would stay in his car and follow the van I rode in with the boys and another youth leader we had. When we got to the ranch, he would stay close to the vehicles, but not interfere with the kids or my work. That was all I really needed to hear from him.

The van ride to the ranch was quiet. The boys in the back either stared at their devices or stared out the window. They had all volunteered, but I imagined it was really the way for them to get out of work at their group homes. I had really high hopes for the day and when we pulled up to the ranch, that feeling only intensified.

Stepping from the van, I found a small blonde woman standing next to the porch steps, with a large, handsome man standing with her.

"Ruth?" I asked.

The blonde smiled and nodded.

"Brooklyn?"

I smiled and walked toward her, opening my arms for a light hug. I had been talking to Ruth daily for weeks and I felt like I knew the woman. It was wonderful to meet her in person and the perfect distraction. Ruth introduced the man next to her and he held out a hand to shake. He then kissed the top of her head and walked toward a barn across from the house. A second man was there, bringing horses into a small paddock.

A third man came running from the house, almost running over Ruth.

"Oh sorry babe, gotta run!" The man exclaimed, before kissing her temple and running to catch up with the boys and the other cowboys.

I turned to look at Ruth, my eyebrows raised. She smiled in response and invited me into the house. Inside, I was taken by the quaint beauty of the ranch home. It was clear hardworking people lived there, with multiple pairs of boots and sneakers lining the wall in the mudroom. Ruth lead me to the kitchen, where there were stools at a breakfast bar.

"So, are one of them your boyfriend?" I asked.

Ruth's face colored slightly, but then she straightened her shoulders and faced me.

"All three of them are," she said, an edge of defense in her voice.

I reached out and laid my hand over hers on the counter.

"No, no, don't misunderstand. I completely get it. And I'm sorry, that question was probably too personal."

Ruth shook her head and smiled.

"We've never really discussed how to behave around other people. I guess it could be confusing," she said.

"No, really, I understand," I said, exaggerating my words.

Ruth's eyes widened slightly as she stood to pour ice tea for us both. She faced me, standing against the counter. With her hand, she motioned for me to continue. I sighed and gave her a small description of The Knights and how we had ended up together. When I hesitated on Aiden's name, Ruth stopped me.

"What's wrong with Aiden?" She asked.

"I don't know if it's Aiden or if it's me. But just when I thought we were getting somewhere, he froze me out. Then there was this other woman," I said.

"Other woman? Oh no, that's not ok. I mean, I don't know

about other relationships like ours. Mine is all I've ever known. But I would probably do something pretty drastic if some woman came sniffing around my cowboys," Ruth said.

I sipped my iced tea, trying to picture the small woman doing whatever drastic thing she could accomplish. Her face looked fierce as she said it and at that moment I had no doubt she would go to blows to protect what was hers. With the way the two men I saw looked at her, it was clear they weren't letting her go anytime soon.

We chatted for the rest of the afternoon, some about her and how she came to be at the ranch. Her story was fascinating and sad. It sounded as if she had escaped a cult like situation and stumbled, literally, across three men that would open their home to her. When she talked about falling in love with them, she got a dreamy look on her face that just made my heart ache painfully.

She asked me more questions about The Knights and I stuck to the good stuff, leaving out the painful pieces. I didn't want to focus on what was hurting me, instead I wanted to share my heart with someone that I knew would really understand me. And Ruth did.

When the day wrapped up, I met with the boys by the van. They loaded up and Ruth walked to meet me and gave me a tight hug. I waved at the three cowboys standing on the porch beyond her.

"Call me, anytime. I know how stubborn these men can me," she said.

The drive back to the group home was a different atmosphere. The boys were exhausted, but chatted between themselves about the things they had learned. They even pulled me into the conversation to talk about how the rest of the week was going to pan out. I couldn't help the bright smile that spread across my face as I thought about how I hoped this gave the boys some peace, at least for a little while.

Brooklyn

THE WEEK WENT by in a flash, with daily trips to Ruth's ranch. I admitted to her on the last day that I was nervous about not having the daily distractions. She had hugged me tight and wished me luck. Now I was sitting alone in my room again, afraid to fall asleep.

Not all of my nightmares had been as severe as the first night. Sometimes I just woke up in a cold sweat, not knowing what had woken me, but adrenaline filling my body to the point of not going back to sleep. I was going on two days without much sleep and I really just wanted one full night before I headed back into the office for normal work.

The guys had been quiet all week. Even though I was the one that left, it hurt that it seemed like they were able to let me go so easily. I was fairly sure Frank was giving Gideon regular updates on my safety, or I knew there would be a Harley parked outside my apartment building.

The good morning and good night messages would come, but there wasn't anything deeper, no emotion in their messages. It made my mind play tricks on me and I was often wondering about the woman from the club that clearly knew all the guys. The idea of her in their home made me sick to my stomach, and I had to breathe deeply to prevent my stomach contents from making an appearance.

When I finally decided I had to lie down, I had to try to get some sleep. I curled up under my blanket and practically hid my head. It reminded me of being a child, never feeling protected by my own mother, and thinking if I just hid under a blanket, the boogie man couldn't find me and hurt me. Now the boogie man was in my head and he was a real man, not a fictional tale I had made up as a six-year-old.

The next morning, I was determined to make the day good and to pull myself out of the funk I was wallowing in. I had a busy week and now maybe I'd be able to think through what to do with the guys. I missed them. That was my first thought. But we had to have some serious discussions if we were going to continue what we had going on. And I would have to somehow deal with the fallout of Aiden.

I went with a power outfit, something to make me feel strong and sexy. Black pencil skirt that stopped just below my knees, a sleeveless red blouse that I tucked in, and black stiletto heels. All things Oliver had bought me when he replaced my wardrobe. I smiled, thinking of him and his unruly curls. My hand involuntarily fisted for a moment as I thought about how I liked to run my hands through it.

Ugh, stop it Brooklyn, I thought to myself as I stomped to the front door and flung it open to find Frank waiting as usual. He smiled at me and I huffed out a breath.

"Are we having a morning?" He asked.

He descended the stairs ahead of me, to ensure I didn't walk out on the street first. He glanced over his shoulder when I didn't answer the question.

"Want to talk about it?"

"Absolutely not," I replied.

"Just trying to be a friend, Brooklyn," Frank said, his voice bristling at my tone.

I sighed, internally reminding myself that Frank wasn't my enemy. And we did have a friendship. He had helped me with my classes without turning me into Gideon.

"I'm sorry. Yes, I'm having a morning. I've been having a week, really. But the ranch was a nice change of pace. I'm just trying to rally, getting back into the swing of things," I said.

"You could always go home," he said. "You know the Knights want you to."

"That's not my home," I replied quietly.

At the curb, Frank opened the sedan door for me and I slid into the car. Once he was behind the wheel, he clicked the doors locked and turned to look at me.

"Do you really think that after this Lyle thing is handled, they would just want you to leave? They care about you, Brooklyn," he said.

"Not like they're showing it right now," I mumbled, looking out the window.

Frank sighed, giving up his therapist act. He didn't try to talk again all the way to the office. In the reception area, he stopped me with a hand on my arm.

"Are you going to your lunch appointment today?" He asked.

"Absolutely. I'm ready to get back into it," I said with a bright smile.

Frank frowned at me, but didn't disagree as I walked down the hall to my office. A week off of my Muay Thai lessons had been enough. If I could have made it back into the city for lessons each day, I would have. But the ranch visits were too important for the kids, and I wasn't going to mess those up.

I opened my laptop and smiled when I immediately saw an email from Ruth. We were building a friendship, but her email was professional and they were offering additional services for whenever we were ready. I forwarded the email to the company President and cc'd my team, letting them know how great the event was for the boys that went. I suggested monthly trips, dependent on the ranch availability.

Funding would become a question, so I started to think about funds I could earmark for it. Having something I enjoyed sinking my teeth in caused my morning to fly by. I was answering emails and composing my funding suggestions when Pam stuck her head into my office.

"Hi. I know lunch is coming, and you were probably going out, but there's a woman here who says she had a meeting with you? I don't have anything on your calendar?"

I frowned, pulling up my calendar as well. I didn't have anything scheduled for the time and nothing with anyone outside of the foundation for the day.

"I don't show anything either," I reply.

"I can ask her to leave. I only came to let you know, well, because she looks like a donor or someone that would attend one of our events," Pam said as she twisted her fingers in front of her.

Pam's paranoia since I had been attacked was at an all-time high. I smiled softly at her, appreciating her wanting to protect me. I stood and straightened my skirt, moving to stand with her at the door.

"It's ok, Pam. I'm sure it's someone that has a date confused. I'll speak with them quickly and get it all cleared up," I said.

Pam nodded. "I put her in the conference room. I'll stay

close by."

I made my way to the conference room. The wall was composed of windows, making it immediately clear who was waiting for me. Eyes turned my way, and it was clear I was being put under a microscope. There was no smile on the face of the small brunette from Club 4 as she watched me walk slowly toward the conference room door.

Suddenly, I regretted not bringing someone with me to the room. I didn't know what she was doing here, but it was definitely about The Knights and it was unlikely to be anything good.

Pam hadn't been wrong. She was dressed like one of our wealthy donors. She was wearing a suit that looked perfectly tailored for her body. She didn't have a shirt under the jacket, allowing a generous view of her cleavage. Diamonds dripped from her ears and circled her wrists. Definitely more than was necessary for an office meeting.

My hesitation caused Pam to rush from the hall, but I couldn't focus on what she was doing. I straightened my shoulders, and I saw an emotion cross the brunette's face, something like humor, but it disappeared quickly. I stepped into the conference room, prepared for whatever the woman was there to throw at me.

"Brooklyn, so nice to actually meet you," she said, her voice taking on a fake sweetness that made my teeth hurt.

"I'm sorry, but you've caught me at a disadvantage. I don't believe we had a meeting," I replied. I kept my business mask on, keeping my roiling emotions off my face.

Suddenly, she raised her hand and wiggled her fingers at someone at the window. I turned just in time to see Frank's mouth drop open and his eyes flash to me. He started for the door, but I held up a hand and shook my head to stop him. This woman couldn't do anything to me in the middle of my office and frankly, something in me needed to hear what she was going to say. Frank shook his head and disappeared again.

"He's like a trained puppy, isn't he?" The brunette giggled.

"He's good at his job," I replied.

Her hand swept across the table, indicating the chairs on my side of the conference room. "Have a seat, Brooklyn. We have things to discuss."

"As I didn't have a meeting on my calendar and I still don't know your name, I don't know what we could have to discuss."

"This isn't about business, dear. I think you know that," she replied. Her voice took on a venomous edge and for a moment, I could see through the veneer she was trying to throw up.

I pulled out a chair and perched on the edge, ready to jump and run if things did go badly. The woman smiled and nodded as she settled back into her chair, getting comfortable now that she had an audience.

"My name isn't really important, but I'll tell you, anyway. You can call me Missy," she said.

"How can I help you, Missy?"

"Oh, I'm just here to chat, sweetie. Seems you were getting quite comfortable with my boys and I thought we should discuss that," she said.

My heart sped up in my chest until I could hear it thundering in my ears. She had called them her boys at the club, too. Gideon, Oliver and Jaxon didn't seem to be happy to see her, and I still wasn't sure about Aiden. I had left before he and I really had the chance to discuss everything that had happened between us.

"Oh, sweetie, you're surprised. I'm sorry," Missy said, though her voice was anything but sorry.

I looked out the window of the conference room, not sure what I had hoped to find. The hallway was empty except for Pam watching from a distance. She had a hand to her mouth, chewing on her nails, her nervous tick. In the back of my mind, I wondered where Frank had gone and realizing he clearly knew the woman.

"I had assumed you'd have questions, but I seem to have caught you off guard. Cat got your tongue?" Missy asked.

I swiveled back to look at her, study her closer. My scars had been the things I hid from the world, the things I thought made me unattractive. Missy didn't have visible scars, though she clearly had work done, without a line creasing her face. If I had to guess, she also had lip filler and a nose job. I wouldn't have thought she was attractive, but I realized that was because her eyes allowed her ugliness to show.

"You clearly have an agenda to come here. Why don't you say what you need to say?" I finally said.

"The Knights and I have history, old history, that ties us together. You're really just a temporary distraction for them. From what I saw, you aren't even good enough for Aiden," she said. "Too early to have bumps in the road, isn't it?"

"Everyone has a past. History. What makes you think they want you now?" I asked.

Missy held a hand in front of her hand, studying her nails for a moment. The move was so orchestrated I almost laughed out loud.

"We have so much shared history, things you will never have with them. You probably didn't even know about our relationship or what they used to do to survive," Missy said.

"I know enough. And I knew they had a similar relationship before me. They had nothing positive to say about the time. If I remember right, you tried to tear them apart," I replied.

"We were basically children back then. They weren't strong like they are now. They couldn't handle me. I'm sure that would be different now. They all have...grown...into delectable men," she said, using her hand to fan herself. "You aren't living with them anymore, are you? Someone is going to need to warm their beds. They loved me. They will again."

Icy rage pumped through my veins. The idea of Missy touching any of my men made me want to launch myself across the table and scratch her eyes out. I swallowed hard, working to control my face, my posture. My hands were gripped in my lap, my knuckles turning white, my nails digging into my skin. Missy's eyes watched me critically and a slow smile crossed her face.

"Oh honey, did you think they loved you?"

CHAPTER
Nineteen

Gideon

THE DAYS WERE BLURRING TOGETHER for me. My brothers always tried to get me to leave my room, but beyond meals, I worked all day at my desk in my room. When I couldn't sleep, I was working. I knew it wasn't healthy. I knew I was obsessing. But until Lyle was found, I didn't see a way for us to get Brooklyn back.

I ran my hands through my hair, pulling it back into a bun, as I watched additional surveillance videos from near the cafe where

Brooklyn had been attacked. I couldn't stop, not believing that the fucker had just disappeared into thin air. Watching the same videos over and over wasn't really going to get me anywhere, but I was feeling at a loss.

Missing Brooklyn was more than I could handle at times. Nothing I had experienced in my life had captured me in such a way. I regretted not telling her, not saying the words that would have told her what she meant to me. Maybe if she knew, she would understand why we were so crazy about her safety.

I was lost in my musings of her when my phone rang. Frank's name flashed across the screen and I frowned. Frank and I had normal check ins, evening and morning. It was the one lifeline I had to Brooklyn, since she wouldn't respond to our calls or text messages. Knowing she was safe, knowing she wasn't alone, gave me a small bit of solace.

"Frank?" I asked, pressing the phone to my ear.

"You need to get to Brooklyn's office now," Frank said quickly.

Before I even knew why, I was running from my room and pounding down the stairs.

"Is she safe, Frank?" I yelled into the phone.

"Yes. But you will not believe who's down here," he replied.

I skidded through our kitchen to the mudroom and launched myself into the garage. I snatched my keys off the hook on the wall and was on my bike before Frank said another word.

"Missy is here. She is meeting with Brooklyn," Frank said.

"Fuck!" I yelled.

I hung up the phone as my motorcycle roared to life. I sped down the drive and the moment the gate had opened enough, I squeezed through. I drove faster than was safe, but the fury and panic in me wouldn't allow me to let off the throttle. We knew Missy coming back when she did wasn't a coincidence. Now I knew Brooklyn was part of her plan.

Getting to Brooklyn's office didn't take nearly as long as it normally would, but by the time I was parking my bike and running for the elevator, I was panting as if I had run the entire way. I paced the elevator as it slowly rose. I watched the numbers, willing it to bypass all the other floors.

When the doors opened on Brooklyn's floor, I rushed through the glass doors, finding Frank waiting for me. The receptionist looked panicked, but she didn't stop us as we went further into the office. We found Pam standing with her eyes on the window of the conference room. When she saw me approach, her face pinched for a moment, but she didn't say anything. We didn't exactly get off well when she had a hand in Brooklyn's cafe attack, even if she hadn't meant to do it.

I wasn't prepared for the emotional blow it would be to see Brooklyn in person. I took in the scene quickly before getting to the door of the conference room. Brooklyn sat on the edge of her chair, her back ramrod straight, her hands gripped in the lap. The tension rolled off of her in waves and it was all directed across the table.

Missy looked cheap, even covered in jewels. Her look felt forced, and I was sure it was all just her way of getting to Brooklyn. The problem was, nothing Missy wore or did would make her more sophisticated or beautiful than Brooklyn. She couldn't even imagine comparing to my girl.

I threw open the door and Brooklyn barely glanced over at me, as if she knew I would be there. Missy's eyes flew to me, widened, and then she smiled brightly. She began to stand up, and I held up a hand.

"Don't even think about coming near me," I growled.

Missy sat back down with a huff and comically pouted. "Oh, come on, my muscle man. Not even a kiss hello?"

Her taunt was said to me, but it was an arrow right at Brooklyn. I took a chance and stepped closer to my girl. I laid my hand softly on her shoulder, feeling how tense her body was. She didn't pull away, but she didn't move into me either.

"Missy, you're well aware it's been years since I've been anywhere near you. You have no place here. You need to get out," I said.

My voice was laced with violence and though I had never put my hands on a woman in that way, I was willing to make an exception for Missy at this point.

"Oh no, Gideon, that's where you're wrong. I have my place. With my boys. And I'm back to claim it," Missy said.

I could feel Brooklyn's body jerk back at her comment, but I didn't dare take my eyes off Missy. She had a sly smile on her face as she batted her overly thick lashes at me. Studying her for a moment, I honestly couldn't remember what we saw in her when we were younger.

"We have no space for you. We're with Brooklyn. Which I'm pretty sure you're well aware of, or you wouldn't be here in her office trying to cause a scene," I said.

That seemed to shake Brooklyn out of her silence. She looked around me to make sure the hallway was still empty. Frank was at the door waiting and Pam was still further down the hall, but no further audience had gathered. I knew Missy was disappointed by that.

"I'm sure you remember the way out. If not, Frank would gladly get you out of my office," Brooklyn finally said.

I squeezed Brooklyn's shoulder, and she leaned into me, putting a hand over mine. I didn't know if she did it because she wanted to, or if it was a show for Missy. Either way it had my skin zinging with energy where she touched me. Across the table, Missy pressed her palms into the table as she stood. She wasn't a tall woman, but she was trying to pull all of her intimidation together and direct it at Brooklyn.

Frank was already swinging open the door as Missy slowly made her way down toward our side of the room. As she neared, Brooklyn stood up, so now she was directly in front of me, her back pressed against my chest. Missy stopped next to us. She pretended to not notice Brooklyn and lifted her hand as if to touch my arm. Suddenly, Brooklyn's hand snapped out, and she had Missy's wrist gripped tightly.

"Do not touch him," Brooklyn said, her voice eerily calm.

Missy's eyes flicked up to me, as if I'm going to save her. I could tell Brooklyn's fingers were tightening each moment Missy didn't acknowledge what she'd been told. Frank stepped into the room, ready to break up what might happen. I glanced out the window again, just to confirm it was only Pam's panicked eyes watching this all unfold.

I decided to dig in and add fuel to the fire. Bending down, I slid my lips along Brooklyn's exposed neck, her tilting her head to give me better access. Missy's eyes were sharp in anger as she watched the display.

"I do not care who you are, where you came from, or what history you have with MY men. You will not touch any of them again. Are we clear?" Brooklyn asked.

"Or what?" Missy spat.

"You do not want to know what I'm capable of," Brooklyn replied, pushing away Missy's hand, finally releasing her wrist.

Frank was now standing directly behind Missy, just waiting for my word. She looked between the three faces in the conference room, clearly judging her chances if she were to try anything else. Luckily for her, she seemed to decide that she had done enough damage. She flipped her dark hair before looking me in the eye again.

"Muscle man, when you get tired of this," she said, motioning up and down Brooklyn's body, "Come find me. I'll remind you what a real woman feels like."

With that, she shoved past Frank and stomped out of the conference room. Once she was in the hall, she straightened her back and started walking with the practice of someone that wanted the entire world to pay attention to her.

"Follow her out. Make sure she leaves," I growled to Frank.

The conference room door swung shut behind him and both Brooklyn and I watch Missy until she's out of sight. All at once, Brooklyn went limp, leaning back against me entirely. I gave myself the freedom to slide an arm around her waist, my hand against her stomach, holding her against me. We stood and just breathed together for a moment.

"How did you know she was here?" Brooklyn asked.

"Frank called," I replied.

She just nodded, before laying her head back on my chest. I inhaled her lavender scent, as if it was the first breath of oxygen I had gotten in a week. Our private moment was broken when we both saw Frank coming back toward the conference room. I knew the moment Brooklyn got into her head, as her body stiffened and she slowly pulled away from me. She went to the door to meet Frank in the hallway.

"She's gone, hired limo. I waited to make sure she didn't have them circle back or something," he said.

"How did she get in here?" Gideon asked.

"I was grabbing a coffee. I don't usually sit in reception the whole day. But today I waited longer. When I went to get coffee, somehow Missy got to Pam and was able to get the meeting with Brooklyn," he explained.

I nodded, but my eyes were on my girl. My body ached for her. I wanted to touch her, taste her, remind her that she belonged with me. I could see the shadows she had tried to hide under her eyes, making me think her nightmares had come back. She wouldn't meet my eye, no matter how long I stared.

"Brooklyn, are you ok?" Pam asked, as she came rushing toward us in the hallway.

Brooklyn turned toward her assistant and held out a hand for Pam to take. She smiled at her and reassured her that everything was fine. When she finally turned to look at me, her eyes were wary and I just wanted them to warm like they did before. She gestured with her head that I should follow her.

She lead the way to her office, which she entered, closing the door after I followed. Immediately, she moved away from me, as if she was afraid I would touch her. The move hurt, but I kept my face neutral and just leaned against the door, waiting to see what she wanted to say.

"I think it's time someone explained to me, in more detail, what that woman is to you," she said.

"Was, what she was to us. She isn't anything present tense," I replied.

"She seems to think she has some right to you, all of you."

"Well, she's delusional. I don't want anyone except you. I know my brothers agree."

Her eyes flashed to mine before she began to pace across her office. When she wasn't looking at me, I watched her body move as she walked. Her legs looked long in her tight skirt and sky high heels. When she turned to walk back toward me, she caught me staring at her ass and I just shrugged my shoulder when she raised an eyebrow at me.

"If that's true, what is she doing, showing up at my office?" She asked.

"Pissing me off to start. But I think she's just trying to cause waves between us. She's trying to make you doubt our feelings for you," I replied.

She stopped in the middle of the office and stared at me again. Her hands were pressed against her thighs, and I knew she was holding herself back from me, causing me to move forward. Before I even thought through my plan, I had an arm around her back, pulling her into me. She gasped lightly, her hands landing on my chest. Even that touch had me biting back a groan.

I ran my free hand up her bare arm and over her shoulder, until I reached her chin, where I gripped it, forcing her to look up at me.

"I know we all fought. I know we have shit to work out. That doesn't change anything about how badly we want you," I said.

"I don't know if that's enough," she said.

"I'll show you what's enough," I said, as I crush my lips to hers.

Despite her protests, she melted into my embrace immediately, lifting to her toes to try to meet my kiss. Her little hands dug into my shirt, gripping it as she tried to get closer. I turned us until I had her pressed against the wall of her office. Her tongue battled with mine, each stroke and caress pushing and pulling against one another.

I needed so much more of her and I didn't think the office was the place for that. Pulling together my willpower, I pulled back. I looked down into her icy blue eyes, blurry with lust and need. Without question, I knew I would give her anything she wanted at that moment.

"Wanna go somewhere with me?" I asked, my voice gravely and deep.

She looked up at me for a moment, before her hand came up to tug lightly on my beard. Such a small gesture, but one for her only, and I had missed it.

"Sure, big man. Take me somewhere," she said.

Quickly, Brooklyn packed up her bag and told Pam she was leaving for the rest of the day. I handed her briefcase to Frank and told him to go back to her apartment, as I would drive her home after our ride. I had a plan to get Brooklyn's mind off her stress, just for a little while.

In the garage, I handed Brooklyn her helmet, and she looked up at me with a large smile. I had promised her a ride, and it was time to fulfill that promise. I got onto the bike and watched out of the corner of my eye as she hiked up her pencil skirt before sliding on behind me. Starting up the engine, Brooklyn's arms slid easily around my waist until her hands were splayed across my front. I couldn't help but take one, kiss its palm, before pressing it to my chest.

On the road, I went directly for the fastest way out of the city. As the buildings disappeared behind us, we wove along tree-lined roads, just us, the wind and the roar of the motorcycle under us. I could feel her laugh and cry out when I would go faster or take us quickly around a curve. I would never put Brooklyn at risk, but she didn't realize I wasn't taking the curves at the fastest speed I could.

An hour later, I pulled us off the main road, to a paved service road I'd been on. When we reached the destination I'd wanted to show her. I pulled my bike to the side of the service road, in case any larger vehicles needed to get by. Turning off the engine, we were dropped into the silence of nature, with only distant bird calls echoing through the air.

I held out my hand, and Brooklyn's palm slid into mine. She carefully climbed off the bike and stretched. I stood up and massaged her lower back for a moment.

"Sorry, I didn't think about how a long ride might be uncomfortable for you," I murmured into her hair.

"It was worth it. This is beautiful," she said.

In front of us was a small meadow surrounded by ancient trees that reached to pierce the blue sky. From my saddle bag, I pulled out a blanket and held my hand out to her. She looked from the meadow, to the blanket, to my hand, the wheels turning in her head. Without saying anything, she reached down to slip off her heels, leaving them next to the bike, before taking my hand.

We carefully picked our way through the grasses and wildflowers. I found a soft patch of grass and laid out of the blanket, and helped Brooklyn sit down comfortably. Sitting down next to her, I didn't try to touch her again. I wanted to make sure whatever happened was her desire.

Brooklyn reached up and removed pins from her hair, allowing the blonde waves to slide over her shoulders and down her back. I squeezed my hands into tight fists to keep myself from touching it. But she was pushing my limits, as she ran her hands through the strands, leaning her head back and basking in the sun rays that came down on our spot.

I could see her glancing at me from the corner of her eye, so I turned my face toward her so she could see me enjoying the scene. A smile spread along her face as she closed her eyes against the sun's strength. Not able to stop myself, I ran a finger along her jaw, causing her to shiver slightly.

"I've missed you, stellina," I murmured.

Her eyes flash open and emotion spilled out at first, before she controlled it.

"Me too, Gideon," she replied.

Brooklyn shifted until she was on her knees facing me. She had a moment of hesitation, but what she wanted won out and she climbed into my lap, straddling my hips. My hands fell to her thighs, finding exposed skin where her pencil skirt had bunched up. Her hands came up to frame my face.

"Can we not talk, big man?"

"Whatever you want, stellina."

Her smile was beautiful as she leaned down to softly kiss me. She focused on my lips first, before her tongue snuck out and slid along the seam, asking for entrance. I immediately obliged, and she slowly slid her tongue along mine, causing me to groan. The sound spurred something in her and she pressed closer to me, angling her head and deepening our kiss.

My fingers dug into the soft flesh of her thighs as I fought to keep myself from touching her further, pushing her too far, making her want to leave me again. The feel of her against me was intoxicating, and I was quickly losing the ability to think straight.

Suddenly, she pulled back and ripped her shirt over her head. She reached down for my shirt and pulled it up and over my head, tossing it to the side with hers. Her hands immediately went to my bare skin, causing goosebumps to break out over my body. She ground against my cock, and I wasn't sure I could handle my control any longer.

"I need to touch you. I can't help it," I said quietly.

"Touch me, god, please, Gideon," Brooklyn begged.

I didn't wait for her to change her mind. My hands ran up her arms, causing her to shiver. I pulled one of her bra straps down, baring her taunt nipple to me. Leaning forward, I sucked the peak into my mouth and Brooklyn moaned above me. Her hands went to my hair and pulled out the elastic I had holding it back. She didn't hesitate to driver her fingers into the strands, gripping my head.

Pulling back, I looked up into her face, finding her eyes bright with desire and her lips slightly parted. We stared at each other for a moment.

"This is a horrible idea. But I have missed you so much," she finally said.

"We can stop. Nothing has to happen," I replied, even if the words practically choked me.

I saw indecision on her face, making me sit back, propping myself up on my hands. If I was going to be inside my girl, she needed to want me there.

CHAPTER
Twenty

Brooklyn

GIDEON LEANED BACK FROM ME, giving me all the space I needed to make my choice. I couldn't stop staring at him, the hard planes of his chest, his abs that looked chiseled from stone. With his hair down around his face, brushing his shoulders, his attractiveness was almost more than I could comprehend.

He had come to save me again. As angry as I had been with them and still was, I knew without a doubt Gideon would always come to protect me. I believed him about Missy. None of the guys had ever lied to me and I didn't believe he would start now. Something inside me needed to mark my big man, to make sure I was all over him, for any woman to know he was mine.

I ran my hands down his chest, running my nails over his abs, watching as he twitched under my touch. I got to his belt, and I began to unbuckle it, holding his gaze. Leaning back to give myself space, I slid my hand into his pant, under his boxer briefs, until I could run my palm along his hardness. Gideon hissed out a breath, letting his head fall back between his shoulders.

Moving to rub my body along his, I ran my tongue along his neck. I tugged on his beard until he looked up at me. I slammed my lips down on his and he leaned into me, his arms banding around my back to hold me to him. Our kiss was messy, hot, and full of emotions that we weren't speaking. I pulled back from him again so I could see his eyes when I spoke.

"This isn't going to fix anything. But I need you, Gideon. Please, make me forget everything else."

His eyes darkened and a split second later, he had flipped us and I was on my back under him.

"You'll forget everything, except how my mouth and cock make you feel," he growled.

Heat flooded low in my belly at his words and I couldn't help the pant that came from my mouth. Gideon's hand went down and found the bottom of my skirt. Not bothering to unzip it or take it off, he pushed it up as his fingers danced up the inside of my thigh. When he got to my lacy panties, he growled again and yanked, ripping them from my body.

He trailed kisses down my neck, pulling down my other bra strap so both of my breasts were exposed to him. His mouth closed hungrily on one peak, and I couldn't stop myself from arching into him. I gripped the blanket on either side of us, losing myself in the sensation of Gideon's tongue as it circled my other nipple, before moving down my stomach.

When his head settled between my thighs, Gideon hooked an arm under one of my legs and banded across my hips, keeping me trapped. Gazing down at him, his green eyes locked on mine, and he slowly licked the length of my center. All the air in my lungs rushed out at once and I pushed down into his mouth. I could feel the vibration of Gideon's chuckle against my sensitive flesh, causing goosebumps to spread along my body.

Gideon wasn't allowing me any chance to hide or slow things down. His tongue pushed into me and I cried out. He replaced his tongue with two fingers that he slid into me slowly, while his tongue pressed against my clit. I was panting, my head thrashing back and forth as pleasure coursed through my body.

I meant what I had said. The physical release, the connection we had like this, wasn't going to fix the problems we had. But remembering how good we were, how good he and his brothers made my body feel, was something I needed after a long week of not sleeping and reoccurring nightmares.

As Gideon increased his pace with his fingers, I pushed away all the thoughts trying to take over my mind, and just allowed myself to feel. He flicked my clit with his tongue, before suddenly sucking it into his mouth and I exploded. Stars flashed behind my eyelids as the waves of pleasure washed over me and Gideon continued to slide his fingers in and out of me, stroking me through my orgasm.

Pulling away from me, Gideon slowly climbed up my body. I could see his beard glistening with my release, and I felt a blush rush up my neck, heating my cheeks. As if he could read my mind, his tongue came out and licked around his lips and a grin spread across his face.

"Taste yourself on my tongue, stellina," he said, pressing his lips to mine, sliding his tongue along mine.

My legs came up to cradle his hips and I moved against the hardness I could feel in his pants. When he finally pulled away, we were both breathing hard and his hair tickled my face, as he lowed his mouth to my ear.

"Did you want more?"

I nodded, biting my lip, holding in the moan that wanted to

tumble from my mouth, just from his words and the way his voice sent a shiver down my spine. His big hand spanned my ribs before palming my breast and tweaking my nipple. The moan I was holding in echoed in the meadow, and Gideon smirked.

"No holding back, stellina. I've missed all your noises," he said.

Without warning, Gideon sat back, grabbed my hips roughly, and proceeded to flip me to my stomach. Using my hips, he pulled me up until I was on my hands and knees, the breeze flowing across my exposed ass and pussy. I heard his zipper, and a moment later, his cock prodded at my entrance.

Reaching down, Gideon buried his hand in my hair, holding it roughly as he worked himself into me. Slow, shallow thrusts caused me to push back against him, wanting him to fill me, stretch me, the way I knew he could. Without warning, he slammed into me, burying himself into me and causing me to cry out his name.

"Fuck, I missed this pussy," he groaned.

He sat still, allowing me to adjust. Even though it had only been a week since I had been with Gideon, my body took a minute to remember how large he was. When he finally moved, he slowly slid from my body, my walls trying to grip him, and shivers ran through me again.

My fingers dug into the blanket, holding on as Gideon fucked me roughly from behind. My neck stretched back as he pulled on my hair, causing my back to arch. I couldn't help myself from pushing my hips back, meeting his thrusts. The sound of our flesh slapping together echoed around us, along with the sounds of birds in the trees.

Gideon let go of my hair and leaned over my back. His teeth and tongue danced along my shoulders and when I turned my head, he nipped my earlobe.

"I want to feel you squeeze my cock. Come again all over me, stellina," he groaned into my ear.

"Oh god, Gideon...." I whined, not even bothering to mask my wanton need.

His hand on my hip curved around until it was between my legs. When he found my clit, he slowly circled it as he continued to slam into me.

"Now, stellina, come, now," he demanded.

As soon as his fingers feathered over my clit, I exploded with a cry. He buried his face in my neck, continuing to pump through to his own release. I couldn't keep myself upright, and collapsed onto my chest, but Gideon held tight to my hips as he spilled into me with a groan.

A moment later, he slipped free of me and he gathered me into his arms so he could spoon me, cradling my ass against his hips. I could feel his hammering heartbeat against my back and his chest heaving as he fought to catch his breath. Grabbing his hand from my waist, I lifted it to my mouth so I could kiss his fingers before twining them with my own. His arms tightened around me as if to ensure we didn't pop the blissful bubble we were in.

The sounds of nature around us lulled me until I was contemplating how nice a nap would be. Gideon used my ruined panties to clean me up before helping me straighten my skirt and put my shirt back on. I couldn't help but eye his body as he slipped his shirt on. When he grinned at me for my staring, I just shrugged, as he did when I caught him checking out my ass in my office.

We sat in silence for a moment, but I knew what Gideon was going to say before the words left his mouth. He nervously ran a hand through his beautiful hair, looking away from me for a moment.

"Come home," he said quietly.

"I'm not sure where home is," I replied.

He grimaced, and I felt bad for hurting him, but I had to be strong, had to do what was right for me as a person and not just as a controllable piece of their lives.

"You know we want you at home, with us. Maybe we weren't very clear about that," he said.

"That's your home, and I was a guest. And that doesn't even address the real issue, does it?"

"We just want you safe, Brooklyn," Gideon said, getting serious now.

I sighed and stood up. "I told you this wasn't going to fix everything, and it doesn't. I do not want my safety, only to sacrifice my independence and making my own decisions."

Gideon jumped to his feet and reached out to me. I didn't stop him as he pulled me into an embrace, because when I was honest with myself, I didn't want to be anywhere other than his arms. My heart yearned for them all, even if that didn't help the controlling issues they had.

"Just drive me back to Ash's, big man. I don't want to ruin this afternoon with a fight. I want to get on your bike, hug you while you race down the road, and just enjoy being near you. We can fight it out later," I said.

He didn't answer, but took my hand and picked up the blanket. We were quiet when we got back to the bike. I slipped my shoes back on and Gideon helped me onto the bike behind him. I was sure to sit as close to him as possible, so I wasn't flashing people my nakedness under my skirt. I crossed one arm around his waist and the other up the middle of his chest so I could lay my hand over his heart.

The ride back to the apartment felt way too short. When we stopped on the curb, Gideon helped me off the bike first, keeping my modesty intact. He dismounted the bike to stand with me on the curb. He nodded to Frank, who was getting out of his sedan on the street. He turned back to me, looking over my head at Ash's building.

"I'd much rather take you back to my bed. Oliver and Jaxon would like that, too."

I smiled sadly up at him. "Not yet. We'll talk soon. I miss you too much to just stay angry."

He stepped into me and I wrapped my arms around his waist. I breathed in his clean smell, mixed with the smell of grass and fresh air from our time in the meadow. I pressed my face against the hard plane of his chest and just tried to be ok with the time we'd had.

"Tell them I said hi," I said, knowing how lame that sounded.

"I'll tell them. But you should talk to them yourself. Oliver, especially, isn't doing great."

I pulled back as my heart constricted. I knew Oliver's emotions were the closest to the surface. Guilt wracked me when I remembered him asking me to not leave again, except that was exactly what I did. We had a lot to talk about and I would have to apologize and make Oliver understand somehow.

"We'll talk soon," I promised.

Gideon nodded and watched as I walked into the building, with Frank escorting me. At the door, I looked back once, needing to see him. He stood, his sunglasses in his hand, allowing me to see the pain on his face. I smiled tightly, not allowing him to see how it hurt for me to walk away.

Inside the apartment, I found a note from Ash, letting me know she had a date and not to wait up. It was all for the best. I wasn't going to be good company for the evening. My time with Gideon in the meadow had been perfect, but when reality set in, the physical needs didn't outweigh the things weighing down everything between us.

I decided I needed to talk to someone that might understand my predicament. After changing into sweats, I sat on the couch and pulled up Ruth's number.

"Brooklyn!" Ruth exclaimed as soon as she answered the call.

"Hi, Ruth," I said, my voice hitching slightly.

"Oh no...what happened?"

Starting with Missy appearing in my office, I told Ruth about the entire day. She murmured here and there, but didn't interrupt as I let out all of my feelings and thoughts about what had transpired. When I got to walking away from Gideon, I had to stop talking. It took everything in me to not have him take me straight back to The Knights' house. I missed Oliver and Jaxon terribly, too.

"Oh, Brooklyn, I'm so sorry. That does sound like a really tough day. Gideon came to the rescue though, didn't he?" She asked.

"He always does. I wasn't even surprised to see him. If I'm in danger, he's just always there," I said.

"I think these men love you."

"They've never said as much," I said.

"Have you told them you love them?' Ruth asked.

"I don't really know if that's what this is. I'm having a hard time understanding my own feelings," I admitted.

"This pain you're feeling. How difficult it is to be away from them. And the fact that you aren't just walking away for good...I think those are signs of love. I'm no expert either, though," she said.

"You seem to understand things in your home, with your men," I replied.

"That's because they've taught me. Two of them at least have the patience of angels. And the third, well, he does the best he can, and we just learn together."

I sighed, wondering if I was robbing my men and I the chance to learn together by leaving when things got difficult. Their desire to control the decisions about my life wasn't something I could learn to live with. But maybe once we could talk and they could really hear me, we could move forward, to build something new for us all.

Ruth and I spoke for a little while longer, changing the subject to the kids that I had brought to the ranch. By the time we hung up, I had a smile on my face, remembering the fun we'd had for the week. I promised Ruth that I would call her again soon and I meant it. I appreciated her friendship and her understanding of my relationships.

That night, I sent a good night text message to my group chat with Oliver, Jaxon and Gideon. I immediately got responses from each of them, making me smile. For the first time since I had left the house, I didn't have a nightmare. The full night's sleep was wonderful, and I woke up with my alarm, feeling refreshed.

I was early to leave the apartment and left before Frank could meet me at the door. When I exited the building, he was climbing from the sedan. He had a disapproving look on his face immediately, and I had to smile at him. His expression changed when he saw actual peace on my face for a change.

Just as I started to walk toward him, a loud crack made me freeze and look around. For a moment I was confused, but when I looked back at Frank, disbelief was on his face. He looked down at his stomach, where he had a hand pressed. When his hand came away, it was covered in red. Confusion clouded my mind as Frank crumpled to the sidewalk.

Dropping my bags, I cried out and moved toward my friend, who laid unmoving on the ground. Just as I moved, someone stepped into my path, causing me to stop short. My eyes were glued to Frank, and I attempted to sidestep the intruder, but they moved with me. Realizing the person was in my way on purpose, I straightened up and glared, only to be caught off guard once more.

"You didn't really think you'd seen the last of me, did you?" Missy said, as she crossed her arms across her chest.

"Missy? What are you doing here? I need to help Frank," I said, uninterested with whatever reason the woman was stalking me.

"Frank will have to just help himself," she said.

As I was trying to put the events together, I felt a sharp pinch in my neck. My hand flew up to touch the spot and I realized there was a syringe in my flesh. Too much was coming into focus, just as black spots started to cloud my vision. I tried to spin, but arms came around me and the voice of my nightmares spoke into my ear.

"It's time to come home, Bee."

CHAPTER
Twenty-One

Oliver

THE SILENCE in the house was deafening. The four of us secluded ourselves to our own rooms, barely interacting since Brooklyn left. I laid in my bed with my noise cancelling headphones on, trying to listen to anything that wouldn't make me think about her. Closing my eyes, I let "Missile" by Dorothy blast into my ears. But even the music couldn't stop me from replaying memories of our girl in my mind.

Even receiving her goodnight text, the night before hadn't quelled the anger in me. I had tried over the week she had been gone, to not be angry, to just understand where she was coming from. It wasn't that I didn't get it. Our relationship was a lot for her. And we acted ridiculously about her safety.

What I couldn't wrap my mind around was, she knew how hard it had been on me when she had pushed us away the first time. I tried to remember the exact words I used when we talked, and I was sure I had been clear. But I didn't say the things I needed to really say. She didn't know I thought loved her. I had allowed myself to be vulnerable with her, and she ripped my heart out again.

I rolled and sat on the edge of the bed, yanking off my headphones. I scrubbed my hand through my hair. It had gotten longer than I usually wore it, mainly because Brooklyn loved to grab it and run her hands through it. Now, I thought I should make an appointment with my stylist and get it trimmed, something to give me a feeling of control.

When Gideon came home from seeing Brooklyn, he was torn between hopeful and miserable. I couldn't help but feel jealous of the time he got to have with her, then I was wracked with guilt for allowing myself to not be in control of my emotions. I knew it was Gideon who was called, because Frank was his contact. It didn't make me feel any better not being able to go to Brooklyn when she needed me.

Missy's harassment of Brooklyn was unacceptable, and we were going to have to work harder to get rid of her. Gideon relayed everything Missy had said, and her desire to create havoc in our relationship was clear. However, she had her own life, her own money, she didn't need our success. I wasn't idiotic enough to believe she had some long-lasting love for any of us, leaving her true motives a mystery.

Aiden hadn't been a help in any of it. He was barely keeping shit together at 4K, to the point where Jaxon was trying to pick up the slack so things didn't collapse. He wouldn't talk about

Brooklyn at all. And when we tried to talk about Missy, Aiden dismissed the concerns as if we were just making a bigger deal of things than necessary. I didn't think he could really say that now that Missy had shown up at Brooklyn's office.

Deciding a shower was the best idea to help me relax, I went into my en suite and turned on the hot water. Steam billowed as I stepped under the spray. Pressing my palms against the wall, I bent my head to let the water flow over my body. I tried to force each of my muscles to relax and release the tension I was feeling.

In my head, I imagined the scene of Gideon and Brooklyn in the meadow. My brother hadn't given us details, but the way he looked when he mentioned it, I knew it had to be good. I remembered the last time I had Brooklyn in the shower and the way Gideon had fucked her against the wall. Looking down, I saw that despite my anger, my body wanted her.

As I fisted my cock, I tried to picture Brooklyn spread out in front of me, just for me to feast on. I stroked, imagining her soft hand wrapped around me. Closing my eyes, I tried to hear her sounds, her moans, her begging for it harder and faster just the way she liked. I leaned my head against the wall as I came, a release that didn't bring any real relief to what was roiling inside me.

I was methodical with the rest of my shower, all the enjoyment missing. When I looked in the mirror and reassessed my curly hair again, I knew I wasn't going to cut it. Not until Brooklyn's hands were in it again, not until she told me it was getting too shaggy. I slipped on my glasses, noting that my blue eyes looked haunted and tired.

Just as I was slipping on briefs, my bedroom door burst open and Jaxon stood in the opening. I froze, looking at the crazy way he looked.

"What is it?" I asked.

His eyes flew around my room for a moment, then he shook his head.

"I knew she wasn't here," he mumbled.

"Who? Brooklyn? Of course not. It's not like I would sneak her in," I said.

"No, I know. We need to go to the hospital," Jaxon suddenly said.

I had been walking to my closet, but spun at his words.

"What the fuck do you mean?"

"There's been a shooting. At Brooklyn's building," Jaxon said in a rush, as if the words pained him.

I stood, rooted to my spot, my brain not firing correctly.

"But you were looking for her, in here? So it's not her?" I asked.

Jaxon just shook his head.

"Who is it then?" I bellowed at him.

"Frank."

Jaxon left the room, and I threw on the first clothes I found to run after him down the stairs. Gideon was on the phone in the kitchen and Aiden was standing near him, trying to hear every word. Now that we were all there, Gideon turned and walked toward the front door, with all of us following.

Outside, a town car was already waiting for us, a member of Gideon's security team behind the wheel. We all piled in and the moment the doors were shut, we were speeding down the driveway. Gideon's call ended abruptly, and he began to punch the dashboard.

"Boss! You're going to hit yourself in the face with the airbag if you don't stop," the driver yelled.

Gideon's fist froze midair as if he debated if getting hit with the airbag would be better or worse at the moment. He decided against it and dropped his hand into his lap.

"What are they saying?" I asked, feeling as if I walked into the end of a movie without any context.

"Frank was shot in the stomach. He's in surgery now. He hasn't been able to talk," Gideon said in a stilted voice.

"Where is she?" I demanded.

The car went into silence, my brothers not wanting to tell me the truth. I looked from face to face. Aiden wouldn't look at me, his gaze glued on the passenger window. Jaxon's face was ashen as he just shook his head at me. And Gideon looked like he was about to punch something again.

"No one knows," Gideon finally answered.

Terror flooded my body, the immediate worst thoughts popping into my mind. Brooklyn shot and dying in an alley, or her body never being found. I tried to push those thoughts from my mind as the car pushed well beyond the speed limit on the way to the hospital.

"No one? You've called her office?" I demanded.

"Of course I called her fucking office, Oliver!" Gideon bellowed.

I just stared at the back of his head, waiting for him to tell me the rest.

"Pam said she hadn't been in today. At all. No one has heard from her," he said in a quieter voice.

I pulled out my phone and stared at our past text conversation. I typed out a text, even if she might not have her phone. Jaxon watched me, but didn't say anything. The text read, Babe, call one of us as soon as you can. We need you home. xoxo.

After hitting send, I laid my head on the back of the seat and closed my eyes. Brooklyn's smiling face flashed through my mind and I swallowed down the lump that was forming in my throat. We didn't actually know anything, and I couldn't let myself get out of control until we had more information. The car swerved around traffic and the three of us in the backseat were thrown back and forth, but I barely registered it.

The car came to an abrupt halt outside of the hospital emergency entrance. The four of us piled out and Gideon took the lead, running into the hospital. At the emergency desk, we were able to find out what floor Frank would be taken to after surgery. In the elevator, Gideon checked his phone again and when the doors opened, we were met by Detective Lee Anderson.

Lee held out his hand, and he and Gideon shook briefly.

"What do you know?" Gideon asked.

"This is an open investigation, Gideon," Lee hedged.

"Don't give me that official bullshit, Lee. Who shot Frank? Where is our woman?" Gideon shot back.

The detective looked uncomfortable, knowingly breaking the rules. But he and Gideon had some sort of agreement that worked both ways when needed. My brothers and I just stared at him until he sighed and looked at each of us.

"We don't know. That's the truth. The gunshot wasn't reported. Maybe it was too early for there to be many people on the street. Frank was found by a neighbor leaving for work. The timing was lucky, because the doctors tell me he would have bled out if he had been left even twenty minutes longer," Lee said.

"And Brooklyn?" I asked.

"I'm sorry, we don't have any leads as yet. She wasn't there. I can tell you, her bags were found near Frank's body, giving the impression she was there when he was shot."

Jaxon's hand went to his mouth, while Gideon turned, looking at the wall as if a hole in it was exactly what it needed. I grabbed his arm to stop him from causing any damage. Aiden looked shell shocked and was running his hands through his hair in jerky movements.

"We haven't found a second blood type on the scene, as far as we can tell she wasn't shot there as well," Lee continued.

"That doesn't make me feel any fucking better, Lee," Gideon said.

The detective just nodded. He turned and lead us to the surgical waiting room. Two uniformed officers were also there and Lee spoke quietly with them. Aiden paced the room, agitated, but not speaking to any of us. Oliver and I both sat while Gideon walked out of the room with his phone to his ear.

"What the fuck do we do now, Jaxon?"

My brother just shook his head, without any more answers than I had. I couldn't stomach the guilt I was feeling, knowing if we had been better with Brooklyn, she wouldn't have left the safety of our home. I took a deep, painful breath as I thought about how we had driven her away and right into the arms of danger.

Aiden

BEING in the hospital felt like déjà vu. Remembering Brooklyn after surgery had me pacing and panic surging in my chest. My throat became dry with the heaving breaths I was taking to control my emotions. I was sure my brothers had no idea what to make of my behavior, but luckily for me, they were too devastated by the news to pay any attention.

I had pushed Brooklyn away, a large contributing factor to her leaving the house. She had every reason to doubt my feelings for her. And every day since she had been gone, I had gotten roaring drunk to avoid thinking about the stupid shit I'd said to her and the way I treated her as if she was just sex.

Leaning against a wall in the waiting room, I stared at my shoes, unable to make conversation with my brothers. I knew they blamed me and now the thing we feared the most had possibly happened. I rubbed at my chest, trying to get rid of the pain that was radiating there.

Gideon came back into the waiting room and this time, he wasn't alone. Ash was on his heels and her face was blotchy from the tears that were still sliding down her cheeks. Jaxon and Oliver jumped up and went to her. Jaxon handed her a Kleenex and Oliver put an arm around her shoulders, consoling her with quiet words.

I knew I didn't belong in the grief, but I slowly made my way over to hear the conversation.

"I didn't know she was missing until Gideon called. I left for work before she did this morning. We said goodbye like always. She was happy. She mentioned talking to you guys, and she missed you. I half figured she wouldn't be there when I got home, because she'd go home with you," Ash said.

I looked at my watch, noting that it was already evening and we had only been notified about Frank an hour before. That was all day for Brooklyn to be missing and we had no leads.

"According to Lee, the original detectives and officers didn't ID Frank right away. Whoever shot him took his wallet, making it seem like a mugging. But when Lee heard the address, he had a bad feeling and got involved. He knew Frank was my guy, so he called me. That was hours after Brooklyn should have been on her way to work," Gideon said.

I scrubbed a hand over my face, the weight of the unknown choking me. Normally, I was always the one in control: my emotions, my actions, my thoughts. Instead, I was raging inside, ready to break apart anything I needed to, to get Brooklyn back, to save her, to see that she wasn't dead in a ditch somewhere.

"We know this is Lyle, right?" I said.

"There's no way it's anyone else," Oliver added.

Gideon nodded. We all knew what was happening, even if the cops hadn't done anything to protect Brooklyn from the beginning.

"I told Lee. He's a good detective. He already has a bolo out for both Brooklyn and Lyle," Gideon said.

"He's not that good, Gideon. If he was, how is this even happening? How is Lyle not already behind bars or in the ground?" I demanded.

All three of my brothers looked at me critically. I knew I sounded a little manic, but I wasn't wrong. Lyle had been running free for weeks. He'd already attempted to kill Brooklyn as soon as he could near her. The city police department did nothing but chase their tails as soon as they lost his trail. It was an incompetence I didn't have the patience for and wouldn't abide any longer.

"We can do better than this, on our own," I said.

Gideon's eyes narrowed critically, but Jaxon started to shake his head. They all knew exactly what I was thinking. We had never gone back into the underbelly once we had dug ourselves out, doing everything we could to save our family. But we came from a life, that transgressions like this against your people weren't tolerated and were met with all the force necessary.

"I don't think you mean that, Aiden," Jaxon started to say.

"Of course I do. We should have done this before she even left the house."

Ash stood in the middle of us, looking between our faces before holding up a hand, like she was in a classroom. "Can someone please explain to me what in the hell you're all cryptically referring to?"

I looked pointedly at Jaxon. Of any of us, he was the most connected to our past, his father playing leader in our bad decisions. It would have to be up to him if he wanted to admit things to Ash.

"We know, or knew people, Ash. People that could work in the shadows and maybe help us find Brooklyn and Lyle," Jaxon said.

"In the shadows? Like black ops or something?" Ash asked.

"Not the legal shadows," I added.

Ash didn't say anything, just nodded slowly until she moved to pierce Jaxon with her gaze.

"If you all care about her like you claim to, then you should be doing anything possible to find her," she said, her voice harsh and determined.

"We will. Let us talk privately, Ash, ok?" Jaxon asked.

Gideon took Ash by the elbow and lead her toward the elevators. She was animated as she spoke, probably not liking that we were cutting her out of our plans. The last thing we needed was to pull someone else down into the darkness with us. None of us would go back there willingly, but saving Brooklyn was all we needed.

When Gideon returned from walking Ash out, he stood with his arms crossing his chest. The four of us just looked at each other.

"It has to be you, Jaxon. You're the only one he'll listen to these days," I started.

"It's been years since I've spoken with him, or any of the crew, for that matter," Jaxon replied.

I watched as my brother scrubbed a hand over his face and rubbed at his mouth. I knew it was difficult for him to put himself back in the place we had worked so hard to be better than.

"We have kept up our side of the deal. Kept our mouths shut, stayed out of his business, and continued the payments. We've never asked him for anything, Jaxon," Oliver said.

Jaxon looked exhausted and wary. "No, we haven't. But now that we are, his terms will change. I'm sure of it. How much more is he going to want from us?"

"Anything. Money is not a problem. If he wants more, we raise the payments," I immediately said.

"What if it's not money this time, Aiden?" Jaxon demanded.

I searched my darkened soul for any objection I had, and there was nothing. Brooklyn brought a light to my world, even if I didn't know how to treat her and keep her close. I wasn't willing to know that light was snuffed from the world and never have the chance to be in her warmth again. There wasn't much Jaxon's father could ask for, that I wouldn't give to save her.

"We'll jump that hurdle when the times comes. I won't be able to live with myself if we don't try everything," I replied.

I could see the understanding in Gideon's eyes and I knew a conversation would be had later once we weren't in fight-or-flight mode. I tried to not think about Brooklyn being taken by Lyle, what he must have done to overpower her. Picturing her perfect soft skin marred by more of his marks made my stomach roil and anger to curl throughout my body. If the police didn't handle things, I wouldn't hesitate to kill Lyle myself.

The nurse, who I recognized from Brooklyn's hospital stay, came in to find Gideon. We gathered around her and she smiled kindly at us, but there was tension in her eyes.

"He's got a long road ahead. He made it through surgery, but he won't be awake for some time. The doctor is going to keep him sedated for at least 24 hours, maybe longer, depending on his vitals," she said.

"What can you tell us about his injury?" Gideon asked.

She studied him for a moment, then looked over her shoulder before turning back. "I shouldn't be telling you any of this really. You aren't family. And the police are already talking to the doctor about the bullet and the patient's status. But I overheard the detective and that sweet girl is missing. I have a feeling you'll be the ones to find her."

"Thank you," Gideon replied, dipping his head under the weight of what the nurse was saying.

She reached over and patted Gideon, which looked ridiculous with her little hand on his muscular arm.

"It was a single gun shot, looks like it was a small caliber weapon, but the doctor can't determine that for sure. The bullet went in, banged around in his gut and didn't exit. He's lucky he didn't lose a kidney, honestly. Leave your number and I'll call you the moment he wakes up."

Gideon left the waiting room with the nurse to give her his details. Oliver, Jaxon and I paced the small area, avoiding speaking about anything that was flooding our minds. I could guess what was going through Jaxon's mind, with the pressure of reaching out to his father on his shoulders. If it had been possible, I would take the responsibility and leave Jaxon out of it completely. Pulling him from under his father's thumb had been hard enough the first time. We would have to watch closely to make sure he didn't fall back into bad habits.

The four of us piled into the small elevator to go back downstairs. I could feel the emotions rolling off of my brothers and they added to my own. We were silent until we got into the town car again. The city passed by in a blur, my eyes not focusing on any one thing as I tried not to allow panic to take hold.

"Aiden, I'm not sure he'll help us," Jaxon said, his voice cutting through the silence.

It was true, we hadn't left the drug ring on the best of terms by stealing a property from under Jaxon's father's nose. And the four of us all leaving prominent posts within the business had left a hole that left things vulnerable to attack. I had kept my ear to the ground those months and years later, to ensure backlash wasn't coming our way. With our regular infusions of cash, the business became the most prominent in the city. That wasn't something I was proud of, but it kept my brothers and me safe.

"We'll make it worth his while," I replied.

I didn't turn, but I heard Jaxon sigh behind me. The words didn't exist to make him feel comfortable with things. I could only believe that he would do anything to help find Brooklyn. Our failure shouldn't be what leads to her death.

The house came into view and it was dark and oppressive, as I looked at it in a way I never had before. My brothers and I had lived without Brooklyn long before she ever showed us what life could be like. But her being gone now made things feel darker and dead. My chest felt tight as we walked in. Gideon flipped on lights as we walked together to my office.

I went to the safe that was behind a painting in my office. Oliver went to the bar cart and started pouring drinks for us all. Once I retrieved what I needed from the safe, I sat behind my desk while my brothers sat around the room. Oliver set my drink next to me and I nodded my thanks to him. As he walked to sit down, I saw his eyes lock onto the bag of flash drives I had set on the center of my desk.

"This is everything I have on the business. The financials, the dirty dealings, the evidence, everything. If he helps us find Brooklyn, I'll give all to him, every last copy."

"That leverage has been what has kept us safe all these years," Gideon said.

"The money has kept us safe. I don't believe he's really afraid of all of this. But if it sweetens the deal, I'm willing to part with it. For her."

"When did you suddenly start caring about Brooklyn?" Oliver demanded.

I leaned back and stared down at the liquor in my glass. The question should have been, when didn't I care about Brooklyn? I hadn't stopped, despite my confusing behavior. The truth was I was torn up about her missing and knowing in her mind I didn't want her, didn't care for her, didn't need her. I looked up finally and met Oliver's eye.

"It's not sudden."

Oliver slammed down his glass on my desk, alcohol sloshing onto the dark wood. I raised one eyebrow at his outburst and watched him.

"Maybe if you hadn't been so good at making her believe you didn't care, she would have stayed here!"

"We're all at fault with the reasons Brooklyn chose to go back to Ash's," Gideon said quietly.

Not allowing himself to be deterred from his anger, Oliver didn't acknowledge the words spoken.

"And what about her leaving here believing you slept with Missy, of all fucking people, Aiden!"

"I didn't fuck Missy. And I never told Brooklyn I did," I replied.

"Your lack of denial clearly was enough to push her into believing you did. Gideon had to convince her that Missy was nothing to any of us, all because you even allowed her to be near you at the club."

"This isn't helping, Oliver. Yelling at each other isn't looking for Brooklyn. We need to work together, not fight among ourselves," Jaxon said.

Gideon stood against the wall, nodding his agreement. Oliver was now pacing, but he didn't continue to yell, so I assumed he agreed for the moment with Jaxon. I threw back the alcohol that was in my glass, wishing the burn in my gut to wash away everything we were facing. But I knew that nothing was going to be that easy. Setting down my glass, I turned to Jaxon, who was staring at the flash drives.

"What's the first step, brother?"

CHAPTER
Twenty-Three

Jaxon

MY FINGER HOVERED over my father's name on my phone screen. I knew what I needed to do, for Brooklyn, for my brothers. But I sat on my bed, frozen in a fear I hadn't felt in years. Getting out from under my father's control had been the freedom I had never dreamed of.

Growing up as the only child of Randy Stoller, I knew from a young age what was in my future. My father raised me on his own to be an obedient soldier. There was never the plan to have me as his successor, because my father was too egotistical to think he wouldn't somehow live forever.

The last conversation we had rang loudly in my ears, as if it had just happened days before instead of years. Randy could barely catch his breath from laughing so hard at our plans to leave the business and start 4K. He all but promised we wouldn't be successful without him. He had demanded to speak to me privately. Aiden wasn't happy with leaving me alone with him, but it was the best way to get the situation over with.

"What do you think you're about here, Jaxon?" Randy asked.

"I think that's all pretty clear, Dad. We're out. We want to go in a different direction, try something legit, clean up our lives."

"Like your buddy Oliver? Who's barely days out of rehab?" Randy had chuckled.

"Oliver isn't any of your business," I said, my eyes narrowing at his gibe.

Oliver had been struggling to detox on his own. Once he fell back for the last time, Aiden demanded he go into a voluntary treatment plan. We all agreed the only way we could really start over was if he was healthy.

"You'll all be back. Oliver first, I'm sure. Then the rest of you. But ask yourself, Jaxon, will I allow you back in?" Randy asked.

There was a gleam in his eyes that made a shiver pass down my spine. Under the fatherly front he often tried to play when others were around, a cruel and evil man lived. I had no doubt he was already thinking of ways to bring the four of us down. Aiden had ensured we'd have enough to keep Randy off our back for some time.

I turned away from him and as I opened the door, I looked over my shoulder at him. "I won't be seeing you again, Dad. Goodbye."

Randy's bellowing laugh had followed me down the dingy hallway of our apartment building. Aiden, Oliver and Gideon waited for me on the street, a cab already pulled to the curb. I nodded once to them and we all piled into the vehicle, leaving everything I had grown up with in the rearview and solidly in the past.

Over the years, we had tried to keep tabs on Randy and his enterprise. I couldn't say I was surprised when local leaders of drug rings started to turn up dead. Somehow, my father was always far enough away that he was never mentioned as a suspect, but there was no doubt in my mind that his team had completed the hits.

Gideon had tried to put a tail on Randy once, only a few years after we left. The tail integrated into the lower levels of the business, just close enough to hear the talk of the dealers that worked for my father. By that time, my father had a number of police officers and city officials in his pocket. Users who were in debt to him, or wanted to protect his product line to ensure they could always get the product he offered.

When the contact from our man had stopped, my gut told me the man was dead. The answer to his disappearance came as a package to Club 4, the man's tongue placed in tissue paper with a note from Randy. It read: Nice try, boys. We didn't need a signature to know where it had come from. Gideon had compensated the man's family handsomely and buried any questions that may have come up about his disappearance.

Shortly after that incident, Randy had tried to enter Club 4 on its anniversary night. We had opened the club two years before and it was at the top of the city's club scene. For the anniversary, we threw a huge three night party with special DJs, contests and drinks created just for the weekend.

Randy showed up with a group of his dealers and tried to get in the door. Gideon had put Randy's photo with security the first night we opened and it was well known that he wasn't permitted into the club. Aiden sent me to the offices to ensure I wasn't a part of what came next.

Gideon and his men pushed Randy and his dealers back from the club. They had been trying to sling their products to the people in line and we had a strict no drug policy for Club 4.

Gideon never told me everything Randy had said, but I was sure it was full of threats, which is when our cash payments to him started. We were three years into those payments and we've never varied, just to keep him away from us.

Now, I stared down at my phone and I knew without a doubt I couldn't call him. There was no guarantee that he would even help us look for Brooklyn. More concerning for me was if he knew there was a woman out there that meant as much as Brooklyn did to us. It would be the leverage he needed to bring us back under his control.

I locked the screen and threw it on the bed. Pacing across the room, I tried not to think of what my woman was going through. There was no doubt that Lyle had her now, but we were in the dark with what his next steps would be. He had tried to kill her twice and I couldn't stomach thinking that the third time was a charm for him.

Groaning, I sat back down on the bed, wishing for nothing more than to have the chance to bring Brooklyn there with me again. I was so angry with myself and my brothers for allowing the fight we had get in the way of how much she meant to us. She told us to not follow her, but I regretted actually listening to that request. I should have gone to Ash's apartment and tossed her over my shoulder if she refused to listen to reason. Maybe we were being too overbearing, but it was only because she was too important to us.

The pain in my chest since she left the house hadn't lessened. There were moments I actually wondered if I was having a heart attack. I didn't tell my brothers, because I didn't want to discuss how badly I was handling her leaving us. And now that she was missing, I could barely breathe without pain lancing through me. It was as if Brooklyn had torn out my heart and packed it in her suitcase that day she left and now I was a hollow being, just wandering the world.

I knew the only thing that was going to fix me, fix my brothers, was Brooklyn. That reminder had me picking my phone up again.

I wasn't going to call Randy. I couldn't give him leverage over us and put Brooklyn in even more danger. But I realized I might have a different way of getting help from some of the same people.

Scrolling, I clicked on a name I hadn't called since I left the business. I knew the number hadn't changed, because it was a business phone. But I wasn't sure who would actually pick up the call.

"Yeah," a voice said after the ringing stopped.

"Cain?" I asked.

Silence was all I got at first until the voice answered with a question. "Who's asking?"

"I need to know it's you first, Cain. You once trusted me with your Spiderman figure, which I popped the head off of," I said, hedging with a hint to our history.

The story had the desired effect, as a loud laugh came through the line.

"Fucking, Jaxon! What in the hell are you calling me for, man?" Cain asked.

"Are you alone?" I asked.

"Weird first question after not hearing from you for, what has it been, 8 years?" He asked.

"Cain…"

"Yeah, man, I'm in the car. Alone. You sound like there's trouble. Did your dad do something?" He asked.

"Can you meet up? Would be best to talk about this face to face."

"Oh fuck, this must be serious if you're willing to risk this. Yeah, my man, I can do that. Where?"

I sighed, not really wanting to have Cain in our home. I was almost positive I could trust the man I had grown up with. We had been neighbors and his father started dealing for my dad. Cain had run with Oliver and me for a while, but his mom took him away when she left his father. Cain came back once he was an adult, messed up after his mother had been killed in a car accident. He immediately fell into old habits with his dad, but I was on my way out with my brothers.

There was a time I wanted to offer a spot for Cain in our business. But Aiden and Gideon didn't know him the way Oliver and I did. The debate was difficult, and the decision was even harder. I would never want Cain to know that we eventually agreed to not pull him out of my father's business, because we couldn't be positive about his loyalties. Now, I was willing to take that risk.

"Club 4. I'll head there. Come to the back and I'll let you in," I said.

Cain agreed, and we hung up. I threw on sweats, changing out of the suit I had been wearing all day. I jogged down the stairs, finding Gideon just as he was leaving the kitchen. He had his phone to his ear, but he was saying goodbye as he turned his focus to me.

"That was the hospital. Frank should be waking up within the next few hours. He has a really positive prognosis. They'll call me immediately so I can get down there to talk to him. Hopefully before the cops," he said.

I nodded and slipped my feet into my Nike running shoes. He eyed my appearance for a moment and when his eyebrow went up in question, I paused to face him.

"I called Cain," I said.

"Shit, Jaxon," Gideon breathed.

"I couldn't call Randy. I have a sick feeling that if he finds out about Brooklyn, he'll use her as a pawn. I can't have my father be another threat to her welfare," I said.

"You really think he'd go that far, after all the money he's made off us?"

"Yes. Without a doubt. He's never going to just be ok with us leaving. Especially not me. If he had a way to get at me, he's going to take it," I said.

The idea made my stomach churn, and I knew Gideon understood my concerns. He nodded and rubbed his hand over his face.

Looking closer, and I could see Gideon was exhausted and cracking at the edges.

"This was the best way I could think to get the resources, but without Randy finding out...hopefully," I said, tacking on the last word, because I knew nothing was guaranteed.

"So you're seeing Cain now?"

I nodded in response, as I turned to go to the hall closet. I found a dark sweatshirt and pulled it from a hanger. When I slipped it over my head, I was immediately hit with lavender and my head swam for a moment. I was confused until I remembered Brooklyn grabbing the sweatshirt once when she was naked downstairs. It had never been washed, because I liked having her smell on it. I held the fabric to my nose and breathed deep.

"Need backup?" Gideon asked from behind me.

"Stay close to your phone, just in case. I don't think Cain will double cross me straight off. But there's no knowing later. He's meeting me at Club 4 now, since we're closed tonight."

Gideon nodded, and I jogged to the mudroom for my keys and then into the garage to get into my Tesla. I was out of the garage before the door had fully opened, racing down toward the gate. Gideon must have opened it for me because I didn't even have to slow when I got there.

At the club, I pulled into one of my normal spaces, noting the strange Dodge Charger sitting in Aiden's spot. When I got out of my car, the door of the Charger opened and out stepped a much older Cain.

His face was the same, but there were lines that hadn't existed since the last time I had seen him. His hair was colored blue and currently sticking straight up in a mohawk. His arms were completely covered in tattoos, and he had a skull across his throat. When he saw me, his face lit up in a huge smile, bringing my attention to the lip ring on his bottom lip.

"You do not look like a richy rich," Cain said.

"I still own a few pairs of sweatpants," I said with a grin, holding out my hand to him.

Cain grabbed my hand and yanked me in for a one arm hug. When we stepped back, I studied his face and couldn't detect any deception behind his eyes.

"Let's move this reunion inside," I said.

Cain nodded and shoved his hands into his jean pockets. He was dressed opposite of my sweats, in dark jeans, a white v-neck and black shit kicker boots. His whole look looked relaxed but dark at the same time, and I wondered if Cain was the only man I knew that could pull it off that way.

Inside the Club, I climbed the stairs to the top floor with Cain behind me. Inside, the main lights were on, with a cleaning crew working on the dance floor. One person glanced up and waved when they saw me. Cain took a moment to look around the building and whistled low.

"Look at this place. Fancy shit, Jaxon."

"It's done the job," I replied.

"More than that, I'm sure," he said.

I continued walking through the owners VIP level to the hall that held our offices. I took him into mine, flipping on the light and immediately went to close the curtains on the window that looked over the dance floor. Cain walked around, slowly taking in the photos I had on my desk and the awards we had received for our philanthropy work.

When I moved behind my desk, I motioned for Cain to have a seat, and he did with a grin. I wasn't sure where to start, so I leaned back and rubbed my eyes roughly.

"What is the deal, brother?" Cain asked.

The word brother surprised me, and I sat up and looked at him suddenly. His face was filled with concern, no malice, no humor. For a moment, I felt a pang of regret for not trusting him more and bringing him with us to get him out of the life. But I pushed it away. If Cain hadn't still been in the life, I wouldn't have had anyone to call to help.

"I need your help. I don't have anyone else to turn to," I said.

"Ok. Tell me what's happening, and I'll tell you if I can help."

"First. Are you still in the business under my dad?" I asked.

A brief flash of anger crossed his face before he answered. "Unfortunately. It pays the bills right now. But I'm always keeping an eye out. Why?"

"This can't get back to my father. Before I tell you anything, I need to know I can trust you."

"You can trust me, just like I trusted you with my damn Spiderman. That was never the same again."

Brooklyn

I WASN'T sure why I had decided to eat cotton balls, but that was the first thing that came to mind as I came to consciousness. My brain felt foggy and confused and I tried to move my body. I immediately realized things weren't what they should be as I started trying to take inventory of myself.

Pain lanced through my head when I tried to move and I stopped and took a moment to breathe to keep my stomach contents where they belonged. Confusion was thick as I tried to picture what the last thing I remembered was. Frank's face came to my mind, but he looked shocked and scared, something I had never seen from him before.

I kept my eyes shut, trying to let the rest of my senses come back first. I recognized that my fingers were tingling and a sharp needle like feeling was moving along my arms and shoulders. When I tried to move my hands, I panicked when I realized my wrists were bound behind my back. I moved slightly, feeling handcuffs circling tightly around my skin.

What the fuck is going on? I asked myself. More images were flashing through my mind and I gasped on my breath, remembering that Frank had been hurt right in front of me, shot I thought. But I couldn't help him. Why couldn't I help him? The memories were going in slow motion and weren't coming back to me fast enough to make sense of what was happening to me.

I was lying on my side, my hip digging into the hard ground below. I rubbed my cheek against the surface of the floor slightly, deciding it was concrete, with no rug or carpet. The atmosphere felt dank and wet, leading me to think I was near water somehow. A chill crept through my body as the sweat on my skin dried in the cold air.

Voices caused me to freeze my movements. I wasn't positive about what had happened, but I knew it couldn't be anything good if I had been knocked out and tied up. Letting my abductors know I was awake was the last thing I wanted to do. I slowed my breathing and tried to listen to the sounds I was hearing.

After a few moments it became clear, there was a door or wall between me and whoever was speaking. It was muffled enough that I could only tell one voice was slightly higher than the other, sounding female. That thought brought my foggy memories back, and I tried to concentrate on what was flashing in my mind. The thoughts didn't make sense, and it felt like multiple events were melting together.

I waited as the voices rose in what sounded like an argument. When everything went silent again, I laid still, wondering if someone would be coming for me. The Knights came to mind, and anguish lanced through me. They would know I was missing by now. How much time had even passed? It was hard to think about them, worried and searching for me.

A tear slid from my eye, landing on the concrete below me. My own stubbornness put me in the position that I could be taken off the street. If I had just talked to my men, worked out the things we didn't agree on, stayed with them in the safety of their home, none of this would be happening. Frank wouldn't have been shot. That image crossed my mind again, and a sob tried to bubble up.

The sound of a door opening had me fighting down my emotions, bringing my breathing back under control. The door slammed and clicking heels came toward me. When the noise stopped, I could sense someone standing over me, and that was confirmed with a huffing sound.

A sharp kick to my foot brought my attention to the fact that my shoes were gone. For a moment, anger blossomed, thinking about the stilettos I had been wearing for work. Oliver had bought those for me and they were my favorite pair. Rationally, I knew the thought was silly, but I loved the reminder of what Oliver had done for me.

"I know you're awake," a voice said, accompanied by a kick to my thigh this time.

The voice started to match with my foggy memory and I realized that I knew who was speaking. Even with that start of understanding, I couldn't understand how the pieces of events matched up. I knew with the kicking, I couldn't keep up the charade of still being knocked out.

I forced my heavy eyelids to open, blinking against the harsh light coming from the exposed bulb above my head. A shadow fell over my face and I had to blink rapidly to try to focus on the figure above me. Missy's sneer was the first thing that registered.

"Finally," she said.

"Missy?" I asked dumbly.

"I figured you'd remember my name," she replied with a sly

smile. "Couldn't stop thinking about what I said to you in your office, could you?"

I swallowed, trying to clear my throat, wanting my voice to sound stronger than possible. "I haven't thought of you once since then."

Missy's sly smile transformed into an ugly scowl, a look I was sure was much more natural for her face. She was dressed similarly to how she looked in my office. Expensive suit, but with more skin showing than necessary. Expensive jewels on her ears and around her neck. Her make up was done to perfection, though a sheen of sweat was showing across her face.

"I put in my time with those four. Long before you were ever a blip on their radar," she said.

"History," I replied.

"They were a mess back then," she continued, as if I hadn't spoken. "All four of them tied up in the drug business with Jaxon's father. At times, testing more product than necessary. But it was ok, I enjoyed the high too. We loved to party in all ways. Tell me, have you had all four of them take you at once yet?"

I wasn't quick enough to mask my thoughts passing across my face. I didn't have all four of them. I had lost Aiden and now I knew I would likely never have the chance to fix that. I saw the triumph in Missy's eyes before she even spoke another word.

"I figured you weren't that special. Really, Brooklyn dear, you're quite plain. And these scars," she said as she leaned down and flicked my collar to the side. "Did you really think men like them would want something tainted and ruined?"

Her words sliced deeper than I wanted to think about. More than once, I had wondered the same thing about the Knights. They could have any beautiful woman in the city, but they had picked me.

"I'm sure you've thought about it. Sorry sweetie, it's just the way things work. Men with the power, money and influence as my boys do, they aren't looking for something broken. They need a woman that's going to make them even stronger than they are on their own," Missy said.

"You don't know them," I said lamely.

"Oh, but dear, I do. I know them at their core. I know the boys they were that started down the road they're on now. They haven't changed as much as they'd like to believe," she said.

She straightened and paced away from me. The moment her back was turned, I took the chance to look around the room. There were two doors, one on either side of the room. The windows were high and small. I was surprised to realize darkness had already fallen. Tears sprang to my eyes again, wondering where my men were.

Missy paced back and when she saw my face, she laughed. I was surprised that her laugh made me think of Tinkerbell. Despite the sweetness in her giggle, her voice came out laced with venom.

"You think they'll be looking for you?"

I closed my eyes and turned my face away from her, hiding my vulnerability. I couldn't have her seeing the pain she was pulling from me. She stalked over to me. Crouching down, Missy grabbed my face and twisted until she forced me to face her again. Her sharp acrylic nails dug into my jaw.

"You'll look at me when I'm speaking, bitch. I deserve your respect," she spat, digging her nails deeper.

My eyes popped open as pain lanced my face where her nails broke the skin. I could feel a warm trickle of blood sliding down my neck. I looked up into Missy's eyes and was surprised to see she looked on the edge of losing control. It was what I needed to realize she felt more threatened by me than she wanted me to know.

"You've done nothing to earn my respect, or the respect of my men," I said.

"They are not YOUR men!" Missy screeched, throwing my head back suddenly.

As my skull bounced off the concrete, stars danced in front of my eyes and darkness threatened the edges of my vision. Pain splintered through my head and I rolled to the side, trying to curl into myself. The sharp toe of Missy's high heel struck me in the back as she screamed. I rolled, trying to avoid her, but she stepped forward and her next blow landed in my stomach, knocking the wind out of me.

When I met with Missy at my office, I knew she was devious. I knew she wanted to cause problems for me and the Knights, had an obsession with them. What I hadn't realized was the threat she saw me as was taking her place in the family with the guys. And she would go to any lengths to get them back.

I gasped, trying to pull air into my lungs. When I looked up, I found Missy pacing, muttering to herself. If kidnapping me hadn't been the first clue, her erratic behavior only pointed to her being completely unhinged. She finally stopped pacing and turned back to me, a facade of control lowering over her face.

"You won't be a thorn in my side much longer. With you out of the way, my boys will remember how much we meant to each other. They will welcome me back with open arms and they'll forget you even existed in their world for a few months."

The faces of the Knights flashed through my mind. I thought about Gideon, lifting me into his arms as if I weighed nothing, or curling his massive body around me in bed. I thought about the way Jaxon looked at me, the heat that was always in his eyes when he would drink in my nakedness. I could vividly picture Oliver's curls gripped in my hand as he licked at my core and see his grin when he looked up from between my thighs. Even Aiden, who gave me reasons to doubt him, looked into my soul more than once.

No. No matter what Missy wanted to believe. I knew my guys wouldn't just forget about me. My heart knew them, each of them, intimately, and their hearts knew me. Without hesitation, I knew they were looking for me now. There was no competition between Missy and I, my guys would choose me every time.

"Just because you keep saying things like that, doesn't make it true," I wheezed out.

I knew it was probably not the right idea to antagonize her, but I couldn't help myself. Missy's eyes flashed, but she kept herself controlled this time.

"You won't be around to find out," she said, before turning and stalking out of the room.

As soon as the door shut behind her, I started to struggle against the bindings on my wrists again. I didn't know what Missy had planned, but I did know she wasn't behind the kidnapping on her own. She had help, and I didn't want to wait around to find out what was next.

Before I had the chance to make any progress, Missy was stalking back across the room again. The evil on her face transformed what could have been a pretty woman to something grotesque. When she got to me, she stared blankly down at me and I waited to see if she was going to speak. Instead, her hand snapped down, and I felt a sharp pain in my thigh. I yelped and looked down just as Missy pressed down the plunger on the syringe she had stabbed me with.

"What the fuck!" I screamed.

Missy didn't bother responding. She straightened and looked at me again. Again, her face was the last thing I saw as my body began to get heavy and blackness invaded my vision. Missy may not have been the one to drug me the first time, but she had no problem doing it now. Fear flowed through my last conscious thoughts of what could happen to my body while I was knocked out.

Gideon

THE SOUND of my cell phone ringing had me shooting out of bed. I yanked the device from my nightstand without unplugging it, ripping the charger from the wall. Since the moment I knew Brooklyn was missing, sleep was the last thing on my mind. Laying down had been a hopeful waste of time.

"Yes?" I answered the phone.

"Mr. Knight?"

"Yeah, that's me."

"Mr. Knight, this is Memorial Hospital. I'm sorry to be calling so late. This is fairly unconventional, as visiting hours are over until the morning. But unfortunately, our patient is demanding to see you and we don't want to sedate him again," the woman said.

"Frank?" I asked.

"Mr. Lewis, yes. Can you get down here tonight?"

"I'm on my way," I replied, hanging up without another word.

I jumped out of bed and quickly threw on sweats. Talking to Frank before the police was important, and the man knew that. I was thankful he was pulling through the ordeal, but at the moment, the most important thing was the information he had about the attack and where Brooklyn could be.

I jogged down the stairs while pulling a t-shirt over my head. I was brought up short by Oliver, who was sitting at the kitchen island, a bottle of whiskey open in front of him with an empty glass in his hand. His blue eyes flashed over to me when I entered, and the pain I saw there was staggering.

"What is it?" He asked, standing up to meet me.

"Frank's awake and he's freaking out at the hospital. I'm going to help."

"I'll drive," Oliver said, turning toward the mudroom.

"You sure, brother?"

I looked pointedly at the empty glass he had set down next to the whiskey. When Oliver turned, he saw where I was looking and he stared for a moment.

"I was remembering back in the day, getting high and feeling nothing. I never want to go back there again, but this pain is more than I think I can handle. I thought about getting drunk, thought I could force myself to sleep through some of this nightmare. But I haven't actually started yet. I'll feel better with something to do."

There was nothing I could say that would make Oliver feel better, so I just nodded my agreement. He grabbed his keys, and we piled into his classic GTO. The roar of the engine was loud, and I grimaced, hoping if Aiden or Jaxon were able to sleep, we weren't waking them up. As we got to the gate, I realized no one in the house had been sleeping, as our group text chat lit up on my cell.

Aiden: Where are you guys headed?

Jaxon: Is there news?

I gave them the update and promised to call as soon as I talked to Frank. Glancing at Oliver in the darkness of the vehicle and I saw his focus trained on driving, but I also studied the dark circles under his eyes and tightness around his mouth that wasn't usually there. We all looked like a mess, but Oliver always seemed to feel things in a more physical way.

Brooklyn hadn't been missing twenty-four hours yet, but it felt like ages. I closed my eyes and leaned against the headrest, picturing her laying in the middle of the meadow I took her to. Her pencil skirt shoved up around her hips, her mouth parted on a moan, her hands in my hair or how she kissed me. The stolen moment felt like a dream now.

We arrived at the hospital and Oliver didn't bother with appropriate parking. Pulling the car into an emergency visitor spot, we quickly ran into the hospital and took the elevator to the ICU floor. When we exited, I found a nurse's station and waiting for someone to come to the counter.

A small redheaded woman rushed around a corner, a bellowing man's voice following her. When she saw us, she focused her frazzled walk in our direction, but slowed when she took us in. Between our size and our disheveled appearances, we painted an intimidating presence.

I tried to force a smile on my face, but when the nurse's eyebrows went up, I knew I hadn't accomplished reassuring. However, it did seem to ease some of the tension from her. She stopped in front of us and looked up, her gaze going back and forth.

"Mr. Knight?"

"Yes," both Oliver and I said at the same time.

"Uh," she said, looking uncertain again.

She glanced down at the file in her hand and back up at us.

"It's me. I'm the Mr. Knight you're looking for. This is my brother," I said, gesturing toward Oliver.

The nurse looked relieved, just as a bellow came from the same man. I recognized the voice and knew it was Frank causing hell in the ICU unit. When he yelled, the nurse grimaced and looked up at me again. I didn't wait for her to explain.

"I'll talk to him."

I moved toward the room that held my employee, with Oliver on my heels and the nurse following behind at a distance. As soon as we turned the corner that lead into his room, something crashed behind a curtain and I rushed in, pulling the fabric back.

Frank was on his feet, swaying dangerously, holding onto an IV pole. When entered, the nurse rushed to his side, trying to guide him back into bed.

"Stop it! I'm not getting back in this damn bed," Frank yelled.

"Frank!"

The sound of my voice caused the man to turn his gaze from the nurse to me. Relief flooded his face, but then anger rushed back and his face went red.

"Where is she? Do you have Brooklyn?" He demanded.

"No. Man, get back into the bed before you fall. You were shot," I said.

I brushed by the nurse and took Frank's arm to force him into a sitting position first. With more strength than I expected him to have, he shoved my hand away.

"I know I was fucking shot. Brooklyn was there. It was Lyle, Gideon. Fucking Lyle shot me and he took Brooklyn," Frank said.

"We had assumed that, mostly," I said quietly, my throat getting tight.

"That's not all. Jesus, it was right in front of us all, and we fucking missed it."

"Missed what, Frank?" Oliver asked from the foot of the bed.

Frank's gaze flew to him, as if he had just realized my brother was in the room with us. His brows gathered together in confusion, and it was then I noticed the nurse removing a needle from his IV line. I stared at her and she just stood her ground, staring back.

"He needs his pain meds managed, and it was time. With all this moving around, he's going to be in horrendous pain," she said.

"Goddamnit, I don't want to go to sleep," Frank said, his voice getting groggy.

"Frank, what was right in front of us? What did we miss?" I demanded.

His eyes focused on me and I could see the fog starting to descend over his mind. I shook him slightly, and his eyes widened again as he forced himself to take a deep breath and say the next words.

"Missy. Lyle and Missy, they're working together. They were both there. She was there," Frank said. His voice began to fade at the end.

My fingers almost slipped from his arm, but at the last moment, I remembered I was the one holding Frank up. With Oliver's help, we helped him lie back in the bed. The nurse pushed us back as she fixed his monitors and checked that he hadn't ripped open any incisions. She covered him up and Frank's head lolled toward me.

"Gideon, I'm sorry. He drugged her. He took her away," Frank murmured.

"I know, Frank. It's not your fault. We'll find her," I said, trying to reassure him as much as myself.

Once Frank was passed out again, Oliver and I went back to the nurse's station to talk to the red head that was waiting for us. She looked exasperated and exhausted.

"Mr. Knight, I understand there's something going on, but Mr. Lewis' health is my concern."

"I appreciate that, ma'am. He should be calmer now that he's told me what he needed to," I said.

"Should I be calling the police?" She asked.

"No, it's ok. I'll pass the information along to the detective on the case."

I didn't mention that I was going home to tell my brothers first. This new information changed everything. Lyle had to believe he had killed Frank, because connecting the dots on him and Missy was probably the last thing he wanted.

"Ok, I'll agree to that because honestly, I'm too tired to deal with the police right now. I'll let Mr. Lewis know that you will come back during visiting hours?" She asked.

I nodded and thanked her. Oliver and I stalked back to the elevator. Once the doors shut and we were alone, Oliver spun to me.

"Fucking, Missy? How is that even possible?" He demanded.

"The same question I have, brother," I said gruffly.

Suddenly, Oliver turned and slammed his fist into the wall of the elevator. He pulled back to do it again, but I grabbed him to pull him back. He bellowed, a deep pained sound coming from his throat. For a moment, I wished Jaxon was with us. He was the one that could always talk any of us down. But Oliver only had me right now, and I had to be what he needed.

I turned, wrapping my arms around him and squeezed him against my chest. None of my brothers were short, but Oliver was the shortest of us. I had at least four inches on him and I was able to control him as he came under control. His head dropped and one of his hands gripped my forearm that was across his chest. I could feel his breathing calming down just as the elevator stopped on the bottom floor.

When the doors slid open, I put my foot at the door to ensure it didn't close on us, but I didn't let go of Oliver.

"This isn't your fault. We couldn't have guessed that our past would collide with Brooklyn's. We will get her back," I murmured.

"You don't know that," Oliver replied dejectedly.

"I don't. But that's what I'm choosing to believe. And you need to as well. It's what will fuel us to keep searching. This information is shocking, but it's also another thread we can follow. We know what Missy wants."

"What's that?" Oliver asked.

I felt sick even thinking about it, but I knew the answer. In the short moments I saw Missy in person, it was clear she had an agenda. When she showed up at Brooklyn's office, that agenda seemed clear to me. But I had no idea how far she would go to achieve her ultimate goal.

"She wants us, Oliver."

Oliver

EVERYTHING FELT SO dark inside me and I didn't know how to fix it. After Gideon held onto me in the elevator, I had to admit to myself that I was on a ledge, just waiting for a small thing to push me over. Brooklyn leaving us had started the unraveling and now, with her missing, there wasn't a string for me to hold on to.

Thankfully, Gideon was quiet on the drive home. I didn't want to talk about the breakdown I had at the hospital. I loved my brothers. They were my family. But they had picked me up before and I didn't want them to have to do that again. As close as I was to losing it completely, I would never turn to oblivion like I had done before we got away from Jaxon's father.

We all dabbled in using back in the day. It was hard not to try the product you were slinging day in and day out. Aiden was the first to know it wasn't for him and he was always business when it came to Randy Stoller and his drugs. Gideon had never been a fan, so he had tried the least, knowing it put him off his game when it came to enforcement. Jaxon and I were the heaviest users. I wasn't just a user; I was an addict. And my brothers and rehab pulled me out of the hole I had dug for myself. No matter what, I wouldn't do that to them again.

The house was ablaze with light when we pulled through the gate. Gideon had shot a text to our group chat to let Jaxon and Aiden know we were coming home with information that was imperative to finding Brooklyn. We pulled into the garage and Jaxon already had the door to the mudroom open, waiting for us.

Inside the kitchen, the whiskey I had opened was sitting off to the side and in its place mugs of coffee had been poured. Aiden sat alert and waiting for us. I couldn't sit. I still felt like my insides were on fire, my mind was having a hard time processing every-thing and I was fighting against screaming with the last pieces of my control. I could see Gideon watching me warily, but I carefully picked up a mug of coffee and sipped the hot liquid to act as normal as possible.

Jaxon, picking up on the tension between our brother and me, watched the both of us from across the kitchen, his arms crossed in front of his chest. Gideon slumped onto a stool, the fight suddenly going out of him. Now that we were safely at home, the four of us together.

"Frank woke up, and he had some alarming news," Gideon started to say.

"We got that from your text, Gideon," Aiden replied sharply.

"It's Missy. She's the partner we couldn't figure out with Lyle," Gideon said.

"What the fuck?" Jaxon exclaimed.

"Are you serious?" Aiden asked at the same time.

I just stared into the black liquid in my mug. In my mind, I could picture wrapping my hands around Missy's neck and choking the life out of her. It was an odd picture for me. I had never been the violent one of our family. But losing Brooklyn was creating something dark inside me, something I didn't know I was capable of. The thoughts should scare me, but instead they only encouraged me to find the deceitful bitch and deal with her.

"Both of them, Missy and Lyle, were there yesterday morning. Lyle's the one that shot Frank, that much we had assumed. But Missy was there too," Gideon said.

"Why would they show their cards like that?" Jaxon mused.

"I've been thinking the same thing," Gideon replied.

"Because they either didn't think Frank would live, or they don't plan on keeping Brooklyn alive," I said quietly.

"I'm going with the first one. I don't believe Lyle would go this far to get Brooklyn, just to kill her. He wants her... for other reasons...," Gideon said, his voice breaking at the end.

The sound of shattering glass made me tear my eyes from my coffee. Across the kitchen, a splatter of coffee was running down the wall, and Aiden was pacing furiously on the other side. His hands were fists at his sides and red was rising up his neck.

"I can't... we can't let him..." Aiden growled.

"None of us want to think about that. But if Lyle has plans for her, that means he's more likely to keep her alive," Gideon said quietly.

"Alive, but broken," Jaxon added.

I thought about the past Brooklyn had, what she had already overcome caused by not only Lyle, but her shitty mother. She had fought a hard battle, through therapy and sheer determination, to be the woman she was when we met her. Even then, she had insecurities that we had to work with her on. But once we showed her that her scars, her past, were not going to push us away, she took on a breathtaking shine. Seeing Brooklyn in her confidence was like watching the first rose bloom after winter, beauty and grace.

"We can bring her back from it," I said. My voice held more conviction than I was feeling.

Gideon's eyes met mine and I could see how torn up my brother was. Could we bring her back? Was our bond strong enough, our caring for her enough, to save her from whatever Lyle would inflict on her? He could break her body and doctors could cure that. But her mind could be a much different story. I had to believe we could help her survive anything he did to her.

"This changes everything. I'll need to call Cain and let him know to look for Missy as well as Lyle," Jaxon said.

Though it was the early hours of the morning, Jaxon pulled out his cellphone and walked out of the kitchen to make his call. He had confirmed that Cain had agreed to help them. I, for one, was thankful we had Cain to turn to, instead of Jaxon's father. I would do anything to find Brooklyn, but the longer we could avoid calling Randy, the better for us all. I had no doubt that he would demand something more than we would be willing to give.

"We have to assume Missy doesn't know we know," Aiden said. He stared off into space, the wheels turning in his head.

"What are you getting at?" I asked.

Aiden turned to focus on me. "We set our own trap for her. Open the door for her to walk through. We know she wants us. Let's make ourselves available and see if she shows."

I couldn't disagree with Aiden's plan. Gideon and I headed back to our bedrooms in silence. I couldn't think of anything to say to him after my outburst. Alone in my room, I felt suffocated by the quiet. I didn't want to sit alone and think about how my room didn't have the same smell with Brooklyn gone. For a few days, her lavender scent had clung to my bed, but it had long since faded and it made everything seem too real.

Instead of sitting alone, I changed my clothes and went to the gym in our basement. I jumped on the treadmill and did a quick warm up before turning to a fast paced run. Too late, I realized that being alone in the gym wasn't the best idea to get my mind off Brooklyn. As I ran, all I could picture was her toned body on the same machine, sweat drenching her sports bra and tiny running shorts.

After almost tripping, I slowed my pace and did a cool down. I was no good to Brooklyn if I couldn't get my mind straight. I had a part to play for Aiden's plan, and I needed to pull down a mask to draw Missy in if she showed. We couldn't be too easy for her, or she'd know something was up. However, we couldn't show our cards and risk her realizing we knew she had a hand in Brooklyn's kidnapping.

In the shower, I replayed memories of Missy from our time together. A lot of those moments were fueled by drugs and fuzzy in my recollection. I tried to figure out if there was ever a sign of her being this unhinged. It was hard to guess if it was our success or the relationship with Brooklyn that caused her to come out of the woodwork. Or did Lyle search her out and pull her into the fray and she played a willing participant? Their partnership was just as confusing to me. I knew what Lyle was likely getting from the agreement, help to scare Brooklyn and getting close to her. But what was Missy getting?

The day passed at a glacial pace, my brothers and I pacing the different rooms of the house. In the afternoon, a dark Dodge Charger pulled up to our gate and Jaxon opened it from inside the house. I waited behind Jaxon as he let Cain into the house. The man's eyes immediately ate up the large entry way and when his gaze landed on me, his mouth split in a huge smile.

"Oli!" He exclaimed, coming toward me.

We shook hands and Cain pulled me in for a one-armed hug.

"Cain. No one calls me that anymore," I said with a snort.

I couldn't believe how the boy we had known had grown into a man. Jaxon had given us a rundown of his meeting, but he hadn't explained Cain's appearance in detail. He did mention

Cain had a mohawk, though today it was down and his hair was slicked back fashionably. His tattoos were all on display and I was instantly curious what brought all the marks on, but Jaxon walked down the hall, immediately reminding me we had work to do. Cain and I followed my brother toward Aiden's office.

"I can't believe this is where you all live," Cain said with an appreciative whistle.

"Life has treated us well," I replied.

"Until now," Cain said, his hazel eyes darkening as he looked over his shoulder at me.

"Until now," I nodded.

Gideon and Aiden both waited in the office. Cain couldn't hide his excitement at seeing them, hugging them both and making a crack at how huge Gideon had gotten since they were kids. The reunion was short lived, and I knew we'd all have a lot to talk about later. Now was the time to talk about the updates we had for him and to hear if he had any leads on our girl.

Cain sat, his legs casually spread as Gideon handed him a tumbler of whiskey. Aiden sat behind the desk, with his fingers steepled and pressed against his mouth. Jaxon and I took the couch to the side of the office, with Gideon sitting next to Cain in a chair.

"Well, boys, though seeing you all again like this is awesome, I guess we should get down to business," Cain started.

"Like I said last night, there seems to be much more to this kidnapping than just Lyle," Jaxon replied.

"Missy. I remember her. She was glued to you guys like white on rice. I was never sure what you all saw in her, but I was too busy trying to get my head right after my mom, ya know?"

"Looking back now, none of us are really sure about that either. We were young, and dumb, of course," Aiden replied.

"Ain't that the truth. Well look, I haven't had much time to look into Missy since Jaxon called last night, so I have nothing on her. But this Lyle guy, man, I don't know how, but the man seems connected," Cain said.

"With who?" Gideon asked.

"He might be on Randy's payroll," Cain said.

My eyes flew to Jaxon and his face went white. How was it possible that our pasts were connecting in more than one way?

"Why would Randy be fucking with us now?" Aiden growled out.

"So I'm not sure he even knows. What I was trying to find was where Lyle was getting funds. He obviously isn't showing up for his parole appointments, there are warrants for him. But he's living on something. I saw someone that looked a lot like him picking up shit from one of my dad's guys. That was before Jaxon called and I got a photo of the prick," Cain explained.

"That could explain how he's staying off the radar of the cops and still making enough money to pull the shit he's been up to," Gideon said.

"If Randy is involved somehow, we need to know that. Is there a way for you to get accounting information, Cain?" Aiden asked.

Cain took a sip from the tumbler before looking at it like he was astonished. "You guys do everything fucking fancy, don't you?"

"Cain..." Jaxon said.

"What's the point of having money if we don't drink well? The accounting?" Aiden said, a wry grin on his face.

Cain looked around the room, taking in the dark decor of Aiden's office before focusing on the man behind the desk.

"Maybe. But if Randy's books man catches me, it'll be a problem. I can't tell him what I'm up to," Cain said, pointedly looking at Jaxon.

"If my father is involved, I don't give a shit if he knows we're working on this. Brooklyn is the priority, and we aren't fucking around with Randy and his business. We just want her back," Jaxon said with conviction I wasn't sure he felt.

My brothers and I all nodded in agreement. Cain let out a low whistle, looking at each of us.

"What is she to you all, anyway? Jaxon made her sound important before, but seems she's more than important."

"She's ours," I replied.

"Yours? Like all of yours?" Cain asked.

"Does that really matter, Cain?" Aiden asked, his irritation shining through.

"Not really. Just curious what this woman has, to have you all willing to dive back into the trenches for her," Cain said. He shrugged his shoulder, indicating he didn't really care.

"Find out if Randy is involved in Brooklyn's abduction, or if he knows that Lyle is connected to her. We don't want to be surprised by anything," Aiden said.

Cain nodded, tossing back the last of the alcohol in his tumbler.

"What's the plan until then?" He asked.

Aiden looked to Jaxon and me, his eyes asking how much we trusted Cain. I was surprised Aiden agreed to Cain being involved in the first place. Though I grew up with Cain, I could admit I didn't know what type of adult he had grown into. I wanted to believe the good kid, with a sense of humor and a trickster gleam in his eye, hadn't been ruined by the life he was leading.

Jaxon didn't hesitate to nod, and I followed suit. Maybe this would help Cain, as well as us. We left Cain behind once, and I felt more than guilt about that when I thought about it. For years, I hadn't thought of him, and until Jaxon had called to ask him for help, I had never known for sure that he was still in Randy's organization. We had gotten out before Randy became too powerful. Now he had an iron grip on his men, Cain included.

"We try to convince someone of the impossible," Aiden said.

Cain looked around the room again and a goofy grin broke out across his face.

"I'm so in."

CHAPTER
Twenty-Seven

Aiden

IT HAD BEEN my idea to pull out all the stops and wading into territory we had fought to stay out of. Brooklyn was worth every step we had to take. Now that we were riding to Club 4 with Cain in the limo, I felt an anxiety in my gut I hadn't experienced in years. It was the same feeling I used to have when we were secretly planning our escape from Randy's business. Since then, I'd felt in control of my life. Until the day Brooklyn was taken.

Cain was calm and cool as we talked about tricking Missy into thinking we were open to her affections. The words were acid on my tongue and I was sure bile was rising in my throat. The idea of letting Missy close enough to touch me made me imagine what it would feel like wrapping my fingers around her throat and squeezing. Even though that image was more palatable in my mind, I knew we needed the information she had.

"Randy always forbids any of us from going to your club," Cain mused, as he looked out the window at the city passing by.

"It was our deal," I said.

"Why did he even abide your arrangement? He's so much bigger than he was a few years ago. You guys have no idea," he said.

"We have some idea. Gideon has always kept tabs on him and the way the organization was growing. We know he has all sorts of connections in law enforcement and at least one legislator in his pocket," I replied.

Cain's eyes flashed over to me, surprise on his face. Interesting, I thought to myself. It seemed Cain didn't even know the full extent of Randy's growth.

"We also didn't want the drugs in the club," Jaxon added quietly.

I nodded. "We have too many liabilities owning these clubs. Having that shit in there and letting people use, or worse, overdose, would only put us at risk."

"We understand why you didn't leave," Oliver added, clearly concerned that we were offending Cain.

The man in question held up his hand and shook his head to stop Oliver. "I've stayed where I had to, so I could survive. I didn't have a group like you four. I've been alone with my Dad, since Mom died. I don't know anything else, so I do what I know. Doesn't mean I don't hate it, or don't understand where you're coming from."

I could tell Oliver was feeling uncomfortable, but our limo was pulling up to the back of Club 4.

"Cain, let's keep you on the owner's level. In case Lyle is

Randy's man, and Missy is working with him, we can't risk her knowing who you are," I said.

Cain nodded, and we all climbed out of the limo together. Gideon lead the way, but Cain knew his way after coming to see Jaxon in our club offices. When we pushed open the door on the owner's level, the music flowed over us and I shuddered, thinking about how we were coming to the club while Brooklyn was being held by her nightmare. Even if I knew we were doing it to try to find her, it felt wrong.

Jaxon motioned to the booth furthest from the stairs, where Cain could sit and be the most unnoticeable. Anyone coming near him would have to be blind to not notice the blue hair and tattoos. I could imagine he had no problems with women, with his chiseled looks and the ease with which he wore the tattoos that covered a lot of his exposed skin. The lip ring was a surprise to me, though.

Gideon motioned for me to meet him at the railing. Standing next to him, I surveyed the packed dance floor. If Missy was down there, it would be hard to pick her out among the writhing bodies.

"I'm going to put the team on alert, get her picture around to them. Tell them to just notify me if they see her and not to give her any indication that they were watching her," Gideon said.

I nodded absently. Watching the people dancing only made me ache for Brooklyn even more. She loved to dance, allowing her self consciousness to fade away as she flowed with the music. It was a beautiful thing to watch. In the two dances I had shared with her, having her body move near mine was more than I could handle.

Oliver took Gideon's place next to me, his hands wrapping around the banister as he looked out over the club.

"Do you think she'll show?" He asked.

I really didn't have an answer for that. Missy exuded confidence and self importance. However, I didn't peg her for being completely stupid. Showing up just days after our woman was kidnapped could be too obvious even for her. I just wasn't sure she could keep herself away from what she really wanted and that was us.

Our waitress, Vivian, was busy flirting with Cain, but she brought all of our usuals and I took a break to sip from my scotch. Oliver didn't move a muscle as he watched the crowd. Jaxon had chosen a seat with Cain, whether to keep an eye on him or keep him company, I wasn't sure. A thought came to me, but before I could really debate the topic to myself, Gideon approached the table.

"I have her picture at the door. I've talked to the team. If she is here or comes in tonight, we'll know," he said, pointing to the ear piece he was now wearing.

I nodded and scrubbed a hand down my face. It was hard not to think about the last time I saw Brooklyn in the club. She had come from our offices, her skin flush and beautiful, all of my brothers around her with satisfied looks on their faces. When I saw her, I wanted so badly to take her into my arms and be the reason she looked so happy.

Instead, my brothers froze, and Brooklyn became enraged at the scene in front of her. A tiny piece of me could find comfort that she cared at all after our tense miscommunication. Miscommunication was the nice way of saying my fuck up. Brooklyn cared enough to be angry about Missy at my side. But that was the first straw that started to take down our house of cards. My brothers blamed me for that. Fuck, I blamed myself.

I finished my scotch, but when Vivian appeared beside me, always the attentive waitress, I waved her off with a small smile. Drowning myself wasn't working. I didn't even like the way it made me feel and I wasn't forgetting any details about Brooklyn that drove my nightmares. Whatever happened after we found her, I didn't want to lose the memories I had of her skin, her taste, her breathy moans.

Jaxon appeared and slid into the booth with us. I looked over my shoulder and noted Cain was missing.

"He got a call, maybe a lead. He was going to grab a cab," Jaxon said.

I nodded and turned to watch the stairs that allowed entrance to our level. One of Gideon's team was there, watching the crowd below. I knew he'd allow Missy by if she appeared, but I continued to stare as if I could make her materialize.

The four of us rotated from the booth, to the railing, to our offices and back. We were all on edge, uneasy with being able to pull off any sort of farce. The idea made me wonder if I should start drinking again. I was sure I could pretend much easier if I was drunk. Missy being anywhere near me made my entire body shudder. Nevertheless, I was willing to do whatever was necessary to find Brooklyn.

As the final call was being broadcast by the DJ to the still full dance floor, desperation clawed at me. I couldn't sit still. Descending the stairs, I began to search the crowd myself. The rational part of my brain knew I was being ridiculous. Missy wouldn't come to the club and not try to get to us. She wouldn't be in the middle of the sweaty mass of dancers. My body just needed the movement, something to focus on.

An hour later, the last of the drunken party people had been poured into cabs and we were left with the employees as they closed up. My brothers and I hesitated on our level, slumped together in our booth.

"Why didn't she show?" Oliver asked.

There were so many answers to that question. The one thing I knew, Missy wasn't stupid. She was conniving, and she was going to fight for whatever she thought she deserved. And right now, she apparently had her sights on us.

"Maybe she thinks it would be best to wait until more time has passed since Brooklyn's abduction," Gideon commented.

"She'll show up, eventually. And when she does, we'll know how to deal with her," I said.

Knowing we weren't doing any good sitting in the empty club, the four of us made our way back to our car. Jaxon checked his phone every few minutes with a sigh, hoping for word from Cain. The man wasn't clear about the type of lead he thought he had, and it was putting Jaxon on edge.

At home, I quietly left my brothers and went to my room. I resisted slamming the door in anger, because breaking things wasn't going to change the situation. Throwing my cup against the wall the day before didn't make me feel better, just created a dent in the wall that will remind me of how I lost my cool. I roughly yanked my clothes off as I walked toward the bathroom, dropping everything at my feet.

I cranked the water in the shower to as hot as I could stand. Stepping under the water, I stepped right to the wall and leaned my forehead against the cool tile. I didn't know how long I stood there, but when I straightened to wash myself, I felt stiff and exhausted. Thinking about Brooklyn and the constant fear made my body feel as if I had participated in a triathlon.

Water still beaded my skin as I flopped onto my unmade bed. I laid there naked, trying to not imagine what could be happening to Brooklyn in the darkness. I would kill Lyle with my bare hands if he hurt our woman. Even if he didn't, his life was forfeit.

Brooklyn

I WASN'T AS CONFUSED COMING from under the effect of the drugs this time. The horror of my situation came back in a blast. Some questions answered from the time with Missy, some additional that I still didn't understand. Waking up still on the cold concrete of the warehouse had my heart thumping loudly in my chest.

I didn't move a muscle as I listened for sounds around me. Everything felt so quiet. As I shifted, I was surprised to find that my bindings had changed. As soon as I realized my wrists were free, I shot up into a sitting position.

Sun streamed through the high dirty windows of the room. I blinked rapidly against the sudden light. As I looked down at myself, horror settled in my gut. My clothes were gone, shreds of fabric sat in a pile nearby. I was left in my bra and thong, which did nothing to hide me from any eyes that could be watching me at the moment.

As the shock of my missing clothing still rolled around in my mind, I took stock of the rest of my body. My wrists were free, but there was something new. My ankle was wrapped in a leather strap that was closed with a fucking padlock. I pulled at the strap, tried to slide my fingers under it, but there was no gap between my skin and the leather.

Tears sprung to my eyes as I pulled and yanked at the rope that was wound around a pillar and then attached to the leather strap with a tight, intricate knot. I stood up and tried to pull with all my strength, but neither the rope nor the leather cuff would give. As I tried to push the cuff down my ankle, it dug in painfully and I cried out.

I collapsed back onto the concrete, the tears I was holding onto, streaming down my cheeks. If there was sun, that meant I had been drugged through the night. I couldn't be sure if it was day two or three. What I did know was my men hadn't found me yet. And things were getting serious.

More questions formulated in my head. Was Missy selling me to a sex ring? Was this just her trying to torture me further? Did her partner have some sick sex slave kink, and I was just there to fulfill his desires? Or was this just the next phase of her staging my murder?

I knew without a doubt, Missy's goal was to get rid of me so she could move on with the Knights. She wasn't stupid enough to believe that they would move on so easily if there was no news of my abduction. Getting rid of me permanently was the only way to cement the next steps in her plan.

A male voice filtered into the room then, someone on the other side of the door. Immediately, a foggy memory triggered something that felt real and tangible, but I could barely reach out and grasp. It was on the edge of my mind and I was positive I could hear it. *It's time to come home, Bee.* The realization of whose voice it was caused me to go frigid. Fear caused me to start clawing at the leather cuff again, shoving my fingers under it, scratching my skin. Anything to try to force myself free.

The door across the room opened and when I looked up, my nightmare materialized into the sunlight. Lyle slowly walked across the room, his eyes eating up my exposed flesh, a delightful gleam on his weasel face. His dull brown hair was slicked down on his head, in an attempt at a fashionable style, but it only made his forehead look larger. It was impossible to look at him and imagine what reason I thought I needed him so badly years before.

Realizing I was on full display for Lyle, I crossed my arms across my chest and pulled my knees up, trying to hide my bottom. The movement seemed to entertain him, as he tilted his head to the side and a sick smile crawled across his face. When he got closer to me, he didn't come within reach at first, instead, he circled me. I moved in a circle, to keep him in eyesight the whole time, afraid to allow him an opening.

"I so hate seeing you like this, Bee," he said.

"If you did, you wouldn't have done it. I knew Missy couldn't be working alone."

"That woman is infuriating, but she has some positives. Her cunt isn't bad either," he said with a shrug.

I couldn't help the disgust that flashed across my face. Instead of seeing it for what it was, Lyle showed his teeth in a smile.

"Jealous, Bee? Well, don't worry. I won't touch her again. I have you back," he said.

"I won't allow you to touch me," I said, my voice coming out with a harsh edge.

Lyle's head went back as he laughed loudly. He had circled

back around to the front of me and, quick as lightning, he stooped, grabbed the rope that was tied to my ankle and yanked. My foot was pulled from me, causing me to fall back. I hit my elbows on the concrete as I struggled to catch myself and not hit my head again. Tingles ran up my arms and I collapsed onto my back.

Before I could back up, Lyle stood over me, his feet planted by my hips, a large knife in his hand. He squatted over my stomach and ran the knife along the scar he had left on me, his gaze shining with delight as he pressed above my breast and the point nicked my skin. I hissed out a breath, but I didn't take my eyes off of him.

When he got to the center of my bra, he slipped the knife under and yanked up hard. The material split and my breasts spilled free. Instinctually, I brought my hands up to cover myself, but Lyle slid the knife under my nipple and I froze my movements. I could feel my nipples budding in the cold air, and Lyle moaned low in his throat as he circled the peak with his knife.

"So responsive, as always, my little Bee," he groaned.

"This isn't for you," I said through gritted teeth.

The knife point drifted down my stomach and over one hip, and Lyle moved down my body. He was too focused on the skin where his blade touched to even respond to me. I tried to lie perfectly still, afraid to anger him further, afraid of what his next plan was. If he wanted to kill me, my mind screamed for him to just get it over with. I couldn't handle him touching me any further.

Suddenly, pain lanced through my thigh and I screamed out. I tried to roll away, but Lyle trapped my leg under him as he carved shallow cuts into my skin. Each time the blade sliced, I would scream, my voice echoing throughout the warehouse. I screamed for Lyle to stop. I begged and pleaded, but he ignored me. His gaze was hot on where my blood ran from his slices.

Once he was done with his marks, he leaned back and inspected his work. Then he pushed my thighs apart, causing me to cry out again as he pressed against the wounds. He slid his hips between my thighs and I tried to back up and get away. He grabbed my hips and anchored me to the concrete, pushing me down painfully as he ground his erection into my core.

I began to gag and I could feel the vomit burning my throat. My mind was going fuzzy with the pain of my leg and I wanted to escape the feel of Lyle's body against mine, even with him being fully clothed. Lyle leaned down and slid his tongue around one of my nipples, and the sensation seemed to snap reality back into place. Before I could react, he bit down around my nipple, breaking the skin.

This time, I didn't just cry out. Acting as if I was trying to cover my breasts, I shifted an arm around my chest. As Lyle sat up to grab it, I slammed my elbow into his jaw. The blow wasn't hard, but it was enough to cause him to sit up and let go of my hips. He sat back and I could see fury dancing in his eyes as he dropped the knife and rubbed at his jaw.

Pulling up the leg that wasn't cut, I snapped out a kick that landed right in his chest and he fell backward. His head bounced off the concrete with a satisfying thunk and I knew that caused more damage than my actual kick did. With him off of me, I carefully climbed to my feet, no longer wanting to be vulnerable to him. I avoided looking at the cuts on my leg, because I knew it would pull me into a spiral of emotions that I couldn't deal with at the moment.

"You fucking bitch," Lyle moaned from the ground.

He was too far for me to reach, or I would have tried to jump on the advantage I had for the moment. The distance was increased as he rolled away from me. He slowly climbed to his feet and turned to glare at me. Before he could react, I snapped out a foot, trying to reach the knife that he had dropped, but my toes barely brushed the handle.

Lyle quickly collected the weapon and stared at me hatefully. I crossed my arms over my bare breasts and backed away from him, afraid of what his next attack would be. As he sheathed his knife and started to back away from me, I watched him warily. I didn't let down my guard until the door closed behind him as he left.

I stood naked, shivering. I dropped my arms and tears sprung to my eyes as I studied the bite on my breast. My breath began to heave out as my mind began to crumble. I didn't want to look at my leg, but the pain demanded attention. On the inside of the thigh that had previously been unmarred, the word MINE was carved, blood still seeping from each slice Lyle had made in my flesh.

I couldn't stop the choking vomit that sprung up my throat. Spinning toward the wall, I let loose the bile that had been threatening since Lyle entered the room. I hadn't eaten anything in hours and I was soon dry heaving.

Moving away from my puke, I spun toward the door, listening for Lyle or anyone else. It was then I started to scream. My desperation bounced around the room as I panicked and cried, hoping someone would hear me. I didn't have any idea of where the warehouse was located, but I couldn't let go of the hope that someone might walk by.

Realizing my blood was everywhere, I paused and looked down at my leg. The cuts weren't horribly deep, but they weren't clotting.

"Need to put pressure on it," I mumbled to myself.

My torn clothing was the only option of bandage I had. I walked as far as my restraint would allow. The cloth was only a few feet away. Having a goal helped clear my thoughts, and I was able to breathe deeply to calm my galloping heart.

Careful of my injuries, I laid on my stomach and stretched my body until I could grab the pile and pull it toward me. A small thrill of victory passed through me as I defied Lyle and got my clothes back. That thrill was short lived as I realized the clothes really had been cut into pieces.

Using my torn skirt, I wrapped two pieces around the word branded into me and tied them off tight. I hissed in pain at the pressure, but not seeing Lyle's claim of me made breathing even easier. My shirt was a loss, but I was able to use the leftover pieces if my skirt to tie around my breasts, giving me the illusion of coverage.

With my last task completed, I sat down carefully and pulled my knees to my chest. I knew Lyle wasn't finished with me. He had been surprised by me fighting back, and I was sure he was reevaluating his plan for me. Making his abuse of me more difficult was the only weapon I had, and I planned to use it to the best of my ability.

Brooklyn

THE DAY DRAGGED ON, with only the position of the sun to tell me the time. I periodically screamed and tried to fight against the restraint. A voice in my head told me it was all futile. However, I was afraid to stop fighting, afraid it would cause the madness in my mind to take over.

I was being dragged down into my past, into the damage I had gone to years of therapy to heal. It was a place I thought I had put into a box and pushed into a dark abyss of my brain. But now that box had sprung open, and I was flashing back to the same defenseless child of a drug addict, who attached herself to a man who wanted her as a possession.

Exhausted, as the sun seemed to be setting again, I curled up on the concrete. I had tried to make a nest of sorts out of the last pieces of my shirt and skirt, but it did nothing to stop the chill that settled into my body. My thigh stung and burned, the bite mark on my breast pulled every time I tried to move.

I laid there wondering if Lyle's plan was to break me, cut pieces from me, little by little. He was a master at psychological manipulation, something I learned and accepted in therapy. I fell under his implied charms as a young girl and let the fog of belonging hide all the horrible things he was actually doing to me.

Things were different now. I was no longer the weak little child, being brought to the group home whenever my mother was too high to remember she had a daughter. I had grown into a woman that had found the strength she had inside. And more recently, the confidence I had always lacked was surfacing. Thanks mostly to my new relationships with the Knights.

The pain was worse when I thought of them, wondered where they were, what they were doing. I had to fight down sickness when I thought about the chance that Missy had gone to them today. Would she act like she was sympathetic about my disappearance? Would she try to comfort them? I believed what I had said to her. They wouldn't take her back just because I was missing. I would have to be dead and even then, I knew how Gideon felt about her. She had no chance with my guys.

My guys. I missed them so much I physically ached with it. I had wanted my independence, the chance to grow and have the strength inside me to survive. I had overreacted by leaving the house the way I did, cutting off communication, while I stewed in my stubbornness. In principle, I was right. They had to let me spread my wings and learn the way I wanted to. But there was a better way of telling them that without leaving them with nothing but a note.

Would I even get the chance to fix what I had broken? I closed my eyes and pictured Gideon in the meadow, as he peered up at me, his head between my thighs. He had made sure I knew that they still wanted me, despite my leaving. I had to believe that would stay true, even with the new scars I would have.

My stomach heaved again as I thought about Lyle's brand on my unmarred thigh. The Knights had always been accepting and even loving about my scars. How would they react to seeing a word carved into my flesh, on display anytime I was naked with them? The idea of them looking at me in revulsion caused despair to worm its way into my thoughts.

Sleep started to take over my exhausted body and mind. I was somewhere between the worlds of awake and dreams when I heard shouting behind the door across the room from me. It was more than one male voice this time, the number of people working with Lyle growing again. The tiny hairs on my body rose when I realized the argument was about who was going to get me next. I scrambled as far from the door as possible, my eyes flying around the dark room for any hopes of protecting myself.

The door opened, spilling light across the side of the room. The figure in the open doorway was shadowed, but it was easy to tell it was Lyle. Behind him, in the bright hallway, another man stood, staring into the darkness hungrily. I knew he couldn't see me, as his face twisted in anger and he started to walk forward. Lyle glanced back once, but he didn't stop the man from following.

I was momentarily blinded as my eyes tried to adjust to the contrast between light and dark. My ears easily picked up Lyle's footsteps as he approached. I loosened my stance, preparing for his attack. He stopped before he was within reach and tilted his head as he took in my appearance.

"You covered up. You'll learn that when I expect you naked, you better be." He moved toward me with his knife out.

I put my hands up in a fighting stance, trying to remember all the things I had been practicing. Lyle hesitated for a moment, and then a condescending grin spread across his face.

"You aren't going to stop me from using my property," he said.

"I'm not yours." I stepped back as far as the restraint would allow.

"You've always belonged to me. From the moment you walked into that group home, you were mine," he said.

I pushed away the inner negative thoughts that started to flow with his words. I had worked hard to overcome the feelings of abandonment and that loss of belonging somewhere. None of it was healthy.

"I belong to myself and no one else."

I sidestepped as he reached out with his free hand. With my front hand, I snapped out a jab and tried to punch him in the jaw. He moved out of the way and the blow glanced his shoulder. It was in that moment I realized I had been too focused on Lyle. Arms banded around my upper torso, trapping me against a body. A scream tore from my throat as I tried to fight free.

"You have so much more fight in you, Bee. Is that from playing the whore to four men? Did they teach you to fight?" Lyle stepped close, his rank breath on my cheek.

His hands found the tie that held the fabric on my breasts, baring me to his hungry eyes again. The knife was out again. I froze as the tip slid down my rib cage to my hip, the blade slipping under the strap of my thong, cutting through the fabric as Lyle yanked. With rough hands, Lyle pulled the material from between my legs.

I tried to throw a knee up, to connect with any part of him, but he saw the move coming. Putting the knife away, his hand slammed down on my injured thigh, his fingers digging into the cuts. I slammed my teeth together to keep the scream that wanted to erupt from coming out.

Lyle's fingers dug in and he laughed gleefully as I tried to pull away. The movements made me press against the man behind me and I almost immediately recognized the hardness the man rubbed against my lower back as I moved. I tried to push myself away from him, but with Lyle distracted, he was taking his chance. One of the hands that held me slipped up until it was cupping my breast. Fat fingers dug painfully and pinched my nipple.

"Damn it, Buzz!" Lyle's voice suddenly erupted.

The hands on me froze, but didn't move. The length against my lower back continued to move, and I physically shuddered.

"She wants it," the voice that must have been Buzz said.

Lyle's hand snapped forward and grabbed Buzz's wrist. He twisted, pulling his fingers from my nipple, cause me to wince, but I stayed as quiet as possible.

"It's not time for you yet. I already told you, you'll get your turn once I get her broken in again. Got it?"

The grip around my waist only tightened and I could see in the dim light that Lyle's eyes had narrowed.

"That's gonna take too long." Buzz's slow speech reflected what was likely his intelligence level.

"Do as you're told," Lyle said.

Not taking any chances, Lyle grabbed one of my wrists and yanked me from Buzz's grip. With his other hand, he grabbed a handful of my hair, pulling my face to his. Though the light was dim, I could make out every pock mark on his pallid skin.

"Behave, or I'll let Buzz have what he wants. Got it, Bee?"

The idea of behaving for Lyle made everything in me protest. However, the lingering pain from Buzz'a hands and his cock jabbing me in the back made me nod my head slightly. That acceptance lit a fire in his eyes and he smashed his lips to mine. I clamped my mouth shut, squeezing my eyes closed, and tried not to breathe in his disgusting odor.

Lyle pulled back, apparently satisfied with my acceptance of the situation. For just a moment, he allowed softness to appear on his face as he ran a finger along my bottom lip. But it disappeared as he looked into my eyes and sneered.

"Don't think I forgot what this mouth is really good for."

Looking over my shoulder, he nodded at Buzz and the feel of cold leather wrapped around my free ankle. I tried to pull away, but Buzz held my leg tightly as he strapped the restraint on. I began to flail and scream. The only thing I could do being held so close was slap Lyle across the face, causing his head to whip to the side.

His head slowly came back to center, and I could see the viciousness in his eyes just a moment before his fist flew. The connection of his knuckles with my cheek threw me back, causing me to fall over Buzz and land in a naked heap. Buzz quickly grabbed the new restraint again and started tying knots with a rope. Vaguely, I realized that I should have figured Lyle couldn't tie such intricate knots.

While Buzz secured my ankles, Lyle stalked toward me with handcuffs he pulled from his pocket. I tried to scramble backwards, but Buzz yanked hard on my ankle, pulling me closer to them. I kicked and cursed at them, knowing it was my only weapon at the moment.

Lyle caught one of my wrists and snapped the cuff around it. I pulled back, but he held strong, causing the metal to bruise my skin. He stood over me again, without worry, as Buzz controlled my legs. I put my free wrist behind my back, even though I knew it was no use. The snap of the second cuff secured my wrists behind my back again.

Lyle kneeled so he was straddling my thighs. He observed my position and turned to tell Buzz to tighten the restraints until I couldn't move my legs.

"Lyle, please, I said I'd behave," I begged.

"Those men changed you, Bee. I can't trust you. Not until I ruin you for them forever." Lyle's angry words caused spittle to fly from his mouth and land across my breasts.

Suddenly, my ankles were yanked until I was forced to spread my legs for both men to see. I watched as Lyle's got gaze landed on the apex between my thighs and he stood to adjust himself. Walking slowly backward, his eyes stayed glued on me until he reached Buzz, who was also staring with his mouth slack and hanging open.

"Don't go anywhere, Bee." Lyle grabbed Buzz by his collar and dragged him toward the door.

I laid on my back, leaning up on my shoulders to make space for my arms. The position pushed my hips up, giving the illusion I was begging for someone to touch me. Which was the furthest thing from the truth. I tested each ankle, trying to get just a tiny bit of slack so I could protect my core, but there was not even an inch to be pulled.

My body almost instantly began to ache. The injury on my thigh burned as if Lyle had touched a torch to the skin. The cold of the concrete quickly seeped into my joints and I couldn't rotate and turn to release the pressure and pain building. Tears spilled down the sides of my face as I tried to control my mind. None of the training I had been doing could defend against this. I began hoping Lyle would drug me so I could sink into oblivion before he acted out any of the things he wanted to do to my body.

The door across the room slammed again, and I was left in fear, wondering who was coming across the room toward me. Unable to see my attacker, I started trying again to pull free of my restraints. Nothing moved and soon Lyle was standing between my spread thighs, looking down at me hungrily, his lips parted on a moan as I struggled. Realizing my fighting was turning him on further, I froze and locked my body rigid.

Slowly, he lowered himself to his knees and ran his hands up the insides of my thighs. I tried to move away, but it was useless. His fingers skated close to my center, but he moved away, causing me to gush out the air I had been holding in my lungs. Lyle mistook my relief as desire as he laid his body over mine.

"Don't worry, Bee. I'm going to remind your cunt who she belongs to. You missed it, didn't you?"

Immediately, I decided I had to change tactics, or I was going to lose the last shreds of me.

"Lyle, please. Not like this. On this concrete, tied up. Please, this isn't like you."

Instead of answering, Lyle buried his face in my neck. I could feel his lips, tongue, and the sting of his teeth as he nipped and sucked at my skin. I cringed, thinking of the marks he was likely making on my body. Steeling myself, I knew I could handle hickies, if I could prevent him from doing the one thing I didn't think I would recover from.

Brooklyn

LYLE TOOK his time exploring my torso, pushing my hair out of the way as his mouth slid along the shell of my ears to the spot behind that was usually very sensitive. Now, all I felt was repulsion. I didn't have a memory of Lyle as a tender lover, so I couldn't predict what his next move was. When he got to the jagged scar that started behind my ear and went down across my collarbone, he stopped and traced it with a finger.

"I'm sorry for this mark. It really doesn't help your looks."

"It's ok." My voice quivered as he kept petting the scar.

"What did those pricks think of this, hmmm? This didn't ruin you for them? I'll need to do better this time," Lyle said, as if he was speaking to himself and I wasn't expected to answer.

"Lyle, please. I'm cold. Let's go somewhere else, where we can talk."

He continued moving down my body, as if I hadn't spoken at all. As he pawed at my breasts, running his tongue around my nipples, tears began to seep from my eyes. Suddenly, he pushed himself up, so he was face to face with me again, grinding himself into me.

"This is why we're not going anywhere else, Bee. You're crying. I need to break you of this new person you think you are. Remind you who you belong to. Then we can move on, back to how it used to be."

His hand appeared with a syringe and an evil look passed over his face. I knew then, I couldn't convince him I was a willing participant in this. He turned to use his teeth to uncap the needle, and I took my chance, rearing up, I sank my teeth into his cheek.

Lyle let out a squeal of surprise and pain as I latched on. A burst of copper hit my tongue as I broke the skin. Lyle tried to sit up, but I didn't let go. Suddenly, he seemed to come to his senses, and one of his hands wrapped around my throat, cutting off the air supply. As my body went into fight-or-flight mode, I released my hold on his face and started gasping for breath.

Fury lined Lyle's face as he leaned up and put more pressure on my throat. Vaguely, I started to realize, this was it. This was how I was going to die. With the panic, gratitude also flared, because I would die without my body being violated. Black dots swam in my vision and my body went limp as the oxygen depletion started to take its toll.

And just like that, the pressure was gone, and I was gasping in oxygen through a bruised windpipe. My vision began to clear, and I focused on Lyle above me. His free hand went straight to the middle of my thighs. He stared down as he forced a finger into me. When he looked up at me again, I saw the bleeding wound on his cheek that was dripping onto his shirt.

"No, no! Stop this, Lyle!" My voice was nothing but a cracked whisper, confirming the injury to my throat.

I couldn't fight, couldn't kick or strike out. My hands had long gone numb under me, useless in the handcuffs that held them. My ankles felt raw against the leather bindings as I continued to pull at them. As all of this ran through my mind, Lyle leaned over me again, this time staying well away from my face. He pressed the needle against my neck.

"Remember who you belong to, bitch."

The liquid burned in my veins as he pushed down the plunger. He tossed the syringe to the side and added a second finger as he ripped into me. The burning tear from my walls made me cry out silently through my injured vocal cords. Tears streamed down my face as I thrashed my head back and forth.

"See, your cunt missed me, didn't she? Those rich assholes probably don't know how to please a woman, really."

I turned my face then and met his eye. Without thought of repercussions, I spit onto his face, the saliva landing on his injured cheek and sliding down. He went red with anger, and I stared at him in defiance. I didn't see the hand coming before knuckles connected with my face, bouncing my head off the concrete.

The blow almost gave me what I wanted: blackness, a way to hide from what was happening. But as I prayed for my mind to go, Lyle continued thrusting his fingers, delighting in sexually torturing a defenseless woman. I turned my head and began to dry heave without control. The drugs quickly began their work and darkness inched into the edges of my vision.

"Fuck, Bee! You feel fabulous. I can't wait till we have more time." Lyle's voice was near my ear, but I was getting too far gone to react.

As he moved toward the door, I barely registered his words. "And don't worry, I won't let Buzz have you until I've had my fill. That'll take awhile, I'm sure."

When the door slammed and locked behind him, I was thrown into inky darkness. I wanted to curl into myself, but Lyle hadn't released my restraints. I wanted to scream, but even my voice wouldn't work. The burning pain between my legs made me wish I could clean myself and pretend this was all a nightmare.

But I couldn't pretend that. And as I fell into the drug induced state, I worried worse was coming. I would be ruined. My body was no longer my own, I was no longer whole. Lyle would do what he intended. He would break me. My thoughts were a mess that couldn't string together and make sense. I could feel my soul shattering while my insides started to go numb.

I knew one thing for sure: I no longer wanted my guys to find me. They could look beyond a few scars, but how could they forgive me for letting another man touch me? How could they forgive and not see me as a ruined woman, undeserving of love? I was telling each of them sorry in my heart as the drugs took over and pulled me into the unconsciousness I had been begging for.

Jaxon

MY CALLS to Cain had gone unanswered, and I was on the verge of fury. Without his leads, we were dead in the water finding Brooklyn. Missy had been our only hope, but she was a no show so far. Aiden had thought about reaching out to her, but we all agreed that would seem too suspicious. Our insistent denial of her before made it impossible to call her as if we had any sort of affection for her.

I had my doubts that I could even pretend well enough to pull anything off. Missy's mere presence made me sick. She was nothing but a reminder of all the things we had worked hard to overcome to have what we had now. She made me think about how close my brothers and I were to a breaking point, all over the drama she caused between us. Always the doting girlfriend, she made sure we were high enough to not catch onto her games until it was almost too late.

I laid in bed, sleep impossible to grasp, staring at the ceiling. I thought about what Gideon had told us about his time with Brooklyn in the meadow. In my heart, I believed she would have come home, on her own, and soon. Maybe Lyle realized that too, and that's why he made his move now. The bastard always seemed a step ahead of us and it was costing us greatly now.

The sound of my phone made me shoot up in bed. Cain's name flashed on the screen and I answered it quickly.

"Did I wake you, man?"

"Do you think I can sleep right now?" I switched on my bedside lamp.

"Fair. I think I might have something." Cain's voice drifted away, as if he was holding the phone away from his mouth. I could hear him murmuring to someone else.

"And? Cain? What the hell you got?" I was practically yelling into the phone to get him back on track.

"Missy. I found where she's staying. The hotel reservation is under a business name. I guess someone that's sponsoring her or some shit. Anyway, I got a guy watching the place. She went in, hasn't come out. Want us to snag her?"

I pinched my nose, thinking about the risk Cain had taken bringing more people in. Taking a deep breath, I avoided asking for the details and wasting the time.

"Snatch her and take her where?" I asked.

"I got a place. I'll shoot you the address. You and boys meet me there and we can decide where to go from there."

I hesitated. I wasn't afraid to do what was necessary to get to Brooklyn, but I had never been involved in kidnapping before.

"Man, she helped take your woman. Why are you even thinking about this?" Cain asked.

I already knew my answer, even if I was taking a moment to think about it.

"Do it. I'll wake my brothers."

'Brothers...," Cain's voice was so quiet I barely picked up the word. Guilt immediately settled in my gut, but I didn't have time to have the conversation I was sure we would need to have, eventually.

"Text me the address once you have her," I said, before clicking to end the call.

I threw on a pair of sweats and a hoodie, trying to dress as innocuous as possible. Leaving my room, I immediately heard the sound of voices coming from downstairs. In the kitchen, I found Gideon and Aiden sitting around the island with a bottle of scotch in the center. I shot a text to Oliver instead of running back up the stairs and then set my phone in front of me and stared at it.

Aiden and Gideon had gone quiet and turned to stare at me.

"Cain knows where Missy is. I told him to grab her. He'll text a location as soon as they have her."

"They?" Aiden slowly set his tumbler down as if he was resisting throwing the glass across the room.

I nodded, not in the mood to argue about the additional liabilities now. Oliver entered the kitchen, his curly hair disheveled, but no indication of sleep on his face.

"We're in the kidnapping business now," Gideon said.

Oliver looked from face to face, trying to figure out what was happening. I quickly recapped the call from Cain.

"She took Brooklyn, or at least helped take her. I have no problems going after her." I crossed my arms across my chest and shot a look at them challenging them to argue.

"I'm not against it. I just want to make sure it doesn't trace back to us," Gideon replied.

"We get the information we need out of her and we turn her over to your detective friend. She's an accomplice, at the very least." I continued staring at my phone, willing it to light up with a message from Cain.

The four of us sat tense around the island, until the sun had started to chase away the night, a soft pink washing into the kitchen. We had long stopped drinking scotch and moved to coffee to ensure we were awake for the message when it did come. When my phone did light up, I jumped up so fast, I slammed a knee into the island. I cursed loudly, but swiped open the phone to a message from Cain. It was an address with no message.

"It's on," I said, turning the phone for my brothers to see.

We strode out of the house less than five minutes later, piling into my Tesla. We didn't need to risk a driver or make any of our employees guilty by association, in case this went badly. I plugged the address into the GPS as I pulled out of our gates.

"That's not far from the old neighborhood," Oliver said, slumping back in his seat.

I nodded, but didn't respond. It wasn't a surprise that Cain would keep his business in the same place he worked. Illegal events were ignored or swept under the rug in that part of the city. No politician or police chief wanted to acknowledge how bad the slums really were. We never set a foot back in the area after we got away from my father. It was a risk going there now, but it was to find Brooklyn. We would do anything.

The house Cain directed us to was nicely kept, despite the area it was located in. The houses on either side looked to be abandoned, which was likely why Cain chose it. No witnesses. I pulled my car around to the back of the house, following tire treads that were years in the making. I parked next to Cain's black Dodge Charger. Before we even opened the doors, the back door of the house swung open and Cain stood in the opening.

He was dressed in a suit today and I had to raise an eyebrow at him as I approached.

"Had to look the part. It's easy to get in somewhere if you dress right. People don't always pay attention to everything else."

He did a little turn, showing the whole outfit, before turning back to us with an ironic grin.

I shook my head, but gestured toward the house. "She in there?"

Cain nodded. "Follow me, boys."

The house was comfortable and obviously lived in. I highly doubted it was Cain's actual home, as he wouldn't bring this type of trouble to where he lived. But it wasn't trashed like a drug pad and someone seemed to clean on a regular basis. Cain lead us through a kitchen, to a door before we would have entered the living room. When he opened it, a shriek we couldn't hear before echoed around the kitchen.

"Get in quick. The door and walls are soundproof. The distant neighbors don't need to be hearing this hag screaming." Cain motioned for us to walk ahead of him.

We hurried through the door and descended the stairs while Cain closed and secured the door behind us. I noticed he locked it with a key from the inside. I guessed to dissuade the prisoner from trying to leave. When we reached the basement floor, the room was dim, but it didn't prevent me from seeing the flailing little wench tied to a chair to one side. She was screaming at a man that sat across from her. With Bluetooth earbuds in his ears and a magazine in his hands, he gave the impression he couldn't care less about her.

When the five of us stopped, we formed a semi-circle behind the man. Cain tapped him on the shoulder and he looked up. He took a set of keys from Cain and disappeared up the stairs. I watched him go before looking back to Cain.

"He can be trusted?"

"Come on, man. You think I don't have people I know I can trust?" Cain rolled his eyes before he turned to settle his gaze on Missy.

She had calmed down considerably, and I could see the wheels whirling in her head as she tried to put things together. The four of us just stared at her, and Cain grabbed the chair his man had just vacated. He turned it so he sat on it backward and a cocky grin spread across his face.

"This is gonna get interesting," he said.

Missy's eyes went to each of us, as if she was trying to determine who she could manipulate. I knew her game too well by now, as did my brothers. We hadn't discussed much about how to play this, making me wish we had some sort of plan. However, when Missy spoke, she set the wheels in motion without us needing to talk before.

"Aiden, baby. What is going on? You could have just called me if you wanted to see me." She tried to bat her eyes at my brother, but the mascara smeared down her cheeks didn't help her sexy act.

"Cut the shit, Missy." Violence rolled off Aiden in waves and his voice was a blow Missy hadn't been expecting.

"I... I don't understand—"

Aiden cut her off with an air of authority. "All you need to understand right now is we could find you anywhere you hid, under any name you stayed under. This wasn't hard, Missy. So, the next part won't be hard either."

I could see as she started to realize there was more going on and she caved into herself, trying to look sympathetic. Her fake tears and begging weren't going to stop us from getting the information we needed. She had long ago burned any bridge to us that would have afforded her the sympathy she was looking for.

Cain looked up at us and then over to Missy, resolve on his face. He stood up and flicked out the blade of a knife. Missy's eyes widened as she watched him pace around her and behind us, a tiger wanting out of his cage. I knew Cain had a dark streak in him. He had survived a long time in a world that had started to eat me alive. But for him, he had found a way to thrive. There was no way he did that without spilling blood whenever necessary.

"What's the next part?" Missy's lip quivered, and I thought some of it was real fear now.

"You telling us everything we want to know," Gideon said.

Missy's eyes flew to him. She immediately softened and all the stages of emotion crossed her face. I was sickened that we never figured this out while we were with her, until it was too late. Missy was a chameleon, changing her tactic to fit whoever she was trying to push. Gideon was a big man, barrel chested, dark with his thick beard and long hair. But he was the last one of us I would ever believe could put hands on a woman. Missy knew that, too.

"My muscle man, couldn't you loosen up these ties? They're cutting into me." Missy blinked innocently up at him.

To Gideon's credit, he didn't even twitch. His gaze was hard on her and his lack of response to her caused annoyance to flash across Missy's face. Cain continued to move around, flipping his knife around as if he was playing a carnival game and was just waiting his turn. When none of us moved to help her or speak, I saw as the facade on Missy's face dropped. A sneer appeared on her face and she leaned back, pressing her surgically enhanced chest out.

"Then what? You guys couldn't find a woman to fuck, so you had me kidnapped and wanted to play out a little role play? I'm down for it boys. I've missed you," she said.

That was too much for Oliver and he stepped forward, his hand going up. Aiden flashed forward and grabbed him by the shoulder. I watched as they communicated through their eyes and Oliver stepped back, letting Aiden take the lead. It was just like Aiden to take the burden, especially from Oliver, after we almost lost him to Missy and the drugs in the first place.

"We will never touch you, let alone fuck you, Missy. Let's stop with the games. Where is Brooklyn?"

The laugh that cackled out of Missy surprised me. Her head tilted back, and the sound rang and bounced off of the concrete walls. When she looked back at us, tears were streaming down her cheeks, a real emotion from her.

"This is about that blonde bitch? Are you kidding me?" Missy moved like she wanted to cross her legs, but she was quickly reminded that her ankles were secured with zip ties to the chair.

"Where is Brooklyn?" Aiden asked again, ignoring her.

She smirked at Aiden and a red flush rose up his cheeks, his fury boiling to a point that even I knew Missy needed to be worried. Sensing the change in the room, Cain stepped forward, his knife gripped in his right hand. Missy's eyes flashed to him, wide with concern again. I had no idea if she remembered Cain from our younger years, but she knew enough that he was dangerous.

He stepped to her, running his left hand down her cheek, softly, almost in a caress. Moving to stand behind her, his hand suddenly gripped her chin roughly, yanking her head back. As she looked up at him, the cool metal of his knife kissed her throat and she squealed loudly and then started begging for help.

"This is how it's going to go. No words will leave your whore mouth until they answer my boys' questions. Clear?"

Missy's throat moved as she swallowed hard. She started to nod, but Cain shook his head slowly and gripped her chin harder, keeping her head right where he wanted it.

"What are you going to do? Cut my throat?" Her voice was nothing, but a hissed whisper.

Cain ran the point of his knife along her throat, up to an ear, before he bent close to her.

"I'll start with this ear, then the other. I'll leave your tongue for last, so you can scream the whole time. Maybe I'll take a finger or two next, then that nose. It's not the first time you've been under the knife, huh?" Cain broke into a smile at his own morbid joke.

"You wouldn't," she said.

"Wouldn't I? You are nothing to me. And you wouldn't be the first body I had to disappear. Do you want to find out how deep I bury them, Missy?"

Gideon

HEARING CAIN'S WORDS, I felt a cold fist settle in my stomach. The darkness Cain was using was the same as what was within me, every day, I chose to not utilize or let out. His was on the surface, so easy to be an advantage and not a liability. I looked over at Jaxon, because I knew Cain was a person he had once known well. My brother's face gave away nothing, so I continued to keep my face neutral as well.

I knew none of us were above torturing the information out of

Missy. The problem was what to do with her after. She was active on social media, was considered an influencer. Her disappearance would be noted, and that was heat none of us needed, Cain included. I had to trust that Cain knew all of these things too, and wouldn't be too risky with his knife.

Missy was contemplating Cain's words. Her eyes stared up at him without blinking for a long moment.

"Fine. I'll answer Aiden's question," she finally said.

"Go ahead, you can speak." Cain looked up at us and we all waited for her answer.

"She's gone."

Cain frowned and looked down at her again. His knife knicking her just enough that a small stream of blood appear and she flinched away.

"I answered the question!" Missy screamed.

"I wouldn't move much more. You're going to make my knife happier without it doing one thing," Cain said, looking up at Aiden with an raised eyebrow.

"That's not an answer, Missy. Don't fucking lie to us. You have no power here." Aiden's hands were rolled into fists, gripped so tightly his knuckles stuck out white against his tanned skin.

"That's where you're wrong, lover." Missy's voice was back to the fake purr she liked to use on us. The sound made my teeth grind.

I knew what she meant. She had the power to keep whatever information she had about Brooklyn from us. The longer she evaded our questions, the longer Brooklyn wasn't with us. A heavy thought also sat in my mind. If we had Missy here, that meant Lyle had Brooklyn to himself and there was no knowing what he was doing to her. I wasn't sure I could stomach even trying to imagine what my girl was going through.

I saw Aiden nod slightly to Cain, and I focused back on the scene in front of me, pushing the overwhelming dread away, so I could work to find Brooklyn. Cain bent to focus on Missy and her breath became shallow as she anticipated the pain he promised with his eyes. His knife skated down her throat and he pressed into her flesh above her collarbone. She cried out as a clean line of blood appeared.

"Missy, where is Brooklyn?" Aiden asked again.

Missy's head fell forward when Cain released her chin, allowing her to make eye contact with Aiden. Her pale skin was marked with Cain's fingerprints, and I knew she would be covered in bruises once we were done with her. She tried to look at the cut on her chest, but Cain grabbed her chin and made her look up again.

"You should be careful how you answer this time, yeah?" He spoke right into her ear, his breath making her hair move and Missy tried to shift away.

She looked into Aiden's eyes, fire lit behind the pain on her face. Anger tightened her features.

"I don't know what you boys thought would happen when you snatched me. Did you think I would just admit to something or give up all my information without something in return? That's laughable. I made it this far, without any of you, on my fucking own. I know how to come out on top, no matter what. You aren't going to get what you want in this basement." Missy's body seemed to relax, and she actually leaned into Cain as if she wanted his hands on her.

"What do you want?" Oliver's voice was quiet, but it cut through to the point.

Missy's smile was a predator, looking over its most recent kill. "I thought I was clear about that, Oli. I want my rightful place back. With you, in your empire, sitting at the top with you as your queen."

"It's about the money then," Aiden said.

"Oh, come on, lover, that's just a piece of it. Of course, a large shiny piece."

"We'll never welcome you back into our lives." Oliver's voice was stone, leaving no room for argument, even if Missy had other plans.

"Oli, baby, you don't know how good we could be again," Missy said. Her smile had softened, and she was back to trying to seduce us into giving her what she wanted.

"We are here for one reason, and that's to find our woman. That woman isn't you," Aiden said.

Cain's laugh boiled up and spilled out into the basement. Missy's face turned into a sneer as Cain grabbed her chin again and leaned down.

"You are barking up the wrong tree there, yeah?"

Missy shook her face free, and Cain allowed it this time. She looked over at me, likely because I had stayed quiet during this entire exchange. It was almost comical to watch her try to put on a face she thought would appeal to me.

"Muscle man, you don't feel that way, do you? You loved me." Missy's bottom lip came out at the end to pout up at me.

Instead of answering her, I looked over at Cain. "What about breaking a finger or two? Maybe that would change her mind."

"Gideon!" Missy's voice rose to an uncomfortable pitch as she screamed at me, at the same time Cain laughed and nodded.

Cain moved away from Missy and she started to thrash again. Her efforts were a waste of energy, as she wasn't strong enough to break any of the ties without a tool. When Cain joined our circle again, he held a hammer in his hand. Instead of approaching Missy, he stood next to me and we all stared at her.

"One more time, yeah? Tell them what they want to know, or a pretty manicure isn't going to save what I do to your hands." Cain made his point by flipping the hammer, catching it again by the handle after it flew through the air.

Missy froze and looked at Cain, real fear reflecting in her stare. She might talk a big game, but Missy was the type to cry for a half an hour if she stubbed her toe. Physically, she was too small and skinny to be built for fighting, and she definitely couldn't sit there and just take her fingers being hammered to mush.

Seeming to understand she was going to lose her hold, real tears began to flood her cheeks. She sobbed and choked as she tried to breathe. The sight would have made me extremely uncomfortable if it had been any other woman. Instead, when I looked at Missy, I saw her for the viper she was.

Her crying jag seemed to slow and Cain moved forward. He used the hammer to push her chin up until she was looking up at him.

"You ready now?"

When she didn't answer, he moved to her hand. He flattened out her pinky, her long red nail at the end. She started to gasp and struggle again, but Cain looked at her with a hard look. Missy froze and cowered, finally afraid of the man that was clearly willing to torture her. Cain looked back at Aiden and nodded to him to ask one last time.

"Where is Brooklyn?"

"With Lyle," she replied, her answer still not complete, still pushing the limits that Cain was setting up.

The man in question looked at her, pity on his face. Without warning, the hammer sailed through the air and slammed into the middle knuckle of her pinky finger. Her wail drowned out the sound of the bone breaking, but I had no doubts that finger was going to need some serious help.

Cain let the finger go and Missy cried as she tried to move it, but the mangled digit just laid there. Out of the corner of my eye, I saw Oliver look away, not able to handle watching the torture. I forced myself to stay focused on the woman in the chair. Even in pain, the moment she thought she had some sort of sway over us, she would try to use it.

"You know there's more to that answer," Cain said, as he came around to stand with us again.

Words began to pour out of Missy then, her crying causing jagged breaks in the story.

"Last I knew, he was holding her in a warehouse I helped him rent. It's on the water. I really don't know if they're still there. I don't know what his plan was after I left."

Collectively, we looked at Aiden, waiting to see where he would lead us.

"Address," he said, his voice rough.

Missy nodded and recited an address. As a group, we turned away from her and headed for the stairs.

"Wait, wait! Aren't you going to take me with you? You can't leave me down here!" Missy's scream raced after us.

Aiden looked at me. "Take her to Lee. Make sure she understands if she talks about this and anything else about us, today will look like foreplay compared to what we do to her."

"I want to be with you at the warehouse." I knew none of us wanted to wait long before going for Brooklyn.

"I know. We need recon first. We'll handle that while you take Missy," Aiden said.

I nodded and turned back toward Missy. Cain threw me a pair of keys.

"Take my Charger. Just bring it back in one piece, yeah?"

My brothers and Cain made their way upstairs as I pulled out my pocket knife and approached Missy. She flinched away from me, expecting a new attack, but I just cut through the zip ties holding her. After she was free, she didn't move, only cradled her broken finger in her uninjured hand. Her eyes watched me closely as I moved around the room, gathering the belongings she had come with.

"Let's go," I said.

"Gideon. Please. What are you going to do with me?" Missy's voice was pleading, but I wasn't fooled for a moment into believing she wasn't looking for her moment to strike.

I motioned for her to walk ahead of me, up the stairs, as I put away my knife. I wasn't worried about handling Missy in a hand to hand attack. Her purse in my hand was too small to hide any sort of weapon, and I was sure Cain checked for that before throwing it to the side. We appeared in the house again and Missy blinked against the bright sunlight that had started to shine through the clean windows.

Cain and his man both stood in the living room, watching us closely. When Missy looked their way, she stepped back rapidly, running into my chest. Cain let a smile that could only be described as psychotic appear on his face. Missy tried to continue her retreat, but I put my hands on her shoulders and pushed her through the kitchen, toward the backdoor. I knew we needed to get to the cars. She turned suddenly and tried to hug me, but I side stepped her before she could touch me.

"Don't touch me." I pushed her again, sending her stumbling back, her arms pinwheeling to keep herself from falling.

"Muscle man, my Gideon. Please. We can fix all of this. We won't go back to what we had before. We would be so much better than that now." Missy put out her uninjured hand, begging me to take it.

When I looked at her now, I felt nothing but a twisted sickness in my gut. There were no pleasant memories or what ifs in my mind. Our time with Missy had been turbulent, dark, and dangerous. Even leaving out the drug use, Missy had my brothers and me at a point where we almost lost each other while we lost ourselves. She cut down the self confidence that grew in young men, creating shells that we had to work hard to recover from.

"No. Outside, get in the car," I finally said.

Her face went blank, all emotion leaving it, in a move that was almost theatrical. Turning on her heel, she stomped toward the backdoor. I unlocked Cain's cars and pointed to the passenger seat. She got in with a huff and I slammed the door. After I slid into the driver's seat, I locked the doors to ensure she didn't try to jump out and take off. She wouldn't get far, but I wasn't in the mood to delay and chase her.

I drove straight from the house to the police station, where I was fairly certain Lee would be working. Circling to the back parking lot, I found an open spot that wasn't noticeable and pulled in. After shutting off the engine, I gripped the steering wheel tightly.

"You understand I'm turning you over to the police for your involvement in Brooklyn's kidnapping."

"You could just let me go. I already told you what you wanted to know," Missy said.

"You deserve to be punished for what you've done." My fingers tighten on the wheel, my knuckles turning white, as I tried not to think about choking the life out of her myself.

"Don't you think this was enough?" Missy's voice rose to a shriek as she motioned to her mangled pinky.

"No, no I don't. And you won't be telling the police how that actually happened. You fell. That's the answer when they ask. Are we clear?" I finally risked a glance at her.

Missy's face was screwed up in fury. No longer were we playing the game of cat and mouse, where she was sure she could win one of us over. Now, the gloves were off and the monster was on the surface, ready to take a piece of anyone in its way. Her eyes narrowed as she met my gaze.

"Why... would... I... do... that?" Her voice was a low hiss.

Suddenly, her uninjured hand snapped out, and she tried to slap me. I saw the move moment before she made it and was able to grip her small wrist in my hand and I began to squeeze. Some of the fight left Missy's face as the pain registered and she squeaked.

"Are we clear?" I repeated my question.

After a long moment of silence, Missy finally replied, "Fine."

I didn't release her immediately. Instead, I pulled her wrist toward me, causing her body to push against her seatbelt.

"If so much of a word is whispered about what happened or about my brothers and I, well, it won't be hard to get to you in jail. You know we know people." I glared, all the hate and anger in me released for her to actually see now.

Missy's throat worked as she tried to swallow. I knew she was trying to come up with a snappy comeback, but I wasn't waiting for it. I tossed her hand away from me, so hard that he smacked into the car door with a thud. Unlocking the car doors, I went around to her door quickly, to prevent her from trying anything.

I kept the grip on her upper arm as we walked into the station. The cop at the front desk eyed us warily, but I asked for Lee by full name and title. Lee came from the back offices and his eyes widened when he saw me and the woman I was holding.

"Lee, you'll want to arrest this woman for the kidnapping of Brooklyn Reeves."

Cain

I WASN'T sure why I was insisting on staying in the search for Brooklyn. Missy had given the Knights enough information to go on without my continued help. But I couldn't help but picture Brooklyn's smiling face in my mind. Something inside my gut wouldn't let me walk away without seeing her safely away from the bastard that took her.

When I agreed to help Jaxon, I had pulled out all the stops in researching and Brooklyn's face was splashed all over her nonprofit website. I could tell she held a lot of inner turmoil and pain, her smile never completely full or her eyes not reflecting the same emotion. It made me feel drawn to her, even though I knew that wasn't a good thing.

The kitchen of what I called my work house was full of the quiet wrath the Knights seemed to have simmering just below their skin. Losing Brooklyn was breaking them in ways I didn't think they spoke about. Jaxon leaned against the kitchen counter, his arms crossed tightly across his chest. Aiden hadn't stopped pacing since we came out of the basement. Oliver sat at the small kitchen table with his head in his hands.

I nodded to my man that was still there and motioned for him to follow me. Giving him the address Missy had told us, I sent him to recon before we could meet him. After he left, I brought my laptop to the kitchen table. I had long set up my equipment to work in the dark places of the internet, and could work my way through most firewalls to find information I needed.

When I settled on the rental lease for the warehouse, I spun the laptop toward the guys to see.

"She wasn't lying about that. She helped him rent the warehouse. It's not in her name, but a shell company I tied to her earlier."

Aiden bent and quickly took in the information on the lease agreement. He stood and nodded curtly.

"We need to go there."

"Going tonight would be better, yeah?" I said.

I could see the indecision on their faces. Without Gideon there to talk strategy, all of their decisions were being based on emotion now. Even with the slight obsession I was harboring myself, my thoughts were based on fact and planning that wouldn't end up killing us all. There was more to me than the drug dealer the Knights thought they were calling.

"Give me the day. I'll call my guys. Lyle could have more people working with him," I said.

"How many men can you really trust, Cain?" Aiden's voice was speculative, as he pinned me with a questioning stare.

"More than you would assume, man," I replied.

Aiden was one of the biggest question marks for me in the group. Jaxon, Oliver and I grew up together. And though I got out for a short time with my mom, I fell right back where we left off after she died. But by then, the two of them had created an unbreakable bond with Aiden and Gideon. At the time, I felt abandoned and probably a little jealous. Now, I couldn't blame them. Finding your crew in my world should be a top priority.

"Without Randy catching wind of it?" Jaxon's voice was quiet from his place by the counter. He didn't look up with the question.

"My men are separate from Randy's operation. They are paid by me."

That caused Jaxon to glance up, his eyebrow up in question.

"There's a lot for us to catch up on." I nodded, acknowledging his unspoken question.

Truth was, I still reported to Randy on paper, and as far as he knew, I was a loyal soldier. He hadn't figured out yet that I was working to carve out my own space in the city. Something I could run on my own, without his tight fist around my neck. It had taken time for me to work through the men I worked with, to recruit the ones I could trust to keep their mouths shut and have loyalty to me and not the most powerful drug kingpin in the city.

"I see that," Jaxon said.

For the next thirty minutes, I ran through my ideas of the best way to breach the warehouse. We would all have to go in armed and that definitely made at least Oliver uncomfortable. The rumble of my Charger announced Gideon's return, and we had to recap for him. He immediately agreed with my plan to go to the warehouse under the cover of night.

As the discussion continued, Oliver shot out of his chair, the offending furniture falling back and bouncing off the linoleum floor. Everyone's eyes shot to him, his curly hair tousled and standing on end from his pulling on it.

"I can't wait. What if they're gone by the time we get there? We're only giving more time for Lyle to hurt her, or worse, kill her." His voice cracked on the last words and I knew it was cutting deep for his mind to be jumping to worse case scenarios.

Jaxon moved toward Oliver, putting a brotherly arm around his shoulders. For some reason, I felt as if I was spying on a private moment and the discomfort made me look away. Jaxon's voice was only a murmur, but Oliver nodded and turned to pick up the chair he had knocked down. When he sat again, he held his head in his hands, as he had been since we came up from the basement.

Clearing my throat, I sat back in my own chair. "Uh ok, so that's it. I think we would do best going in with minimal numbers, unless something indicates Lyle has a bigger team. I'll have my men on standby, on the off chance this fucker found loyal soldiers somewhere."

I watched as Jaxon and Aiden shared a look. Before Jaxon spoke, I already had a good idea of what he was going to say.

"Cain, this isn't your fight. We appreciate everything you've done to help us get this close. But you can bow out now, not put yourself or your men at risk."

There was no way I could tell Jaxon that it wasn't just about the favor he had asked me for now. I couldn't tell him I badly wanted to see Brooklyn, in the flesh, with my own eyes. My protective instincts were deafening in my mind. I would cut off my own trigger finger before backing off. I was also pretty sure the Knights wouldn't be pleased with my new obsession with their woman, so I had to keep that to myself.

"You're basically blood, man. There's no way I'm not helping you get her back." And that wasn't a lie either, just not all the reasons I wanted to help.

Jaxon jerked his chin in a nod and we decided to go back to their house to wait out the day. I had packed a duffel for my move over to my work house. I hadn't had a moment to unpack and settle in, so I grabbed it and followed the Knights out. They climbed into Jaxon's Tesla and I threw my duffel into the back of my Charger. Before following the guys, I turned back to my man that was standing at the door of the house.

"Pull together the team, just the main guys. I don't want anything loud, yeah?"

"Got it, boss," my man said before disappearing back into the house, shutting the door with a click behind him.

During the drive to the damn mansion the guys lived in, I went over the roster of men in my mind. I definitely trusted them to not alert Randy to what we were working on. I would have to pay them handsomely to get involved with something that could be risking their lives. My hope was this bastard Lyle didn't have a bigger team than just the Knights and I could handle. I had no problem putting my life on the line and I knew none of Brooklyn's men did either.

The gate was open when I arrived, and Jaxon stood by the garage. He motioned toward an empty spot in the huge building that should have been called a hanger and not a garage. I pulled the Charger in, the deep sound of the modified exhaust reverberating inside until I switched off the engine. Jaxon came in and shut the door behind us.

When I got out of the car, he indicated that I follow him. I grabbed my duffel and trailed after him through a door I hadn't seen before. It didn't lead into the house, but into the backyard. My previous visit hadn't warranted a tour of their mansion, so my eyes widened when I saw the huge pool and Jacuzzi that could probably fit fifteen people. Jaxon lead me to a building, detached from the house, on the other side of the pool.

Pushing open the door, Jaxon entered and flicked on a light. Inside, was a small kitchenette and living room with a big screen tv on one wall. A door off the living room revealed a large bedroom with a king sized bed and a huge bathroom fit for a luxury spa, fully stocked with products. I whistled low as I slowly walked around. Jaxon propped himself against the kitchen counter and watched me.

"Look, we don't know how long this will take. We don't have a guest room inside the house. It's Brooklyn's room now. If you want to stay, the pool house is yours for as long as you need it." Jaxon gestured casually around the small house.

I was vaguely uncomfortable with the offer, but I could admit that it would be a good idea to stay close, in case the coming raid didn't go as planned and we didn't find Brooklyn. I was committed to helping them get her back, and from there, I wasn't sure how our relationship had changed.

Nodding, I went into the bedroom and dropped my duffel at the foot of the bed. Back in the main room, I went to the small bar cart and opened a decanter. Holding it up to my nose, I recognized the same expensive booze I had come to expect with the Knights. They had built themselves up from nothing, to become the Club Kings of the city and beyond. I could admire that, even if there was a bit of jealousy there.

"Let's get inside and finalize plans," Jaxon said, walking toward the doors that led back to the pool area.

Inside the house, the first floor was silent and still. All of the guys have gone their own direction. Jaxon nodded toward the stairs, and I followed. He opened a door, but frowned when he didn't find whoever he was looking for. Understanding lit in his eyes and he turned toward a door we had already passed.

This time, when Jaxon entered the room I followed. I was immediately hit with the strong smell of lavender. The bed was huge, larger than anything I had ever seen. Across the room, Oliver stood in front of the window, staring out over the backyard. He didn't move when we entered, and Jaxon went to lay a hand on his shoulder.

"What do you think he's done to her? What he's still doing?" Oliver asked.

Assuming it wasn't me he was talking to, I didn't answer, just continued to look around the room that I was certain was

Brooklyn's. According to Jaxon, she hadn't been living here when she was taken. A fight between them all had sent her packing, and they all regretted it. Whatever the reason, she was still gone. But the room held the memory of her, in her scent, her robe draped over a chair, her clothes still in the closet.

"Cain?" Oliver's voice pulled me from my mind and I looked back over toward the window.

"Yeah?"

"I'm not saying this is something you would do, but with your experience, what do you think he's done to her?" His voice was so broken, it almost hurt me to make eye contact.

"Man, there's no guessing really, ya know?" I hedged my answer, because I knew the things I was thinking were worse than what they could handle imaging.

"Cain!" Oliver's voice rose and banged around the walls of the room.

"From the reports, it's clear he liked to physically abuse her. And from what Jaxon told me, that abuse was sexual in nature a lot of the time. If we get her back alive, which I believe we will, you should be prepared, yeah?"

I could tell my words hit their mark and cut deeply as Oliver flinched and looked away. Jaxon's eyes were just angry, but he wasn't shocked by my words. He had already assumed everything I had said. We all knew what we were going to find when we got their woman back.

Brooklyn

SOMEHOW, the day had passed without another visit from Lyle. I hadn't expected him to get his fill of me so quickly. Every creak of wood, scrape against concrete or what sounded like foot-steps, had me jumping and waiting for him to appear in the room I was held in. My fear was deep and all-consuming, wiping away any thoughts of being rescued or if I would have a life after this. I knew this was the end of me and my subconscious was accepting that.

Dusk began to settle in the room and my entire body felt frozen and on fire at the same time. I was sore in the places Lyle had abused and injured me. But each of my cells was freezing from being naked on the concrete for so long. Even when the sun was up, there wasn't enough light coming into the room to even slightly heat anything. Part of me was angry with the cold, because it continued to remind me I wasn't dead yet. I had to believe that whatever was after death didn't hurt this badly.

My brain was foggy and my thoughts were confused. I was beyond wishing for food or water, knowing Lyle wouldn't give them to me until he absolutely had to. Starving to death would be a long and painful process, so I held out hope that Lyle would end things before it got to that point. There was a disconnect in my mind, causing me to lose time and feel like I was floating above my body at times.

I heard the murmur of voices and this time I was positive I hadn't imagined the sound. Sliding back as far as the ankle restraints would allow, I tried to pull my thighs together. The tightness of the ropes hadn't given at all, no matter how much I pulled. I had no chance if Lyle came back in. I was on display and wide open for him to take whatever he wanted. I wanted to roll over and vomit again, but my stomach was twisted too tightly from the dry heaving I had done the night before. There was nothing left to come up.

In the darkness, I heard someone unlocking the door and suddenly a rectangle of light splashed across the concrete. A figure stepped into the doorway, creating a silhouette that I immediately knew wasn't Lyle. The bulk of the body was too large to be my psycho scrawny ex boyfriend. When the door shut with a thud, the tiny glimmer of hope I had was dashed. The figure slowly walked across the room until he was standing at my feet.

"Lyle thought he was going to make me wait," Buzz's voice cut into my brain.

The words were confusing to me for a moment, but the discussion between the men the night before came back to me. Lyle had promised Buzz a turn with me, though what the man didn't know was Lyle wouldn't share me, no matter what happened. I assumed Lyle wasn't in the building, or Buzz wouldn't take such a chance to try to get what he thought he was owed.

"He'll be angry," I croaked, my voice a shell of what it normally was.

"Fuck him. You aren't going to tell him what I do to you, or I'll make it worse." Buzz kneeled at my feet and I could feel his fingers running around one of my ankles, tracing the rope there.

"He'll know." I badly wanted to rub my throat, try to bring my voice back somehow.

Buzz's fingers left my ankle and worked up my calf, over my knee, to my thigh. When his thumb brushed near my center, I tried to buck away, but that only made Buzz chuckle darkly. He leaned over me then, making his face clear in the darkness. His sneer was predatory, and I tried to buck up to headbutt him. He was too aware of my antics, probably after seeing the bite on Lyle's face, and backed up to avoid the blow.

"You are a wild one. Lyle will enjoy breaking you of all that. I know that's what he plans. But I want you a little wild, makes me hard." Buzz ground his crotch into my stomach and I once again could feel his hardness.

I turned my face away from him, not giving him the satisfaction of the tears that were in my eyes. It was the only piece of defiance I could still have. Fingers grasped my chin, and he forced my head back toward his. He smashed his lips onto mine and I immediately bit him, causing him to pull back and a string of curses left his mouth. Instead of stopping, he grinned down at me with a trickle of blood creeping down from his lip.

To my horror, he began to fumble with his belt, the sound of his zipper as loud as a gunshot in my ears. I heard another noise that I thought was an animal. For a moment I wondered what kind of animal was in the warehouse, but then it occurred to me that the growling and crying was coming from my ruined throat. I thrashed my body the best I could, ignoring the pain as the hard floor cut into my hips, shoulders and arms, where they were secured behind my back.

Buzz tripped in his excitement of trying to get me. It was then, when I could see behind him, that I realized the door was open again. A shadowy figure, hunched, crept up behind Buzz. My eyes were locked on the figure, unable to decipher if they were another of Lyle's people or Lyle himself. As it approached, the figure straightened to a towering height, and I knew it wasn't Lyle.

The flash of silver was almost lost in the darkness, but I didn't miss the way Buzz's body froze in an instant.

"What the fuck?" Buzz's voice was high pitched and laced with fear that felt like a balm over my body. I wanted him to be as afraid as I felt.

"Did he touch you?" The voice wasn't recognizable to me, but I knew he was addressing me.

I shook my head, assuming the figure could see me. Lyle had probably given instructions to other people to ensure I wasn't touched, and this man just caught Buzz before he could get his pants completely down. Suddenly, Buzz's body disappeared, as the large figure tossed him to the side. I could hear Buzz sputtering on the ground and the figure followed. The sound of flesh hitting flesh reached my ears until only the figure stood alone against the light of the doorway and Buzz's body was a crumpled ball on the ground.

The shadowed figure walked toward me and I could see a blade in one of his hands. I started to struggle again, afraid that he was going to use the metal on me. Abruptly, one of my ankle restraints went limp, and I was able to pull my legs closed. My hips ached, and the movement felt difficult. My other ankle went free as well and suddenly the man was kneeling near my feet, slowly coming closer.

"No, no, stay away," I tried to say. My voice came out rough and unrecognizable.

All at once, the room became awash with light. I squeezed my eyes shut, unable to handle the amount of light shining on my face. I felt a touch on my shoulder and I shimmied away, making small noises of protest.

"Shhhh, it's ok. I'm here to help," the man said.

I peeked one eye open, forcing myself to handle the light so I could see my newest attacker. This man didn't look like anyone I would assume was with Lyle. Kind hazel eyes peered at me, though the rest of him looked rough. Most of his exposed skin was covered in tattoos, including a skull on his throat. A lip ring glinted in the light, something that caught my attention for a moment. His flop of blue hair did little to make him seem less imposing, especially with the bloody knuckles he now had.

He reached out one of his hands again, the other holding a phone to his ear, and I cried out and moved back, unable to accept that he was actually there to help me. I felt like I was in the middle of a nightmare, a game concocted by Lyle, to break me down until I gave in and became the obedient little girl he wanted. I knew this man was another test, something I could fail and pay the price for later. If I took his help, Lyle would make me hurt in ways I wasn't sure I would live through.

Aiden

WE COULDN'T HANDLE WAITING around the house longer than necessary. Cain was right, that we needed to wait for the cover of darkness, but sitting in the house, thinking about what could be happening to Brooklyn, was making us all too unstable. I dressed in all black, slipping my small handgun at the small of my back. I didn't have need of it on many occasions, but there was no way I was walking into the warehouse without being armed.

Sitting in Cain's Charger, the five of us were silent, willing the sun to go down faster. We were parked in a place where we could see movement to and from the warehouse. We hadn't seen anyone come or go and we weren't sure what kind of sign that was. Cain had a group of men posted two blocks away in a black van, waiting for our call if we needed back up.

The moment the streetlights came on, my brothers and I climbed from the car. Cain followed closely, ready to go to war with us if necessary to get Brooklyn back. I could appreciate the help. We had no idea what Lyle had cooked up with Missy and possibly Jaxon's father as well. The possible connections were something we would have to worry about later. Right now, we dealt with what was right in front of us and that was the possibility of rescuing the woman that had captured all of our hearts.

Gideon took the lead at the door, opening it and swinging his gun down the two halls before we followed him in.

"That was a bit too easy, yeah?" Cain's voice was a low whisper behind me.

I nodded, but didn't answer. I did think the doors would have been locked, keeping secure what Lyle had taken. If the doors were wide open and no one was inside, did that mean we were too late?

"We need to split up," Gideon said.

We didn't know the layout of the warehouse and the idea of splitting off from my brothers made me anxious. I could see from how Oliver shifted nervously that he wasn't thrilled with the prospect either.

"Teams?" Cain suggested.

I nodded my agreement. Gideon and I paired off while Jaxon and Oliver headed off in a different direction. That left Cain alone, but he grinned like a goofball and ran off. The hallway Gideon and I went down had an old office and supply storage. Both rooms were filled with leftovers from whatever company used the building before.

We took a second hallway that lead to a loading dock and

rolling door. As we were about to enter, voices could be heard and Gideon stopped, causing me to almost run into his back. He peered around the corner and then motioned that there were two people inside.

"Lyle?" My voice was barely a breath, but Gideon heard and shook his head no.

There was no reason for us to confront them until necessary. If we made too much noise, we could alert Lyle to our presence. Backtracking, Gideon and I found ourselves back at the door we started at. The hallways and rooms were fairly dark, with the building seeming to run on limited power, likely another way to not draw attention.

Without an idea of where to go, we went down the hall that Cain had taken. Suddenly, all the main lights came on in the building. The surprise had me pulling my weapon. Standing back and to back with Gideon, we waited for any sort of attack that could be coming. When no one seemed to attack, we slowly began to move again.

A vibration in my pocket had me hesitating and pulling out my phone. Cain's name was on the screen, and I quickly answered.

"Hmm?"

"I found her. But you need to get here. Send someone to my car for the keys in the glove box. She's in handcuffs." Cain was speaking rapidly and quietly.

"Got it. I'm headed to you." I clicked end and turned to Gideon.

"Go back to the car. Keys in the glove box. Need them. Be quick. Cain found her," I said.

Gideon started to turn down the hall instead of toward the door. I grabbed his arm and made him swing back to me.

"I know you need to get to her, but we need the keys. She's handcuffed. We don't know her mental state. I need to do this."

After everything that had gone wrong with Brooklyn and me, my insides were screaming to save her, to fix it, to protect. So much of what caused her to leave was my fault. I had agonized over how I would ever make it up to her. It could already be too late, but I wouldn't let myself think about that.

Gideon's face took on a desperate look, and he pleaded with me without words. I just motioned toward the door and took off at a run down the hall. I knew Gideon would get the keys because we needed them for Brooklyn. I could barely breathe as I ran, looking for the door that was open.

When I found the room, I froze just inside, taking in the scene in front of me. A man was crumpled in a corner, looking knocked out, so I didn't spare him more than a glance. At the wall, Cain was crouched, with a hand out as if he was approaching a wild animal. Against the wall, in a tiny ball, was a naked Brooklyn. Her arms trapped behind her, she tried to stand, but collapsed again. She was begging, but her voice didn't sound right and when I got closer, I saw why. Her throat was ringed with dark purple bruises.

White hot fury shot through my system as I took in her injuries. I couldn't even speak, my own voice trapped in my throat that felt like it was closing. Cain looked up at me as I approached. All of a sudden, Brooklyn's eyes locked on me and she burst into tears and slumped against the wall.

"Aiden... Aiden," she cried through her tears.

Snapping out of my ice, I ripped off my shirt and crouched in front of her. I pulled the fabric over her head, to at least cover her as best as I could, before carefully reaching down to pull her into my lap. Her blonde hair was matted and blood stained in places. There was a piece of fabric tied around one of her thighs and it was blood soaked. I feared what was under it.

Cain had left, keeping guard at the door. Brooklyn tried to burrow into my chest, but when I lifted my arms around her, she froze. I carefully laid my hands on my thighs, allowing her to take the comfort she needed, however she could. Heavy footsteps behind me caused Brooklyn to shoot away from me and land in a heap on the ground again.

"Sweetheart, no, it's ok." I reached out to help her up.

When Brooklyn was able to see who had approached, she began to cry again in earnest. Gideon rushed to her, immediately pulling out the keys and going behind her to release her wrists. She cried out in pain as her arms dropped. Carefully, I helped her thread her arms through my shirt, and Gideon immediately scooped her into his arms.

"We need to get her to the hospital," I said, my voice feeling thick in my throat.

"There's going to be questions," Gideon replied.

"Fuck the questions. She needs a doctor."

Brooklyn had laid her head on Gideon's shoulder, and seemed to pass out. I touched her cheek lightly, and she jumped. When she opened her eyes and was reminded she was safe, she relaxed again. Gideon and I made eye contact over her head, and I could read the pain all over him.

We made our way to the doorway just as Oliver and Jaxon appeared. Oliver had a split lip and his hair was in disarray. Jaxon's knuckles were busted. Neither of them paid attention to their injuries. As soon as their eyes landed on Brooklyn, they both rushed forward. I put up a hand to slow them down.

"She's a bit jumpy. Give her space until she's more awake."

"We're here, baby," Oliver murmured when he was within earshot.

Brooklyn weakly lifted her head again and looked around. She didn't show any emotion when she knew she was surrounded by us. Her eyes were empty and her face was a void. Her withdrawal made me nervous, but I had to push away all of my pain to care for the woman in front of us.

Cain walked back to the man that was still knocked out on the ground. I heard the click of the cuffs and then a whoosh of air as Cain kicked the man in the gut. When he met my eye, I could see the fire in his gaze. If we didn't have to worry about the cops coming to the warehouse, the man likely wouldn't still be alive.

"I'll wait with the trash, take my car, take her to the hospital. Send your detective, Gideon, yeah?" Cain said.

Jaxon walked over to Cain and they shared a few quiet words before they shook hands and Jaxon pulled Cain in for a hug. Even though I didn't know the man as well as my brother, I was tempted to hug him, too. By the looks of things, the man he had beaten had been trying to drop his pants and I couldn't let my mind go to the things he would have done to her if Cain hadn't found her.

My brothers and I surrounded Gideon and Brooklyn as we made our way to the door. When we swung it open, Brooklyn's head shot up and her eyes went wild as she looked around.

"Where is he? He's going to come. He's going to kill me!"

"Shhhh, stellina, no. He's not here. We looked. And he'll never get near you again. I promise you that." Gideon moved, so he was whispering directly in her ear. I could see her body tense at his closeness, but his words did calm her slightly.

In the car, Jaxon took the driver's seat and Oliver immediately went to the front passenger seat. I slid into the backseat and waited for Gideon to hand Brooklyn in. But when he tried to put her down, she screamed, the sound coming out raw and broken. She clawed at him, trying to make sure she stayed in his arms. He spoke to her quietly again, rocking her almost like a baby, before clumsily sitting down with her in his lap.

Oliver had turned almost completely around in the seat, panic on his face. I could see tears in his eyes and I looked away, choked by my own emotions. Gideon's neck was covered in scratches, some that were welling with blood now, but he didn't loosen his grip on Brooklyn. She was curled into his lap, pulling my shirt over her legs, trying to cocoon herself in the fabric.

The silence in the car was practically unbearable. I looked up at Oliver again, who hadn't turned back around. I realized I didn't know how his lip got split.

"What happened to you two?"

Oliver didn't register my question, still staring at Brooklyn. But Jaxon spoke from the driver's seat as he sped through the warehouse district.

"We ran into two in a loading dock. Somehow, we didn't see them or hear them before they realized we were there. The lights came on, surprising us, and then they attacked. They weren't very skilled fighters, so it didn't take long. Oliver's face was a lucky punch."

"Sounds like the same guys we saw, but didn't approach. Where did you leave them?"

"In the loading dock. Neither of them had much to say." Jaxon sped through a stop sign and followed the road that spilled into the city.

The words none of us were saying were that Lyle wasn't in the warehouse, which meant he was in the wind again. There were so many unanswered questions that I could only hope Gideon's detective friend could get answers out of Missy or one of Lyle's men.

Brooklyn

I KNEW THEM, by their smells. I could hear their voices, but I wasn't sure I trusted just that. I had heard their voices in my mind before. But their smells, that wasn't something that could be faked. My face was pressed against the skin of Gideon's throat and I just kept trying to breathe, his clean soap smell; faint, but it was there and it was uniquely Gideon.

The further we got away from the warehouse, the more safe I felt, but my levels of despair were raising to tsunami levels. What was going to happen when the Knights found out about what Lyle had done to me, to my body? Would they look at me in disgust and push me away the moment they found out? How could they love my body as they did before, if I couldn't even stomach the idea of seeing myself in a mirror? What about the lost time, where I had no idea what had happened to me?

The car slid around a corner, and Gideon grunted as we were thrown against the door. I lifted my head slightly to look around the car. I was afraid to have Gideon set me down before we were away from the warehouse. Now that we were putting distance between me and my living nightmare, I was feeling more comfortable.

I started to move, to sit on the seat, but Gideon's arms tightened around me. Without thinking, I tried to pull away. Gideon's face came down until his mouth was near my ear, his breath tickling my neck. The feeling caused me to freeze and fear to course through my body.

"Stellina, it's ok. Just sit still until we get to the hospital." His voice was whispered and soothing.

"Gideon." It was all I could choke out without pain to my throat.

"Yes, I'm here. We're all here. We have you. You're safe." He said the words as if it was a mantra he wanted me to remember.

He didn't understand the anguish in my voice. I knew who I was with. I knew I was away from Lyle for the moment. The pain that I was feeling was more than physical or about my safety. It was knowing that it was inevitable that they would know what had happened to me. My skin itched and felt stretched too far. I wished I could put distance between myself and Gideon, that I could hide in Aiden's shirt and disappear.

When I heard how Oliver and Jaxon had been attacked, I wanted to express how thankful I was that they were both alright. When I saw them, I knew something wasn't right, but it was too hard to focus and see the injury on Oliver's face or the bruising on Jaxon's knuckles. They had put themselves at risk to save me. I had known they would, but I felt the weight of guilt for what they must have had to go through to find me.

When the bright lights of the city began to flash by the window, my head started to lull to the side, my body was exhausted, drained from being on edge and trying to recover from my injuries. I was jolted awake when the car came to a stop outside the hospital. I could see a doctor and nurse waiting with a wheelchair at the door. When we stopped, they started forward.

"We called ahead, sweetheart." Aiden's voice caused me to jump and when I looked over at him, I saw the hint of pain on his face before he controlled it.

His torso was bare, reminding me I wasn't wearing anything but his t-shirt. I fumbled with the hem of the shirt again and looked at the doctor.

"We can get you a blanket before you get out of the car," Aiden motioned toward the emergency room entrance.

I didn't try to speak, just nodded, thankful he understood my worry without me having to explain it. Aiden, shirtless and imposing, climbed out of the car and approached the doctor. The nurse nodded and rushed back inside. A moment later, the woman appeared with a hospital blanket. When she tried to step toward the car, Aiden intercepted her and held out his hand. There were words exchanged, but Aiden wasn't backing down.

The nurse relented and held out the blanket to Aiden. He turned and came to the side of the car Gideon and I were sitting on. Carefully, he popped open the door and unfolded the blanket.

"Just step out here, sweetheart. No one will see you and we'll get you wrapped up."

Slowly, Gideon turned me toward the door. He held out a hand, and I grasped it as I lower my legs, until my toes could scrape the sidewalk. The process was slow, but none of them tried to move me faster. Oliver and Jaxon watched silently from the front seats and Aiden stood with the blanket wide open the entire time.

As I stood, my legs started to buckle, but Gideon's hands were on my hips immediately, keeping me standing as he climbed out of the car behind me. My hands landed on Aiden's warm chest as he wrapped the blanket around me. Despite the situation, I could tell my touch had an effect, as goosebumps pebbled across his skin. And in that moment, I wanted so badly to lean into him and just let his warmth suffuse me.

The sound of car doors slamming caused me to jerk back, and Gideon's arms came around me to steady me. Oliver and Jaxon came to stand on either side of me, both of their eyes taking in our surroundings. I realized they were keeping watch, that even here at the hospital they were worried about my safety. Aiden finished wrapping me up and stepped back to give me my space.

"Go ahead. We'll stay with you the entire way." Gideon's soft voice flowed over my shoulder.

"Just look at me, look into my eyes. Don't pay attention to anything else around. Let us worry about everything else," Aiden said.

His gray eyes locked with mine and I was lost in the emotions swirling there. I could see the concern and the hard edge of anger. His features softened, encouraging me to move forward. Carefully, I stepped forward, feeling my body and what I was able to do. I hissed quietly at the stretch of the cuts on my thigh. Aiden immediately stopped, and I looked down at the ground.

A soft touch under my chin forced my face up. Aiden was closer now, and he was demanding my full attention.

"I can carry you, or we can take all the time you need."

I shook my head and took another step, Aiden stepping back at the same time, as if we were locked into some sort of dance.

"Sir, you can't leave that car there," the nurse called to Jaxon.

I looked over at him, fearful that he was going to leave my side, leave me vulnerable. But all he did was look at me with an encouraging smile before looking at the nurse.

"Once she's settled in a room, and we know she's completely safe, I'll move the car. Or you can do it."

The nurse scoffed, but the doctor just shook her head to stop the conversation. The distraction of the conversation helped me forget about walking and before I realized it, Aiden was moving to the side for the wheelchair. Since my arms were trapped inside the blanket, Gideon helped me sit and then bent to slowly put my feet up, mindful of my injuries.

When the doctor turned the wheelchair and started inside, the Knights stayed around me, with a shirtless Aiden leading the way inside. It was a tight squeeze in the elevator, but none of the guys would wait for the next one, insisting they were to stay at my side until I was safe. The doctor took us to a quiet floor, and Aiden spoke with a nurse at a desk in quiet tones, giving them all of my information. He pulled out my wallet, which Lyle must have left on the sidewalk, giving my insurance card over.

I was wheeled into a stark white room with one bed and no windows. Gideon, Jaxon and Oliver followed, while Aiden found a shirt and worked out the paperwork.

"Miss Reeves, I'm going to help transfer you to the bed. Do you think you can climb up on your own?" The doctor pushed the wheelchair next to the bed and locked the wheels.

I looked over, but before I could answer, Gideon came to my side.

"May I, stellina?"

I looked up at my big man, read each new line on his face, the way his hair was hastily pulled into a bun, the dark circles under his eyes. I was surprised by the sudden ache that squeezed my heart, thinking I was completely lost, that my ability to care about anything was gone. But here I was, thinking about how sad I was that Gideon had suffered.

"Please." My voice was the same harsh croak, but Gideon smiled and his big arms slid under me.

Without effort, he placed me into the center of the bed and the nurse removed the wheelchair, leaving more room for Jaxon and Oliver to be inside with us. I looked at them all and took a moment to really see what hadn't registered before. Oliver and Jaxon looked as bad as Gideon did, Oliver worse with the split lip and bruise starting to blossom on his face. They had all suffered, been in pain while I was gone, and it was my fault. And I knew that the pain was going to get worse when they knew for sure what Lyle had done to me.

The doctor started with softly touching my throat, causing me to wince. She then probed the bruises on my face and ran her hands over my scalp, which caused me to hiss in pain when she came into contact with the knot Lyle had caused.

"I don't feel any obvious breaks, but we'll need an x-ray to be sure. I need to remove the blanket, is that ok?" The doctor looked around the room after asking me the question.

I couldn't make eye contact with the guys. When the door opened and closed softly, I knew without looking that Aiden had joined us. Eventually, I nodded and started to pull my arms from my wrapping, waiting for the doctor to move on. She pointed toward my thigh that was wrapped in a red stained piece of clothing. It was the first moment I was so terribly afraid of, knowing the Knights would see the brand, something they would never be able to unsee if they stayed with me.

Nodding, I squeezed my eyes shut. The doctor was gentle, and the nurse joined again, assisting and holding my hand. I knew the wound was exposed when I heard a hushed curse and a gasp of breath. Something metal loudly clanged, and it made my eyes pop open and I jumped in the bed. Gideon was standing with his back to me, his shoulders heaving with his breathing, the small metal side table laying across the room on its side.

"Gentlemen, if you can't control yourself, you're going to have to leave." The doctor didn't cower when Gideon turned and fixed her in his fierce gaze. Instead, she turned to address me in a softer tone. "These are likely going to need stitches —"

"No." The one word held power, and it stopped the doctor in her tracks. Aiden moved closer.

"Sir, these are still bleeding. They need to be closed."

"Are you a plastic surgeon?" Aiden asked.

"Well no, but —"

"Then you aren't sewing one stitch into her skin, are we clear?" Aiden was right next to me now, his hands on the plastic railing, his grip causing the material to squeal.

"I'm not sure who you think you are, but you can't decide on my patient's medical treatment." I had to give the doctor credit. I couldn't imagine anyone else standing up to Aiden when he was being so imposing.

"We need the best plastic surgeon in the city. I don't give a shit how expensive, we'll pay whatever we need. And that will be the only person putting stitches into her. Close it for now, without anything that will scar," Aiden immediately said.

The doctor sputtered and looked to the nurse, but there was no support there. She looked at Aiden again, looking as if she was going to continue to argue. But Aiden held up his hand, shutting her up before she was able to open her mouth.

"There is no fucking way I'll sit by and have her living with that on her body. You get to calling who you need to." Aiden crossed his arms across his chest, staring down at the doctor.

She looked down at me and I nodded, not making eye contact with anyone, but showing my agreement with Aiden. If Lyle's brand could be removed and leave me without more scars to live with, I wanted that. The doctor sighed and leaned down near my ear, clearly trying to have a private conversation with just me.

"I'm sorry because I need to ask a question and you may want to be alone for the conversation."

I knew what she wanted to ask me, what tests were probably necessary, the invasion of my body that was going to continue.

Without looking up, I took a deep breath, to force a few words through my injured throat, "Please leave."

CHAPTER
Thirty-Seven

Oliver

FOR A MOMENT, I wasn't sure who Brooklyn was speaking to. She wouldn't look at any of us. My brothers and I all stood and stared at her. The doctor, who seemed to know something we didn't, stood next to her and wasn't budging. The rush of anger that I felt wasn't fair, I knew, but I couldn't help it.

"Sweetheart, let us help," Aiden said.

Brooklyn didn't look up at him, just shook her head.

"You can't. Please go." Her voice was a small whisper, the only sound she seemed to be able to make without much pain.

The bruises ringing her throat, the cuts on her leg, the injuries we hadn't seen yet, made me want to find Lyle and tear him limb from limb. In the same thought, I wanted to crawl into the small hospital bed with Brooklyn and cradle her bruised body against mine, and try to heal everything for her. Now, she was telling us to leave her again.

Without a word, I turned and grabbed the door handle, yanking it with more strength than necessary. The hospital door bounced off the wall with a slam and I stalked out without looking back. Jaxon called my name, but I didn't slow until I got to the elevator and was stabbing the down button.

All three of my brothers arrived before the elevator did and we piled in together. On the ground floor, we stood aimlessly, none of us really sure what we were supposed to do now.

"I'm going to move Cain's car," Jaxon murmured before walking back into the night.

Aiden scrubbed a hand over his face, exhaustion seeping into his features as he leaned against the wall in the waiting room. Gideon collapsed into a chair.

"Did you see that?" Gideon's voice was strained.

"We all fucking saw it," Aiden said.

I didn't respond, just started to pace back and forth between the chairs. Seeing the injuries to Brooklyn made bile rise in my throat. The condition she was in told me that Lyle was likely not planning on letting her go or live any normal life. He wanted a prisoner, and he treated her like one.

"Why do you think she wants us to leave her again?" My voice was more demanding than I meant for it to be.

"I'm afraid there's more she doesn't want us to know," Gideon said.

Jaxon entered the hospital again, this time with Cain in tow. I stopped pacing long enough to hear him tell us what happened at the warehouse.

"I had my guys give me a ride over after we saw the cops go into the warehouse. They brought out the three guys we handled. No sign of Lyle. I didn't hang out to chat with them. I wouldn't say we have that kinda relationship, yeah? Where's Brooklyn? She getting tests or something?"

Gideon stood with his phone and walked away from us, which I presumed meant he was calling his detective. They had Missy in custody and now three of Lyle's men. They needed to track that bastard down. I watched Gideon from a distance and I could tell he was getting heated on the phone, nothing less than what the police force deserved. They couldn't even be trusted to find a missing person, let alone a kidnapper.

"What do you think Gideon meant? That's there's stuff Brooklyn doesn't want us to know?" I asked.

"She was naked, Oliver," Aiden said as he turned to look out the window.

In a whirlwind, it occurred to me what he was implying. I began to gag and sprinted for the exit of the hospital. Outside, I took deep breaths of the cold air, pushing down the vomit that threatened to rise up. I knew exactly what Aiden was implying and my head throbbed with the reality of what Brooklyn had endured when we weren't there to protect her.

Turbulent guilt roiled in my stomach, and I looked up into the night sky. The city lights prevented anything from shining down, but I tried to imagine the stars, the freedom of the night sky. A scrape of a shoe behind me made me look over my shoulder. I wasn't even surprised to see Jaxon just outside the doors.

"Are you ok?" He asked.

"Stupid ass question, Jaxon."

"I know. None of us are ok. Least of all Brooklyn." He moved forward until he was standing next to me.

"I was so angry with her, a part of me still is, for leaving us again. But I never would have wanted something like this to happen to her." I covered my mouth, upset that the words were even uttered at all.

"Of course not. We all know that," Jaxon said.

"But does she? Does she know we don't blame her? That we aren't angry with her?"

Jaxon looked over at me, his eyes understanding as he studied me. I was sure I looked a mess. I hadn't looked in a mirror, but knew my mouth was sore and I tasted blood sometimes when I swiped my lip with my tongue. I had to look away as tears stung my eyes.

"We'll tell her, as soon as she lets us talk to her," he said.

The overwhelming feelings I had for Brooklyn were hard to become accustomed to. I had never been in a relationship with someone, other than my brothers, where I would lay down my life for them. Being in love with her seemed like a lame way to look at it, but there weren't really other words for it. Since Missy, I had dated randomly, but not one woman touched me as deeply as Brooklyn had since the moment I met her. Once she was healed and on the road to recovery, I was going to have to make sure she knew what I felt for her.

A small woman exploded out of a cab and ran up to us. It took me a full moment to realize it was Brooklyn's roommate, Ash. She had been crying, but was pulling it together when she stopped in front of us.

"Gideon called me! Where is she?"

"I'll take you," Jaxon said, putting a supporting hand on her back as he lead her inside.

I followed quietly behind and stayed in the waiting room while Jaxon and Ash disappeared in the elevator. I hoped Brooklyn felt supported with Ash there, hoped she let her in, lean on her. Because I knew with what my girl was going through, she was going to need all the people that loved her.

Brooklyn

"DO YOU NEED A SEXUAL ASSAULT EXAM?"

The doctor's voice was soft and kind. When I quickly met her gaze, her sentiment was in her eyes as well. Maybe I didn't know everything that had been done to my body, but I knew who was responsible. Why did I need tests? Why did I need someone poking and prodding at my body even more?

Before I could answer, there was a soft knock at the door. The doctor went and blocked the view from whoever was on the other side. She turned to look at me.

"Your roommate, Ash, is here. Would you like to see her?"

I nodded and gripped my hands together tightly in my lap. Ash pushed past the doctor as soon as she could and the door was shut again. My friend rushed to my side and dropped into a chair so she was at my level. When I didn't look over at her, shame drowning me, Ash's hand found mine. She pulled one of my hands free and laced her fingers with mine.

Immediately, I burst into tears. I looked over at my best friend and I could see tears were streaming down her face too.

"I didn't think I'd see you again," she said.

"I'm soo..rrr...yyy," I sobbed.

Ash stood and leaned over to hug me, cradling my head against her shoulder.

"You have nothing to be sorry for. Don't you dare say that. You were taken, kidnapped. You couldn't have done anything."

We cried together for a few moments when a clearing throat caught my attention. It was the doctor standing at the end of my bed, watching me sympathetically.

"I'm sorry. I know this is really hard. But we can't wait for too long to handle the exam."

"What exam?" Ash asked.

"Maybe rape," I whispered.

To her credit, Ash kept her face schooled and looked over at the doctor.

"She'll need that as evidence to prosecute this motherfucker, right?"

"Unfortunately, rape cases tend to be he said, she said cases. Physical evidence gives power to the victim to ensure whatever the attacker tries to claim isn't given weight. The evidence is something you should want to obtain, Ms. Reeves." The doctor reached down and carefully laid her hand on my leg in comfort.

I looked over at Ash, not sure I could make the decision on my own. My mind understood the practical need, to ensure that Lyle got whatever punishment possible. But I wasn't sure I could put my body through the process of an exam.

"I'm right here, honey. I'll stay the whole time. This is important. I know it's hard and scary. But Lyle needs to be nailed to the fucking wall."

The sound of curse words coming from Ash was almost comical, and if we were in any other situation, I would have laughed. However, the determination on Ash's face gave me enough courage to nod my head slightly to the doctor. The woman squeezed my shin slightly before leaving the room to get a nurse. Ash sat back down, holding my hand the whole time while we waited in silence.

Some time later, a nurse came back into the room with the doctor. They had a bag and a number of instruments, including a camera. I stared at it, wondering what the point of that was, and the doctor caught my attention.

"We need photos of the injuries, Ms. Reeves."

My body shuddered as I thought about the documentation of the worst moment of my life. Ash squeezed my hand and brought it to her face to kiss my knuckles kindly.

"Do you want me to get any of the guys?" She said.

I shook my head forcefully. "I don't want them to see any of this."

"Sweetie, they are down in the waiting room. I don't think they're going to leave." Ash reached up to brush my hair out of my face, but the doctor quickly asked her not to.

"I can't...I don't want to see the disgust on their faces." Tears began to slip down my cheeks again.

"Oh, Brooklyn. They aren't going to look at you like that. You know that. I'm pretty sure those men love you."

"They won't anymore," I said, my voice barely audible.

Ash didn't respond, but I knew she had heard me. Her face took on a hard look for a moment, but she clearly knew the argument wasn't what I needed at the moment. The doctor and nurse collected the bloody clothing I had put around my wound, as well as Aiden's shirt. Both went into an evidence bag and were sealed.

"The shirt, it wasn't from..." I tried to say. I was worried about Aiden's DNA getting mixed into the investigation.

"I know. We'll note that. But just in case anything carried over from you to the shirt, we want to be sure we have it," the doctor said.

I nodded and watched them proceed. First, the doctor took photos of my leg and I turned to squeeze my eyes closed. Ash let me squeeze her hand as I tried to ignore the click of the camera shutter. The doctor asked me to look straight, as she wanted to get photos of the bruises around my throat. She carefully moved my matted hair away, and the camera began to click again.

When it was time for the pelvic exam, I laid back as instructed, with Ash by my head. The doctor talked to me quietly as she opened swabs and took the samples she needed. Then she prodded my vagina in ways that caused me pain, and I began to hyperventilate and cry. Suddenly, I was back in the warehouse and Lyle was touching my body, causing tearing and pain. I tried to close my legs, but the doctor called my name a little louder this time.

"Ms. Reeves! You're ok. You're safe. I know this hurts and I'm sorry. I just need to make sure you don't need any sutures. I will give you an antibiotic ointment to help prevent any infections. We're also going to test for STDs."

I covered my mouth as I cried out, realizing that illness hadn't even entered my mind.

"Ash... I'm going to throw up." I pointed toward a small bowl they had sitting at the side of the bed.

My friend hurriedly grabbed the bowl and brought it to my face. I started to dry heave, nothing but bile coming up in a burning wave. Between the heaving, I sobbed, thinking about the implications of what Lyle could have done to my body, things that would last the rest of my life.

"Can you tell... if he..." I couldn't spit out the words, I could barely allow the image into my mind.

"Unfortunately, there's no way to know that at this moment. The swabs will be tested for semen and we can make sure you get those results." The doctor spoke quietly, as if she was trying to keep me as calm as possible.

My heart pounded in my ears and I couldn't understand how I couldn't know what had happened to my own body. How strong had the drugs been if I had stayed passed out while my body was violated? Having to be tested for STDs caused another thought to pop into my head. Though I had an IUD and had unprotected sex with the Knights, I realized I couldn't risk anything.

"I need the morning-after pill," I said.

The doctor nodded and tapped into a handheld tablet before handing it over to the nurse. She continued her exam, combing through the short pubic hair I did have and collecting other samples from around my vaginal area. The process was demeaning and painful. The tears continued to come as I laid there, at the mercy of the doctor.

Two hours later, the doctor finally announced they were done with all the evidence collection. My thigh was covered in gauze and a clear adhesive to keep it dry until the plastic surgeon could arrive. Apparently, Aiden had the money or pull necessary to get someone out of bed and driving to the hospital immediately.

After wheeling me in and out of the room for an x-ray of my neck, I was getting settled in a bigger room on a different floor than ICU. I wondered how much of that was also Aiden's influence, as we walked by many rooms that held multiple patients. I wouldn't argue with privacy, not after the horror I had been through and the waking nightmare my life felt like.

"Would you like to shower, Ms. Reeves?" The nurse asked.

The idea of washing away the filth I felt all over my skin was the best thing I could think to do at the moment. I nodded, and the nurse gave me a soft smile. With the help of Ash, I was led to the bathroom behind a door that hadn't been opened. The nurse handed me two towels, washcloths, and a set of scrubs. Ash sat on the toilet while I stepped under the spray.

As the hot water washed down my body, I felt myself start to shake. Sobs that were stuck in my chest began to bubble up and I couldn't stop them from erupting. I leaned against the wall and slowly slid until I was on the cold ground of the small shower.

"Brooklyn, what can I do?" Ash asked from the other side of the shower curtain.

I couldn't breathe enough to answer her. I slammed my hand against the wall, slapping at the tiles, screaming through my wrecked throat. I bent and rocked in a ball under the water, crying for myself, what I had lost, what I could never get back. I cried for how Lyle had ruined another part of my life, ruined another chapter, when I had worked so hard to make myself someone that could love and be loved.

The shower curtain was pulled to the side, and I expected to see Ash standing there, but instead, it was Jaxon. He was naked, except for his boxer briefs and I felt confusion distract me for a moment. But in the next instance, he was on the ground with me, wrapping me in his strong arms and rocking with me as I cried. I didn't want his pity. In my mind I wanted to push him away and wallow in my misery. My body didn't agree, and I laced my fingers with his and pulled his arm around me tighter.

"Shhhh, love. I'm here. Cry, scream, get it out however you need to," he said, his mouth moving against my wet hair.

I leaned us to the side until I could press my hot face against the cold wall. Jaxon didn't stop me, just moved with me, keeping close, but not touching me except his arms. I wasn't sure I was prepared to be fully embraced by any of them, wasn't sure they would want to once they knew what had happened to me.

"Why are you in here?" I asked.

The question came out harsh, my limited voice not helping how the words cut.

"Where else would I be?" Jaxon said.

"Running away from me. I told you, I warned you, I'm not

worth the trouble." The tears began to flow faster again, causing me to sniffle and moan as my bruised face hurt and my throat burned.

"You're hurting right now. You know how I feel about you. I'm not running. I'm here to help." To accent his words, his arms flexed around me and I finally gave in and let myself fall into his body.

The moment Jaxon's skin was against mine, I didn't feel as dirty. He represented good, clean, happiness and light. If I let him, he would infuse it all into me while we sat there. If I let myself open up, tell them my feelings and what was going on inside, maybe we could move on.

But I knew it wasn't that easy. I could pretend with just Jaxon, inside the shower, that things were going to be ok. He didn't know everything yet. He still cared about me now, didn't look at me in disgust or feel that I was ruined. I knew it was coming. Lyle's goal was to ruin me for the Knights, and he has succeeded.

Slowly, I calmed down. When I was ready, I tapped Jaxon's arm, letting him know I wanted to stand up. Together, with me leaning on Jaxon, we stood under the shower spray. Without saying a word or touching me more than needed, Jaxon began to wash my hair.

I turned to rinse the shampoo, and I kept my eyes clenched shut, so I didn't have to look into his eyes. The silence was trapping me inside my inner thoughts and it was driving me crazy.

"Did Ash call you?" I asked.

"Yeah. She didn't know what to do." He turned me again so he could work conditioner into my ragged locks.

"And you did." I said the words as a statement, not a question, because the truth was he did exactly what I needed in that moment.

"I took a guess. You could have told me to fuck off." I didn't open my eyes as he spoke, but I could picture the small smile he likely had on his face.

"I guess I could have," I said with a shrug of my shoulder.

"I will always be there for you because I know what it's like to have no one there for me," Jaxon murmured.

My eyes were closed and my head was down, but I heard his words clearly. I wanted to lean into him, lay my cheek against his chest. But I couldn't handle the contact and he didn't try to force his touch on me.

After letting the conditioner sit on my hair for a few minutes, Jaxon massaged my scalp under the water. He stood close to me, the hair on his chest tickling my breasts, his thighs brushing against mine. Though I noticed all of these sensations, I couldn't feel anything at the moment. I did feel pain in my heart, knowing I had lost what I had with them.

I took the body wash from Jaxon, afraid I would breakdown if his hands ran over my body. I avoided my injured thigh, but scrubbed the rest of my skin roughly. As the skin began to become pink and then angry red, Jaxon's hands reach out for mine, stopping my movements.

"You're clean, love."

I knew he was wrong. I would never be clean again.

Jaxon

IT TOOK everything in me to control my feelings. When I rushed to the room at the request of Ash, I hadn't been prepared for what I'd found. It was clear Brooklyn, my love, was far away from me, even while she stood in front of me. To shoulder what she was processing, I had to push my own heartbreak and anger to the side.

Her face held none of the hope, happiness, or what I believed was love, that I had come to adore. Once the shower was over, she wrapped herself in the small hospital towel and walked away from me, never actually meeting my eye. I quickly dried with the towel that was left. Dressing without my boxer briefs, I slipped my clothes back on.

In the mirror, I found my face with a hollow look. I had wanted to reach out to her, not just physically, but reach her in the pain she was in. Leaving the bathroom, I found Ash helping Brooklyn climb back into the bed. A new doctor was there, and I hesitated, trying to determine if she wanted me to stay. When she didn't ask me to leave, I leaned against the wall, out of her line of sight.

"Ms. Reeves, I'll need to examine the wound. If we want to minimize scarring, it needs to be handled soon," the doctor said.

I realized it was the plastic surgeon Aiden had demanded. The man was older, gray hair salting the hair he did have left on his head. He wore glasses and was reading Brooklyn's chart. I had some doubts this was the best plastic surgeon out there, but I trusted Aiden's judgement.

Brooklyn just nodded and lifted up so Ash could pull her scrub pants down again. With the wound exposed again, the doctor studied the cuts on her thighs.

"Fairly clean cuts. I think we can stitch this up with minimal scarring. And I think we can make sure this isn't a word ever again." The older man looked up into Brooklyn's face with a kind expression. I watched as she swallowed hard and nodded her agreement.

"Just give me an hour. I'll gather my supplies and support and we'll get started. We can do local numbing, but this is going to be a long process and could be painful. I can offer something to help you sleep through it."

Brooklyn began to shake her head violently.

"No. No medications. I don't want to be put to sleep like that." Brooklyn forced as much emotion as she could behind her words.

"Ms. Reeves, I don't want to put you through more than necessary. I —"

I cut in because I could see how much fear was in Brooklyn's eyes. "Sir, she said no. Let's leave it at that."

Brooklyn didn't look over at me and I could have sat and begged her to just look into my eyes. I wanted to see her face when she saw me, actually saw me with her. If there wasn't fear in her eyes, they were hollow, void of emotion. It was something I had never seen before and I could admit it scared me. We could help her through anything, if she'd let us. But I had a feeling she was disappearing before my eyes.

The doctor finally agreed to not put her out for the work on her leg. He excused himself to get the tools he needed, leaving Brooklyn alone with Ash and I. Standing against the wall, I fidgeted, thinking I should leave the room again. Ash made the choice for me by standing up and stretching.

"I'm going to get coffee. Jaxon will stay with you, so you aren't alone, right?" She directed her question to me.

"I'm staying as long as she is," I said.

Ash nodded before squeezing Brooklyn's shoulder and walking toward the door. When she passed me, she patted my shoulder reassuringly, and I appreciated her support. Silence stretched through the room after the door shut behind Ash. I had never struggled to talk with Brooklyn before. Now I felt nervous and unsure of how to even start.

"Who's the guy? The blue hair?" Brooklyn was the first to speak, her voice soft and barely audible.

I moved toward the bed, but didn't touch her, just stood closer, so we could talk.

"Cain. An old friend. From a time long ago."

Brooklyn's eyebrows scrunched together, and I knew she was putting pieces together.

"From before? What did you have to do for his help?" Her voice quivered, but she still didn't look up at me.

"We would have done anything we had to. But Cain really is a friend. And he didn't make it hard on us," I said.

"I didn't want your lives to be hard because of me. You shouldn't have had to search."

"Love, this wasn't your fault. I'm sure I'm not the first to have said it, and I'm sure we'll have this conversation again. This wasn't your fault."

Brooklyn slouched down into the bed slightly, folding into herself. "I'm not worth the trouble."

Her voice was so quiet, it was as if she were speaking to herself. But I heard the words loud and clear. They made me think of the Brooklyn we had first met. Though, even then, she wasn't this broken. She had worked hard through therapy and creating the life she wanted, she recover from her past. Now she was back there, falling further into the abyss than she had been when I first laid eyes on her.

I reached over and tilted her chin up with one finger. She didn't fight me. Eventually, her eyes opened, and she looked up at me.

"No matter what, you're worth it to me." I let my finger trail over her cheek before pulling away.

Her eyes didn't react to my words, but her body shivered slightly from my touch. I knew she was still in there, still could feel the things we had together. Her body knew me, despite the abuse she had endured. Her skin knew mine, knew how we had shared breath in hot moments, but also laughter and secrets. It gave me hope, knowing that she would remember those things.

Eventually, she pulled away and looked down at her hands in her lap again. And I let her, stepping back and leaning against the wall again. I allowed her to sit in the silence she seemed to need, while I took my fill of her with my eyes. It was hard to realize she was back. She was safe and sitting right in front of me.

Ash came back with two steaming cups of coffee. She handed one, black, to Brooklyn, who wrapped her hands around the cup, holding onto it for dear life. When she carefully sipped, she closed her eyes and swallowed slowly.

"I thought maybe the warmth would feel good on your throat." Ash motioned toward the coffee.

Brooklyn let out a little broken moan and a small smile for her friend. We stayed in silence until her original doctor came into the room. The doctor was tapping away on her tablet when she entered, but looked up and gave Brooklyn a bright smile. She glanced around and back at her, with a question in her eyes.

"Should we speak in private?"

Brooklyn didn't look my way, though I knew the question was about me being in the room with her. After she had asked us to leave, I was sure the doctor had questions about the relationships we had with her.

"No. It's ok," she said, her voice a husky whisper.

"Alright then. Well, good news, there's nothing broken in your neck or spine from the injury there. You definitely have some tissue and muscle damage, which will take time to heal. I suggest alternating heat and ice for a few days and we'll give you some mild pain killers to help with the pain. You'll definitely not want to use your voice much, but don't stay silent for so long that it's extremely painful when you try to speak again. You want to use the muscles, even for whispering." The doctor turned her tablet while speaking, showing an x-ray image to Brooklyn.

"How long do I have to stay?"

"As soon as your leg is fixed up, I would be ok with discharging you into the care of your roommate, if that's what you'd like to do and if she's good with that?" The doctor looked at Ash to confirm.

"Of course I would be, but, well..." Ash looked over at me as she trailed off. Her eyes floated back to Brooklyn, and she took a deep breath before speaking again. "Honey, I think you'd be safer with the guys. We don't know where Lyle is. Gideon said the cops are looking for him in full force, but there's no knowing if he'll try to attack again. Don't you agree, Jaxon?"

I froze, looking between Ash and Brooklyn. Of course, my first priority was Brooklyn's safety. Having her back under our roof, where we could protect her with all of our resources, would make that task easier. Frank was one of Gideon's best. However, that didn't stop the man from being shot on the street and Brooklyn taken in broad daylight.

"It's up to Brooklyn. Her room is waiting for her at home," I finally said.

Brooklyn didn't look at me, only at Ash. It hurt to see anguish on her face, as if coming back to our house hurt her physically. Ash just looked down at her with a soft, encouraging look. Enough that she was trying to push her toward our home, but not enough to be refusing to take her back to the apartment.

Suddenly, an idea popped into my head. Before thinking, I blurted out, "Ash can come stay with us too."

Ash's eyes flicked over to me in surprise and the statement finally got Brooklyn to willingly look at me. She was also surprised, but I could see a little relief as well. I knew my brothers would agree to anything to get Brooklyn back under our roof. We didn't actually have any additional rooms, but Oliver and I could give up our office for a guest room. We didn't use the room as often as Aiden used his, so the transition wouldn't be hard.

The doctor, not understanding any of the context of what was not being said between us, cleared her throat. "I would insist that Ms. Reeves go to the place she is comfortable, can rest, recover—"

"And be safe," I interjected.

"Of course. I'm sure the police—"

"Haven't protected her yet." I rolled my eyes.

"Sir, I understand your frustration, but this really is Ms. Reeves' choice," the doctor said.

I wasn't trying to force anything on Brooklyn. It was no secret. I wanted her under our roof, where we could keep her safe, be near her, be in her presence. And to bring our family back together, because that's what we had created together. My phone had been vibrating in my pocket constantly since I came up to the hospital room. I quickly typed out a text about inviting Ash to stay with us so Brooklyn would come home. I didn't wait for a response or approval before dropping my phone back into my pocket.

"You're right. It is her choice. Brooklyn, please come home."

Instead of trying to get her to look up at me, I crouched next to the bed. Her eyes flicked over to me and held. I reached a hand out and cupped her cheek. She didn't look away as she leaned into my touch for a moment. A flicker of life came to her eyes for a moment, before it faded and she pulled away.

"Ok. If Ash can come, I'll go to stay with the Knights," Brooklyn said.

She didn't call it home, but she agreed to come. That was the first step, in what I was sure was going to be a long road to getting back to what we had.

CHAPTER

Forty

Brooklyn

"YOU GOTTA BE KIDDING ME!" Ash's exclamation made me wince.

The few days in the hospital had melted together, and I was discharged before I knew what was happening. The guys had kept their distance, but I always knew they were in the building somewhere. Ash only left my side to go home and pack our things, so when I was discharged we could go straight to the house. Gideon reassured me that he would stay with her the entire time, but I didn't feel ok until she was back in the hospital.

The detective Gideon knew had come to see me twice, though there was nothing I could tell him that he didn't already realize. But he had wanted a statement from me anyway, with specifics. Gideon had been in the room, having shown the detective in. I could see the hurt on his face when I asked him to leave so I could speak with the detective alone.

With the story out in the open and on the record, I knew it was only a matter of time before the Knights knew everything. Which was the reason I was on edge as the town car we were in stopped in front of the house. Ash's excitement did nothing to make me feel more comfortable. I was extremely grateful to her for agreeing to give up her normalcy to stay with me at the Knights' house.

Aiden was at the open door, dressed more casually than normal in distressed jeans and t-shirt. He slipped on flip-flops to come open the car door before the driver came around with our bags. Ash jumped out of the car first and Aiden reached in to help me climb out. His hand in mine felt strong and warm, making me wish he would hold me just for a moment.

Gideon joined us and took the bags from the driver. He guided Ash into the house and I slowly limped to follow. The plastic surgeon had done wonders on my leg, but it hadn't been a short process. I was supposed to be off my feet as often as possible to prevent any pulling at the tiny sutures.

By the time Aiden and I entered the house, Gideon was halfway down the lower hallway with a chattering Ash.

"Where is she going to sleep?" I turned to look up at Aiden.

"Oliver and Jaxon's office turned guest room."

"I didn't mean to be so much trouble." My voice was quiet as I looked away.

Without warning, Aiden wrapped an arm around my shoulders, pressing his chest against my back. His voice was low and his breath caressed my ear as he bent to whisper to me.

"We would take on the world if that's what we needed to do. You are trouble we want to have."

"We?"

Aiden's body froze behind me, but he didn't let me go. I couldn't forget that Aiden and I weren't on the best of terms before the kidnapping. He had been in the warehouse, was the first I saw beside the blue-haired Cain. It was his arms that comforted me and held me as I fell apart. Those actions were of someone that cared for me, but it was hard to not feel the sting of our last encounter alone. I could easily still see how he iced me out after we had sex on the hood of his car.

"We have a lot to talk about, sweetheart. Now isn't the time. Let's get you settled upstairs."

Using his arm and body, he turned me from the downstairs hallway to face the stairs. I froze when I saw Jaxon and Oliver at the foot of the stairs. Behind them, in the entrance to the living room, was the man I knew now to be Cain. He had visited once in the hospital, but didn't stay long. Barely speaking, he stood and assessed my injuries with his eyes, nodded, and left the room. I wasn't sure what to make of him yet, but his presence told me he was still staying in the pool house.

"Welcome home, babe," Oliver said.

I forced a smile on my face for his sake. He returned a tentative smile, which told me I probably looked like a freak show standing there with a random expression on my face. Aiden finally released me and I made my way to the stairs. I let Oliver wrap me in a hug, allowing his warmth and his familiar vanilla scent to surround me. Jaxon kissed my temple before stepping back and letting me climb the stairs on my own.

My bedroom door was open when I got to the top of the stairs. Everything was as I had left it, minus the note I had left on the bed for the guys to find. I didn't really feel like being reminded of that at the moment, so I turned to the dresser and pulled out a clean set of pajamas. When I turned toward the bathroom, Gideon was at the door with my suitcase. He hesitated and waited for my invitation.

I waved him in and he set the suitcase down near my closet. He lingered over it and I laughed uncomfortably.

"You don't have to unpack my bag, Gideon."

"Sorry, stellina. I'm not sure what to do." He stepped back toward the door and crossed his thick arms across his chest.

I stood and stared at my bare feet for a long moment. Gideon's boots came into view and his hand came up to cup my cheek, angling my face up. His eyes searched mine for a long minute, and neither of us spoke. His thumb softly caressed my cheek and I couldn't bring myself to step away. I was caught between feeling like I didn't deserve his comfort and wanting to climb up his body to take advantage of everything he was offering.

I noted the red scabs on his neck and vaguely remembered clawing at him at one point. Guilt suffused into me and I looked up into his eyes.

"I'm sorry I hurt you." I motioned toward the scratches.

Gideon absently ran a finger down one of the injuries and just shrugged his shoulder. "I'd go through a lot worse for you."

Before panic could set in, Gideon leaned in and pressed a warm kiss against my forehead. I closed my eyes and took a deep breath, allowing the tingling to flow through me that came just from his sweet kiss on my head. He stepped back, letting his hand drop from my cheek. Back at the door, he turned to look at me again.

"I'm really happy you're back, stellina. I missed you."

I opened my mouth, closed it, then opened it again, not sure what the appropriate response was. Would I have eventually come back to their house if we had worked out our disagreements? Or would we have taken things much slower, with me living at the apartment? I didn't know the answer to that and I didn't want to feel like the only reason I was living in their house again was for protection.

No matter what, I had missed them, but when I looked up to

tell Gideon exactly that, the doorway was empty. My chest felt heavy, surprising me that I could even feel anything after everything I had gone through. I was a swirling mass of emotions that I was trying to not feel all at once.

Turning toward the bathroom again, I put my clean clothes on the counter and turned on the shower. Under the steaming hot spray, I let the water flow over my body. My thigh was still wrapped in a water tight bandage that wasn't to come off for a few more days. But I badly needed to scrub the rest of my body. Once the shower was heavy with my lavender scented products, I could feel some normalcy in my mind, even if it was only a small sliver.

I dressed quickly and wrapped my towel dried hair on the top of my head. When I came out of the bathroom, Ash was sitting on the edge of my bed, flipping through a magazine. Her head popped up the moment I opened the door and a huge grin appeared on her face.

"This place is crazy, Brooklyn. It's huge. But like feels like a home, know what I mean?"

"Well, it is a home," I said, shooting her an ironic look.

"I know, I know. But the club kings of the city just seem above family life. I see now I was quite wrong." She slid back onto my bed, propping herself up on my pillows.

I moved around the room, moving things here and there, though nothing needed fixing. The guys had left everything just how I liked it, not even considering turning my room back into their guest space. I went to my suitcase and bent to grab the zipper, but instead, I slipped to the side and caught myself with my hand, my head swimming.

"Brooklyn!" Ash jumped from the bed and rushed to my side.

I shook my head slightly and lowered myself to a sitting position before I tried to stand. Ash crouched in front of me, looking into my face, searching for what was wrong.

"I'm ok. Just moving around too much, I think," I said, pushing her hands away from my face.

"Brooklyn?" Oliver's voice came from the hallway and I could hear his feet moving fast.

When his face came into view, it was clear that he had heard Ash's cry when I fell. He bent to scoop me into his arms before even checking me out. Carefully, he placed me on the edge of the bed and his hands came up to frame my jaw. He tilted my face up, with his thumbs under my chin. His gaze was critical, but I could see the worry creasing his forehead. Without a thought, I reached up and rubbed against the wrinkles and Oliver froze.

"I'm ok." My voice was a whisper, as I snapped my hand back.

"She's doing too much. She needs to rest," Ash said from behind Oliver.

I nodded the little that Oliver's hands allowed and waited until he saw everything he needed to. When he released my face, his hands slid down to my shoulders to squeeze before he stepped back.

"I'm ok. You don't need to hover, Oliver." My words were meant to be in jest, but when I saw him flinch, I knew they came out more harshly than I intended.

I motioned for him to come back toward me. His first step was small and careful. Reaching forward, I boldly grabbed his belt loop and pulled him until he was between my knees. These men, my men, had come to save me, despite the risk to themselves. My heart thudded when I thought about what could have gone wrong, but we were lucky and safe under their roof again. I needed to remind myself what good I had in this house.

Slowly, I wrapped my arms around Oliver's torso. I pressed my uninjured cheek into his chest, waiting for him to hold me. I wasn't left to wait long, as his arms hugged me closer to him. It was the feeling of coming home, not the house, not the huge room, not the extensive wardrobe that hung in the closet. It was them, their skin, their smells, their warmth. They were home.

With that realization in my mind, I held Oliver longer than I intended, but he didn't try to pull away. His hand came to the nape of my neck and began to massage the tension there. I sighed, melting a little under his touch.

"No wonder you wanted to stay here." Ash laughed behind Oliver and I could feel my cheeks heating a little.

"She's safer with us," Oliver said, his voice a little defensive.

"That's not the only reason, Oliver," I said, pulling away to look up at him.

His smile was easy, and I couldn't help but give him a small smile in return.

"We have plenty of time to talk about the other reasons, babe. I should let you get some rest. Has nurse Jaxon been in yet to give you meds?"

"I've been called much worse." Jaxon came strolling into the room, his hands full of pill bottles that he set up on my night stand.

"Why do I feel like I'm living through the movie Groundhog Day?" I said.

"Let's make sure this is the last time we have to repeat this." Jaxon went to the mini fridge, which was already stocked, and brought a bottle of water and two pills to me.

When I just raised an eyebrow at him, he sighed and showed me the bottle. "Pain killers. The doctor said we needed to stay ahead of the pain, so you don't suffer."

"Yes... nurse," I said, gulping down the pills with the cool water.

"I'll make you pay for that later." Jaxon's voice pitched low into a playful growl, causing me to cough on water.

"Hey, you're not supposed to kill her, you're supposed to help heal her," Ash said, before bursting out into laughter.

"Whose side are you on?" I asked, after I could stop coughing.

"I'm just here to watch the show, girl."

Brooklyn

I WASN'T sure how many days I had stayed in my room. The black-out curtains stayed drawn, and I only got up to go to the bathroom. Jaxon came in like clockwork to ensure I was taking my meds. Gideon brought in three meals a day, though I wasn't finishing everything on my plate. Ash came in and laid in the bed with me during the day, giving me support in a silent manner.

Silence was my only companion. After the first day, everyone stopped trying to talk to me. They realized I wasn't ready, so they came to check on me, but no one forced me to speak. My throat was feeling better every day, however I hadn't tried to use my voice in a few days, so I wasn't sure I was sounding any better.

Gideon had just left my lunch. He quietly left, closing the door behind him. I sat up in bed and picked at the pear salad he had brought me. My fork was between my mouth and my bowl when my door opened again, startling me. I dropped the fork when I saw Cain standing in the doorway. The rough-looking man had avoided speaking with me since I got home, not that I had given him too many chances.

"How long is it you're going to hide yourself away in here, huh?"

"Excuse me?"

My voice was a whisper, as if I had forgotten how to use it. Cain didn't seem to allow an argument as he stalked into the room, going straight to my curtains. He ripped back the material, allowing the offending sun to blind me.

"What are you doing?" I exclaimed, my voice gaining some strength.

"Opening the window."

"Obviously. Why?" I crossed my arms across my chest, realizing I was wearing my camisole nighty and nothing else.

"Because the sun is good for you."

His overly obvious answers were starting to annoy me and he seemed to know it as he took up a spot next to the windows. I couldn't help myself as my eyes roamed over his body. He was dressed in sweatpants and a t-shirt. His feet were bare, which caught my attention immediately. His blue hair was swept back, but fell forward into his eyes when he moved. The shaved sides of his head had dark stubble, that I was pretty sure he liked to keep clean, but hadn't made it to the barber lately.

Hazel eyes locked onto mine and I couldn't find the strength to look away. I stared back into his face, refusing to back down or lose whatever battle of wills we seemed to be having. A small grin appeared on Cain's face, and his lip ring glinted in the sunlight.

He stepped forward, walking slowly toward the bed, until he was perched on the edge, looking at me.

"The guys treat you like you're made of glass. Not forcing you to leave this room for days. I have no such inclination."

I sputtered for a moment before remembering how to speak. "What is it any of your business?"

"Oh, it's not, really, yeah? But for some reason, I feel the need to push your buttons."

Deciding I didn't want to seem bothered by him, I picked up my fork again. Though I didn't really feel like eating, I had to admit that the salad was delicious, as was almost anything Gideon put on a plate for me. I felt bad for not eating the food he was taking the time to prepare. I knew if he was bringing me three meals a day, he was likely not going to work, making me even more of an inconvenience.

After I was halfway done with the salad, I looked up to find Cain sitting in the same place, watching me eat. I raised an eyebrow and waited for him to say the next quippy remark he was coming up with. He just tilted his head and stared back.

"What do you want, Cain?"

He moved until he was lounging across the foot of my bed. My mouth dropped open, shocked at his audacity to make himself so comfortable in my room.

"How long are you planning on doing this?" He repeated his original question.

"Doing what?" I pushed my hair out of my face and fidgeted with the lettuce left in my bowl.

"Having your own private pity party, yeah?"

I put my bowl on the night stand, before turning to glare at Cain. "Pity party? I could barely speak. My throat was almost crushed. I had to have intensive surgery on my leg to remove a fucking brand. Not to mention all the bumps and bruises. Am I allowed to rest and heal?"

Cain rolled his eyes and flopped onto his back before letting out a huge yawn.

"Look, thank you for helping find me. I really can't express my appreciation enough. But I don't know who you think you are, coming in here and trash talking. You have no idea what I've been through."

Casually, Cain rolled toward me, propping himself up on his elbow.

"Enlighten me, princess."

I leaned back against my pillows, looking away from his eyes that were searching for pieces of my soul. I hadn't talked to any of the guys about what had happened, not in detail. I was still waiting for any sort of results from my exam, to tell me if the worst had happened and I had even more to be ashamed of.

"Look, we don't really know each other. Wouldn't it be easier to tell a stranger the truth, someone that has no reasons to judge? And wouldn't it feel good to talk to someone?"

"I've talked to Ash," I said.

"Have you, really? Seems she's just as lost as everyone else on what is going on in this room, yeah?"

He wasn't wrong, but I wasn't interested in confirming that for him. Ash was there when I was examined, but I hadn't really talked to her about it. She had tried, been the best friend I needed. I just wasn't able to form the words to tell her what happened in that warehouse.

"That's what I thought," Cain said, as if he was reading my thoughts.

"I'm not ready, ok?" My voice was stronger, though not quite able to yell, even though I badly wanted to.

"If you stay in here, in the dark, not talking to anyone, you'll never be ready. Everyone in this house is just waiting for you."

With those parting words, Cain rolled off the bed in a smooth motion and walked toward the door. It wasn't until he was gone that I realized he had left the curtains wide open and hadn't even closed the bedroom door. I just stared into the hallway, wondering where the guy got off with trying to push me around.

I slid out of bed and tried to decide if I was going to close the door or the windows first. As I stood in the middle of the room, movement at the door caught my attention and I turned to find Oliver standing just outside my room. His eyes were hot as they roamed my body and I was reminded again that I was wearing nothing but my camisole nighty that barely covered my ass.

I didn't think I was ready for that kind of attention, but Oliver's gaze caused warmth to lick within my cold interior. I fought the urge to cover myself and just motioned for him to come inside. He didn't say anything, just stepped forward and shut the door behind him. I went to the window and pulled the curtains mostly closed, but still allowing a little light into the room.

When I turned back, Oliver was relaxing against my pillows. I didn't hesitate. I climbed under the blanket and laid against his chest. His arms came around me and I sighed.

"You sure this is ok, baby?" He asked.

I nodded, nuzzling my face against his shirt and then moving up under his chin. It was more than ok. I wasn't entirely ready to talk, but I wanted their comfort, their nearness. I wanted to belong in their world again, to know that they wanted me and cared about me. There was no knowing how long that would last, but I wanted to soak up what I could while I was free to do so.

"I want to help, just tell me what to do," he said.

"You're doing what I need right now." I pressed a kiss against his chest and laid my head back down.

We laid in silence for a few minutes. Oliver's hand rubbed up and down my back and I let my hand rest on his abdomen. It felt like a surreal, normal moment and I didn't want to do anything to disrupt it.

Oliver was the one to break the quiet. "I know Gideon has told you stories of when we were kids and the world we grew up in. We saw many illegal things, dangerous things, immoral things. Some of them we participated in. We knew it was wrong, but it was the world we knew. We never realized it was possible to change our fate."

"And you did, as soon as you had the opportunity," I said.

Oliver nodded, his face lowered into my hair. "We did. Sometimes I still have to think about what we did. The number of lives we hurt by dealing. The women we saw come and go from the apartments Randy and his men had. How we could see how bad the life was for them. But we didn't do anything, didn't stop the things we knew were happening. When I think about those things, I feel guilt. Ugly, deep rooted, guilt for my hand in those things."

I tried to imagine my Oliver, the fun, silly, handsome man, doing things that made him feel ugly. I imagined a younger version of him, working in the dark underbelly of the city, just to make ends meet. It was hard to think about him, taking the drugs he dealt, being high and out of control at times. I couldn't see him as someone that was a threat to others, or that didn't do the right things for the people around him.

However, what I didn't feel was ashamed or disgusted by him. That was a life he was forced into, what he was born into, without a choice or say. When he was old enough, he, along with his brothers, created the life they lived now. They became the people that I knew they were. The strength to overcome their origins was something I admired and appreciated.

I knew why Oliver was talking to me about this now. He was trying to tell me he knew what it was to be ashamed. But I wasn't sure I was able to admit to him what had happened to me, even once I could admit to myself that it wasn't my fault.

"You were practically children, then. You turned things around and you do wonderful things now with the power you have," I said.

"We've tried to do what we can to make up for our sins. You know these things about us, but does it change how you feel? Do you think of us differently?"

I shook my head, my throat suddenly clogged.

"I'm sure you know why I'm telling you this. I want to make sure you understand that we know darkness. We've lived in it.

And just how it doesn't change your feelings for us, what you've been through in your life, doesn't mean I love you any less."

He said the words so simply that I wasn't sure I heard him correctly. I froze in his embrace and waited to see what he would say next. His breathing had gone shallow, and I realized he didn't mean to say the words when he did.

"You can't put that back in the bottle." My lips moved against his skin in a quiet whisper.

"I... uh... well... it's not that I don't mean it, because I do. I just didn't mean to blurt it out when you're laying in bed recovering. I was thinking more romantic, candles, dinner, ya know... the whole thing..." his voice trailed off as he fidgeted uncomfortably.

I let the feelings roll around in my mind. Did I love Oliver? Yes, I was sure I did, even if I wasn't sure I even knew what real love was. I knew that he and his brothers occupied my mind all the time. My life felt like it was black and white before they walked in and it sprung into technicolor. For the first time, I could see a future, bright and loving and real.

That was before. Before Lyle had defiled my body, breaking me all over again, and the Knights were left to pick up the pieces. Telling them now that I loved them didn't seem genuine. I wasn't in the right headspace to dive into those feelings. And I wasn't sure what I needed to get back to that place.

Oliver

"THERE'S something else I need to tell you."

It took a lot to find my voice or the courage to speak. How did I just drop the bombshell of love on her, the first moment she let me near her again? I felt like a fool, but she wasn't pushing me out of her bed, even if she didn't really address what I had said. She was right. I couldn't take the words back now, not that I had planned on that.

"Go ahead."

Her normal voice was slowly returning, but she still spoke quietly. Her breath slid across the skin of my neck and made goosebumps rise along my arms. I ignored my body's reaction to her nearness, knowing that wasn't what she needed from me at the time.

"We don't blame you for what happened. The fight we all had was our fault and our lack of communication with you. And I lay a little heavier blame on Aiden's head, but that's a different conversation. I just wanted to make sure you knew we weren't angry. What happened wasn't your fault." I squeezed her tighter against me as I spoke, trying to infuse my words into her.

"I do, blame me, I mean. I'm angry at a lot of the decisions I made. They made me vulnerable," she said.

"There was no way for anyone to know the lengths Lyle would go to get you. He shot a man in broad daylight."

She nodded under my chin, but I had a feeling she wanted to still argue the point. I let it go, knowing I would remind her as many times as possible that she was the victim in this, not the one that asked to be kidnapped. She was also the victim of whatever Lyle had done to her while he had her tied up in the warehouse. Those were things we still didn't know, because she was refusing to talk about it. I wasn't going to be the one to push her on those details.

"What about Missy? We haven't really talked about how she got arrested?" Brooklyn asked.

"With Cain's help," I replied.

Brooklyn nudged me with her knee, before laying her leg across me, keeping pressure off her injury. She waited for me to continue and I tried to decide on the best way to tell her what Cain had done in the search to find her. Eventually, I decided on the truth, because Brooklyn deserved that. And I wasn't ashamed of anything we did to bring her back to us.

"Cain kidnapped her from the hotel he found her staying in. We questioned her, again with some persuasion from Cain. She eventually gave us the information we needed to find the warehouse. Gideon drove her straight to the police station himself to have her arrested for your kidnapping. I sort of tuned out on that process, because I was focused on finding you."

"He's interesting, isn't he?" She asked.

"Cain? I guess. We have history. Some of it not great. I'm glad he was able to help us."

Brooklyn shifted uncomfortably, and I loosed my arms to allow her movement if she wanted. Once she settled back into my body, she spoke again.

"He was in here earlier, giving me hell about lying around."

"He did what?" My voice came out harsher than I intended.

Cain wasn't dangerous, not to Brooklyn. I wasn't worried about that. I had noticed the way he looked at her and it was curious that he was still staying in the pool house, though our needs for him were done. Our history with him, feeling as if we had left him behind, influenced the decisions we were making now. However, if he overstepped with my girl, we'd have words.

"It's ok, honey. He didn't upset me. In a way, he's right. I need to get out of this room at some point."

"Not before you're ready. None of us are going to push you," I said.

Brooklyn sighed and rolled away from me. I immediately missed her warmth, but I stayed still instead of following her body. She laid, staring at the ceiling for a long moment before turning her head so she could look at me. Indecision was written all over her features, so I just waited, not sure what the right thing to say would have been.

"I don't know what will make me ready. I feel like I'm going to be stuck like this forever," she said.

I rolled until I was leaning on my elbow, my head in my hand. Reaching out, I slid one finger along her cheek and she leaned until my hand cupped her cheek. She pressed her hand on mine, not allowing me to let go.

"I don't want to be like this. I want things to go back to normal. But I'm not sure that's possible."

"We can create a new normal, if that's what you need," I replied.

"I was happy with what we had. And it was still new. We were still figuring things out. How do we figure things out when everything is so complicated?" Tears were welling in her ice-blue eyes and they tore at my heart.

I decided to take the chance and slide closer to her. She didn't move to put distance, but her eyes flared slightly and I knew deep down, the feelings we had for each other weren't complicated. Nothing that had happened made those feelings less. She just needed to be reminded and know that we all felt the same as we did before.

"Does this feel complicated?" I rubbed my thumb along her cheek as I looked into her eyes. She shook her head.

"What about this?" I let my fingers trail from her cheek bone to the shell of her ear and down her neck. She craned her head to give me access. When I settled my fingers along the sensitive skin behind her ear, she shook her head no.

"It's only complicated if we make it that way." I had moved forward until my lips moved against her ear. She shuddered a little before turning her face toward mine.

"I don't want to make your lives difficult," she said quietly.

"It's harder without you, baby."

She leaned her head back, her hands coming up to frame my face. A tear slipped from her eye and I caught it on my fingertip. I so badly just wanted to make everything better for her, but I knew she had to decide how the process was going to go. Nothing I said could force her forward.

"I'm scared, Oliver. I've never lived in a world where I could be loved right, or where I was accepted for me. You have always looked beyond my scars and what was in my past. But, it's different now. I'm different now. And I am so scared you can't see past what's wrong with me now."

I heard her words, even understood her fears. In my mind, I dismissed them immediately, because I knew in my heart that we could work through whatever there was to come. If we stuck together, leaned on each other, became the family I knew we could be, we could handle anything. But I had to make Brooklyn believe that.

"Baby, give me a chance. I might just surprise you." I let a small smile appear on my face.

The indecision didn't leave her face, but she slowly closed the distance between our faces. When she softly pressed her lips against mine, it was hard to hold back and let her steer. I had missed her, but more than that, I had been paralyzed with the fear that I would never see her again. Never kiss her exactly like she was kissing me now.

The kiss was innocent and sweet. When she pulled away, it was almost reluctant, but she did end the connection. I immediately craved more, but I reigned in the crazy, and just studied her face. Some of the indecision was gone, but the light in her eyes was still not bright.

"I think, if I'm going to talk about this, I need to do it once, with everyone," Brooklyn said.

I nodded. "I can gather the guys. You want to talk in here?"

"Sure. But not right now, I just want to lie here for a while, is that ok?"

She rolled until I was spooning her. Grabbing my hand, she pulled my arm around her waist from behind. I slid closer to her, until her ass was cradled against my hips, a move I almost immediately regretted as the warmth of her seeped into my sweatpants. Mentally, I started thinking about baseball, bowling and Olympic curling, anything and everything boring enough to keep my libido controlled.

Brooklyn settled in and soon her body went soft, her breathing evened out and her hold on my arm loosened. Knowing I couldn't sleep with how worked up I felt, I carefully extradited myself from her body and slid to the side of the bed. I waited a full minute to ensure she stayed asleep before climbing from the bed.

As I quietly closed her door, Jaxon approached from the stairs. He waited until we were halfway down the hall before he spoke.

"Did she talk to you?"

"Not really. She's really scared we're going to not want her or something. It's crazy," I said.

Jaxon followed me into my room, where I sat behind the desk that now resided in the corner of the room. I needed to get away from Brooklyn's scent and get control over my emotions.

"It's not really crazy when you realize she was conditioned to believe she wasn't worth anything. I know what that's like." His eyes were focused on the far wall and I knew he wasn't seeing my room, but the past.

"You know your dad is a piece of shit, Jaxon. He just wanted to keep you under his thumb."

Jaxon nodded and rubbed a hand over his face before turning to focus on me.

"We need to talk about Cain," I said.

I shouldn't have been surprised that Jaxon looked like he knew the conversation was coming. My brother was one of the most perceptive people I knew.

"He's attracted to her." His words were said simply, with no tension attached.

"How do we feel about that?"

"It's not really for us to decide, is it?"

I thought about that. Would I easily accept another man in Brooklyn's life if she wanted that? I knew I would do anything to make her happy and after what we had been through, it would take a lot for me to tell her no again.

"I guess not. What about Aiden and Gideon? They don't know Cain like we do. How do you think they'll react?"

"Pretty sure they both have noticed something, too. Neither of them has tried to kick Cain to the curb yet, so maybe they're fine with the idea," Jaxon said.

Remembering what Brooklyn and I did talk about before she fell asleep, I knew this wasn't something we would have to deal with anytime soon. She was having a hard enough time coming back to us fully. Adding another man to the mix was not likely something she had on her mind. A piece of my mind disagreed with that, thinking a shake up was exactly what our girl needed now.

Brooklyn

IT WAS dark when I woke up and I was alone. I hadn't really expected Oliver to stay with me while I slept away the day, but having him touching me, even in an innocent way, made me feel normal. I stretched and thought back to Cain, giving me a hard time about hiding away in my room. It was very presumptuous of him to think he could lecture me on anything, but that's what he had done.

My mind flashed back to the first time I saw him, as he swept in to prevent Buzz from raping me. I couldn't see what he had done to Buzz, but I knew he hadn't been kind. The man didn't know me personally, and yet he was willing to put himself at risk to rescue me. And I hadn't even thought to thank him properly.

With my mind made up, I climbed out of bed and changed into bike shorts and an oversized sweatshirt. In the bathroom, I found my hair to be a complete disaster, so I took the time to comb through the knots, until the blonde length fell down my back in a silky wave. I was quiet as I left my room, afraid if I ran into any of the guys, I would lose the nerve I had built up.

Somehow, I made it to the backyard without seeing anyone. Lights were on in the pool house and I could see a figure move behind the curtains. I swallowed hard as I raised my hand to knock. Before I made contact with the wood, the door swung open and Cain stood there, surprising me and making me jump back a step.

It took me a long moment to register that he was wearing nothing but gray sweatpants that hung low on his hips, leaving his v on display. My guys had some tattoos, but Cain was covered and I couldn't help but to stare. I had seen his sleeved arms and the skull on his throat, but I hadn't imagined he had such intricate art all over his torso.

"Just let me know once you've had your fill, princess."

His words jarred me from my silence and I snapped my mouth shut, which until that moment I hadn't realized was hanging open. My eyes met his and there was humor there, even though his lips didn't show the hint of a smile. He lifted an arm and leaned it over his head on the door jamb, leaning to one side, which only accentuated the muscles he had on view.

"Sorry, uh, to interrupt your night." I was gripping the bottom of my sweatshirt in my fists, trying to control my nerves.

Cain didn't seem to notice or care that I was nervous. He reached out and grabbed one of my wrists and pulled me into the pool house.

"Come in." He said the words as if he had given me a choice, but I was already in the middle of the living area with him closing the door behind me.

I spun and came face to face with his chest as he approached me. Instincts screamed at me and I backed away until I was hitting the small kitchen counter on the other side of the room. That didn't stop Cain, who continued to prowl toward me, until he was within arm's reach. Again, his hand snapped out, and he pulled at my wrist, making me release my sweatshirt. He repeated the move with my other wrist until my hands were relaxed at my sides. His fingers were rough against my skin, but for a moment, his thumb swiped along the inside of my wrist and a shiver ran through me.

"Better?" He asked.

I knew my mouth was hanging open again as I searched for words. The man was imposing, and he had completely thrown all of my determination out the window by being so forward. Instead of trying to answer him, I just nodded my head.

"Good. Now, to what do I owe the pleasure of this visit?"

His words snapped me into the present, making me remember why I had come down to the pool house in the first place. But now the words seemed to have escaped me and a long moment of silence spread between us again. Cain just cocked his head to one side as he studied me, waiting.

I forced my eyes to not linger on his naked body, but only on his face. That didn't really help make me feel any more calm. There was something about the energy he exuded. Tough, electric, but also aloof, as if anything he did was without care. I knew in the tough life he lived, there couldn't be anything he did without complete purpose. That's how he had to be to survive. But on the outside, you couldn't tell that the wheels in his head were turning.

It also didn't help that he was devastatingly handsome. My guys were the most beautiful men I had ever met or seen in my life. Each of them was so devilishly delicious without even trying. It was one of the things I found so alluring about them. Cain was a different beautiful, with rough edges and colorful swirls all over his body, a body that looked to be carved directly out of a slab of marble.

I cleared my throat, realizing that I was making everything way more awkward than necessary.

"I wanted to come and thank you for real, instead of snapping at you. I realized that it's been a week or so and I should have said this before. But thank you for what you did to help the guys find me. And thank you for stopping Buzz..." I trailed off and looked down, not wanting to put to words what almost happened to me.

Cain's heat hit me before I realized he had approached me. My head snapped up just as one of his fingers came under my chin, angling my face up even further. He continued to have the detached look in his eyes, but he studied me closely.

"For some reason, princess, I think I would burn the city to the ground if it meant saving you again."

I couldn't think straight, and his body was entirely too close to me. I forced myself to take a step back, and Cain's hand dropped to his side.

"I... I'm not sure... why?" I asked.

"That's the question, isn't it?" He said.

I felt so confused. The feelings that were rioting around inside my stomach were familiar to me, but they were usually always associated with one of my men. I remembered the conversation with Jaxon in my office when he explained how our relationships worked. I could be with the brothers, but other men were off limits. And just at that moment, I felt a sliver of regret for that rule.

"Um, ok. Well, I need to go. Thank you again. And thank you for not making Jaxon go to his father. I wouldn't have been able to forgive myself if that was how far he had to go to save me." I started toward the door.

"Anytime, princess. And feel free to come visit me whenever you feel like."

I glanced back toward Cain and a lopsided grin was on his face and I knew he could read my emotions all over my face. I rushed out of the pool house and quickly closed the door behind me. Away from the effect of Cain, I took a deep breath of the clean outdoor air. With my heart under control, I made my way back to the main house.

As I opened the back door, Jaxon came around the corner and froze. His eyes widened when he saw me, but he didn't approach. I hated the way they all seemed on edge around me and I knew my self imposed quarantine had created a tense situation. I took a chance and walked to him and wrapped my arms around his waist. He hesitated for just a split second before his arms came around my back, pressing me to him.

"Where have you been, love?" Jaxon asked.

"I went to see Cain. I needed to thank him."

Jaxon snorted, causing me to pull back to look up into his face.

"I'm sure he enjoyed that." He grinned down at me.

"What do you mean?" I asked.

I knew how Cain made me feel, but he was distant with me. However, I thought about what he had said and I knew there was something else going on inside his head, even if his face didn't show it.

"Nothing. We'll talk about it later. How are you feeling?" Jaxon asked, his eyes searching mine.

"I'm ok. Cain lectured me, kinda kicked my ass into gear, I guess. He made me realize I needed to start moving on, somehow."

"Cain can be an ass, so don't let his words weigh too heavily on you," Jaxon said.

I shook my head before laying it back against Jaxon's shoulder. "He wasn't wrong."

Jaxon was silent, but his hand rubbed my back softly and it made me melt into him just a bit more. It was then I realized I smelled something delicious and my stomach suddenly growled. Jaxon released me and put his hands on my shoulders to move me back.

"Hungry?"

"Yeah, I guess so." I smiled up at him.

"Gideon's cooking, because nothing else seems to help him. Let's go get some food in you."

Jaxon's hand slid down my arm until he could intertwine our fingers. He squeezed my hand, and I squeezed back, assuring him that his touch was completely welcome. It actually made me realize what I needed, and I would need to talk to them about it. After I told them the truth of everything that I had been through.

As Jaxon led me toward the kitchen, my cell phone chimed in my pocket. Pulling out the device, I realized I had missed a call from the hospital. I stopped walking and Jaxon looked back at me.

"I need to return this call. I'll come to the kitchen after, ok?"

Indecision crossed Jaxon's face for just a moment, but he cleared it before I could comment on it. He nodded, lifting my hand to his mouth. The kiss he pressed against my knuckles was innocent, but the feeling rocketed through me. My reaction to it almost brought tears to my eyes. For just a moment I didn't feel broken. I just felt like the woman that couldn't get enough of the man standing in front of me.

Jaxon left me alone in the living room and I sat down on the couch, not sure my legs would hold me up during the phone call. I listened to the message left by a nurse quickly and punched in the number she left. When I reached the automated system, I impatiently clicked through the options, just needing to get to a live person. When a woman's voice came across the line, I was almost breathless, my heart thumping in my chest.

"This is Brooklyn Reeves. I was calling for my test results."

"Oh, Ms. Reeves, thanks for calling back so quickly. I still have your file in front of me. Your doctor made sure to flag these results. She understood that it was highly sensitive information that you needed immediately," the nurse said.

"Thank you. All I need to know is if the test was positive or negative, for fluids..." I trailed off with the last word, feeling bile rise in my throat. I took a few deep breaths to control my physical reaction before I even knew the results.

"Yes. The test came back negative for any fluids..."

I didn't hear anything the nurse said beyond that. Her voice became a drowned out sound that I didn't register or consciously respond to. I knew I said thank you at some point and hung up the phone. I went completely lightheaded and bent to put my head between my knees. My breathing was ragged and I couldn't seem to process.

"Brooklyn?!"

Ash's alarmed voice broke through the haze and suddenly my best friend was on the ground in front of where I sat on the couch. I looked up and her face was stricken with worry. I rubbed my face and my hands came away wet, making me realize I was bawling. I wasn't sure I could form the words to tell Ash the news. I was on the verge of hyperventilating, as I was bombarded with thoughts and memories of the nightmare I had been through.

"Are you ok? What can I do?" She asked.

The back French doors opened and suddenly I was yanked to my feet. The shock of the move made me look around wildly, only find Cain with a serious look on his face, his hands under my arms, keeping me upright.

"Breathe with me, princess." His voice was rough and demanding.

He grabbed one of my hands and pressed it against his chest, which was thankfully clothed. Taking a deep breath, he allowed his chest to rise and fall with my hand, feeling the movement.

"Cain, I don't think —" Ash started to say, but Cain's eyes cut to her and she quickly closed her mouth.

His hazel eyes flashed back to mine, and he took another deep breath. This time I tried to follow his lead, take a shaky breath of my own.

"Good, now again," he said, his voice flowing over me like a caress.

I followed him through three more deep breaths before I

started to find a normal rhythm again. However, Cain didn't release my hand, or remove the hand that was now on my waist, holding me closer to him than necessary. As I calmed down, my senses started to come back, and I blushed, feeling exposed and in the wrong place immediately. I stepped back, forcing Cain to release me.

"Have you had panic attacks before, princess?" He asked.

"I haven't in a long time," I replied, my voice barely a whisper.

"Are you ok?" Ash asked, moving to my side.

I looked at her and took another calming breath. I leaned over to her ear, wanting to tell her what had happened without Cain hearing. He didn't seem annoyed or put out with the secret, just watched calmly as Ash burst into tears herself and turned to hug me tightly. I returned her embrace, so thankful for her and the support she had provided me when it had put her out so greatly.

Movement behind Ash caught my attention, and I found Jaxon standing outside of the living room. I had to wonder how long he had been standing there. He didn't approach, just watched me carefully. I released Ash and rushed to him, throwing myself into his arms. He took a small step back to keep us from tumbling, before hugging me and burying his face in my neck.

"I need to talk to you guys, privately," I whispered to him.

Jaxon nodded and looked up at Cain.

"Thank you for helping her through that. Dinner is served in the kitchen. If you could send the guys in here, I'd appreciate it."

Cain nodded, no argument as he left the living room. Ash slid out as well, squeezing my shoulder as she made her way to the kitchen. A few moments later Aiden, Gideon and Oliver appeared. I released Jaxon and motioned for them to all sit down. I stood in the middle of the room, their eyes all on me and suddenly all words seemed to have disappeared from my mind.

Brooklyn

"SWEETHEART, ARE YOU OK?"

Aiden's voice cut through the static in my mind. I looked at him and for a moment, it felt like it was the first time I had seen him in ages. He looked disheveled, which for Aiden was a huge red flag. Bags were settled under his eyes, indicating he wasn't sleeping. Despite all of that, he took my breath away, and I wanted to go to him.

I nodded my head to answer his question, but then stopped

and shook it no. When he raised an eyebrow at me, I just shrugged, because I wasn't sure what the answer was. I did know that to survive this, I needed them. They reminded me there was something decent in the world to survive for, something to wake up for every morning. The feelings I had for them were proof that I could feel something, despite what had been taken away from me.

And my feelings hadn't changed. If anything, they were even stronger, knowing what they went through, the lengths they went to, just to save me. My eyes fell on Oliver, the man that told me he loved me. And it was real love, I knew that. Even if I was confused about what love felt like to me, I was confident about Oliver's feelings for me.

With all of that in my head, I still knew there was a risk. Once I told them everything, there was a risk that I wouldn't be worth their love any longer. There was a chance that I was too damaged, too dirty, too scarred to be the woman in their lives. I brought problems to their doorstep just by being in their home.

I pressed my hands against my stomach, trying to calm my nerves. Even knowing everything I knew, I still had a sliver of hope. A small piece of me hoped they would look beyond everything and still see me, the woman they were drawn to while dancing in their club. The one they touched and kissed and did beautiful things with. My sliver of hope wanted all of that to be enough.

"I heard from the doctor. But before I explain why they called, I feel like I need to tell you everything," I said.

The four of them looked at each other before focusing back on me. None of them spoke, but there was tension in their bodies and I knew this couldn't be easy for them to hear. I started from the beginning, because there was no way to skip around and leave things out. We couldn't mend things and be together if there were secrets.

I told them about seeing Frank be shot and how suddenly Missy was there and how everything went dark. I explained how at first I was clothed, and Missy had come to harass me. When I talked about how she planned on being rid of me so she could be back with them, all four of them started to argue, mostly cursing at Aiden and his idiotic ways.

"Enough!" Aiden's voice reverberated throughout the room and it shook me to my core.

We all focused on Aiden, and he stood to walk toward me. He put his hands out, as if he was approaching an injured animal. I didn't move away, even if part of me wanted him to suffer for what he had put me through before I had left the house. But a larger part of me wanted Aiden back, wanted him with me, close and connected.

"Brooklyn, I'm sorry. First and foremost for what happened between us. I shouldn't have iced you out. It's the last thing I really wanted to do. I've been torturing myself since and it was my own dumb actions."

I nodded and swallowed hard. The memory of us having sex on the hood of his car, how hot it was, flowed over me. I held onto the moment when we seemed to be connecting and then suddenly Aiden turned to ice, breaking my heart. Looking into his eyes now, I saw the door wide open for me, all of his emotions on the surface, available for me to see and hold on to.

"Secondly, as my brothers have so enjoyed pointing out, I fucked up royally with Missy. When she showed up at the club, I should have had her booted immediately. But I was so busy drowning the hurt I had caused that I didn't really register she was there, or that she was there to cause you pain. I never would have allowed a moment of that to happen if I had been in my right mind."

Aiden had reached me and had softly put his hands on my arms, not pulling me in, not pushing me away. Just holding me still, as if he thought I wanted to bolt from the room. Maybe I did, in a way. This was all so heavy and deep, emotions I wasn't used to warring inside of me. But that's what my men did to me, and it was perfect.

"I'm sorry, sweetheart," Aiden said again.

"Thank you," I said, my voice barely a whisper.

Aiden's eyes seemed to light with relief and I moved before he did. I wrapped my arms around his neck and hugged him tightly. His arms around my waist lifted me to my toes as he hugged me. I could feel his body tremble around mine, and I knew we were both at the edge of restraint.

He carefully released me and held my hand for a long time before returning to his seat. I took a deep breath that seemed to shudder. That was one hard part of the situation down. I could easily forgive Aiden. He had hurt me, but we all had our damage. We just had to work together to communicate and not cause pain we didn't intend. Which was just another reason I needed to finish telling them everything from my time with Lyle.

When I continued, I started with Missy injecting me with something again and how I didn't wake again until I was almost naked and partially tied down. Gideon stood abruptly, and I stopped talking. He motioned for me to continue, but rage was written all over his features as he paced behind the couches. I watched him for a moment, debating how much detail I should go into.

"Just tell us, stellina. Whatever you need to say, whatever you want to tell us, it's ok." His words were meant to be encouraging, but he was clearly too angry to stay still.

I didn't see the need to go through each individual detail. What was the point in torturing all of us with reliving it?

"Ok. I'm going to cut to the chase. You saw the cuts in my leg. Lyle's whole goal was to ruin me for anyone else. He wanted to break my body to make sure no one would want me. He thought he would break me down until I accepted him back. He touched me... everywhere..." I trailed off, as my breathing felt heavy. I closed my eyes to get my bearings, when a loud crack made me jump.

Aiden, Jaxon and Oliver had jumped from the couch. All three of them turned to stare at Gideon. It took just a moment to realize, the hole in the wall next to him had been made by his fist. All thoughts flew out of my head as I rushed to him.

"Gideon!"

I grabbed his hand and looked at his knuckles, where blood began to well. Jaxon appeared next to us with a bar towel in his hand. I carefully pressed it to his knuckles and put pressure on the wounds. Ash came rushing into the room, with Cain nonchalantly following.

"What was that?" She asked.

"I told you, we need to stay outta their way, yeah?" Cain said.

I looked over to my best friend. Seeing the indecision in her face, I gave her a small smile.

"Everything is fine, Ash. Just give us some time."

Ash was definitely not sure about leaving me alone, but Cain steered her back toward the kitchen and we were alone again.

"The wall had nothing to do with this." My quip didn't elicit even a small smile from Gideon.

None of them were talking, and it was starting to freak me out just enough that I started to babble.

"I know this makes me more damaged than what you signed up for. I know this changes everything. And I'm so sorry. I tried to fight, I really did. After Lyle had his hands on me… and in me…" I choked on the words, but I had to get everything out. "He drugged me again, because I bit a chunk out of his face and I wasn't cowering down."

"You did what?" Oliver asked, shock causing him to blurt out the words.

I continued to focus on Gideon's hand, keeping pressure, and that helped me focus on pushing out the words without another panic attack.

"I was strapped down. I couldn't hit him. So, when he got too close, I latched onto his face with my teeth. He didn't like that. So, he drugged me again. I didn't see him again before you guys showed up. His guy, Buzz, didn't get the chance to hurt me before Cain found me."

I guided Gideon to sit down on the couch and was surprised when he willingly followed my lead. Once he sat down, I kneeled between his legs so I could tie the towel around his hand.

"When I was drugged, I didn't know... I've been scared and worried. But the tests the doctor did came back, and Lyle didn't rape me. So at least you know that."

With everything out, I started to stand, my body shaking as I released all the pent up tension I had been holding onto. It was better to have the truth out to them, no matter what they decided. Gideon's hand snapped out and wrapped around my wrist. Without warning, he pulled me into him, causing me to climb into his lap.

"What did you think we were going to say to all of this?" He asked.

I stared into his eyes, the green a swirl of anger and pain. I felt horrible for being the reason he was suffering and I wanted to put their needs above my own. I wanted to wipe away the knowledge of what had happened, what was putting this rift between us. I just wasn't sure what to do, beyond being honest about everything. As an answer to Gideon, I just shrugged, because I didn't want to put into words my worst fears.

Gideon's arms came around me and crushed me into his body. I gasped as I was pressed against all the hard planes of his chest as he secured me to him. Tucking my head under his chin, I just let the tears fall. For the moment, I didn't know if this was a goodbye hug, or more. I just let myself feel the comfort and heat coming from Gideon's body.

A hand on my hip made me look over and Jaxon was on his knees next to me. He pressed his face against my side, hugging himself into me. His short brown hair was longer than usual and in complete disarray. I swept my hand over it before cradling the back of his neck. Oliver moved to sit next to Jaxon on the ground, bending to lay his head on my uninjured thigh. Aiden moved to sit next to Gideon, where he could slide a hand just under my sweatshirt and span my abdomen.

I knew then, in that moment, that they weren't saying good-bye. They were telling me I was still theirs; they were still mine. I could feel each of them touching me, trying to connect and comfort me. The tears came faster now, and I buried my face in Gideon's chest, soaking the front of his shirt.

"Stellina, we are here for you. Nothing you've said changes one fucking thing, you understand that?" Gideon's voice was a rumble under me.

I couldn't even form words, just nodded and tried to breathe through the grief and ease of fear that passed over me. Gideon's hand came to my chin, and he pulled me up to look at him. There were unshed tears in his green depths and I couldn't handle it anymore. I crushed my mouth to his in a messy, needy kiss. He didn't hesitate to respond, immediately forcing my mouth open and sliding his tongue along mine. His hand slipped to the back of my neck, anchoring me to him, as he explored my mouth, as if it was the first time all over again.

When he finally pulled back, kissing each of my lips and then next to my mouth, continuing up until he kissed each of my eyelids.

"Whatever you need from us, just ask." His voice had gotten gravely with desire.

For a moment, I caught my breath and looked at the four of them. I wasn't even sure what I wanted at the moment, my mind was muddled with hot thoughts caused by Gideon's kiss. But I had a feeling I knew what we all needed.

"Wipe it all away. I need you all to make my body yours again, make me only yours again." My voice was quiet and everyone was still for a long moment.

Then Oliver bounced to his feet. Jaxon followed. Aiden stood and held out a hand to me. But Gideon shook his head and stood in a swift movement, cradling me against his chest.

"Her room." Aiden's voice was more of a command than a request, but no one argued.

Oliver and Jaxon lead the way, with Gideon carrying me and

Aiden behind us. When we passed the kitchen, Ash's mouth dropped open and then she smiled softly. Cain's face was a mask of nonchalance, but I didn't miss the flash of heat in his eyes. I couldn't handle facing that too.

All I wanted was what I had thought I had lost. I needed my men.

Gideon

THE MOMENT I pulled her into my lap, I knew I needed to feel more of her. The fury inside my chest hadn't loosened, but that wasn't Brooklyn's fault. I pushed the images of tearing Lyle limb from limb away, putting them into a box to handle later. My hand ached like a bitch, but that was only helping me focus and contain the emotions that didn't need to spill over, not now.

She pressed her face into my throat as we climbed the stairs. I didn't miss the look Cain gave us as we walked by, and I knew we'd have to discuss him at some point. The guy clearly had it for our girl, but the question was what Brooklyn wanted. I didn't know Cain as well as Jaxon and Oliver, but my brothers trusted him, so I was inclined to trust him as well. He hadn't left the pool house yet, on the premise that he wanted to help find and handle Lyle. I could admit that his type of help may be exactly what we needed.

Those were all things for later. My girl needed me and I was going to give her everything she asked for and probably more. Oliver pushed open her door, and we all strode into the room, with Aiden shutting and locking the door behind him. For the first time in days, I grinned, knowing why Aiden was making sure to lock the door. Normally, we didn't lock any doors in the house, there was never anyone to keep out. But right now, we needed the privacy to take care of our girl.

I carefully set Brooklyn on the edge of the bed and she looked at all of us. Her cheeks were flushed and her eyes were bright, back to the color I was so used to, instead of dull and sad. She bit her bottom lip, and it made me want to dive at her, and just take everything I needed so badly. But I held myself back, knowing this was for her, what she needed, to find the road to healing and to bring her back to us.

Jaxon stepped forward, his hand cradling her face. He pulled her bottom lip from her teeth and leaned down to kiss her softly.

"Tell us what you need, love," he whispered.

She stood up and swept her sweatshirt up over her head. My mind went slightly blank as I realized she wasn't wearing a bra or anything under. Her nipples hardened almost immediately and Jaxon palmed one, running a thumb over the peak. She moaned and gripped his shoulder.

Aiden stepped forward, and she turned her full focus on him. I knew there was some making up that needed to happen between the two of them. Jaxon stepped back and let them have the moment.

"Aiden," she said as she reached out a hand and gripped his t-shirt, pulling him into her.

"I'm here, sweetheart. Even when you thought I wasn't, I was." He tapped his chest. "In here."

It was the closest I'd ever seen Aiden tell anyone about his true feelings.

Brooklyn smiled sweetly at him before lifting his t-shirt. He obliged by putting his arms up and helping her remove the garment. It landed on the ground with her sweatshirt and she hugged herself to his naked torso. Aiden wrapped his arms around her, rubbing her back with his hands, causing a groan to rise from her throat.

"I missed this. I missed you," she said.

"I'm sorry, sweetheart."

"You already apologized. You don't have to keep saying it," she said, before a small giggle.

The sound was like a tinkling bell and it made me smile in response, because it felt like forever since we'd heard any happy sounds from her. Watching her suffer in silence for days was almost too hard for all of us to handle. Seeing her recovering, slowly but surely, was more than I could ask for.

"I'll say it every day, because I'll forever feel it," Aiden said.

Brooklyn pulled away and looked up at him. "There's better things to feel, aren't there, babe?"

Aiden nodded and leaned down to capture her mouth in a rough kiss. She met him, pushing up on her tip toes, deepening the contact. Jaxon joined them, moving behind Brooklyn, hooking his fingers in the bike shorts she wore. The shorts didn't leave much to the imagination anyway, but having them off would be a much better view.

"Ok, love?" He murmured in her ear.

Without breaking contact with Aiden, she nodded and shimmied her hips. Jaxon was careful of her injured leg, that was still wrapped in a waterproof bandage. We would all have to wait for the healing to be done, to know if the plastic surgeon did the job he was well paid to do.

Jaxon left her thong in place, taking things at a slow pace, but as he stood up, he brushed kisses along the back of her thighs, his hand dipping between her legs as he moved up, just brushing a caress against her center. A small moan escaped her and it made me feel hot all over.

Aiden ended their kiss and brushed a hand over her cheek, pushing her hair behind her ear. I could see the adoration in his gaze and I wondered if Brooklyn realized he had never looked at a woman like that in his life. Even the only other long term relationship he'd been in, with Missy, did he ever look at her with love on his face. It made my chest ache.

As she gazed up at him, Oliver moved to take Jaxon's place behind her, his hands spanning her ribs and slowly moving up. He bent to kiss her neck, along the bruises that were changing colors but healing, and she craned to the side to give him better access. Her eyes fluttered closed as his hands closed around her breasts. One of her arms came up to cradle his head against her neck.

Jaxon moved to her side, taking her chin and pointing her face toward him. She opened her eyes just long enough to smile sexily at him, before he pressed his mouth to hers. The kiss became rough as they battled for pleasure. Aiden, who was still standing close, ran his hand down her stomach until he got to the material of her thong. I couldn't stand away from her any longer and moved closer to the group as Aiden asked her if she was ok.

"So ok. Please don't stop. Claim me, in all ways," she begged in a breathy voice.

When she saw me close, she turned slightly toward me, not wanting to break contact with any of my brothers. She tugged on my beard until I bent toward her and she softly caressed my lips with hers. The touch was hot and begged for more. I deepened the kiss, slipping my tongue between her lips, sliding along hers, creating a sexy dance between us.

She was breathless when she pulled back. Her pupils were blown with desire. When Aiden moved her thong to the side and slid a finger along her wetness, she moaned and threw her head back against Oliver's shoulder. Jaxon leaned down and captured one of her nipples in his mouth. Her hips began to move, grinding against Aiden's hand.

"So greedy, sweetheart," he said in a low voice.

"I want it all." She said the words as she gripped his wrist, not letting him pull away from her pussy.

Aiden chuckled before leaning forward to kiss her again. I knew the moment he pushed a finger into her because Brooklyn let out a groaned word of encouragement, and her hips bucked harder against his hand.

"More." The one word was all we needed to hear.

I ripped my shirt over my head and her hand immediately came down on my chest, nails digging in as Aiden added another finger to her. Not wanting to wait to hear the sounds she made when she came, I joined Aiden's hand and found her wanting clit. Circling it with the wetness of her pussy, Brooklyn cried out and lifted her hips, trying to get more contact.

Pressing down on her clit, Aiden continued to pump two fingers in and out of her. Her back bowed, seeking more contact. Jaxon moved to her other side, to lavish the same attention on that breast. That seemed to push her over the edge and her voice ripped out of her throat on a cry as she came on Aiden's fingers. Her body stilled and her chest heaved and I couldn't help but to stare.

When she opened her eyes and brought her head up, there was a tear slipping down her cheek.

"Did we hurt you, stellina?" I suddenly worried that we pushed her too fast, but she shook her head.

"God no, that felt fantastic." Her smile was slow, but another tear slipped down her cheek.

I reached up and cupped her face, wiping away the tears with my thumb.

"Then what is it? Why are you crying?" I asked.

She took a deep breath before leaning forward into Aiden, who wrapped an arm around her neck, cradling her to him.

"I was afraid I couldn't feel any sort of pleasure anymore. I thought maybe he did break me and I would never feel you again." Her voice was slightly muffled by Aiden's chest.

The sadness in her voice was too much. I closed in and pressed into her side, kissing her bare shoulder. Oliver, still at her back, hugged her from behind. Jaxon embraced her from the other side and we created a cocoon dedicated just to her. I trailed kisses up her neck, to the sensitive skin behind her ear.

"Do you feel that, stellina?"

"Mmmm." Her voice was nothing but a sigh.

Aiden tilted her chin up, so we could all see her face and she could see the intent on ours.

"We have all night to show you just how much you can feel."

Brooklyn

THE AFTERGLOW of the orgasm Aiden and Gideon had given me was still washing over my body, and I still couldn't believe how good it felt. Just the idea of losing what we had together caused me pain. If I had been right, if I had been too damaged to feel the pleasure they brought to me, I wasn't sure how I would continue to live with myself. They had awakened something in me, that I hadn't realized I was capable of. I couldn't lose that now.

Aiden's words caused a new flush to heat my skin. His words were heavy with promise and I had no doubts about what they intended to do. And I wanted all of it and more. I wanted things we'd never done before, new memories to wipe away the nightmares I had endured. I needed them to mark me, make me theirs in every way, remind me who I really belonged to.

"Make me forget," I said.

My words were all the guys needed, and I was swept up in Gideon's arms. I couldn't suppress the giggle that popped out of my mouth and his sudden eagerness. He laid me in the middle of the bed, moving me delicately and carefully.

"I won't break, big man."

"We can be rough later, stellina." His voice was thick with promise.

As he slid his hands down my body, he hooked his fingers in my thong and started to slide it down my legs. I was blissfully nude while they were mostly clothed. I was about to remark on it, but Gideon began to kiss my ankles. I looked down, seeing that he was paying extra attention to the bruises that were starting to heal.

Oliver removed his shirt and climbed onto the bed next to me, stretching out, where he could curl an arm around my waist. I looked over at him and realized that he looked like a weight had been lifted off of him. He ran his fingers over my lips before dipping down and catching my mouth in a deep kiss. His tongue slid sensually against mine and a small moan bubbled up from my throat.

He leaned back and looked into my face before putting his lips to my ear.

"I love you."

The words were just for the two of us and I had to fight the tears that wanted to surface again. Even after I told him everything, he still loved me. My heart swelled, and I was close to just blurting out the same words. But I held back, still unsure of how I was supposed to feel, or how I knew my feelings were real. So instead, I smiled as brightly as I could before kissing him roughly.

Gideon was making his way up my legs and was kissing the burn scar on my exposed thigh. Moving to my injured thigh, he ghosted a kiss over the bandage, but didn't risk causing me any pain. When his shoulders started to push my thighs apart, I pulled away from Oliver and looked down. Gideon's hair was up in his normal bun, but I wanted his hair falling over me. I reached down and pulled at the elastic until his hair brushed my thighs and he was looking up my body to meet my gaze.

Without taking his eyes off of mine, his tongue snaked out and licked along the seam of my pussy. I gasped, and my back bowed. His thick forearm came down around my hips, to anchor me to the bed.

"You're not getting away that easily, stellina. I plan to take my time."

I looked around the room, finding Aiden sitting relaxed in a chair next to the bed. Jaxon was at the foot of the bed, staring at my spread thighs. I could see his erection, thick in his sweats, and my mouth went dry. When I looked back over to Aiden, I saw his hand was stroking his cock that he had pulled from his pants.

"Aiden, I want to suck you." I motioned for him to come to me.

His eyes widened, but he immediately stood and climbed onto the bed. I reached out and pulled his sweats and boxers down his thighs. His cock was rock hard and curved toward me. Gideon was blowing on my clit and I had to focus to lead Aiden's hardness to my lips. I looked up at him as I circled his plush head with my tongue.

"Fuck, sweetheart." Aiden's voice was low and seductive, making me tremble.

His hand came down to the back of my head and he slowly fed his length into my mouth, stopping before hitting my throat, not forcing more on me than necessary. I hollowed my cheeks and sucked and he groaned again, before slowly pulling out of my mouth and thrusting back in.

Gideon didn't hesitate to take advantage of my distraction. Pulling apart my outer lips, he slid his tongue from my clit to my entrance and back again, before sucking my clit into his mouth. I cried out around Aiden's cock, but he didn't slow as he fucked my face. I felt hands on me, but the hold Aiden had on my head prevented me from turning to see who it was. A hot mouth closed around my nipple and I bucked up, arching my back.

Jaxon came into view, next to Aiden, his cock in his hand as well. While Aiden fucked my face, I reached out toward Jaxon and wrapped my hand around his length, joining him in the stroking. He moved forward to make it easier for me to please him, and I slid my hand down to squeeze his balls before stroking him again. His eyes were on mine and he bit his bottom lip as I twisted my fist over the head of his cock.

"Sweetheart, I'm going to cum," Aiden said.

I nodded slightly, telling him to cum in my mouth. I wanted to taste him, I wanted every drop and feeling of him exploding on my tongue. He thrust through my lips a few more times, more roughly, making me want more before he pressed into my mouth and I felt him begin to spurt. I started to swallow, and he threw his head back as he finished.

Between my legs, Gideon slid a finger into my pussy and began to fuck me slowly. I fidgeted, trying to tell him I wanted more. A second finger was added and he bent his knuckles, to hit the perfect spot inside me. At the same time he circled my clit with the tip of his tongue. I couldn't contain the wanton nature rising up in me and I started to gyrate my hips against his face. Gideon didn't mind and let his pleasure known as he growled against my pussy, the feeling shooting sparks into my clit.

His teeth closed around my nub just as Aiden pulled his cock from my mouth. My orgasm was like a tidal wave and I screamed out as Gideon lapped me softly, drawing out my pleasure. Once it began to slow, I blinked down at him, finding a smile splitting his handsome face. I buried my hand in his hair and yanked until he was crawling up my body.

When he pressed his mouth against mine, I tasted my pleasure on his tongue and it made me hotter than I could imagine. I wrapped my legs around his hips, but was met with the barrier of his sweats. I didn't have the ability to wait, my body was begging for more. Reaching down, I pushed at the waist of his sweats and I shoved a hand between us, until I could circle his cock with my hand. Gideon pulled back and hissed out a breath.

"Our girl has no patience," Oliver said with a laugh.

"Give her what she wants, brother," Aiden said from the chair he was sitting in again.

Gideon didn't need the encouragement, he was already pushing his sweats to his thighs. Once his cock was free, I immediately guided him to my entrance and tilted my hips up for him. He leaned on one of his elbows, curling his arm around my head, keeping me in place as he notched himself.

"Ready?"

"Gideon, please." My voice was whiny as I begged, but it only caused a grin to appear on his face.

With one hard thrust, he sheathed himself deep in me, his pelvis hitting mine. I couldn't hold back the sounds as I cried out from the pleasure of having him stretch and fill me. He pulled back and thrust again, harder, and I lifted my hips to meet him.

"Your pussy is heaven," he groaned into my ear.

"Harder, big man, harder please," I panted.

He crushed his lips to mine, kissing me roughly before leaning back on his knees, his cock still deep inside me. The new angle made him rub against different sensitive areas and I gasped. Oliver and Jaxon were on either side of me, and as soon as they had access, they started running kisses along my neck to my taunt nipples. Oliver sucked one deep into his mouth while Jaxon's teeth closed down softly, causing electricity to shoot directly to my center.

The additional stimulation made me want so much more.

Planting my feet on either side of Gideon, I gyrated my hips, fucking myself with Gideon's cock. He bit his lip as he allowed me to move as I needed. Aiden came to the side of the bed, watching as Gideon's cock slid in and out of me. I could see his cock was starting to thicken again, and I knew he wasn't done with me either. Aiden added his fingers, pinching my clit as I rode Gideon.

Having all four of my men touching me, sucking me and being inside me at once was exactly what I needed, even if I hadn't known how it would help. I could feel pieces of me coming back to the present, as if they were stuck in the horror I was running from. They began to fall into place as I looked at each of their faces, their eyes bright with passion, the wanting of me and my body.

With my mind muddled with passion and what I was starting to call love, at least to myself, I began to feel a third orgasm cresting. It felt far away, but Aiden didn't let up on my clit. As I started to shake and slow my movements, Gideon grabbed my hips and started to thrust roughly into me, as if he knew he was helping me chase the pleasure.

Oliver ran a tongue around my nipple before rising up to capture my mouth, his tongue battling mine immediately. When he pulled away, he looked into my eyes knowingly.

"Let him have it, baby. He wants your pussy clamped around his cock."

It was as if the words pushed me beyond control and I began to fall into the tidal wave of sensation. I was pretty sure I cried out, but I couldn't be positive. Gideon growled as I clamped down on him. His paced picked up, and he fucked me harder still until I could feel him spilling deeply into me.

For a moment he collapsed onto me, holding himself on his forearms not to crush me. I cradled his head against my chest where he laid it, my heart thundering in my ears, and I was sure he could hear it as well.

"You ok, love?" Jaxon asked.

"Mmm, so ok."

"Good, because we aren't done with you." Jaxon laid on his back next to me and tapped Gideon's shoulder.

I realized Jaxon had lost his sweats at some point and his cock was hard and laying against his stomach. My mouth began to water as I looked at him and I knew I wasn't done with them either. Gideon carefully pulled out of me, and I didn't hesitate to crawl over Jaxon. With my hips in his hands, he lead me to the position he wanted me in, his cock easily sliding into me with the mix of Gideon and my wetness.

Aiden came behind me, running his hands down my back and over my ass. When his fingers wandered down toward my puckered hole, he pressed his mouth against my ear.

"How do you feel about trying something new, something only for us?"

It was exactly what I wanted. Their claim on my body to wipe away everything else. It was something I had never done, allowing a man to take me anally. But I knew without question that I trusted them to be careful with me and to never cross lines I had. Without fear, I nodded my head and leaned back against Aiden's shoulder.

"I want you everywhere."

Aiden

MY BRAIN SEEMED to freeze for a moment as she agreed. She turned her face toward me and I could see the desire burning in her eyes without a hint of trepidation. I knew it wasn't the time to tell her that my brothers and I had never been with a woman like this either. It was something that would be only ours, and I needed that as much as Brooklyn.

Her mouth around my cock had been hot and I could find my pleasure between her lips anytime she wanted. But this was a completely different thing. Jaxon and I made eye contact over her shoulder, and he gave a small nod, agreeing to the idea. Gideon left the room for a moment and reappeared with a bottle of lube.

With the door locked again, I allowed the lube to slide between her cheeks before I rubbed it into her puckered hole. She moaned in surprise, but she pushed back against me as she also rode Jaxon's cock. His knuckles were white with his grip on her hips, trying to make things last.

I kissed her shoulder and neck as I pressed a finger into her. She groaned but seemed to know that she needed to relax. As my finger passed the ring of muscles, her movements on Jaxon became more frenzied. I took that as a good sign, so I added a second lubed finger, carefully stretching her as she moved. I stared as my fingers disappeared into her forbidden entrance and my cock throbbed with the idea of being there.

No one could have convinced me that this would have been how the night had gone. Brooklyn's admissions to us meant absolutely nothing to me. I would support her in whatever way she needed. But what Lyle had done to her didn't change her in my eyes. If anything, she was even stronger and more resilient than we had known. And her forgiveness for me was more than I should have ever hoped for. But I couldn't help but to hold out hope for this woman that had captured my heart.

"Aiden, I need..." she said suddenly, and her hips moved faster.

"Ok, sweetheart, let's see if this feels good."

I didn't want to force anything on her, but she seemed to know what she wanted. I poured a large amount of lube on my hand and stroked my cock. Moving closer to her, I let my cock slide down her crack. She leaned toward Jaxon and froze. He reached up and pushed her hair behind her ear before pulling her down for a kiss. The angle made it even easier for me to see as the head of my cock pressed against her back entrance.

With just a little movement, I held my breath as the head popped past the muscled ring.

"Oh god, Aiden. Fuck... so full... so good." Her voice was breathy and sultry, causing me to move forward.

I couldn't look away as my cock disappeared into her. When I was fully seated, I froze and waited to see how Brooklyn felt.

"Shit, brother, I can feel you... inside her..." Jaxon said. Sweat had popped out on his forehead.

"Are you ok, sweetheart?" I asked.

"I... yes. I feel so full, but in such a good way. I want to move." She took that moment to flex her muscles around us, squeezing down, causing us both to hiss.

Carefully, Jaxon and I worked on a rhythm, thrusting in and out of her. Her eyes were closed and her hands gripped Jaxon's as she tried to keep her balance. The feeling was beyond incredible. She was tight as a fist around my cock, but then I could feel Jaxon moving just beyond a thin barrier, causing even more friction.

"I'm not sure how long I can last like this," Jaxon admitted.

I grunted my agreement as I slid deeply into her. Brooklyn continued to make little mewling noises, and I could feel her walls spasm around us. Oliver crawled toward us and added his hand to the mix, sliding it below her and massaging her clit.

"I don't know if I can again," she moaned.

"I know you can," Oliver replied.

Our movements became more frenzied, but I was careful to wait for her. I wanted to feel her clamp down on my cock while it was deep inside her, before marking her with my cum.

Jaxon groaned, not able to hold out much longer. "Please, love, cum for us."

Brooklyn's hips bucked against Oliver's hand and our cocks once, twice, and then she screamed. She tightened like a vice around us and I immediately came spilling into her. She bent forward, and I followed, as to not hurt her. I kissed her shoulder and murmured sentimental words that didn't make any sense, but my brain wasn't working.

As I carefully pulled from her, she completely collapsed onto Jaxon's chest. He wrapped his arms around her and I laid to the side. I turned her face toward me and her beautiful eyes fluttered open. I pressed a hard kiss against her upturned lips.

"Thank you, sweetheart."

"For what?" She asked.

"Sharing that with me."

Brooklyn

I WAS IN A PLEASURABLE SHOCK. I couldn't believe I had just had two of my men in me at once. And I knew I wanted to do it again. I laid against Jaxon's chest and listened to the thundering of his heart. He had a fine sheen of sweat over his skin, and I let my tongue dart out and circle his nipple.

"I can't even think about moving, love," he groaned.

A laugh erupted from me, louder than I intended. Gideon sat in the chair next to the bed, his eyes hooded, locked on me. I smiled at him and he returned it. Rolling to the side, I found myself between Jaxon and Oliver. I stretched a little, checking in with my body to figure out what was sore. I was surprised to find that I didn't feel that bad.

"How about I help you shower?" Oliver asked.

I looked at him. His whispered words during everything weren't forgotten in my mind. They echoed and found a place to sit so I didn't have to search for them. The idea of a quiet moment with him was exactly what I needed. I nodded and let him pull me from the bed. Aiden and Jaxon looked completely spent, sprawled on the bed. As Oliver lead me into the bathroom, I froze at the door and turned back to them.

"Stay, please?"

"We'll be right here, stellina," Gideon replied.

I nodded and smiled before going into the bathroom. Oliver only turned on the lights that dimmed and turned them down, so they weren't so glaring. He adjusted the water and held me in his arms as we waited. I pressed up on my toes to press my lips to his. Reaching up, I gripped his curls, keeping him connected to me. His kiss was hot, but also it felt different now, more emotional and a connection was there that I hadn't realized before.

We stepped into the shower and the hot water fell from the rain shower head. I leaned back, allowing the water to run over my hair and down my back. Oliver took the moment to lean forward and kiss a tender path along my throat, up to my ear, where he nipped. I gasped and turned my mouth to his for another kiss.

I could feel how turned on he was, with his cock pressed against my stomach. Sliding a hand between us, I stroked him and he softly bit my bottom lip.

"Are you sure you can handle any more, baby?" He asked.

I looked up at him, knowing I wanted him more than anything at that moment.

"Oliver.." I faded off.

"It's ok, I know you're probably exhausted—" he started to say, but I reached up my free hand and covered his mouth.

"I'm never too tired for you. I love you."

The words were out before I realized I wanted to say them. His blue eyes widened, and he didn't speak right away, just stared down at me. My heart swelled, as if it were going to burst as we just looked at each other. It took me a moment to realize I was still covering his mouth, so I slowly let my hand drop to his chest, where I could feel his heart hammering.

"You aren't just saying that, because I did?" He asked.

I squinted, staring into his eyes for a moment. There were so many emotions swirling there, and it all dawned on me at once. I had a lot of physical scars to show the terror I had been through in my life. There were a lot of mental scars too, but I wasn't the only one with those injuries. Except for his brothers, Oliver had never had someone truly love him in his life. And now, he was worried my confession was forced.

"Oh, Oliver. I love you so much. I know I haven't always made the right choices. I'm not always sure how relationships and communication work. But my heart is yours. I promise you that."

As soon as I stopped speaking, Oliver had me pressed against the wall, his mouth covering mine. He teased his tongue along the seam of my lips for a second before I opened for him. His hand cupped my face as he kissed me deeply, spilling all of his love into me. I gripped his wrist with one hand and his shoulder with the other, keeping myself on my feet.

"Oliver, make love to me, please." I said the words against his mouth and he barely broke contact to allow me to breathe.

His hands went to my ass, and he easily lifted me. I immediately wrapped my thighs around his hips, crossing my ankles behind his ass. He lined his cock up with my entrance and pressed forward slowly, savoring each inch as he stretched me open for him. He sucked on my bottom lip as he completely sheathed himself and held still for a moment.

"No matter how often I get to do this, you feel so fucking amazing," he said, his words flowing directly against my mouth.

"Please, move Oliver. You feel so good inside me," I begged.

His fingers dug into my ass as he carefully swung his hips, his pelvis rubbing against me in the most delicious way. I dug my heels into him, urging him on faster, but he wouldn't be rushed. He kissed across my cheek, to my ear and to the sensitive spot behind it. I shivered as my nipples rubbed against his chest.

Oliver didn't slow, continuing with the pace he wanted as he fucked me against the shower wall. My moans were echoing throughout the room, and I knew the other three could hear me in the bedroom. But they didn't try to intrude, as if they knew we needed this alone time to reconnect on our own.

He was deep inside me when he growled into my ear. "Touch yourself, baby."

I released his shoulder with one hand and slid it between us, finding my nub. It was so incredibly sensitive, almost painfully so, and I wasn't sure I could orgasm again. But Oliver was determined. He lifted me slightly higher, so he could reach my nipples, and sucked one into his mouth. His teeth scraped the taunt bud before he switched to the other side.

"Make yourself cum on my cock. I want to fill you so badly." Oliver groaned against my neck.

I knew he was getting close because his thrusts were becoming harder and I wanted to cum with him. I pressed down harder on my clit, sending a jolt of pleasure through my core, just as Oliver changed his angle again and his thrusts became more forceful.

"Oh god, baby, just like that." The words tumbled from my mouth and I wasn't sure I was even coherent.

I pinched my nub and felt the crest of erotic pleasure flow through me. I screamed out as the orgasm made me clench down on Oliver. He bellowed his own release, and I could feel him spurting deep inside me. He buried his face in my neck for a long moment before letting his cock slide out of me.

"I love you, Brooklyn."

"I love you, too," I immediately replied.

Relationships, communication, love. They were all things I knew little about. I had gone most of my life believing I wasn't good enough for anyone. Even therapy only made me feel good in my own skin, which was an improvement. What I did know was when I was with Oliver, my heart alternated between thudding in my chest or stopping. I knew when he touched me, it felt like he did so with reverence. When I wasn't with him, he was always on my mind.

With soft hands, Oliver cleaned my body, dipping between my legs to clear away all the remnants of our activities. I leaned back under the water, my breasts pressing against him as he rinsed my hair of the conditioner he had massaged in. Even the task of getting clean felt hot with Oliver in the shower with me. But I was well spent and ready for bed by the time we were done getting clean.

He wrapped a fluffy white towel around me and I quickly towel dried my hair. Oliver stood next to me, towel slung low on his hips, watching me in the mirror. I stopped and turned to look at him.

"What?"

"You're beautiful."

I smiled wryly and looked at myself in the mirror. Healing bruises ringed my neck, dotted my face and chest. I tried not to think too hard about where those marks came from. It was definitely not the vision of beauty I wanted to be. But I wasn't going to argue with Oliver. If I was beautiful in his eyes, that was good enough for me at the moment.

We joined the other three in the bedroom. I carefully climbed over Jaxon, to lie between him and Aiden. Gideon reached over Aiden to squeeze my hip as I got comfortable with my head on Aiden's chest. Jaxon spooned me from behind. Oliver leaned over to give me a kiss on the shoulder before getting comfortable behind Jaxon.

"Jaxon, can I be the big spoon?" Oliver asked.

Jaxon didn't answer, just grumbled and buried his face into my hair.

In the middle of my bed, surrounded by the skin and smells of all four of my men, I found a contentment that I had searched for in my life. My heart slowed and calm blanketed us all. Aiden's breathing slowed under my ear, and I knew he was falling asleep. Gideon had shifted and I could see him with his arm over his face, just like he always slept. Jaxon's grip on me hadn't loosened, but I wasn't sure he would, even once he fell asleep. Oliver reached over to massage my hip, before he also started to doze.

I couldn't imagine a better way to fall asleep, to live, to love. Only good dreams would come, as my men would keep the nightmares at bay.

CHAPTER
Forty~Nine

Cain

POURING ANOTHER SHOT OF WHISKEY, I sat at the kitchen island, getting sloppy drunk. I hadn't realized that not being with Brooklyn, while the Knights were, would make me feel a depression I didn't know I was capable of. I hadn't touched her, except in non-sexual ways. But I was feeling some sort of hole in me that I had never tried to fill. And now that hole felt like a crater, growing by each moment.

Her muffled cries filtered downstairs as Ash wandered back into the kitchen. She froze and turned her head toward the stairs for a moment before laughing. The sound cut off when she turned and saw the state I was in.

"Maybe slow down on that?"

"Nah, I don't think I will." My words came out clearly in my mind, though I was sure they were slurred.

She went to the fridge and pulled out a bottle of water before turning to study me.

"What exactly is it with you and my friend?" Her words didn't sound like an accusation, but I knew it was.

There wasn't much I could tell her that wouldn't make me sound like a jealous asshole. It wasn't that I cared that she was with the Knights, it was that I wasn't with her too. It was that she didn't have room in her life for me. It was that just by reading about her, looking at her picture, searching for her, stitched her into my brain.

Since I wasn't sure what I could say, I just shook my head and poured more whiskey down my throat. It was smooth, only the good stuff for my friends. And it was fabulous to crack their booze to get drunk while they got to have Brooklyn in bed. I heard one of the guys cry out and I knew what that sound meant and I dropped my head into my hands.

"Well, you have it bad, don't you? You thinking five isn't a crowd?" Ash asked.

I shot her a dirty look, and all she did was laugh at me. I wasn't sure who made the decision about five being a crowd, Brooklyn or the guys. Without even asking, I knew I'd kneel at her feet if that's what she wanted. I did have it bad, whatever it was. Which was why I was sitting in the kitchen, torturing myself with her sounds of ecstasy, that I wasn't party to.

Feeling as if I was lower than I needed to be over a woman, I carefully stood from the stool I had been sitting on. I started to walk out of the kitchen, but when another of her moans came to my ears, I turned and grabbed the whiskey bottle. I practically ran for the backdoor, to get back to the pool house, with Ash's laughter echoing behind me.

Lyle

A KNOCK at my hotel door had me pulling a gun from my duffel. I waited to see if the person was going to leave, but the knocking started again, more insistent. I growled, before stalking to the door with the gun pointing toward the entrance of my room. There were very few people who knew where I was hiding out, and none of them would be banging on my door.

With the gun pressed against the cheap wood, I hovered my

eye over the peephole. When I saw who was on the other side, I cursed loudly.

"Lyle, open the damn door!" Missy's grainy voice easily carried into the room.

I threw the lock and tossed the door open. Missy only had a second to look surprised, before I grabbed her by her arm and dragged her into the room. Slamming the door behind me, I locked the deadbolt again before turning and fixing Missy with a dirty look.

"Bitch, what are you confused by? Do you think I'm staying in this shit hotel for the hell of it? Using my name where everyone can hear you? How fucking stupid are you?"

Missy's attitude slipped a notch as she understood the implication of my words. A flash of fear went across her eyes and that was the only time she didn't seem like a complete dumb ass.

"Baby, I'm sorry. But do you have any idea where I've been the last four days?" Her voice wasn't apologetic at all, and it was grating on my nerves already.

"I hadn't thought about it," I said.

Turning away from her, I flicked the safety on my gun and slipped it back into my duffel bag. Missy was stripping out of her clothes, and I raised my eyebrow at her.

"What happened to your face?" She asked, with a hand on her naked hip.

I lifted my hand to the bandage that covered the bite on my face. Fury rose in my gut as I thought about how Brooklyn had slipped from my grasp again. After I left her to get my face patched up, I was ready to come back and sink into her, whether she was awake or not. Instead, I almost drove into a sea of emergency lights, from cop cars, firetrucks and ambulances. Parking far enough away to not be seen, but to see what was happening, I was furious to see my guys being taken out on stretchers.

There was no Brooklyn, which told me she was already gone. I had screamed and pounded on the dash of my car so loudly, I caught the attention of the closest emergency worker. When I realized, I sped away and got myself lost in the city. I slept in my car the first night, then brought myself to this shit hole motel that I kept in mind for hiding out. Since then, I had been living on vending machine food and one order of Chinese I took the risk of going to pick up.

Looking at Missy, I tried to remember when I told her where I would hide out if things were to get hot. Apparently, I let it slip at some point, because here the bitch was. Just having her in my space was pissing me off. She didn't wait for me to answer about my face before she stomped into the shower. A moment later, I heard the water come on.

"Baby, can you bring me a towel?"

I kicked my duffel. What the woman didn't understand about keeping it down, I had no idea. I didn't have any clean towels anyway, since I hadn't answered the door when housekeeping knocked. Of course, there was no way of knowing how clean the linens were when you checked in. That was what came along with staying in a shit motel when hiding out.

I went to the bathroom and shoved the door open. Missy peered around the dingy shower curtain, looking for her towel. Her eyes widened, and I knew I looked as deranged on the outside as I was feeling on the inside. In my mind, I wasn't seeing Missy. I was picturing a naked Brooklyn, tied down, at my mercy. Broken, bruised, she would have been ruined for anyone. But that wasn't what happened.

Before Missy could react, I had my hands around her throat. She tried to dig her fingers under mine, but it was useless. Her fake nails scraped at my skin and I was amazed by her strength. I loosened my hold just enough so she could drag a breath in. I didn't give her a chance to gather herself, instead I dragged her from the shower, one hand on her throat, the other gripping her hair.

When I got her into the bedroom, I tossed her onto the flimsy mattress, where she landed in a heap. She began to cough and sputter, but her back was to me. As she lifted herself up on her hands and knees, I could feel myself getting hard. But it wasn't her that I wanted. It was Brooklyn and that had been stolen from me again.

I pushed my workout shorts down until I could free my dick. Without giving Missy a warning, I pushed her face into the mattress, but held her hips up with my other hand. I slammed my dick into her dry and she began to cry out. I yanked her head until I could muffle her screams into the mattress. It also helped that I could pretend she was whoever I wanted her to be.

Brooklyn should have been the one taking my dick. She should have remembered her place and given it up willingly. But instead, I knew she was back behind those walls, with those rich fuckers, thinking she was better than me. The bitch had no idea of the lengths I was willing to go to.

Despite Missy acting as if she didn't want it, I could feel how wet she was becoming, and when she came, she tightened down on me and caused my orgasm to rush through my body. But before I spilled into her, I pulled out and painted her back with my cum. I let her go and Missy fell to the bed in a heap, her body heaving with tears.

I stared down at her, and a small sliver of pity stabbed through my mind. No matter what the woman did, she would never be who I wanted, who I deserved. Brooklyn's face appeared in my mind again, and I gritted my teeth against the fury that coursed through my body. It was time to take the fight to the next level, and the rich assholes wouldn't see me coming.

Acknowledgments

Thank you so much for reading Finding Brooklyn, book 2 of The Club Kings Series. I hope you enjoyed the story of Brooklyn and The Knights continued relationships and the threats they had to overcome to be together. If you'd like to follow my upcoming works find me on Facebook at https://www.facebook.com/char lottestpierreauthor or at my website https://charlottestpierre. com/ .

This book wouldn't have been made possible without my editor DJ Cooper with Angry Eagle Publishing. She has been an inspiration, a sounding board and great friend through this writing process!

Also a huge thank you to JS Designs for the beautiful cover that perfectly fit the story of Brooklyn and her Knights.

The beautiful formatting of this book was done by Emcat Designs and I just love how their work gave everything that extra pop!

Thank you to my family for all of the sacrificed weekends and evenings where I was doing nothing but typing away. I couldn't do anything without you and the belief you have in me.